ISBN-13: 978-0-9832063-4-7

Printed in the United States of America

Fomite
58 Peru Street
Burlington, VT 05401
www.fomitepress.com
Author photograph by Robin Perlah

For Tim, who has always recognized the writer in me

To Miriam —
Dance laughter &
good health
Susan

Acknowledgments

Thanks to Seth Steinzor, who read this book as it was being written and encouraged me along the way, and to my mother, who also read the chapters hot off the press as long as she was able...to Kevin Bradley, without whose patience and skill I would not have developed a web presence...to Robin Perlah for helping me in a variety of ways...and to Marc and Donna, my publishers.

I am ever grateful to Tim for enabling me to write these many years, and ever delighted by Evan and Chloe, who both have grown up to appreciate the value of writing and have become able writers themselves.

My God, What Have We Done?

Susan V. Weiss

Fomite
Burlington, Vermont

Part I

Atomic Honeymoon

For our honeymoon, my husband and I went to Los Alamos National Laboratory, birthplace of the atomic bomb. We used frequent-flier miles to fly to Albuquerque and, once there, drove around New Mexico, from the state's sleepy largest city to opulent Santa Fe and, on our fourth day, to Los Alamos.

My schoolteacher husband, who usually dressed conservatively in khaki pants and button-down shirts, all at once became sporty in our low-riding rental car. He'd bought what may have been his first pair of sunglasses in reaction to the unrelenting light. Even the dull stucco and concrete glared back at us too brightly.

All of the businesses on Albuquerque's main streets were closed in the afternoon when we arrived. The city seemed fatigued, as if it needed to nap. Only the sun kept working non-stop, a perpetual machine. "Where is everyone?" we asked each other and eventually a few passersby, who explained that the stores would open again at three o'clock.

"Kind of like a siesta," I said to Clifford.

"I guess."

Yet at three, when we returned to the dormant downtown, all of the doors were still locked and the streets nearly vacant.

"Maybe it's a holiday," Clifford suggested. "A New Mexican holiday that we don't know about."

"But then why wasn't it mentioned in any of the guidebooks?"

I almost always had the last word. Clifford just wasn't an arguer. He was a peaceful man who heard the chirrup of birds even in the middle of a city. Although I envied his serenity, I sometimes wished I could get him to grab onto some of my challenges, to declare himself, to fight back.

"Well, we got our money's worth mile-wise," I said, "but we would have had more action if we'd gone to… Chicago."

Clifford agreed.

Santa Fe, however, was a lively place with hundreds of stores that were always open, selling luxuries that we couldn't afford. The quantity of jewelry peddled in the shops and on the street made me feel drab and plain and poor. After wandering away from yet another table glinting with bursts of silver, I was soon overtaken by Clifford, who'd stayed behind to buy a pair of earrings I admired. He watched me remove the pair I was wearing and replace them with the silver disks studded with variegated turquoise, boasting two of the state's most prominent natural resources.

"I do," I said, lacing my arms around his lean body. I could close my eyes and still see the ups and downs of his lipline, each of the intersecting planes that made up his face, its newness gone after months of knowing him.

"You already did," he reminded me.

Clifford wanted to get away from the culture of shopping and the smell of money. So we headed north to Los Alamos, number one on my honeymoon wish list of destinations. My older sister Sylvia had scolded me when she saw the city associated with the bomb on my itinerary.

"Come on, Pauline. Why would you go there?"

Sylvia had invited me to her house for breakfast without forewarning me that she meant to critique my honeymoon plans. But I was ready with an answer. "It's the tragedy of what became of all those scientists' vision. Poor Robert Oppenheimer. He thought they were developing a weapon that would put an end to war. Forever." The surface heat of my skin made me feel that I was about to ignite, like a small test bomb.

"What's Clifford going to think? He's probably looking forward to hikes in the mountains or romantic dinners at expensive restaurants."

Clearly she didn't know my Clifford. I stabbed a spoon into my grapefruit, launching a trajectory of juice exactly into Sylvia's left eye. She flinched and then, to my surprise, she retreated. "Sorry. It's your honeymoon, after all. Not mine."

Sylvia and Howie had spent a week in Paris for their honeymoon six years earlier. Every left turn and every rest stop had been scheduled in advance. I remember thinking that they'd probably ordered their meals ahead of time and found their food waiting for them when they entered each five-star restaurant recommended in the guide books.

In fact, I hadn't needed to justify my desire to see Los Alamos. Clifford was just as glad to leave all of the plans to me as long as they included a visit to the primitive dwelling caves at Bandelier National Monument at some point during our travels. I could already picture him inspecting the remnants of that long-ago settlement, eyes squinting to see back in time. I could hear his impassioned regrets about the plight of those vanished people. A deep river of feeling ran through him. Whenever he would recall a heroic baseball play or Mrs. Quill, his inspirational second-grade teacher, his eyes would get misty.

As we lowered ourselves into the blazing white vehicle that was temporarily ours, I noticed Clifford's face becoming rumpled and worried. Since the beginning of our relationship, he'd done all of the driving even though he suffered from an undiagnosed inability to read a map, a handicap that caused him endless embarrassment. After a lengthy review of the logical route to wherever we were going, he'd always pull over on the shoulder of the road a few minutes later, enormously lost, hoping that another look at the map would get him at least a mile or two further towards our goal. I tried to act as navigator, but despite my promptings he would take sudden, inexplicable turns based on mistaken intuition.

A crisp, unused map of New Mexico was open on my lap as vastly as the desert reached out around us. If I needed any more detailed directions, I could refer to one of our many other maps of New Mexico or the Southwest, or to the three atlases that had been among our wedding gifts, as if our guests didn't trust us to buy maps for our trip.

"Oh look! Forests," I said, interpreting the green shading sharing the desert with the sand.

"I know. The Santa Fé National Forest." Despite Clifford's confusion about deciphering maps, he enjoyed studying them with motives other than planning a travel route. In contrast, I hadn't looked at any of our New Mexico maps until we arrived in Albuquerque.

"And there's a river."

"Uh-huh."

"In the desert?"

"That's not as uncommon as you might think," he told me. Because Clifford was a history teacher, geography was among his areas of expertise.

The road map, as I scanned it, seemed to depict the different emotional states that had lately overtaken me. The open land, limitless and desert-dry, represented my vision of the years ahead now that I was married and didn't know what to expect of my future. The forests, dim and enclosed, depriving the hiker of orientation, corresponded to my current claustrophobic panic about living out my life with one man.

I'd arrived at the altar exhaustedly after years of serial romances that never outlasted the narcotic effect of new love. At the same time I was tired of plummeting from ecstasy to the bottom of the drop, I missed the tummy rush and wondered whether stability would always seem to me monotonous and stale.

And yet I couldn't have imagined a better match for me than the man I'd chosen to marry. Clifford was the nourishment I needed even if I still sometimes craved the quick, candy thrill of a first kiss. I squeezed my new husband's thigh and felt his warmth even through his khaki pants.

We'd agreed to overshoot Los Alamos, which was on the way to Bandelier National Monument, and return after seeing the ancient ruin. Clifford couldn't imagine visiting the site any time other than early morning, primetime in a culture that predated electricity and even candles. Los Alamos, on the other hand, was a round-the-clock enterprise. I'd read about the fizzlers and stinkers—code names for physicists and chemists—loping home at the wee hours to reacquaint themselves with their disgruntled wives.

From the ground I looked up at the cave mouths, each speaking a timeless truth unchanged after all these years. The entrances were so small that it was hard to imagine entire homes lurking beyond them. The only way to inspect the interiors of the caves was to climb up one of the wooden ladders leaning against the mountain-side. Had the cliff-dwellers, too, used ladders to mount the smooth rise up to the row after row of openings?

"Why don't you take off your sunglasses?" I suggested as Clifford peered into one of the imperfect circles. I waited while he removed them, then took a picture of him on the ladder so he could prove to his middle-school students what an adventurer he was.

"What's it like in there?" I called up to him.

"Have a look yourself." Above all else, Clifford was considerate. He climbed down off the ladder to give me a turn even though there were several other ladders nearby rising to several other caves. That morning we were the only visitors.

I tried my best not to hurry Clifford through the only activity he'd requested for the entire trip. In truth there wasn't much to see. The greater impact of the ruin, rather than its entertainment value, occurred afterwards, when the tourist was left to ponder the merits of civilization and the ebb and flow of culture.

Finally Clifford was satisfied that he'd seen enough, so we got back in the car to drive the remaining few miles back to Los Alamos. I tried to imagine myself living in one of the caves, skin-to-skin with my extended family. Though I frequently yearned to be rid of dozens of earrings, my appliances, my car that was always on the verge of a breakdown, I questioned whether I could tolerate the stark simplicity within the rock walls. And yet what might I accomplish away from the distraction of modern props and toys in this universe both so close to and eons away from the nuclear lab?

The town of Los Alamos wasn't at all what I'd been expecting. It was a new town. Of course. Until the Army colonized that flat of land close to the Jemez Mountains, the only residents had been the students and faculty of a private boys' school eventually displaced by the government. Only after the lab's many secrets had become public did anyone not involved in the Manhattan Project move to the town.

For us, this was a day trip. We would be spending the night back in Santa Fe so there was no hotel to check into, no figuring out where to leave the car. And while the history of the place might propel visitors on a long journey of speculation—what would our world have been like without the bomb?—the only real tourist site was the museum attached to the laboratory.

Clifford took two or three photographs of me standing beside the *Los Alamos National Laboratory* sign, grinning as jubilantly as I should have been in our wedding pictures. Though my husband didn't have to persuade me to look happy, my friend Rob, the volunteer photographer at our wedding, had kept coaxing me to smile while I tried to disguise my doubts and deficiencies, which must have been as visible as my ivory tea-length dress.

I plunged myself into the complexities of the museum exhibits, needing to escape the constant throb of

"I'm married, I'm married." The prospect of waking up every single morning for the rest of my life next to the same man was, frankly, frightening—more frightening to me than the inconceivable destruction schemed by those scientists, citizens of a contrived community that existed solely to create a weapon that could obliterate the world.

Clifford followed my lead throughout the museum. After all, this was *my* peculiar obsession that had drawn me away from more typical honeymoon scenarios: drinks out on a hotel terrace, mountain vistas viewed through our four eyes, ambrosial dinners concluding in bed. My husband read the text associated with each exhibit, looking seriously thoughtful as if it were his task to evaluate the merits of each scientific stride along the road to Hiroshima. I, however, was much less interested in the science underlying the development of the bomb than in the psychic life of the plotters and in the strange routines of this hidden city with its unreal address.

So I wandered through the museum, pausing at exhibit after exhibit that detailed the scientific steps along the way to the grand finale. I overheard a museum guide replying to someone's question about the current work in progress at Los Alamos. Once her listeners had dispersed, I confided to her how intrigued I was with Robert Oppenheimer. "I'm not even sure why. I don't remember when I first heard of him or know what it is that so attracts me to him."

She nodded as if she'd heard this before or as if she shared my fascination with the lanky overseer of the bomb. Still nodding, she said, "This country played a dirty trick on him."

I waited for further commentary but she offered none and finally stopped nodding. Perhaps she'd strayed too far from her script. Abruptly she began to provide me with information about the museum.

"We show a film here that'll give you a sense of what life in Los Alamos was like in those days. Better hurry. It started a minute or two ago."

By now Clifford had ventured off on his own. I scanned the large room with its predominantly glass and metal displays, acrylic dividers, and chrome guide rails, and soon I spotted a likeness of Oppie fractured into parts as in a cubist painting. The multiple images created by so many reflective surfaces complicated the simple act of walking from where I stood to where Clifford stood. I was misled into false turns and stepped into at least one parallel reality in this physics funland before I managed to reach him.

"Come on. The movie's already started."

"What movie?" he asked.

I dragged him away from a gigantic model of an atom beside which was posted a tiring explanation of how so small and simple an entity could wreak mass damage. After a hushed greeting that I couldn't quite hear, we were admitted into a darkened room. We entered during a segment of antique footage—semi-sepia, two-toned shots of shirt-and-tied men sitting around drinking cocktails. This was the secret society of the bomb, a place where all residents had vowed never to reveal their whereabouts or their purpose in vacating their lives. In the midst of the desert, away from the enforcement of norms concerning proper attire, they would dress for a typical work week in blue jeans and cowboy boots. In the next segment, a cluster of scientists was conferring in the lab, looking like ranch hands.

"Isn't this fascinating?" I whispered to Clifford, who didn't agree, at least not out loud.

"I wonder where the old film came from," was all he said.

At the first appearance of Oppenheimer, known to his peers as "Oppie," I gasped as if the forty-million dollar star of the show had just come on the scene. What a man! What a mind, and an imagination that I could well appreciate even if it was in a realm so unfamiliar to me. What else but imagination could impel one towards the thunderburst of power harbored by particles so tiny that specialized instruments had to be designed merely to see them?

During every interview with Robert Oppenheimer, every filmed meeting of him and his colleagues, every shot of him arriving or leaving, walking from here to there, he had a cigarette in his mouth or held between his fingers. In his later years he alternated between cigarettes and a pipe.

My husband had been a smoker when I met him but had since quit.

Oppie was angular, both his features and his gestures, though his thoughts seemed infinite and fluid, as if they had no edges or endpoints.

Like Oppie, Clifford had a pointy nose and prominent cheekbones. His profile was a composite of stern, straight lines and square angles. I could tell that he wasn't budged by the pathos of Oppie's predicament or the similar change of heart suffered by some of his crew, who devoted themselves to the making of the bomb and then ardently opposed its use.

Probably I should have felt contempt for a man who had contributed to the invention of such an evil force without giving much thought to its real-life application. Instead, I was smitten by the owner of a soul that cringed at war, a man who could become a moral being long enough to demonstrate horror, maybe even remorse, for the outcome of his work.

As engrossed as I was in the movie, I was aware of the unaccustomed sensation of a wedding ring on my finger. I kept sliding it to slightly different locations along my joint. Soon the movie arrived in time at that moment when the first mushroom cloud of mutating potential blossomed, electrifying the desert sky. At that instant following the detonation of the Trinity test bomb, Robert Oppenheimer had no quotable reaction, according to the movie. The recollections of those present suggested that both he and his brother Frank, beside him at the time, exchanged terse statements acknowledging that the bomb had been successful: "It worked," something as plain as that. Most likely they were in shock from the incomparable spectacle they'd just witnessed.

The movie concluded with the dropping of the bomb on Hiroshima by the Enola Gay. My wedding ring felt uncomfortably tight, so I began to rotate it around my finger. I glanced at Clifford and just then heard the co-pilot's legendary reaction to the explosion: "Oh my God, what have we done?"

◆◆◆◆

The Angels Speak

Soon after Clifford and I had begun dating, we went to an experimental theater performance in Philadelphia about the life of J. Robert Oppenheimer. *The Angels Speak* may have marked the beginning of my curiosity about this ultimately tragic public figure. The fledgling playwright, aspiring to push the limits of theater, had written a script that was described as a mix of dialogue and opera. The characters included not only Oppie, his family, friends, and colleagues, but incarnations of virtues such as truth and beauty.

Clifford pored over his program while I toured the surroundings from my seat. The theater had been converted from some kind of assembly room, I guessed. A barely adequate stage elevated just a few inches above the floor had been outfitted with a wraparound curtain in a deep shade of red.

"What time is it?" I kept asking Clifford since he could always be counted on to wear a watch.

He tried to disguise how late it was by rounding off the minutes. "Not much past eight-fifteen," he said as I pressed towards him to read the watch myself: a few minutes before eight-thirty.

By now the eight o'clock curtain time was too far past to be excused by an inaccurate clock backstage or a missing prop. "This is so obnoxious," I complained. But the half-hour wait didn't bother Clifford in the least since it allowed him to think ahead to his lesson plan for the next school day.

Meanwhile I continued to scour the theater for details of interest to me, like the predominance of women in the audience, a seaside mural still visible through the sloppy top-layer of ivory paint, and the popularity of plastic eyeglass frames. No one else seemed annoyed by the play's late start. In the row in front of me and to my left, two women were talking about their boss. Though I was usually entertained by gossip even about people I didn't know, their discussion was absorbed by the wordless buzz of blended conversations around me.

"Go say something," I said to Clifford. "We can't just sit here so sheepishly." He would be a much better audience ambassador than I, determined as he always was to avoid conflict.

"Why don't you give it another few minutes?"

Since we'd just begun dating, I didn't want to portray myself as extreme in any way. So I flipped my hair over my shoulder and sat back in my folding chair. My attempt at patience, however, lasted briefly. "Maybe I'll go ask what's happening."

Clifford tried to dissuade me from getting out of my seat. "Just relax," he told me even as I could feel my entire musculature contracting into a taut, second skeleton.

"I wouldn't be surprised if this is part of the play," I said, "and we're being tested."

"That's crazy, Pauline. It's just a disorganized, small-change theater company."

Before I had decided whether or not to hunt down someone who worked at the theater, the house lights went off, the wafture of mildew from the upholstery became more noticeable in the darkness, and the play commenced with an ultra-soprano solo. The vocalist listed the many milestones of Oppie's career, concluding with his humiliation by the Atomic Energy Commission and the subsequent collapse of his spirit "………*like an audience that sits passively waiting for a play to begin,*" the actress sang.

Even though Clifford was staring fixedly at the stage, I was certain he could feel the intensity of my eyes on him as I waited for acknowledgment that my prophesy had come true. I'd been right. The late start time had been a ploy to get us to look at our willingness to accept without question whatever was inflicted on us.

But by now the subject was too emotionally charged for Clifford to dare to look at me. Finally I just had to say it. "I *told* you." I wanted so badly to stand up and announce to the crowd that I had suspected exactly this. Begrudgingly I forgave the actors and behind-the-scenes supporting cast. Being kept waiting intentionally was much more acceptable than being forced to wait because of ineptitude or rudeness. I could not as easily forgive Clifford, the pussycat lazing too close to the tigress in me. Soon, though, he kissed my cold cheek and I formed a wish that I could be more like him.

Every few minutes a speedy change of scene was accomplished with a few large props and an adjustment in the lighting. Within the first ten minutes of the play, Robert Oppenheimer had progressed from a young child to a university scholar.

"*A hero, accused spy, populist rich guy,*" sang a tenor whose vocal range was more within the bounds of my tolerance than had been the first soloist's.

Soon a gigantic cyclotron was wheeled onto the stage, and a slew of personified atoms enacted the acceleration taking place inside the chamber. They seemed to be enjoying their tumble through space and didn't at all give the impression of being exploited. A clever trick of costume design allowed each atom to split into two while an offstage chorus of voices chanted, "*Fission, fission, fission…*"

Each actor must have assumed at least a dozen roles since numerous friends of Oppie appeared during the play, though some of them were represented by hand puppets. Oppenheimer's wife Kitty was characterized as two personas: the temptress who'd captivated her man corresponding to the front, and the sullen, unpopular first lady of Los Alamos to the back of the actress who played her. The professional stature of Oppie himself was symbolized by boosting the lead actor up on stilts. Certain of the characters appeared always with wings—the angels of the title, I guessed—though I couldn't tell what qualified someone to be an angel in the play. Perhaps, I decided, the qualifying factor was unrelated to the subject of the play; for instance, maybe all of those who'd been cast as angels had names beginning with the same letter or were double-jointed.

My attention strayed to the thick curls of paint separating from the ceiling. When I looked back at the stage, a line of actors all shrouded in black judges' robes was entering. Their angry eyes directed at Oppenheimer, they sang, *"You love her, you love her, you love her…"* At each repetition of the phrase, another woman would emerge from behind a judge, and together the women formed a circle around Oppenheimer.

"Oppie's like a movie star," I said to Clifford, who nodded. Even in the dark, I could see his smile.

"You love her you love her….THE BOMB!" the judges accused, and instantly a swirl of smoke obscured all of the players.

I leaned into Clifford. "I thought he was tried for being a communist, not a lady's man. Are you following this, Cliff?" I asked him then.

"'Following' may be too strong a word."

The play explored Oppie's personal and family relationships and his disputed communist affiliations, but the nontraditional form and ambiguous lyrics left me unsure whether I was making anywhere near the right inferences. Had Oppie had an affair with a co-worker, or was his love of work being personified in the form of an erotic brunette? In one scene, Oppie's Cal Tech cronies were costumed in aprons fashioned out of masculine-looking fabrics: browns, grays, plaids. A laboratory explosion, symbolized by a diffusion of opaque smoke, allowed the actors to exit the stage and the next set to be erected.

During intermission, the woman sitting directly in front of Clifford turned around and asked, "Might I borrow your program?" Then she smiled. She was about seventy, and since hers was a face you couldn't imagine saying no to, Clifford obligingly took our shared program off my lap and handed it to her. I continued to watch her as she stood without even glancing at the program and, securing it between her arm and her side, left her row of seats. She approached a young woman in the aisle and after a short exchange between them, the young woman gave her another copy of the program.

"What's she doing?" I asked Clifford, as if he would know.

"Maybe this is part of the play, too. Maybe she'll collect everyone's programs and then not return any of them."

This possibility wasn't that farfetched, but I wasn't ready to surrender my template of reality and to begin seeing everything as a staged interaction. "I want my program back," I said.

"I'll get you another."

When the house lights were switched off and Clifford hadn't yet returned, I guessed that no more programs were left and that he was postponing having to tell me so. Eventually he reappeared and settled back into his seat as inconspicuously as possible.

"Where's my program?" I asked.

Clifford must have felt immensely relieved when someone in the row behind us shushed me. Oppie, on stilts, was singing his first number, a medley of all the languages he'd studied. Meanwhile a circle of female admirers embellished the number with vibratos and tremolos, each of the women eventually spinning away from the orbit around him until only Kitty remained—Kitty, who soon became his wife.

At the time, I had no premonition that Oppie, Clifford and I would come together again in more intimate circumstances. How could I have foreseen that this high-profile scientist would spend some of our honeymoon with us?

Not until well into the play did I stop brooding about Clifford's refusal to ask what was causing the delay. All of my hopes of being rescued from an oncoming train, if need be, had vanished. And yet a life with Clifford would surely be serene, a still lake rather than a wildfire. I'd never known a man as gentle-hearted. He was abundantly generous with both his time and his money. Unlike so many of my emotionally erratic boyfriends, Clifford was a man I could actually consider marrying.

I'd decided during the last year that, yes, I did want to get married, that I did want to experience such an enduring social institution. I'd already known for a while that I wanted children. Over the years, I'd encountered many women who felt morally obligated not to introduce more children into this wretched world or who were repulsed by the physical act of giving birth. But from the time I was about six and doted on the itty-bitty three- and four-year olds in the neighborhood, I had wanted to be a mother.

Clifford and I had been keeping company for about nine months when I realized that he was unlikely ever to broach the subject of marriage. So I brought it up, in abstract terms at first. "Have you ever wanted to get married?" I asked him one Saturday while we were bravely chewing our way through peanut-butter sandwiches on heavy-grained bread. As soon as I heard the question spoken out loud, it sounded so obvious. Clifford, however, seemed not to read too much into my words.

"Yeah. I guess," he said.

"When was the last time you thought about it?"

I still hadn't decided whether or not Clifford was objectively handsome. But when he smiled fully enough to reveal shallow dimples, as he did now, I couldn't stop looking at him. "I'm thinking about it right now!" he confessed. "Pauline….?"

"What?"

He took another bite of his sandwich, so I had to wait while he ground down the heavily textured bread.

"Do you want to marry me, Pauline?"

I couldn't tell whether he was asking me hypothetically or presenting me with an authentic marriage proposal. And so I faltered.

"I think so. I mean, yes, I do."

"It's OK," Clifford quickly said. "You don't have to answer that."

"I don't? Why not?"

"Because…I didn't mean to put you on the spot."

Clifford fled what he must have perceived as a developing controversy by biting into his sandwich again. I didn't want to consent to a marriage that wasn't completely mutual. I wanted Clifford to reiterate, not withdraw, his proposal.

By the time he'd finished eating his sandwich, we managed to establish that he was really asking me to marry him and that I was accepting his proposal. This wasn't exactly a memory that I would willingly preserve or recount to our children. In fact I tried to forget the awkwardness of the scene and hoped that it wasn't predictive of a shared lifetime of miscommunication—miscues, retractions.

My disinterest in owning an engagement ring didn't bother Clifford at all. I thought that the money we might spend on a diamond could be used instead to accelerate us towards the purchase of a house. "My practical darling," he said, nuzzling into the protected warmth where my neck joined my shoulder. "Don't you want something, anyway, to wear on your finger to let the world know that you're attached?"

"Like what, Cliffie?"

Clifford reached across me and rummaged in the glove compartment of his car. We were paused at a red light en route to the grocery store to stock his kitchen, so empty that it appeared to have been burglarized.

"Like this," he said finally as he offered me a large metal washer that had probably been in the glove compartment for years. The light turned green so I slid the washer myself onto my left ring finger.

"Problem," I announced.

"Too big?"

"Too wide." But not wanting to quash Clifford's playful side, I suggested "I could wear it on a chain around my neck."

"It's not the same."

"Closer to my heart," I told him.

His eyes brightened. He found a dirty piece of string, also in the glove compartment, and for the time being we agreed that I would wear the string around my neck, the washer hanging from it like a charm.

Inside the store, while I dedicated myself to selecting basic provisions that every kitchen should have, Clifford wandered up and down the aisles picking up packages of dried peas and bottles of soy sauce and inspecting the labels. What he was up to I couldn't guess, and I hated to interrupt his visible concentration with a question. The outcome of his search was a bottle of Italian wine that he set in the cart without comment.

When we arrived at his apartment, Clifford immediately took the wine out of one bag of groceries and removed from around its neck a wire collar with a decorative plastic charm, a cluster of grapes printed on it.

"Will you? Do you?" he asked as he slid the wire onto the finger still slightly pink from my first engagement ring.

All of my doubts about marriage at that moment eluded me. I gripped his head in both my hands and kissed him with more hunger than I ever had. While our lips were still melded wetly together, I said into his mouth, "I do."

◆◆◆◆

Settling in for the Summer

Clifford and I had met while both of us were living in Philadelphia, but soon afterwards he accepted a job offer in Boston. Every other weekend from then on, we took turns visiting each other.

Probably our relationship would not have endured without the glamour of all the travel or the recuperation time between our visits. After each weekend that we spent together, I'd start to experience a creeping malaise that spread over me much like a rash. If I'd been a turtle, I surely would have withdrawn into my shell. Instead I boarded a departing plane out of Boston or else stood at the glass pane overlooking the plane back to Boston that Clifford had just boarded, waving goodbye as if he could see me.

For the first two days of our separation I'd do my best to tolerate the incessant commotion inside me. The ranting monologue, always rendered in my own voice, repeated phrases of doubt and refinements of my fear:

"What if I stop liking him?" or "I'm meant to be alone." But worse than this plague of words was the void enlarging between my stomach and my heart—an unreachable emptiness that, more often than not, felt more comfortable than the prospect of a lifelong commitment.

"Maybe I really prefer being by myself," I said to my friend Alia.

"Or maybe Clifford just isn't the one," she suggested.

My barren heart warmed to the comfort of her kitchen, the clutter of pasta tubes strewn over the counter, bubbling soup on the stove.

"No," I said slowly. "He's so much better than any of the others."

"You're wondering why you're not feeling...more fulfilled—is that what this is about?" Alia asked me.

"Well, or just..." I couldn't bear to articulate the possibility that perhaps I was simply incapable of contentment.

"Just what?"

Alia was one of those people who, if she missed even a word spoken by a character in a movie, would keep asking, "Take the boat to....what'd he say?" And she'd repeat her question until finally someone filled her in on the missing word or two. So I knew that I was going to have to work my way through to the end of the thought.

"Just maybe...maybe I'm not comfortable being happy."

"That's pretty serious for a 'just.'"

"Yeah."

While we were talking, Alia was diligently sorting through single grains of rice and removing an infestation of maggots. By training, she was a scientist in some excruciatingly specialized field of biology. She applied the same care to hunting down and segregating maggots from rice as I imagined she once had to dissecting cellular organisms. For as long as I'd known her, though, Alia had worked as a service bartender at an expensive restaurant—making drinks for waitpeople to serve without ever having to deal directly with customers herself. Though the sight of Alia with a tweezers and magnifying glass was consistent with the scientist in her, the thrift suggested by saving a cup or two of bulk rice didn't match my understanding of who she really was. She'd once told me that, some years ago, she and the other working women and the single mothers on her street would pool money from their paltry paychecks and welfare checks to pay for a cab to pick up and deliver lobster dinners—the most exorbitant meal they could think of.

"Do you think of Clifford as cute?" she asked me now.

"Cute? I don't know."

"Do you like looking at him?"

"Yes," I finally admitted, bothered that she'd had to ask. Weren't Clifford's good looks evident? His changeable eyes—sometimes brown, sometimes green—

seemed deep as still water. His heart-shaped face tapered to an impish chin.

The upcoming weekend would be my turn to fly up to Boston. My time with Clifford had become slightly unreal, set apart from the monotony and routine of daily existence. We ate out, we stayed up late, we attended plays and other such extravagant forms of entertainment. The only routines that seemed to have penetrated our weekend were toothbrushing and the need to buy gas for our cars.

And yet I anticipated our visits with dread, I think because we'd already agreed to get married and each day advanced us nearer to that daunting end. Marriage, a rite sanctified across cultures. An institution that according to statistics, despite its eons of endurance, was quite likely to fail. Would stepping across that nearly mythical divide somehow alter my feelings, I wondered, and the sensation of togetherness that so compelled me at the same time it strangled me like a too-tight waistband?

By then I'd permanently installed a toothbrush and duplicates of all my toiletries at Clifford's Boston home. I'd also left a few articles of clothing there. Packing had become a mindless process that required not much more than ten minutes. I'd become efficient, or maybe indifferent enough to how I looked around Clifford that I didn't give much thought to my weekend attire.

He didn't comment that Friday on my traveling ensemble—a silk shirt, overalls, and purple dress gloves—that I'd worn just to be silly. I wasn't sure whether to interpret his non-response as oblivion or embarrassment or disapproval.

"Hungry?" he asked.

"Hungry minus two of those little packs of peanuts," I said.

This meant that we had a little time before my blood sugar would plunge and I'd become savagely irritable. Unlike me, Clifford could go hours without eating even when he was extremely hungry.

Entering the restaurant where Clifford had made reservations earlier in the week was like crossing into a cave. The low ceiling implied that he was much taller than he actually was, and the moist air seemed a perfect growing environment for stalactites. "I read a review of this place that claimed it was one of the ten best restaurants in Boston," Clifford told me. "'Flavor without pretension' is how it was described."

While we waited for our food to be served, he asked, "Do you know your summer work schedule yet, Pauline?"

"Public health organizations don't have summer work schedules, Clifford. They're not like schools."

Maybe I could have reacted with less annoyance to his fairly benign question. Clifford's ever-tolerant acceptance of my temper bothered me even more than his question.

"Well I asked," he said, "because I was thinking maybe you should stay up here all summer. That way we could spend more time together and see what it's like to actually...live with each other, instead of always being on vacation."

I didn't suggest that Clifford spend the summer with me in Philadelphia since we'd agreed, once we got married, to live in Boston.

The waitress arrived with two huge plates only half-filled with our dinners. "You mean so we can see if we want to change our minds?" I asked. Though Clifford wasn't directly expressing his doubts about me, I could imagine him interrogating me: Do you always leave your clothes on the floor? Do you scribble notes on unpaid bills even if provided with a pile of scrap paper? Is your reuse of coffee filters an immutable habit, or might you be lured away from this form of thrift? Clifford's face was partially blocked by the waitress's extended arms and the tilt of her upper body. Still I could tell, when he answered, that my question had flustered him.

"No, that's not what I meant. I was thinking about… about having a different kind of—"

"Can I get you anything else?"

Clifford took advantage of the opportunity to disengage from our escalating conflict. "Some hot sauce."

"Hot sauce with ravioli?" I asked, trying to meet eyes with him through the criss-cross of the waitress's arms.

"Oh…and some water, please."

The instant the waitress turned away, I reeled Clifford back into our interrupted conversation. "A different kind of what?"

"Hmm?"

"You know, what you were saying before."

"Sorry. I don't remember."

"Well I do. You were saying that if I came down here for the summer, we could have a different kind of... Then the waitress bought our food."

The mention of food suggested to Clifford that he start to eat, further delaying the completion of his unfinished sentence.

"Come on, Cliff. What were you going to say?"

"All right. I guess I was thinking about—"

"Everything OK?" The waitress had dutifully returned with Clifford's hot sauce and water. I, too, would have liked a glass of water—no longer provided automatically since a drought some years ago—but didn't want to invite another interruption.

"Fine," Clifford and I answered at once. Had it been a less predictable response, I might have believed that this synchronicity was actually meaningful, evidence of our attunement to each other.

"OK, Clifford. The waitress is gone. We have our food. You have your hot sauce and your water. You went to the bathroom at the airport. Now please finish your thought."

"It's just...I've been wondering if you could possibly be as wonderful as I think you are."

I slammed back against my chair. This was not at all what I'd expected to hear. I felt defeated by the incomparable burden of sustaining his illusions of who I was. He didn't really know me after all. I thought of the beige tweed skirt my mother had sent me for my last birthday, a skirt I never would have bought myself, never wore, and that clashed with everything about me.

I said with nothing but sincerity, "I'm not."

Clifford took my hand—the hand with the fork in it rather than the hand that was free—and corrected me. "Oh, but I think you are."

For just the briefest moment I thought I understood that his statement wasn't about delusion or denial but about love. With genuine humility in the presence of someone with a bigger heart than mine, I looked down at my plate, at the messy sprawl of chicken bones and carnage.

I was thirty-one years old and Clifford was my eighteenth boyfriend, excluding kindergarten lovers who had given me plastic rings and misspelled pledges to love me forever. I'd calculated that, beginning when I was a nubile seventeen-year-old, I'd been with each mate for an average of nine months or so. From Clifford's point of view I wasn't a very good risk. He, in contrast, hadn't dated all through college and since then had had only one significant relationship, which lasted four and a half years. When I asked him why it had ended, he answered quite simply, "I don't know." No allusions to either party's childhood traumas, no analysis of their patterned interactions. Nothing that suggested any understanding of cause and effect as they applied to love. So I suppose that from my point of view, Clifford wasn't a very good risk either.

Since the restaurant was at basement level and had

no windows, we didn't know how heavily it was raining outside until a pair of very soggy customers breathlessly entered our cozy little grotto. The force of the downpour, audible during that moment when the door was open, seemed unmistakably punitive to me, and I wondered fleetingly whether an entire city might be suffering for my own failings or whether all of us within the city limits right now were equally to blame for the decreasing longevity of love.

"Why don't we get the check now?" I said, wanting to be ready to run before everyone in the restaurant jammed the door, desperate to escape the water that had begun seeping in from somewhere and was rising.

A threesome seated near the door was moved to another table. Soon someone emerged from the kitchen with a machinelike contraption attached to a length of hose. Once the customers sitting towards the front of the restaurant were evacuated to other tables, the little machine was plugged in and began emitting a drone.

"It's a sump pump," I heard a nearby diner say. The wet sound I'd been listening to was the slurping of shallow water into a hose, which I imagined drained the floodwater into the Boston Harbor. Despite the effort of the noisy little pump, I could feel that the carpet below our table was saturated.

The same waitress who had checked in on us so often during our meal took at least ten minutes to finally deliver the bill. By then she was wearing high yellow plastic boots, which she must have kept at the restaurant, suggesting that this flood wasn't an uncommon occurrence.

I asked Clifford, "Did the review say anything about a problem with flooding?"

"No," he answered earnestly, then said, "Maybe this is what they meant by charm."

Neither of us tended to laugh out loud. But with full-sickle smiles, we both leaned forward until our noses touched, the equivalent of a shared laugh. Clifford offered to get the car while I waited in the cave.

The next week, back at work, I broached the subject of taking the summer off as if it were a theoretical possibility.

"Well, *if* you were to need to take more than, say, two weeks off, there are two ways you could do it," my supervisor, Sara, began to explain.

"And what would those be?" I asked with theoretical interest.

"You could apply for a leave of absence…"

"Uh-huh."

"Or else you could use all of your vacation time, sick days, and personal days, and after none was left, do some work from home, or from wherever you'd be."

The first option sounded so much easier, though a leave of absence would interrupt my income and impose on my co-workers, who were likely to have to compensate for my absence. "Go ahead," and "Off with you," they said, conspiring in my presence to throw me a send-off party. So I requested a leave of absence for six weeks in the summer, beginning at the end of June.

I loaded all the available space in my small car with things that I decided I'd need that summer. My ironing board, for instance. Clifford didn't own one, and many of my clothes were made out of crisp, impressionable cotton. The small electric keyboard that I'd been meaning to teach myself to play. After all, I wouldn't be working for those six weeks, Clifford would be at a summer job, and I didn't know anyone in Boston except for him (though halfway through my fiancée-in-residency, I discovered that a second cousin on my mother's side lived in a Boston suburb).

When Clifford greeted me at the curb outside his building—he must have been on the lookout from a front window—he raised his eyebrows suggestively but uttered not a word about all my cargo. Once we'd finished carrying it inside, I realized that I, a passer-through, now had more belongings in the apartment than Clifford did.

"I cleared out a drawer for you in my dresser."

Poor unsuspecting Clifford. Didn't he understand that I'd need much more than one drawer? My clothes, my books, my folders messily filled with notes on some-day projects—all of these, I hoped, would create a semblance of familiarity in my new home, linking me to the life I'd soon be forsaking for the frightening unknown territory of marriage.

For the next few days, I spent a lot of my time establishing myself in the apartment—displacing or rearranging Clifford's harmonicas and paperweights and loose keys. Most of the books on his two bookshelves had been with him for years and never been subject to any kind of purge. Among them were his college textbooks—*Learning along with Your Students, History Awakes!*—and even childhood books that his mother had shipped to him during one of *her* book purges.

"Clifford, do you think you could sort through your books and make some room for mine on the shelves?" Clifford was always so obliging that I had to be sure not to ask more of him than was fair.

From his response, I couldn't tell if I'd succeeded in being considerate. "Sure," he said as always, no matter how unreasonable the demand.

The several very tall stacks of books and nearly vacant bookshelves that resulted from his sorting process that night left me feeling terribly autocratic and a failure in my desire to be less demanding of him.

"Cliffie, you don't have to get rid of that many books."

He added one more to a cast-off pile. "No, this is fine. I never look at any of them."

But after Clifford went to bed that night, I reviewed his choices and found at least a dozen books that either I wanted to keep for myself or believed that Clifford should hold onto. Discarded along with the political science books and education texts was an ancient-looking booklet titled *My School Year.* I opened it to the front page and was met with a black-and-white school photo of Clifford, probably in third or fourth grade. He looked irresistibly boyish—brash and bashful at once with a missing front tooth, a perky nose, his army-close-cut hair and cardigan sweater. I learned from the page titled "All about Me" that his favorite color was red and his favorite food was hot dogs.

"Hello, my sweetheart," I said quietly and kissed his picture lips, then gently set *My School Year* on top of the pile of books to be saved. I wished that I could have known him back then, this adorable little boy who grew to buy one postcard from every place he ever visited, who collected unwashed seashells in a shoebox, who would soon become my husband.

◆◆◆◆

Settling In

The mesa was the open hand of the desert, a gesture of welcome to the men assigned to find a site for the new bomb laboratory. It was the perfect place, they all agreed after rejecting a series of almost-perfect places that in the end had been judged unacceptable. From the beginning, New Mexico had been on the shortlist. Jemez Springs, perhaps. Almost perfect.

Then Oppenheimer led them up a steep and rocky road to that pause in the mountains, a two-by-six mile reach of flatland overseen by giant trees, the desert beyond at once desolate and thriving, insistent sagebrush growing in the cold out of infertile sand.

Since his youth, Robert Oppenheimer had been charmed by the New Mexican landscape. During early visits to the Los Piños Ranch, he'd learned to ride horseback and to navigate the directionless desert, to traverse an infinitude of particles everywhere on the ground like toast crumbs. Every summer he found his way back there along with his brother Frank, and each year they'd get to know new regions of wilderness farther and farther from the ranch where they stayed.

The pearl moon low in the desert sky became Robert's muse when, as a young man, he began composing verse. His poetry often conjured memories of summers in New Mexico. The spartan lifestyle on the ranch was well worth the boundless freedom. The Oppenheimer brothers could ride for miles with no more than chocolate bars in their pockets and never encounter any restrictions like those imposed at home and at school. They could be themselves, without the distortions of ambition or pretense.

So in 1942 Oppenheimer led them—the strange pairing of military men and academics—to that same corner of the country, and when they arrived at the mesa, all of them recognized it as the site they'd been seeking: surrounded by a margin of isolation, forlorn by human interest and separating the distant residents from the bomb that would one day be tested. While the men toured the area, noted the trembling railroad bridge over the rio and the snarl of woods beyond the clearing, teenage boys huffed about in the snowy autumn air wearing shorts and thin veneers of perspiration.

"The boys' Ranch School," Oppenheimer explained. "They own the land," though he couldn't explain why the boys were dressed so scantily in the cold.

"Isn't this the desert?" asked Major Dudley, piqued that his own choice near Jemez Springs had been rejected. "I thought deserts were as hot as hell."

"We're up in the mountains," Oppenheimer said, though everyone except Dudley seemed already to know about the effect of mountains on climate.

Suddenly Edwin McMillan turned around, having sensed something of considerable height and authority standing behind him. He was met with the Jemez Mountains, and he swore later in privacy to his wife that they'd been watching him.

"What is it?" asked General Leslie Groves.

McMillan was a scientist. How could he explain the unshakable sensation that they were not alone? For one long moment he let himself feel the air and the light. Oppenheimer remarked that McMillan was unusually quiet for the rest of that afternoon.

Within two days, the Army had purchased the property, enigmatically dubbed "Site Y." The boys in shorts were given till the near-end of winter to leave. By then the ground was melting into mud.

Housing was built quickly and cheaply, quality not being a concern since the Army's intention was to finish this bomb short of two years. After that, the houses could collapse or rot. The planners lacked the foresight to imagine that there might be bombs beyond this first one and that the need for secrecy would have to be sustained as long as national boundaries existed.

The standing buildings previously belonging to the school represented a head start: the staff's homes could house the higher on the hierarchy of scientists; the common kitchen would of course be useful for community meals and other civic gatherings; the dormitories would be occupied by the legions of young, unattached men; the stables would, as always, be used for horses so the scientists could gallop away from their cloistered community, as if they were free-riding explorers of the tiniest world within the world. By invitation only, these men, these women, these wives and children came to live here with no address.

Teams of carpenters, builders and plumbers were transported to Los Alamos, believing that they would be constructing a government retreat where residents would be working on electric rockets—so the story went, the intentional misinformation broadcast by the general's staff. What'll they do for fun? the work crew may have wondered, unable to imagine the hundred-plus-proof parties that the scientists would be throwing on Fridays. The paranormally strong alcohol distilled for laboratory use combined well with pineapple juice, perhaps no one's first choice for a mixer but one that was usually available at the Army Post Exchange.

Dick Glazer, one of the University of Chicago graduate students brought to Los Alamos to perform some of the more menial calculations, said of the plywood barracks, "I'd do better sleeping in my car." They hadn't even bothered to slap clapping over the rough structures, and every building alike was painted Army green. But after all, Glazer wasn't there for a luxury-hotel getaway, or for the novelty of southwest nature-shades of brown, or to gawk at the sky that, here, appeared to approach its actual dimensions.

Being asked to participate in the Manhattan Project was an unquestionable honor, a chance to collude with some of the great minds of the time, to share in their vision of a world without war. Many of those involved in the project were European runaways who barely got out in time. Jewish, or sympathizers. Free thinkers. For them, Los Alamos was their battleground where they would concoct a bomb to stop the spread of Hitler's epidemic empire and, with its terrifying potential, deter all further wars.

Any mail received by residents of Los Alamos was addressed to Box 1662, Santa Fe, and after dropping into a bottomless hole in the postal system, the cards and envelopes were routed to that place that seemed to have been erected on the edge of time.

So the existing boys' school buildings were used, and new plywood barracks were built. While some of the school facilities were designated as work areas—offices for those who needed them, meeting rooms conveniently accessorized with the boys' left-behind chalkboards—two major laboratories were added to the compound. These had to be constructed of materials sturdier than plywood, with impenetrable walls that could contain vagrant, high-speed subatomic particles and any trade talk that lurking spies might overhear. Espionage was a worry. Even after Little Boy and Fat Man were dumped onto their targeted victims, even after the war was won, everyone's ears would be checked for traces of what they might have heard.

The laws of nature applied inside and outside those government-funded structures, those horse stables, those laboratories so far from the universities where the work had begun. The whole universe, after all, was ruled by those laws. How small the earth could become, summed up on paper in equations made up of harsh and ugly sounds. A world so small one could almost cease to recognize it as home to humankind, and to the birds and fish and the colossal redwood trees.

Oppie had at first projected that sixty scientists would be needed to design the bomb. But soon that number increased, and increased again, and the population up on the Hill continued to grow for months after the spring start of the work, when runny mud, dried, dulled the flanks of the construction vehicles. In fact a small town of scientists—thousands—would be required, and Oppenheimer recruited them in batches, having to twist some arms more than others but aware that his own name lent the project prestige. Then as the German army continued to advance, even the unswayables were swayed: the pacifists and the stay-puts who hated to leave their comfy homes.

They straggled onto that flat span of space, many of them arriving alone, some of the younger men arriving in groups as if they'd already organized themselves into bunks. As many as eight men slept in each dormitory room, sharing a crude kitchen well-matched with their limited cooking skills. On that first night, they waged tugs of war over ownership of the blankets even though all were identical military issue.

"No, see, that one already has moth holes."

"What difference does that make?"

But desert nights could be cold. These men, atomic scientists, knew all about small spaces and what could fit through them.

Dorothy McKibbin checked in on them as they were slapping each other with their blankets. All that energy, like frisky atoms. "You men getting settled?" she asked. The official greeter down in Santa Fe, she was unofficially the matriarch of L.A. The men looked up, saw her, and at once let the blankets slacken and hung their heads like naughty boys.

"You finding everything you need?"

"Everything except, maybe, a nice warm cuddle," one of the men said flirtatiously.

Dorothy winked. "Lights out," she said.

The new plywood structures still smelled of wood and paint. These barracks were thought good enough for the rank and file, the young ones, the no-names who hadn't yet established reputations.

The more eminent scientists, especially those with families, were given small houses once inhabited by the faculty of the Ranch School. Other houses were built for the scientists and their families as well as for the officers based there to remind the men that this was, ultimately, a mission of war. All of the rearranging of atoms, the measurement of unfathomably small specks of matter and squeaks of energy—this was, to the military, not so much research as the manufacture of weaponry dictated by the machinations of state. And despite repeated declarations by the scientists, however heartfelt, that this was an example of how science could be applied to a moral end, General Grove and Lieutenant Colonel Pash saw Los Alamos as just another military victory: the subjugation of science—now locked up in cages in the form of these hot-shot scientists—to the big boys, the muscled uniforms with guns and guards to protect them.

What would they have done without the women? Dorothy McKibbin, from her desk in the Santa Fe headquarters at 109 East Palace, extended hospitality to the newcomers. She told them where to shop and how to dress for the desert. Rose Bethe, whose husband Hans had been appointed head of the Theoretical Division, arrived early so she could oversee housing arrangements down to the locks on the doors. The pediatrician's wife, Shirley Barnett, helped bring order to Oppenheimer's office. None of his former colleagues and students could quite imagine him in an administrative role until the women organized his drawers, created files, and made lists for him of all that needed to be done. "Maybe Oppie hasn't been miscast after all," those same skeptics said then.

During one of many planning meetings, a Los Alamos wife suggested that the town needed a café. Before long, Oppenheimer, the Scientific Director himself, was involved in deciding what to do with that suggestion, whether or not they should open a café, and if so, where to locate it. Soon he'd be asked to come up with menu selections. "Honestly, General, shouldn't someone else be doing this?" he could have said, and yet he wanted to keep his people happy. If having a place to go each week that simulated a restaurant would help with morale, then he was all for it.

While Los Alamos homes were equipped with kitchens so families could carry on with their domestic routines, the single men, including the packs of cogitating graduate students and rookies, were expected to eat their meals together, preparing them in this or that communal kitchen. During the first weeks, as the selected citizens began to arrive, everyone ate in the large dining hall where the boys used to eat in rows. All of the scientists, their families, the officers, and the office support staff sat at the long rectangular tables across the room from the janitors and handymen who'd been misled as to the existence of this small, unknown town in the desert and who were, apparently, incurious or strangely willing to believe whatever they were told. "Just for now," Colonel Pash assured them, feeling that it was his duty to inaugurate each meal with a word or two spoken to the group. Everyone sat at the tables in the dining hall, fed cafeteria-style the plain food prepared by temporary food service people who'd nearly been blindfolded to preserve the site's secrecy before being conveyed in buses to Los Alamos from neighboring towns.

Why would these nail bangers and food scoopers agree to uninspiring jobs and such rustic living conditions? Work was scarce in San Ildefonso and Tesuque, the nearest towns. Here, in the sudden city, they were housed in Army-green boxes. To General Groves the expense was well worth it, as was the hiring of maids to clean the houses powdered with desert dust, keeping the at-home wives feeling pampered until the cocktail hour, when they'd swim away through glassfuls of spirits to fantasies of where else they'd rather be.

Meanwhile Pash fussed with security on the Hill. Fences, passes, rumors. Several versions of secrecy emerged:

1. intentional misrepresentation of the nature of the project (electric rocket technology);

2. acknowledgment that Los Alamos was the site of secret research, though that research wasn't identified;

3. news that a fireworks manufacturer was thinking of relocating to the desert and that people had been attracted to the area because of real estate prospects;

4. and finally, that Los Alamos didn't really exist. After all, the project couldn't be identified, the place couldn't be named.

The Oppenheimers didn't sell or rent their Eagle Hill Road home in Berkeley, expecting their sojourn in the desert to be temporary, however long it lasted. Neither did any of the other rooted families dispose of their homes. But a good number of the team were still in the gypsy stage of their lives, moving from one academic setting to the next, stopping for a while in this boarding house or that rented room. These young men brought with them to Los Alamos everything that they owned, each one's possessions typically fitting into one large suitcase and an attaché case. The Oppenheimers and others entitled to actual houses had more to bring, more to leave behind, and somewhere to leave it. Though Kitty, Robert's wife, wanted to hang some of their valuable artwork on the desert walls, Robert insisted on leaving their entire collection of paintings at home. "You'll see," he told Kitty. "The views there are much more beautiful than anyone's rendering of the real thing."

Robert didn't, though, interfere with her choice of other, more portable home furnishings, like tablecloths and matching napkins, or the satin pillowcases that she loved to feel against her cheek. The houses were supplied with cookware and appliances. And though Kitty preferred her own pots and pans and washing machine to any the Army was likely to provide, she conceded the impracticality of moving hers to Los Alamos.

Phyllis Fisher thought that she might as well package all of the food in her refrigerator and take it along. She'd had barely any notice when they'd be leaving and had, she admitted, shopped a bit excessively that last week, considering she knew that the moving date couldn't be far off. A handful of string beans—why waste them? Lolling leaves of lettuce twice wrapped—in newspaper then in a blue bath towel that was being packed anyway; half a jar of chunky peanut butter, half a button mush-

58

room that she swaddled in layers of cloth napkins, thus smuggling into her Los Alamos home some of her favorite table linens.

As more and more of the bomb team arrived and joined the work-in-progress, the town began to organize around the steps of scientific inquiry.

Question: Which is more efficient, to construct a bath house with multiple units or to continue building a bathroom in each living unit?

Hypothesis: Individual bathrooms are cheaper.

Supporting evidence: The cost of larger parts—those intended for commercial purposes—that would be needed to accommodate use by numbers of residents is greater than the cost of plumbing supplies needed for residential purposes, even when multiplied by the number of living units. Also, individual units, in the long run, are easier to maintain.

Theory: Contrary to one's first, reflexive reaction, one must conclude that housing will be cheaper if smaller, individual living units are favored over dorm-style units.

Question: Should a weekly community meal be scheduled or left to the initiative of the citizens?

Hypothesis: Group meals should not be scheduled.

Evidence: A tendency became quickly established for the boys to break away from each other at the end of the work day. Too much time together, too much new data that their minds had to chew up and swallow. They needed, in the evenings, to be alone as much as they could in a postage-stamp-size town with no escape.

Theory: Planned meals would be too regimented for a community stressed by the pressure of deadlines and the onus of war. Therefore, dining together on a regular basis should be optional.

However, they all gathered on Friday nights, needing to put those overworked brain cells to bed, knock 'em out so they could start anew the next week. Oppie's martinis were cold and strong and could be counted on to fuel fascinating conversations even among these party guests who lived and worked with each other throughout the week. They didn't need paid entertainers when instead they could reach inside themselves and find the clever jokes, amusing anecdotes, even a snippet of song performed in a wobbly falsetto. All of them were willing, at least once, to play the fool.

By eleven o'clock on those nights, the thinkers, drinkers, and all the rest were flattened into two dimensions, and only copious amounts of water and desert manna could possibly help them to sleep through the night without vomiting and to wake in the morning without the grip of a headache pressing on their skulls. And during those bleary moments before sleep, when whispers of air coming in through the window might remind a man of all the places his ancient soul had traveled, he was likely to hear phrases from Beethoven on a keyboard and be unsure whether or not to trust his inebriated senses.

While everyone else slept or cranked out pre-dream ideas that could be applied to work, Edward Teller sat at the piano he'd made great efforts to ship to Los Alamos then to have hoisted up the hill, no doubt believing that the project would keep him there a while.

◆◆◆◆

Fusion of Two

When did the celebrations of our life rites—weddings, funerals, graduations—become social occasions that had to be planned with exquisite artistry and precision? And why, during these months of planning, did each departure from tradition have to be justified? I sensed that my wedding ceremony was supposed to be the culmination of everything that had preceded it—every awkward date, each splendid kiss—at the same time it had to express all of my wishes for the future and to acknowledge the inevitable, lurking possibilities of woe.

As the wedding date approached, scenes from my life began to flash before me as if I were about to experience a kind of death. I was afflicted with frequent recollections of all those rough bumps on the road through childhood. The triumph of trading a small, sparkling stone I'd found at day camp for a plain but weighty dalmatian rock had been displaced soon after by an indescribable remorse—a lesson about the unrelatedness of size and value. I also remembered that a chunky girl whose arms were scaled with eczema had been the only person in the fleet of eighth-grade girls in gym class willing to stay behind and hoist me up from a fall that had seriously abraded the skin on both my knees. Not all of these long-lost memories dated back to my youth. The premature death of my cousin Heidi when we were both in our late twenties warped the predictable timeline of life enough that I found myself wondering what would I do if Clifford were to suddenly have a heart attack.

So far I hadn't let the horrors of bridal dresses and catering arrangements deter me from getting married. But was this massacre by so many solemn memories supposed to be a warning? I didn't believe that marriage was for everyone, and now, on the eve of my own wedding, I was tormented with doubt that it was really right for me.

Clifford's aunt and uncle owned a summer home in the Berkshires. The house itself was a plain structure that had withstood generations of threats by carpenter ants and wood rot. Its design made me think of the numerous historic houses I'd toured as an unwilling child. The first time Clifford and I had stayed there, I was sure that I felt the breath of a family forbearer on the side of my face—though it was probably mildew. Aunt Laura and Uncle Bill offered us the house for our wedding, knowing that its allure wasn't the building itself, erected by lay carpenters, but the luscious five acres on which it sat. Only at the far rear of the property did the dense population of trees qualify as woods. The distribution of trees everywhere else on the land—twenty-three different species of trees, Clifford's uncle had told me—created more variants of shade than I could have imagined, and as many growing environments. The perennials bloomed in arrangements that appeared more accidental than planned. Aunt Laura suggested that we cut as many bouquets as we'd like. I could have harvested half of the flowers and still enough would have remained to preserve that wild, overgrown beauty.

Fortunately the size of the house limited our guest list, and my mother's vision of my wedding as a major social event was not to be realized. One night during my summer in Boston, we phoned my parents to let them know about our plans. My mother had been prodding me to hurry up and set a date; many places had to be reserved years in advance, she'd warned.

She's not going to like this," I said to Clifford.

He squeezed my hand in his, still damp from after-dinner dishwashing, and said, "We'll tell her together."

"I don't know... I don't want to drive all the way to New York just to deliver the news."

"No no. Phone conference!"

Clifford knew my mother well enough to predict that she wouldn't be nearly as unpleasant to me if he were listening in. I made the call from the living room, comforted even as I dialed by the regularity of Clifford's breathing into the mouthpiece of the phone in our bedroom.

As soon as my mother answered the call, I announced, "Mom, Clifford's on the phone with me."

"Clifford! How nice to hear your voice," she said, even though Clifford hadn't spoken yet.

"How are you?" Clifford asked. Ever since he'd met my parents, he skillfully avoided addressing them by any form of their names, not sure what to call them.

I didn't wait for her to answer. "Mom, we have some news... We've set the date. And we're getting married at Clifford's aunt and uncle's home in the Berkshires."

"That's right," Clifford added, probably just to remind her that he was still on the line.

My mother said nothing. Her silence, though, seemed soft and submissive rather than stern.

"The place is really charming," I told her. "There are acres of gardens and birds, and the air sparkles."

"Really. Where will your guests stay? Are there any hotels nearby?"

"Plenty of hotels!" Clifford exclaimed. "People come there to vacation. The whole area is really beautiful..." He trailed off where normally he would have inserted a name.

"Yes, I imagine it is. Well, we'll still need a caterer. Or will we be foraging on the grounds?"

"You're right, Mom. We'll need food."

"We'd like a simple menu, though," Clifford said.

"And you'll need flowers."

"Actually, Mom, we're going to have cut flowers from the gardens. There are hundreds of them!" Even as I said this, I so wanted to offer her something, some part of the planning that would belong to her.

She summoned my father to the phone and I repeated our news to him, including the wedding site.

"Sounds good," he said. "You love each other, right?"

My father seemed to be missing the point of the call, but both Clifford and I answered his question with an unequivocal "Yes!"

"Don't expect your aunts in Cleveland to come," he said. "They don't travel anymore."

"Mom?" I wasn't sure if she'd handed the phone to my father or was still with us.

"What, Pauline?"

"Will you help me pick out a dress? You could come up one weekend and we could go shopping."

"I'd like that."

I was thirty-two years old. Old enough to have radically strayed from a young bride's ideal of what a wedding should be. After talking with my mother, I was certain I would get the inconspicuous, almost tentative ceremony that both Clifford and I preferred. Most everyone we had invited planned to come—a much higher acceptance rate than the eighty percent I was advised to expect by people who paid attention to such statistics. Apparently the setting had enough appeal that the weekend was to serve as a vacation for some of our friends.

My family—my two brothers, my sister and her family, and of course my parents—described their travel arrangements to the wedding as carpooling though I counted only one less vehicle than the number of families included in their caravan. At the same time I was pleased that all of them would be attending, I cautioned myself not to expect that they would have changed in honor of the occasion. Riley would conduct business surreptitiously during the ceremony; Philip would mutter bits of snide commentary about how artificial marriage was; and Sylvia would probably preempt anything I might say with knowing pronouncements about marriage and motherhood, her two indistinguishable sons still clinging to her like a nursing litter. My mother was sure to criticize everything about the wedding except for Clifford, who she'd try to establish as her ally while my father would converse with only the male guests, either about golf or about money.

No one except Clifford's cousin Meg, Laura and Bill's only child, could stay in the house with Clifford and me since we'd be occupying separate bedrooms according to his aunt's wish, a sleeping arrangement that reduced the number of rooms available for out-of-town guests. I would have liked my groom to defy this prohibition either by climbing up the drainpipe and diving into my room through the window or by marching down the hallway at night and boldly opening my door. Yet even if he'd been that much of a rebel, I was certain that Clifford would be snoozing by nine-thirty with an open book askew on his tummy. He was an early-to-bedder but fortunately could be easily wakened if I wanted to visit when getting into bed hours after him.

On the night before our wedding, we met in the upstairs hall outside the bathroom. The ceiling, floor, and walls intersected at imperfect right angles and cast shadows that seemed to have no source. Clifford was wearing his underwear while I resembled Emily Dickenson in a wholesome-looking cotton nightie that I'd owned since high school.

"Cliffie, do you—"

"No, go ahead, Pauline. You finish up in there."

"What?"

"Weren't you going to ask me if I wanted to use the bathroom?"

Perhaps the intuitive, wordless understanding that characterized so many couples came over time. Though I didn't want to compromise my privacy, I aspired, in fantasy at least, to an intimacy of such a degree that both partners seemed to be connected to a single mind.

"No. I was going to ask if you know where the wash cloths are."

Clifford would always give me food when I was thirsty, a glass of water when I needed a nap. But in my deepest heart, I believed that his willingness to give me something was more important than what he actually gave me.

I'd decided not to hide myself from my groom before the ceremony. In my off-white wedding dress, I had brief, fragmentary conversations with most of our guests. "Introduce me to anyone I don't know, all right?"

I said to Clifford, who had either washed his face extra thoroughly that morning or was radiating joy. He looked as fresh and as trusting as he did in that distant school photo I'd found of him.

"Who's that?" I asked. Though we'd purposely created a small-scale event, I spotted guests who were strangers to me.

"You know Cousin Meg?"

An outburst of my mother's laughter assured me that she must be enjoying herself.

"Yes. Is this her man?"

"No, this is her roommate."

"Did we invite him?" The roommate looked as miserable as I imagined a man could be.

"No, but he just lost his job, and she thought a party would cheer him up."

I looked over again at the suffering roommate. "Except that it doesn't seem to be working."

"Well, on top of losing his job, he has an abscessed tooth, I think she said."

"OK, but let's keep him out of the pictures. You, though—I want you in every picture. I don't ever want to forget what you look like today."

"Really?" I wondered whether Clifford was surprised that he could look in any way memorable or just surprised that I would think so.

He suddenly disappeared. Then, in response to a cue that I missed, all of the guests quickly seated themselves in the rented chairs. The flawless blue sky seemed to mock our decision to conduct the ceremony indoors, but the weather that time of year was too unpredictable to risk rain and mud and ruined party clothes. My friend Flora, who'd introduced Clifford and me, began to play a gentle melody on her flute. I panicked, then, when Clifford materialized suddenly in front of the justice of the peace. I was tempted to wave at him just to remind him to expect me soon.

"C'mon, honey." My father said, drawing me towards him and positioning us for our entrance.

So often, since I was a younger woman, I'd rehearsed my walk up the aisle, a poignant journey away from being primarily a daughter and towards becoming a wife. With reluctance I'd unlatch myself from my father's arm and then, having advanced into womanhood, I'd proceed past him to my waiting man. The wedding march, as I envisioned it, was like a relay race in which I was the baton.

Sylvia and her boys were gathered in the hall where Dad and I were about to be launched. When I should have been listening for the musical phrase that signaled us to start walking, I was instead analyzing the vibrations being emitted from Flora's flute in a variety of frequencies. Flora wasn't actually making music; she was disturbing the molecules of air and producing a ripple effect. Just as I was about to try to visualize the endless fidgeting of atoms that comprised my guests, the chairs, the very floor we stood on, my father jostled my arm and thrust me forward, following beside me but half a step behind. I looked straight ahead at Clifford, who seemed engrossed in his own thoughts.

"Hold your flowers higher," Sylvia coached me in a stage whisper. I raised the bouquet to the level of my chest, but she scolded, "That's too high." Meanwhile my father's effort to propel me forward was becoming more aggressive.

"Let's go, honey. That man of yours isn't going to wait forever."

So I started forward, smiling, I hoped. Everyone had turned around to watch me, a dreamlike combination of faces from many different times and places in my life. My Philadelphia neighbor, a floral designer, was sitting next to Clifford's auto mechanic, who'd become something of a friend. How so many chairs had been fit into the room was a mystery to me, but I was sure that none of the guests had much leg room.

I felt my father tighten his grip on my arm to prevent me from falling. Without much grace, I regained my balance and then glanced behind me. I had stepped and stumbled on a red plastic building piece—some kind of block that I might some day, as a mother, be able to name more exactly. "Sorry," Sylvia mouthed from her martyrly, motherly post out in the hall.

What were the chances of my foot landing precisely on that spot on the floor? As I felt my mind gearing up to actually attempt the calculation, I redirected it to the sensation of my father's arm looped through mine. My father: solid, scent-free, and predictable—accompanying me, leading me, presenting me, finally, to Clifford. Then he let me go with no more than an incomplete kiss somewhere in the air between his lips and my cheek.

Clifford seemed to have returned from his mental wanderings as I had from mine, and at that moment we stood together, united on the verge of a life change that might gulp us down into its belly. While the justice of the peace expertly read the service that combined standard wedding text with the personalized vows that we'd written ourselves, everyone else in the room besides Clifford—even the justice of the peace, who was just inches away—receded or vanished. Getting married meant that the world around us must fall away, and that, in our closeness, we were truly alone.

While Clifford struggled to slide the ring onto my finger, the justice of the peace recited verses from "Asphodel, That Greeny Flower," by William Carlos Williams, as we'd requested. He looked at us, noted that both our rings were in place, and nodded.

"We step ahead together into the unknown, where the ups, downs, and turns may make this journey different than we planned. We will stay on the path, the two of us, helping each other up when either of us falls, waiting up when one of us lags behind."

Towards the end of the pledge that we chanted in unison, I noticed that I was performing solo and that Clifford had rushed through the words much faster than I. The travel motif had been his idea; still, I wondered if he wasn't embarrassed by so publicly declaring his commitment. Clifford was, after all, extremely shy and always aspired to be as inconspicuous as possible.

Then suddenly I felt so exposed. Shouldn't this be a private matter? Why were we speaking of such personal sentiments and translating them into vows in front of an audience, the price of admission having been a gift and good wishes to endure the test of the future? I heard a muted groan from Cousin Meg's roommate, the one with the abscessed tooth.

Some part of me dissociated from myself and kissed Clifford, grinned with immeasurable delight, and withstood the unexpected heft of Sammy—Sylvia's youngest, whom she'd released—against my abdomen, his version of a congratulatory hug. My insubstantial, alterself walked out of the room linked arm in arm to Clifford as each flute note collided into my brain with a most unflutelike impact.

My friend Rob took pictures throughout the ceremony and the party. If not for those two hundred and eighteen images that I later reviewed, I might have disbelieved that any of those moments had actually occurred, or that I'd been present during them. Because ever after that day, the only memories of my wedding that I could trust were the sweet, sad scent of the flowers in the room and Clifford's wistful eyes when he said, "I do."

◆◆◆◆

An Unlikely Marriage

Groves had resisted ordering a uniform shirt in the next larger size. The placket of his shirt gaped open between the buttons, but all he needed to lose was a pound or few and then the shirt would fit him just fine. And anyway, the sleeves of the larger size would be too long, the neck probably too large for him.

He sucked in his tummy, removed his cap and replaced it snugly on his head. Even though this Dr. J. Robert Oppenheimer wasn't himself a military man, Groves had discerned in him a meticulous nature, at least when it came to grooming. Oppenheimer's suits were obviously expensive and custom-tailored to fit his thin figure. His shoes seemed to hold onto their shine even in the dusty desert. That hat of his, what was it if not a deliberate fashion accessory?

"A pitcher of water," Groves commanded Colonel Kenneth D. Nichols, his officer-in-waiting.

Groves wasn't thirsty yet, though thirst was inevitable

in this climate. But he wanted Dr. Oppenheimer to feel valued and attended to. The general's strategy would be to coax the doctor of physics to his point of view; let the doctor then persuade his rank and file that everyone participating in this Project Y would be best served if the scientists' jobs were established as military commissions. So they'd all become officers and be issued uniforms. During his preliminary talk with Dr. O about this matter, Groves could tell that the doctor was on the line—unsure but convincible. If the issue applied only to him, he most likely would go along with militarization of personnel. The general's best guess, though, was that Oppenheimer knew his men wouldn't like the idea. Not at all.

Colonel Nichols, bearing water, and Dr. Oppenheimer entered the general's office together.

"Doctor." Groves extended his hand.

"General." Oppenheimer met it with his own.

Groves expected the doctor to take off his hat, but he didn't. Fair enough. The general was wearing one, too. He nodded towards a chair. In the background, Nichols was pouring water, two glasses of it that no one had yet asked for.

Groves started right in. "The advantage," he said, "of going military is that everything gets spelled out. There's not a chance of favoritism or exceptions or anything that could get in the way of the work, Doctor. It'll put the weight on my shoulders. They're a lot bigger than yours," the general joked. "I'd rather see you free to do what you do best instead of having to come up with a new set of rules and consequences."

Oppenheimer had arrived with a cigarette in his mouth and was already smoking his next. "You see, General, it's really not about me. Not more than one or two of my men favor the prospect of being drafted. It would be more accurate to say that the majority of them are vehemently opposed to it." Even with his soft voice and measured words, he was a formidable man.

"I didn't think you objected, not last time we spoke."

"Oh, I don't myself." The doctor smiled but soon reinserted the cigarette between his lips. "Give me my khakis and my five stars."

"Five stars?!" The general himself had only recently been promoted to Temporary Brigadier General. And his rise in status hadn't gotten him the battlefront assignment that he'd wished for. Groves knew that the administration of a project he couldn't openly boast about brought him no prestige. At least not yet. But if this bomb could be actualized, if it could win the war (Groves stopped short of Oppenheimer's assertion that the bomb could end *all* war), then he was as good as in command of the battlefield that would determine the outcome of this worldwide conflict.

"Water?" Nichols asked. In the presence of the esteemed physicist, he couldn't help but wonder what makes water water, and where it ended and the glass began.

Oppenheimer seemed to think deeply about the offer. "Yes," he finally said. "And some hot sauce, please." He was known to like his *comidas* spicy. His dinner guests had to remember to ask him to serve *los habeñeros* on the side.

Colonel Nichols left the room, subvocally chanting, "Hot sauce, hot sauce," without having asked, maybe not even wondering, what the hell Oppenheimer needed it for.

Groves wanted his discussion with the doctor back on track. "This is a military project," he said, "overseen by the Army and being conducted for the sole purpose of winning a war."

"I'm aware of that, Leslie."

Still the general went on with his point, somewhat distracted by Oppenheimer's use of his first name. "It's *not* a scholars' playground, a chance for your people to satisfy their own career needs."

Oppenheimer slid forward in his chair, almost off the edge of the seat. "But without my men's love of the mental challenge, without their intellectual pride, you're gonna end up with a stalled donkey cart."

Groves was ever surprised at the doctor's way of expressing himself. The poet-physicist, he'd heard him referred to. Groves knew, too, that Oppenheimer could claim to speak as many languages as the general had fingers on his hands. But the one tongue that Dr. O hadn't mastered was Army Efficiency—as few words as possible, direct, and suggestive of control. "So where does that leave us, Doctor?"

"Leslie, I'm telling you. You'll never capture the stars in your butterfly net."

Groves tried to look away, to experience some fascination with the plank floor that would equal the intrigue of the man before him. "Dr. Oppenheimer." Groves gave up on his escape plan. "You have the bluest blue eyes I've ever seen." *It's as if he's looking right through me*, the general thought. *As if he can read my mind.*

Just then Nichols returned with a dose of hot sauce at the bottom of a glass tumbler. "Here you are, Doctor. I had to borrow it from one of the men's homes."

Nichols and Groves watched Oppenheimer with un-disguised curiosity, both far from predicting what he would do with the stuff. Dab it on his neck like perfume? Inhale it to decongest his sinuses? Silly guesses, yet there was no food in sight and none had been ordered.

"An enchilada, Sir?" Nichols asked.

Oppenheimer laughed, coughed, continued laughing but almost at once reverted to coughing. "Five packs a day," he bragged or confessed. Then he turned those indescribably blue eyes on Nichols and answered, "No thank you, Colonel Nichols. I'm not a big eater. I rarely eat breakfast," he explained. "I nibble now and then during the day if something's within reach, but I don't usually sit down to a meal until dinner. I like a good steak." He smiled in anticipation of the steak he'd have that same day for dinner.

Oppenheimer lowered the ring finger of his left hand—the finger reserved for a wedding band—down into the glass and dipped it into the shallows of the red-hot sauce. "Mmm," he said before sucking the saucy heat off the finger where he wore his pledge to his wife.

Twice he repeated this lowering, dipping, sucking sequence and then drank some of the water that Nichols had served him.

The meeting had taken a wrong turn, General Groves realized when he suddenly revived and saw himself and his assistant watching one of the most deft of scientific minds titillating his taste buds with Papa John's Pepper Sauce. Was every little thing this man did the object of other people's interest? Would I, the general asked himself, be so enthralled if Dr. Oppenheimer raised a hankie to his nose and tooted his horn?

"Dr. Oppenheimer," he said now in his most authoritarian voice. "Dr. Oppenheimer, we will please get back to the matter of establishing your crew as Army officers. I don't want any ambiguity about whose project this is."

Oppenheimer's eyes emitted a chill, like the ultimate snow-topped mountain the climber was hoping to reach. "Not mine...not yours either. It's all of ours, Leslie."

A little blip upset the general's heartbeat.

"This is a patriotic undertaking," J. Robert went on, "in which we all share. You can't tell me you're going to bureaucratize love of country, can you?"

General Groves was ready with a quick retort. "Exactly how long have you loved your country, Doctor? Because that little affair you had back in the thirties, you remember —her first name Communist, second name Party, I believe —makes me think that you're about as faithful as..." Groves wasn't nearly as quick or as apt in his choice of words as was Oppenheimer.

Yet the general, of all those who had decided whether or not to grant Oppenheimer security clearance, had been most willing all along to give him the benefit of the doubt.

"That wasn't a love affair, General. More like a mild flirtation. I never slept with her. You know that."

The poster on the wall that Oppenheimer was facing appeared to be the only effort to decorate the general's office: a repeating image of a man standing as straight as possible, the image echoing backwards and creating the impression of a line of just-such straight-backed men, all standing at attention. Oppenheimer half-recognized the artistic style, but the corner with the photographer's name was blocked by a box full of folders waiting on a table. Waiting to be filed. Waiting for this office, for all of Los Alamos, to become workable.

Nichols was asked to leave. "Of course, Sir," he replied.

The two great men, each larger than himself, seemed to fill the room entirely. An electric tension sizzled at the boundaries where the two nearly touched.

Oppenheimer returned to studying the poster on the wall. Black, white, and hundreds of gradients in between. The repeating self made him think of the march of progress that brought each man to the present moment. It made him think, too, of the many selves each shed along the way.

Groves stood and went over to the open window. But when he pushed up on the sash, he discovered that the window wouldn't budge. That was probably the exact amount of airflow that had suited some English teacher or other on one of the cooler days here in autumn. Because this building had been a facility for the school. Sometimes the general mistook the dust in the air for chalk particles.

"I've got it, General Groves."

Good, Oppenheimer was back to addressing the general in a fitting fashion.

"I think we can resolve this matter very shortly," he went on.

Now finally General Groves would get to see for himself how a first-rate mind solved problems. He'd get to watch Oppenheimer in action as the administrator, the one who must keep the fire burning but at the same time keep it contained.

"I'm listening," Groves said.

For the first time during the appointment, Oppenheimer laid his cigarette in an ashtray on the general's desk. He seemed to be preparing to use his right hand for some purpose that the general couldn't guess, though he did notice the staining of Oppenheimer's nails and fingertips, the indelible evidence of nicotine. No wonder the fellow was so thin. With a cigarette always traveling towards and away from his lips, how could he find time to eat?

"Odds or evens?" Oppenheimer asked.

"Eh?"

"Your choice—odds or evens?"

"Odds," Grove answered—even though he would rather not have participated in this childish game.

"Best two out of three," the doctor decided.

One, two, three, shoot! Again. One, two, three, shoot! Even, both times, so Groves suspected that some trick of physics had allowed Oppenheimer to forecast the outcome of this war. Finger play was most certainly not the way to settle such high-level disputes. And yet Groves didn't want to be perceived as a sore loser.

"So…no military commissions?" he asked, defeated.

Oppenheimer, whose brain had suddenly switched into a state of trance, wandered through untranslated texts in the many languages he'd studied, meandered around mathematical laws of being, and finally returned to the room. He said, "I'll tell you what, General. Let's leave the men out of this, keep it between you and me. You can make me an officer." Oppenheimer saluted, his cigarette in the gesturing hand coming close to singeing his porkpie hat. "And then, once we're closer to testing the gadget, we'll commission 'em all."

Groves nodded, slowly at first then more rapidly as he neared acceptance of Oppenheimer's proposal. "All right, Doctor. We'll do it your way."

"*Our* way."

What does that mean? Groves wondered. "I'd like to see your boys moved up onto the Hill. All this commuting between here and Santa Fe… We're losing time."

Surveying the room, Oppenheimer caught sight of the camera eye that had been watching them all along.

He stared back at it until it blinked, he was sure. Must be the shutter. They were being photographed at intervals, he guessed.

"All right then, Leslie," and Oppenheimer rose.

"Robert." Groves rose, too. Better to compromise on these lesser issues, he decided, like addressing each other by first names, and to save his insistence for disputes that he cared about wholeheartedly. Groves was learning about a new brand of power and that power didn't always mean being right.

As he exited the office, Robert was finally able to see around the boxes to the bottom of the poster that he'd admired. *The U.S. Army. This is where you've been headed all along.* A recruitment poster, Oppenheimer realized. And hadn't he just been recruited himself? He looked again at the Army men, one self or many, lined up, ready to serve, and he thought, I'm one of them now.

◆◆◆◆

Los Alamos Primer

Robert Serber spoke with a stutter. Nonetheless, Oppie chose him to deliver the introductory lectures on the top-secret project that had brought them all there. Serber had proven himself in a similar role the summer before at Berkeley, when he'd led a seminar on these same arcane topics. He was shy and slender; standing in front of a blackboard, he was grounded by the piece of chalk in his hand.

By April of 1943, the first staff had arrived at Los Alamos. The big boys of science were assembled in the lecture hall of what used to be the administration building in the boys'-school days. And though their number was to double again and again as the real scale of the project was realized, even now they comprised a sizable group.

"Can you hear me?" Serber asked those in the back row. Some of the men nodded; others shook their heads, so Serber cranked up his volume. "Is this better?"

he inquired, receiving a unanimous nod.

"This is to fill you all in, and also—" Serber interrupted himself with a nervous giggle "—to begin discussion about the design. Of the bomb."

Many in the audience were taking notes. Those who weren't, gifted with remarkable powers of retention, could soak up Serber's lecture without losing much more than a word or two. Oppie had seated himself in the audience, conveying to the men that he was one of them even though he had the title of Scientific Director.

Serber's wife, Charlotte, had been forbidden to attend the meeting for security reasons though Robert would have liked her to be there. He wasn't much of a public speaker and would have benefited from an encouraging nod or a wink whenever his eyes might find their way to hers. He contented himself with a photograph of him and his wife posing on a bench after a game of table tennis. The photograph was clamped onto a clipboard on top of all his pages of notes, and only now did Serber decide that he should have practiced releasing each sheet of notes from the clip without displacing the photo, which kept fluttering conspicuously to the floor.

"Now that we're all here—finally—in one place…" Serber grinned, anticipating a laugh from his audience. Someone coughed. A pen dropped onto the linoleum floor. A distant shout attenuated into silence. "…we can put all our pieces together and see what we've got." Serber scanned the group, searching for one set of sympathetic eyes.

"We all agreed, early on, that the release of energy from a chain reaction of atomic fission would be the basis for this bomb." No one wrote this down. Again Serber grinned. "I'm stating the obvious, I guess.

"The thrust of our work now is to determine how to start this chain reaction and which element will work best. And all of the mathematical calcu—" Serber's stutter stalled on the next syllable until finally he escaped, then risked returning to the word to repeat it. "—calculations to get the timing right, the critical mass, the requirements of the container."

Serber unclamped his first page from the clipboard, reinserted it underneath the rest of the notes, then stooped to retrieve the photograph of him and Charlotte. This was to become a recurring sequence of actions—unclamp, reinsert, stoop to retrieve the picture.

The men were absolutely, respectfully quiet. But the beat of a hammer, of multiple hammers, intermittently filled in the breaks between Serber's pages and sometimes rivaled his words. Improvements in the building hadn't been completed yet, and while Serber led this first of a series of colloquia, construction was going on in the reading room next door.

"We've got to get it right. In as little time and with as little material as possible. Some of you know there's not much plutonium around. Microgram amounts. And it takes a while to produce it, and the process is costly. If we plan on the bomb—"

Oppie leaned forward in his seat and spoke directly into John "Mathematics" Manley's ear. "There are workers in and out of here, so let's keep them guessing. Tell him not to use the word 'bomb.' Use 'gadget' instead."

Manley got up and walked along the wall to the front of the room. He then went up to Serber and in a whisper conveyed to him that henceforth the bomb should be referred to as the gadget. Orders from the top.

Robert Wilson, professorial looking even at his young age, turned and said something to Hans Bethe, who nodded vigorously in reply. Serber feared that he was losing them. Or could it be his glasses? Charlotte had coached him to straighten them every now and then since the black frames tended to tilt crookedly on his nose.

"I hear we're having chicken for dinner," Serber announced.

"With the giblet gravy?"

Bethe's German accent distorted the word "giblet," so Serber had to ask, "What gravy?"

"The gib-let gravy."

"Is that how they served it last week?" Serber asked.

"I don't like it." Phil Morrison looked like he was fifteen years old. "Too much fat."

At last Serber had inspired the participation of his audience. He sat back, relaxed, listening to the commentary on the food service. But when his roving eyes arrived at Oppie, he came awake again and interrupted the others, saying, "We have to get back to the work."

"Please chime in at any time if you have something to add," Serber thought to say, beginning to feel like a failed performer, a comedian who just plain wasn't funny.

"Everyone's work has been so compartmentalized that I'm not sure you all understand... What we're doing here will make a difference in the outcome of the war." He'd snagged their interest, he could tell, because even the sound of breathing had ceased. "You know?

"We can stop the Germans. But only if we get to the——." he stopped himself on the verge of uttering the forbidden word. "If we get to the gadget before they do."

The men were able to figure out what Serber was referring to as soon as he introduced the new code word. No one was hearing all of this for the first time, after all; each of them had been involved in some part of the work that had been progressing in locations scattered across the country and overseas.

"Centralize," Oppenheimer had urged the Army officers who were suddenly partners with him. "You've got these guys in Chicago, another bunch at Harvard. And at Berkeley, Cal Tech, MIT," drawing on his fifteenth cigarette of the day at eleven o'clock in the A.M. Plus all the immigrant physicists leaving Europe just one step ahead of forced conscription or exile.

"Bring 'em all together," he'd said, because one brilliant mind combined with another brilliant mind produced so much more thought than the sum of those two brilliant minds in isolation.

He'd spirited them away from their academic dens, their laboratory hideaways, appealing to their intellectual conceit and patriotic infatuation with democracy. At U of Wisconsin, the few faculty remaining suddenly looked around, amazed at how many of their colleagues had magically disappeared. A similar amazement was experienced by the stationmaster at Princeton, who'd never sold so many one-way tickets to Lamy, New Mexico, of all places, way out there in frontier land.

So as Serber stuttered his way through the particulars of what had been accomplished so far, this or that man would nod at his part of the puzzle. And then he would widen his eyes in awe at leaps and strides he'd known nothing about until then.

"We'll be meeting in smaller groups for more specific briefings, but for now..." Serber looked at his notes. "This is the broad outline of what we've got."

Seth Neddermeyer stood up eagerly from his chair. "I've been thinking. There are problems with this gun-assembly model. But if we were to form the uranium into a sphere..."

An intolerant groan that could be traced to no one in particular informed Neddermeyer that his idea was unpopular. But he went on anyway to sketch what such an implosion model might look like. Not only was he competing with the resistance of his audience, but with the noise produced by the workmen in other parts of the building.

"Think about it," he went on. "If the timing works

out, the mass of fissionable material could be reduced by at least a third."

Many of the others had been expecting this. They'd heard his more informal campaign to promote the implosion model and were skeptical about its advantages. While Neddermeyer's height implied a certain authority, his arms gangled long and gawkily, and his hands were in constant motion, like those of a young boy.

Interpreting a flicker of Oppie's eyelids, Serber presumed to say, "We'll keep working on that, for sure." He reached up to level his black glasses.

A background drone, which no one had been conscious of until it ended, abruptly stopped, and a mild curse could be heard coming from the reading room. The new residents weren't yet accustomed to the power outages that would soon become a feature of the lifestyle on the Hill. Along with these maddening plunges into darkness, they would learn to tolerate water shortages; even when the water flowed, discharges of rust and sludge made it unusable. Alcohol shortages, too. The war, enough of a reason for a body to crave a strong drink, had interfered with the usual access to liquor. This wasn't the first time, however, that some of the lab rats had resorted to drinking the super-proof ethanol.

The average age of the population of Los Alamos was twenty-nine, skewed downward by the slew of young bachelors working alongside the Nobel laureates. These recent graduates relied for entertainment on the stupefaction brought on by drink. A party was successful if, the next morning, a scientist-sorcerer woke up still inebriated and could sleep-walk through his first few hours back at the lab.

One of the construction workers, on his way into the lecture room, was barred entry by the uniformed guard. "I gotta get at some wires that cross through here overhead." he boomed. Some of the younger men found the quickening drama in the doorway more engaging than the scientific lecture intended for them. Many of them were whispering to each other, swapping punchlines. Any ladies on the premises? some of them wanted to know even though this mass meeting didn't seem to be the occasion when they could ask about single females or visitors from outside of L.A.

While Oppie might treat such questions with paternal indulgence, the others might not. So the men tuned into the technical chit-chat and sat raptly through marathon descriptions of structure and procedure—who would work where and with whom.

"Should we have some discussion?" Serber asked tentatively, first looking at Oppie for approval and then renewing his confidence with a peek at Charlotte's image. The problem was that every time he sought a glimpse of her picture, he had to suffer the spectacle of his own dominant, dark-framed glasses, his toothy smile and his prominent knees and elbows.

Oppie nodded. Everyone in the room must have perceived that minuscule gesture because, without further word from Serber, Edward Teller stood up. "Are we going to build this bomb with papers and pencils?"

Most everyone knew what he meant. The country's supply of enriched uranium totaled not much more than a pound, and the entire stockpile of plutonium would fit on the head of a pin.

While Teller was still standing, two others rose. "Physics is a lab science, too," accused David Harkins, and the assemblage of eyes all together traveled towards Oppie, a theoretician who was known to be lacking in hands-on lab hours.

Everyone looked to Serber for a response. But his face, suddenly rubbery, was misshapen with apprehension. Fortunately for him, Oppie got up and, rotating a half-circle around as he spoke, a bit like a chicken roasting on a rotisserie, answered the complaint. "That would be a problem, you're right, if General Groves weren't overseeing the establishment of two production sites— one for the production of U_{235}—that's in Oak Ridge, Tennessee—and one to produce plutonium. That plant is in Hanford, Washington."

Oppie had anticipated a swell of small discussions, and he waited until the wave of reactions subsided. "Still," he told the men, "both commodities are precious. We won't have enough to play around with." Before the volume of protest could quiet down, Oppie spoke again. "I'm expecting one serious trial detonation."

In the reading room, some of the workmen were shouting loud enough to each other that Oppie paused, unwilling to compete with the noise. Shouting about power and strategy and safety, almost as if they were talking about the bomb. Those attending the colloquium were beginning to squirm.

By now Serber had receded as some of the notables took their turns at talking. Isidor Rabi, visiting from the East, had helped Oppie chart an organizational structure (to the relief of those who'd long been awaiting just such a who's-who and what's-what); he spoke now about how well a similar structure was working at MIT. "Tell them about the team crossover," Oppie directed him. Oppie was now running the show, inviting questions, doing his best to fuel the enthusiasm of the group.

"All right, you great men of science," he said with a smile. "This work is every bit as vital as the warfare being waged on the battlefields. And just like the soldiers, we're accountable. Colonel Pash—I'll call him in in a minute to say a word or two—has the job of drawing a box around us and keeping us inside it while letting no one else in. Got it?" His next inhalation burned up half the length of the cigarette he'd just lit. Some in the audience glanced at Oppie's other cigarette already burning in an ashtray at his feet.

He landed his hand flat on the crown of his porkpie hat. This must have been a prearranged signal because at that exact second, the officer who had been guarding the door disappeared. In no more than a minute he returned, this time behind Colonel Boris Pash.

The colonel, by positioning himself in the southwest corner of the large room, required everyone in the audience to swivel around in his chair. Some, instead, lifted their chairs and turned them just enough so they were facing the colonel. Pash wasn't used to such prolonged commotion during what should have been a swift transition. Impatient, he began to address the men before the racket had ended.

"You all, by now, have your passes. Carry them with you. I don't care if you step outside to put out the trash; have your pass with you. Same goes for all your family members."

Pash went on to explain why the streets had no addresses, the radio station no call numbers. "We've made it as difficult as possible for you to inadvertently spill any of our secrets. You'll have a hard time finding your way out of this little hole in space, and no one can find a way in."

The men were unsure if they were being instructed or threatened. Pash's military uniform suggested a whole army on-call to enforce his will. The wayward whispers, all side conversations had completely stopped. The men listened with eyes that took it all in and expressed a rare and profound terror.

At the end of each day of lectures, Serber met with Condon, deputy director of the lab. Condon would spread Serber's notes across the top of a weighty oak table, ask Serber questions, clarify this or that point that could have been interpreted in more than one way. During these consultations, the two men produced crude drawings of atomic activity and of possible bomb designs. Afterwards, Conlon would solicit supplementary information from those who'd been appointed division leaders. The final document, plump with as many pages as a book, became known as *The Los Alamos Primer.*

After the fifth day, the last in the series, Serber sighed, deflating back to his pre-colloquium size. The strain of enlarging himself and projecting leadership had exhausted him. Slope-shouldered, he rose from his throne and draggled after the others out of the room. Plaster dust—finer, more nomadic than the desert dust outside—tickled his lungs, and finally he coughed.

The workers rewiring the reading room and patching up the walls seemed to him twice his size. They were on a break, he observed, and standing in social clusters, laughing Spanish laughter, some of them. Serber thought that he himself had never perspired so, even during his most exorbitant output of effort as a graduate student under Oppie's wing. This world, the world of application, of war and weaponry, was so much less real to him. This world of workers who sweated enough fluid to hydrate a herd of cattle. The men seemed fiendish to Serber. Laughing, perspiring. He saw now what they were up to and very nearly gasped at the bunch of them hoo-hooing over his picture of Charlotte. He hadn't even noticed that it had escaped the grip of his clipboard and then flitted away, airborne.

"Wonder what she sees in him," one of them said.

◆◆◆◆

This Isn't Me

This isn't me, eating meals with him from a common pot.

This isn't me, drinking his coffee when I can't find where I put my own. We take overlapping showers, use the same bath towel, blink at the same intrusive streetlight that requires us to pull the shade down as far as it will go.

This isn't me, reading with a constant companion on the other end of the couch, though he's most often silent, reading like me.

This isn't me, sharing a bed with him every night.

This isn't me, I told myself. But then where was I? Or who was this impostor who was supposed to be me?

For most of my life, I'd yearned to belong to a "we." This was an instinctive longing based on fantasy, like the longing someone can have to go to Paris without ever having been there before. I'd never felt part of my family as a child even though all of us lived in the same house and had the same last name. Only my undeniable resemblance to my father stopped me from believing that, somewhere out there, my real parents were searching for me and would eventually track me down. How else could I explain my sixth sense that my birth into this family was an error evidenced by the number of differences between me and the rest of them? I was acutely aware of every trait that distinguished me from all three siblings and from my parents, even if I'd inherited every gene that determined my father's face.

"I don't have to ask who this is," a teacher had once said to me when meeting my father for the first time.

"I'm Pauline's father," Dad had said as if he hadn't heard the teacher or had never noticed our uncanny resemblance. So when we got home after the open house that evening, I rummaged through our chaotic box of family photographs and showed one to my father, holding it two inches from his eyes.

"What's this?" he asked, craning his head backwards to achieve the focal distance that would allow him to see the picture.

"It's us, you and me." My hope was that he'd comment on our lookalike faces, maybe even with a suggestion of affection or pride.

"Oh…yes, it is. That was taken during one of our fall leaf-peeping trips." He even tweaked my cheek. Still, his response had fallen short of the one I was hoping for.

Ever after that day, I'd relied on my own invented logic that transformed family distance into an asset. I was assured by the differences between me and each of my family members. I had learned to equate dissimilarity with love; for me, differentness was essential to relationship.

Over the years, I became quite skilled at finding differences between myself and everyone else—my schoolmates, later my roommates, my co-workers, my lesser friends, and most of the men who were willing to see inside me. Whether I actually experienced these differences or tried to create them remains unclear to me now.

"You're not interested in the arts, but I am. And you're very...physical. I'm not really at home in my body, you know?" I was trying to explain to a tall, black-haired man with a beard, after one date, that I didn't think we were well-suited to each other. We were parked outside my apartment. My hand had been choking the door handle even before the car stopped. "I just think we're not compatible," I concluded.

He leaned towards me in the nearness forced by his small car. "Oh, but I don't agree," he said.

"You just proved my point," I said and pushed open the car door.

It hadn't taken me long to figure out the most obvious differences between Clifford and me: he was neat and orderly and I was a slob; he preferred to make decisions quickly, even at the risk of making the wrong decision, while I was usually indecisive; he saved time and spent money, while I was willing to invest a great deal of time in saving what to him were negligible amounts of money. But I knew also that some unidentifiable similarity bound us more deeply than those superficial differences.

Clifford allowed me to displace nearly all of his furniture with mine and to rearrange the dining room table, the couch, the bed. In the corner of our bedroom that overlooked the back alley, I set up a job-seeking station for myself. After Clifford went to work in the mornings, I'd scan the classifieds, compose cover letters and make phone calls. My formal training was in public health, but early on I'd veered away from the more conventional career paths and begun applying some of my skills to the field of homelessness. My travels around town that last summer had been skewed by my professional mindset; I observed men and women with lopsided shopping carts that were difficult to steer, and I knew what the large pieces of cardboard tucked inside them were for.

One person referred me to another referred me to another, and on and on. While I was on hold during one of these serial calls, I turned around in my chair to entertain myself with a view of the buildings behind ours and saw a man urinating directly across the alley from me. I hung up the phone, stepped out onto the balcony and yelled, "Hey!" thinking that being watched by a woman would deter him.

But he turned and looked up at me, grinning so familiarly that I began to wonder if I might know him. "How you doing, Missy?" he asked. Meanwhile he was packing himself back in his pants and zipping up.

"I'd rather you not do that right outside my home."

"I get it. I'd rather not do it here, too, you know,

Missy. But I got nowhere else to go."

"Come on, now. There are plenty of public bathrooms."

By now the man was strolling closer to my building. He was overdressed for the weather—layered with shirts and vests and an open jacket, probably wearing his entire wardrobe all at once. "You ever go into those places?"

"Course I do."

He disregarded my answer and went on to explain. "Dirty, dirty, dirty. I gotta use one hand to hold myself, another to hold onto my bag, and that don't leave no hand to hold my nose closed."

"Wait there…OK?" I told him, and then I hurried into the kitchen and brought back the other half of an avocado and tomato sandwich I'd made for lunch, wrapped sloppily in a plastic bag from the produce section of the grocery store. "You eat yet today?" I asked, offering the sandwich out at arm's length.

His grin grew even wider, wider than his face. "Missy, I not eat today or yesterday before that." He extended his arms, ready to catch the airdrop about to descend on him.

Not a good idea, I knew, to feed the hungry outside one's own door. They came back like squirrels, increasingly aggressive, certain of sympathy. Still, I tossed the half-sandwich over the balcony rail with an incantation: "Here's hoping we both find jobs tomorrow," even though our prospects were hardly alike.

Each day when Clifford came home, I'd provide him with an unsolicited narration of my entire day. Afterwards, I'd interrogate him about what his day had been like since he didn't tell me unless I asked. This imbalanced evening exchange continued after I was hired to be a street worker for a clinic serving primarily the homeless. I'd roam the streets, distributing condoms, sample sizes of hand sanitizer, and pamphlets on a variety of health-related topics. As I was handing out these goodies, I'd introduce myself to the citizens of the street and attempt to seduce them into an appointment for free testing for sexually transmitted diseases and for tuberculosis. Few of them were aware that a resurgence of TB was threatening certain immigrant populations and the homeless, as well. Upon hearing this news, all of the coughers among them would promptly vow to come to the clinic that very day without suspecting that their smoking habits were more likely than TB to be causing their incessant hacking and the compulsive clearing of their throats. Cigarettes had become unbelievably expensive. They were, however, one of the cheaper forms of entertainment available to my friends in the street.

Usually, the crowd of outreached hands would quickly disperse. Not always, though.

"TB, they's no cure for that!" He was probably much younger than he looked. A tangle of coarse dark hair, like the ends of unresolved electrical wiring, stuck out from under the brim of his felt hat, the kind my father had worn in his youth. This man's companion, a woman who no doubt was also much younger than she looked, was attempting to lead him away.

I wasn't supposed to hand out diagnoses, but I wanted to liberate this man from the inescapable doom he foresaw in his future. "You're OK. Really," I told him.

Clifford praised me every day again for my bravery and my guts, for mingling out on the streets with people whom others would mistake for dangerous. Yet he lacked any protective urges or tendencies to worry about me. If I told him I was taking a bus home, at night, from a crime-infested part of town, he'd suggest, "Take a jacket, Pauli. It's supposed to get cold."

"Good idea. I can conceal my gun underneath it."

I was headed for a farewell gathering for someone at work. Large squares of electrically colored paper, each with a bold heading printed on it, were laid out on the floor surrounding him. Clifford was planning one of his U.S. history musical chair sessions, I could tell. His own curriculum invention for tricking middle schoolers into memorizing names and dates.

"Call me when you're done and I'll come pick you up," he said, raising his eyes. That evening they were green, probably because of his sweater vest, which I interpreted as green and he described as blue. His uncharacteristic offer surprised me even if it was just an offer, not an expression of any concern about what might be prowling in the dark doorways I'd pass on my way home.

The exhilaration of shearing through the chill of night with my coat unbuttoned, wide open like wings, allowed me to rise high in the big sky of the future. At that moment, anyway, I was lofting on a strong current of optimism. How different this feeling was from the worries that used to nibble at my insides when I'd walk unnoticed through the night before I'd ever met Clifford. Those last, uphill strides as I neared my old building had always reminded me of the ever-greater effort I needed to get through the days. Would I always feel this wretchedly alone? Would I end up a single mother, determined to have children but unable to find a suitable mate? And then I'd met Clifford, and once we'd agreed to get married, I understood that I'd never again be alone—both a comfort and a menace. I'd lived by myself for five years by then and hadn't had to take anyone else into account when deciding what to cook for dinner or how to spend my money.

Now that I'd moved to a new city, I noticed hints of that old lost-at-sea feeling. Yet even to myself I couldn't confess to being lonely. After all, I was newly married, a condition that was supposed to cure me of the ailment of lovelessness forever. But I missed my longtime Philadelphia friends. My conversations with Alia on the phone consoled me while they lasted, but as soon as I'd hang up, the gate would close and all communication cease.

Lately, though, I was getting used to a lamp on and the somewhere sound of Clifford snoring when I arrived home. He was waiting for me—Clifford in his green, or blue, vest. He'd arranged a radial of apple wedges on a plate for me and drizzled honey over them.

That night I'd gotten a ride home from one of my

co-workers. Of course I, too, could have driven but always shirked the bother of parking and benefited from the willingness of other people to drive.

"I thought you were going to call." Clifford's array of colored paper was compacted into one stack, edges aligned.

"Oh. Well I got a ride."

"From who?"

"You're unusually curious tonight," I said, seating myself snugly next to him on the impractical off-white couch. I could feel the pulse of his heartbeat in his chest. Clifford smelled like dew more than sweat, a fresh, almost innocent exuberance that he produced when he strained either body or mind. His arm reached around me and brought us even closer.

*   *   *

Three weeks later I learned that I was pregnant.

A central heat emanated from the place where I supposed my womb would be. Already I felt that I was enlarging, and soon I developed a new gait, my hands curving protectively over my belly. Every nerve ending in me picked up on a signal that I'd be having a girl. At last I could buy a pair of the little ankle-strap baby shoes like the ones I'd seen in windows in Philadelphia's Italian neighborhood. Or maybe not quite yet. But I did wander into more than one baby store and buy a cuddly bunting—even though her birth was scheduled for late summer—and a diaper bag with numerous pockets, each with a designated purpose.

My mother, too, bought a diaper bag for me after I told her on the phone of my pregnancy. She and Dad drove up from New York to personally deliver the gift to Clifford and me and to give us a tour of every compartment and feature. "Look, it's a foldable changing pad!" my mother exclaimed. "And look at this! You can heat up this gel pack in your microwave and it'll keep the bottle warm for at least an hour."

"Nice!" Clifford said.

"We don't have a microwave, Mom. And I'm going to breastfeed."

Clifford slid forward on our couch and laid a restraining hand on me, as if I might spring up and attack my mother. "Still, it's a nice bag, Pauline, don't you think?"

I was shamed by his graciousness. While we critiqued the diaper bag, my father was standing by the window at the front of the room, looking downward two stories. "You know, in all the time I been watching, not a single parking space has opened up on this block. How do you do it? No parking lot, no driveway."

My first motherly sacrifice was to suffer through three months of merciless nausea, baffled that other women's pregnancies were characterized by distinct food cravings. For me, the frequently prescribed saltine crackers and even water weren't neutral enough.

One afternoon, having stayed home from work with the queasies, I rode a bus to Garber's, a wonderful hardware store with bins of window pulleys and chains, bulk screws of every size, and quaint kitchen aids. I was going to buy myself a really good tape measure and a garlic press. After reading the thermometer mounted outside our kitchen window, I put on a long navy wool coat—the warmest coat I owned—over the shredded orange sweatsuit that had become my maternity uniform, providing warmth, comfort, and expandability. Still unfamiliar with the city, I had to vigilantly watch the passing scenery through the window or else risk getting off beyond walking distance to the store. The only other time I'd been there, Clifford had driven and I'd dozed most of the way. So the only landmark en route that I was likely to recognize was the sleep shop immediately next to the hardware store. Only then had Clifford nudged me to let me know that we'd reached our destination.

Two blocks before Garber's, I could see the tall red letters painted on white brick shouting "MAT-TRESSES," and pulled the stop cord.

The rush of icy air into my lungs tasted brazenly metallic. I might as well have consumed a plateful of heavy Mexican food or deep-fried squid. I didn't get enough warning to be able to find a secluded escape place, an alleyway or a hidden niche. So right there on the sidewalk, as if an exorcist's client expelling the devil himself, I bent forward and wretched up the emptiness inside my stomach. Again and again my body was seized by convulsions. My gut muscles began to ache. I gagged, drooling. A sudsy afterflow of bile dripped down onto the front of my navy-blue dress coat.

And yet I felt full and glutted with contentment. This, I thought, *this* is me.

◆◆◆◆

The Miracle of

Finally they meet. Those two invisible bits of matter. Out of their collision emerges an astonishing new force beyond motion and heat, a life where before there was none.

The scientists at Los Alamos squabbled about which bomb model would work best, the gun assembly model or the implosion model. Each presented design challenges, not just to Oppie's boys but to the international community of scientists. To be sure, the Germans and the Russians were likely working on nuclear weapons, too, but the lab at Los Alamos was ahead in the race.

The favored frontrunner, the gun assembly model, worked by propelling a slug of uranium or plutonium towards a larger sample of the same to instigate a chain reaction—a continual displacement of neutrons and the accompanying release of the energy that bound them in place. Multiply that energy by gazillions and it could destroy a world.

But the critical mass to get the chain reaction going had to be determined beforehand by difficult computations in the lab.

In the summer of '42, Richard Tolman suggested another way of initiating a chain reaction: implosion. An inward assault of neutrons on nuclei would, as in the gun model, result in the discharge of uncontrolled energy and destruction of a magnitude as great as the atom was small—unfathomable even to those big-brained scientists fussing over unseen particles that eluded a microscope's keen eye.

For months they experimented on a smaller scale, attempting to forecast which combination of model and material would generate a military weapon like no other before. Plutonium had never existed in nature and was expensive to manufacture, as was its costly cousin, uranium$_{235}$. These were the only elements that, when bombarded and split, could produce the blast of power that would silence the enemy.

And so finally they meet—invisible bits of matter, the two becoming more than the sum of them. Scientists would argue that nothing more was created than was already there: carbon and hydrogen and oxygen, the ingredients of life. But to the more innocent eye and mind, something quite inexplicable was occurring at that instant of union.

Is it the tininess of the cells that so evades our imaginations, or the number of times they must be multiplied to yield a beating heart, the number of times an atom must divide to produce an explosion that could efface an entire city? The third, unthinkable dimension, of course, is the enormity of that explosion—the fire, the light, the resplendent colors that tinge it with beauty, almost. A wondrous but lethal spectacle against the sky while the proud parents stand by, counting ten fingers and ten toes, shielding their eyes with pieces of glass and hoping that Fermi's calculations were correct, that the atmosphere couldn't possibly ignite and consequently disappear.

The splitting again and again of atoms, the division again and again of cells within a host chamber, the uterine cavity... Meanwhile, the co-creators have been nurturing their offspring throughout its development with refinements in design, experimentation, prenatal vitamins. But even if the atoms behaved as expected, the real enemy was time—would the bomb be ready before the world was snatched away by a huge, greedy hand? And even if tested, could the bomb be relied on to perform a second time? Could the process of gestation be relied on to stay on track and lead to a perfect baby with no missing parts, and a heavenly breath as fresh as flowers or as rainwater before it hits the ground?

Trinity—mother, father, and child. Any one of the whiz kids, Oppenheimer, and the bomb.

♦♦♦♦

The Gadget

Our second act as parents, after attaching a name, Jasper, to our baby son, was to relocate to a bigger apartment. Breaking Clifford's lease cost us a month's rent, but we hadn't been paying that much for the three tomb-like rooms with tilting floors and woodwork that had been vandalized by gnawing rodents. "More likely dogs," Clifford had said, but I was sure that any dog that could inflict such damage on the old varnished wood had to be rabid, not much better than a rat.

In our new place, Jasper had his own room that came instantly to smell like baby's breath—sweet and blameless. The two windows, on adjoining walls, were both so close to the corner that the intersection of those swaths of incoming light didn't benefit much of the room. Jasper's crib, for instance, was outside of this blessed rectangle, so whenever he slept, he seemed to have been damned.

"Much better for napping," Clifford pointed out,

trying to depict our son as less of an exile.

"I guess." These days I was being especially agreeable. Clifford had lost the baby-naming competition. He wasn't fond of the name "Jasper" but hadn't come up with any favorites to promote.

"What about David?" he'd asked brightly, as if it weren't such a common name. To him, Jasper sounded very dated. "Or maybe not dated, but from some other unidentifiable culture. You know?"

"No, Clifford, I don't." Since the baby would be inheriting Clifford's last name, I felt entitled to a louder voice in the process of choosing his first name. We had both agreed, though, on "Sonia" if the baby were a girl.

Our apartment occupied the second floor of a three-family house. Normally, engrossed in the business of mothering, I forgot about our first and third-floor counterparts. But now and then, when I'd detect the wafture of a voice from downstairs or feel trampled by footfalls on the floor above us, our lives felt too compressed and crowded. I began to understand the longing that some young families experience for a house with margins of yard and garden around it.

My parents generously offered to pay for a washing machine and a dryer, a house-warming gift even though technically we weren't living in a house. The gift was in observation of a tradition begun with Sylvia, when she and Howie, as newlyweds, moved right into their own four-bedroom house. Being spared two visits a week to the Queen o' Clean Laundromat was the most welcome gift I could have imagined. Though the baby and his clothes were tiny, he produced a constant barrage of dirty laundry. And of course there were his diapers. Having a washing machine in our basement enabled me to use cloth diapers instead of disposable. The challenge, though, was negotiating ownership of our new appliances with our neighbors. Even if they understood that the washer and dryer belonged to us, they didn't necessarily believe that it was wrong to run a load, if they could get away with it. Sometimes I'd sense the house quaking and decide that one of my neighbors was running the dryer. Occasionally at such a moment I'd sneak down the back stairs all the way to the basement but never managed to catch anyone in the act. My sleuthing wasn't very aggressive; I didn't want any of the other tenants to report to Mr. DiNatale that I'd installed the washer and dryer in the basement since he was the one paying for the water.

How had this newfound ease in doing laundry become such a luxury that the drudgery and repetition of the task didn't trouble me in the least? All the years when I had been single, laundry was probably my most procrastinated chore; consequently, only after three weeks, when not even the makings for an outlandish outfit remained clean, I would haul an enormous sack of dirty clothes to the public laundry. The only reward for all those years of sitting for hours in the indescribable air of the laundromat was the copy of *The Confessions of St. Augustine* that I acquired, abandoned by another customer. The fact that reading such dense text could have diverted me in that setting is testimony to the utter misery of being in the laundromat.

Somehow, now, laundry presented new challenges. The baby's clothes required the germ-fighting properties of hot water, which would shrink all of our clothes to uselessness. My bright cotton clothes were sure to bleed their color onto the neutral tones of Clifford's shirts. By the time I'd separated all of the laundry according to various categories, the resulting loads were way too small to bother with. Yet we didn't own enough clothes to wait out the accumulation of bigger loads of wash. The solution might have been to manually wash these small loads in the bathtub, except that our apartment didn't have a bathtub.

One evening while browsing through the latest batch of unsolicited catalogues, I came upon a picture of a table-top washing machine. The description below the picture boasted that this miniature wonder, operated by a hand crank, could launder one pound of clothes in less than ten minutes. Why wait for your mini-loads to grow into larger, more unwieldy loads? the catalogue asked. The savings in electricity and the non-drain on the environment made this small appliance positively virtuous.

"Look, Cliff." I thrust the catalogue in front of my husband, covering over the magazine he was reading.

"What?"

"Look at this manual washing machine."

Clifford dutifully read the copy then said, "I don't know, Pauline. It seems more efficient to me to do fewer, bigger loads."

I put both my hands on his cheeks and rotated his head until he was facing me. "My dear, it's a new world of laundry we're living in. No more mixing the underpants with the red-satin tunic."

"Really?"

I realized I'd already decided to buy one—an Ergo-Eco Cranking Clean Machine, as it was called. No doubt Clifford, too, recognized my resolve because he ceased to argue and simply asked, "How much is it?"

"Sixty-nine dollars. Plus shipping. Much cheaper than a washing machine."

"Which we already have," he reminded me.

"Maybe having one of these, though, will make our regular washing machine last longer. Ever think of that? Huh?"

Clifford removed the catalogue from his lap and returned to reading the magazine. Immediately I phoned in my order just before 8pm, when the order line closed for the day.

My husband was not a consumer. Aside from food and fuel for heat in the winter, he wouldn't have purchased anything for himself. His clothes were a collection of cast-offs and gifts, including many from me during the last year. Clifford didn't know the origins of most of his clothing, or his bed sheets, his rugs, or even his furniture. However, he never would have interfered with my own occasional extravagance, especially since I bought most of my clothes at thrift stores and had acquired nearly all of the baby's furnishings second-hand.

The Ergo-Eco Cranking Clean Machine, in reality, was even smaller than I'd supposed. Though its dimensions had been included in the catalogue description, my imagination had slightly enlarged it. The dainty white plastic item that I unburied from under countless Styrofoam pellets looked like a doll accessory. The prospect of cranking the handle for eight minutes when I could just as easily have let that same small wash load soak in the bathroom sink was beginning to seem ridiculous.

The night when it arrived, Clifford and I assembled a load of laundry and step by step followed the instructions for washing it in the Ergo-Eco Cranking Clean Machine. While taking his turn at cranking, Clifford actually became enthusiastic about our new purchase. He liked the fact that it didn't rely on electric power, and he observed that the clothes were getting much more agitation than they would in the sink.

Its name quickly became cumbersome, and we renamed it "the gadget." This nickname would serve another purpose besides saving on syllables. We wanted to avoid referring to it directly in my parents' presence when they visited, so they wouldn't learn that their expensive gift to us had been displaced by a much simpler machine. I fit the gadget into Jasper's closet, on top of boxes of thrift-store baby clothes he would grow into.

Anything larger than his infant figure, even clothes

meant for a one-year-old, looked enormous. I couldn't imagine him wearing them, only shifting around in their spaciousness. Would his little fisted hands ever be bigger than a bird's heart? Would his soft-soled feet exceed the size of a rose? Yet in just a few weeks, some of his first gowns were already straining across his chest. When I held him close, I could feel the rhythm of his rapid heartbeat.

"If my heart rate were this fast, I'd be in intensive care," I said to Clifford.

"That's normal for an infant." I was impressed at the scope of Clifford's knowledge until he added, "The pediatrician told us, don't you remember?"

All I remembered about Jasper's first examination at the doctor's office was my heart-stopping fear that the doctor would discover a serious deformity in my child's anatomy, or an irregular heartbeat or a sluggish reflex. I'd nearly wept at the news that Jasper was healthy in every way. Only then had I come close to comprehending the incomparable miracle of conception—not so much the kindling of a new life as the complicated sequence of steps, the differentiation of cells, the continuous fission and growth. So much potential along the way for error, and yet here we were with a perfect son.

Still, I could hardly fathom that this soft-edged, helpless baby would someday be capable of thinking through mathematical puzzles and hurdling over the schoolyard fence. Among the gifts mailed to us by our long-distance friends and families had been an assortment of contraptions meant to keep Jasper amused as well as to usher him hastily through two years of developmental phases.

One weekend my parents drove from upstate New York to see me and Clifford, but primarily to spend time with their grandson. While my mother and I sat on the floor of Jasper's room, passing him back and forth, performing harmonized renditions of songs that I'd learned as a child, my father was directing Clifford, who was oiling the hinges of the doors to all the bedrooms. Gradually under Dad's tutelage, my husband was developing a small repertoire of handyman skills.

"The trick," my father was saying, "is to drizzle the oil in very small amounts at the same time you move the door on its hinges."

I heard an outcry and guessed that either Clifford had whacked my father's face with the door or his version of a small amount of oil had been excessive.

"Don't squeeze the can so hard," my father scolded.

"I'm sorry. It's all over your shirt." Then Clifford said, "We'll clean it up in the gadget."

"What's that?" my mother asked me at the very same time Dad asked Clifford the same question.

I continued singing and made myself louder. "C'mon, Mom," I urged her. "Join in." But she asked again, "What gadget?"

Clifford knew that he'd violated the secrecy that prevented my parents from discovering our replacement washing machine. So honest by nature, he was unlikely to improvise a lie; instead he prolonged the silence by saying nothing at all.

"Top secret," I said, thinking the words would pass as a joke. Why my parents were so intensely curious about some non-specific thing was hard for me to understand, unless its very mystery was irresistible to them.

"No, really," my mother said, passing Jasper to me and making the mountainous ascent to her feet. Gradually she and my father converged and were standing as one confrontational unit before me. So naturally, I got up and sidled closer to Clifford, hoping that our union had the same intimidating effect on them as theirs did on me.

And then my parents started guessing. "Is it a medical device?" my father asked, only to be challenged by my mother.

"That wouldn't make sense. Why would they use a medical device to clean your shirt?"

"Some kind of pre-wash, then."

"But that isn't any kind of gadget. A washboard?" By now they were conversing with each other even though neither of them had the answer to the unknown they were attempting to name.

Finally, Clifford put his arm around me and said, "Some things are private between husband and wife."

That was all. Both my parents lowered their heads in shame. We all continued to stand there, not speaking or looking at each other. Soon an audible splat inside Jasper's diaper and the minuscule belch that followed presented us with a new pursuit: getting the baby cleaned and changed.

Just several weeks after the gadget had become an indispensable member of our household, it was unofficially retired. Excavating it from the nursery closet—and having the foresight to do so when Jasper wasn't asleep—had gotten to be a major nuisance. The exercise involved in cranking the gadget's handle, even when Clifford was around to alternate shifts with me, was exhausting. Its original box had been disposed of in the interest of security, so until we moved, the gadget remained as part of the accumulating heap in Jasper's closet, increasingly concealed beneath an excess of towels, fresh diapers, outgrown clothes, and the preciously scented receiving blankets that had been wrapped around his newborn body.

◆◆◆◆

Kitty Cat

Most days she could will herself to wait for the hour hand of the clock to arc around slowly towards five. She may already have poured the vodka, gripped the glass in her hand ready to be raised. But she would wait until five o'clock exactly to touch the rim of the glass to her lips. Whatever she had done while waiting for the cocktail hour had not been related to food. That five o'clock shot was poured down the chute into a thoroughly empty stomach. Two sips, maybe three, and she was rocketing away to another state of mind.

Usually she'd reach for the phone. "Are you stopping by?" She didn't have to identify herself since everyone in Los Alamos was familiar with Kitty Oppenheimer's drinking habits and that voice skidding all over the musical scale. "How 'bout just come say hello to little Peter."

Asked where her child was just then, Kitty had to admit, "I don't know," only because the days were all so similar to each other that she couldn't remember if this

121

was the day when Peter had accepted a sentence in the playpen or was playing just outside the wooden bars or if today Pat Sherr had put him in a stroller and was walking him a while.

"Oh never mind." Kitty wasn't going to bother charming anyone who had no intention of keeping her company. She pushed down the phone button and dialed another number, and bypassing the pleasantries that would cost her too much effort, she began bluntly, "Shirley, can you get yourself over here? Please. I need some company."

Once Shirley got there, Kitty could say to her all the things she would otherwise say to herself. She'd start by spewing curses at this life, the repetition, the possibility of returning to work in the blood lab. "Robert might as well set up his bed in the "T", the Tech Area. Half the time he gets home and I'm just about ready for sleep. Do you think his son ever sees him?"

Do you? Do you? Kitty hardly was aware that she'd repeated this question and had to wonder why Shirley finally exploded with an emphatic "YES. I'm sure he does, though not as often as he'd like. Or you. Kitty, why don't you let me watch him tomorrow morning, give you a little time off?" This was the wife of the bigman, after all, and everyone agreed that she should be treated indulgently, especially since she could sometimes blow up as dangerously as several sticks of dynamite.

Kitty, cross-eyed, was studying the level of clear vodka against the clear glass.

"Let's go outside," Shirley urged her, and led her by the elbow out the back door that opened out into the sandy soil of the yard. "Why don't you start a garden, Kitty? Find out what'll grow out here. We all know about your green thumb."

"Yes, a garden," and Kitty gazed at the gritty ground and transplanted from her fancy some of the orchids she used to cultivate. They were a specialty of hers, though no one except for her seemed to know that orchids actually thrived on neglect. They only needed watering now and then. Most undemanding beauties.

"That commie doctor," she said. "Robert would be home earlier if it was she who was waiting," Kitty accused. An undemanding beauty for sure, that doctor. A visit from Robert every other month was enough for her.

"Kitty, whatever are you talking about?"

The glass in Kitty's hand tilted, lunged, like a stunt plane until she returned it to a state of balance. "You know. Jean Tit-luck." Kitty sniggledy-giggled. Sipped the last of the glassful in one long swallow. She handed her empty glass to the young doctor's wife then kneeled on the ground.

"Grab me that stick, will you?" she ordered Shirley. With it she drew the shape of a garden bed, an irregular oval that she began carving into sections, stating out loud what would be planted in each.

"Sounds lovely," Shirley said.

Kitty stood, her jean knees as particled as sandpaper. "Where's my boy?" she asked suddenly, stunned by the edge where the air stopped and her own self began.

"Peter!" she called. "Peter, where are you hiding?"

Kitty unbuckled her belt and treated herself to an extra-deep breath before buckling it back up again. "Hand me that glass, will you?"

"Kitty, I'll help you find Peter, but then I've got to go."

"Sure you do. It's all right, though. I'm jolly fine."

Kitty couldn't actually see, from her house or her yard, the enclosure all around the compound, topped with two lines of barbed wire. Yet she felt herself captive to this new life dedicated to saving the world by destroying it. Work on the "gadget" proceeded unevenly. Some nights Robert declared that success was right around the bend, but after setbacks, he had more than once confessed to his wife a fear that the bomb wasn't viable because of some nearly imperceptible oversight or miscalculation.

Kitty was sharp. She could follow most of his narration, even the technical descriptions of various gun-type assemblies that had been proposed. General Groves, however, had come close to forbidding the physicists to discuss their work at home. Even the coded references to the "gadget," the "device," might be too revealing, he feared, since an untrustworthy eavesdropper might not be tricked into believing that the gadget being discussed by husband and wife was the family washing machine, or the toaster.

So Oppie and Kitty began to make up a language all their own that allowed them to converse about scattered neutrons, about the shape of the hull, about the endpoint bomb that everyone was pushing towards. And Peter wasn't skilled enough in speech to understand that he was being purposefully excluded from his parents' dialogue. Peter, casting aside his miniature spoons and grasping at handfuls of soft green beans and the chicken his father had cut for him into very small bites, ate dinner in the company of government secrets.

The boy appeared now at the front door, knocking as if he were a guest. Hedda had escorted him home all the way from her house, where he'd wandered. "It was the smell of the cookies baking," she explained, that had attracted him. Peter was carrying a large one, and his mouth was encircled with crumbs. "I told him to save this one for after supper."

Kitty barely knew Hedda or much about her, only that she lived behind Bathtub Row and worked with the dentist on staff. And now here she was feeding Kitty's son, giving him instructions about what to eat and when. As a bluster of resentment was making its way into words, Kitty seized Peter's hand and pulled him into the house.

"Thank you, Hedda. We were wondering where he'd gotten to," Shirley said.

Kitty reclaimed her glass, half-filled it and poured a long drink for both Hedda and Shirley. "No thank you," both women said when served their rockless vodka, an amount that would have lasted each through at least two cocktail parties.

"Peter," Kitty scolded. "You know you're not to wander off like that!"

But when Peter crumpled into a naughty boy, sulking and scowling, Kitty soothed him. "Did the lady take you into her house? Were you scared?" He reached out for his mother's glass, wishing to sip the diamond-like liquid and learn what glitter tasted like.

"No, Peter," Hedda intervened, doubting that Kitty would say it.

The distant sky beyond the mountains swooped down and into the house. Kitty staggered backwards three steps and collapsed onto the couch. "I'm tired," she declared. The lonely days lasted too long.

"How 'bout a nice bath?" Shirley suggested. If she and her husband had been among the privileged few with a bathtub in the house, she'd have been bathing regularly, even more than once a day.

"No bath, no."

Shirley decided it was time to phone Robert's office and the many labs, to keep phoning until she found him and could urge him to come home.

"So long," Hedda said, leaving the door open. Peter followed after her outside.

Minutes later Kitty spied Jane Wilson and her husband—off from work early, thought Kitty enviously—walk by, arm in arm. "Come on in!" Kitty called to them all the way from the couch. Robert (but not her Robert) leaned his head and shoulders into the house. "Hello, Mrs. Kitty!"

"Robert, come right in here and tell me what you did today about the containment of the stray neutrons."

Shocked at her indiscretion, Robert Wilson instinctively backed away as he fumbled for what to do and say. "Ah… That's actually not my department," he said, and "Gotta go, Mrs. Kitty." He managed to add, "Meow," his signature farewell to her.

When Kitty's own Robert appeared, abnormally early, Kitty had no idea that he'd been summoned by Shirley Barnett, who was concerned for her and for her son. Kitty lit up a cigarette at the risk of being ignited by all that she'd drunk. She danced over to her darling.

"Get it all figured out, did you? Is that why you're home?"

At a glance, Oppie rated this only a class-C crisis. He'd seen worse. In fact, he was already figuring that he could turn things around and get back to work for another hour or two.

"Tell you what," he said in his cheeriest voice. "How 'bout you take a little nap—would you like a little nap? And I'll look after Peter," meaning that he'd find another of the unoccupied wives to look after him. "Then when I get home from work—"

"But you *are* home," Kitty argued. She lay back down on the couch. "Or are you telling me"—her sloppy smile was oozing all over her face — "that I'm imagining all five-foot-ten of you?" She rolled one-half a turn, right off the narrow couch.

Robert squeezed her hand, his Kitty little loyal wife,

and continued. "When I get home, we'll have a cocktail and watch the sunset." He knew that the enticement would be the drink more than the incomparable sight of the sunset that, at this altitude, brought them within arm's reach of the sun.

Kitty had cozied herself into a sleeping position on the floor, following the soporific summons of the alcohol. "I am rather sleepy," she confessed.

"Not here, dear. Let's get you upstairs."

When Peter roamed back into the house, Kitty was again upright, even if her posture was maintained by the support of her husband's arm around her.

"Are you…dancing?" Peter asked wondrously.

"That's right, Sport," his father said. "I'm dancing your mum up to her bed. Nap time." Then when he noticed the look of horror, almost, on his child's face, he added, "For your mother. Nap time for Mum."

That's what he'd called his own mother—Mum. Frail, breakable Ella with an indomitable will. Her fierce pride in her older son had inspired him to achieve. Or had his achievement come first and her natural reaction of pride afterwards?

Robert helped Kitty up the stairs, one at a time. She didn't weigh much so was easily led to bed, a drowsy dreamer before she'd even closed her eyes. "We were back on Eagle Hill Road," she murmured. "We were eating toast, and the butter was right there on the table but we both forget to spread any of it on the toast."

"Oh my," Robert said. He removed her one shoe, the

only one that she was wearing, and dragged the coverlet underneath her to the foot of the bed then laid it on top of her.

"G'nap." He touched her forehead with a tender kiss.

"Meow," she answered sleepily.

Shirley was still downstairs, waiting to confer with Robert, who thought she'd escaped when he arrived, as if they were a tag team. But no, she'd stayed to supervise Peter. Would she stay a while longer, or perhaps take the child with her to her house? he hoped.

"This doesn't happen every day," he told her, aware of the gossip circulating about his wife's instability, her mood flares.

"I'm sure not." But Shirley wasn't so sure. She helped out sometimes in Oppie's office and had been present more than once when he'd received a call at cocktail hour, either from Kitty herself or from her guardian of the day.

"Robert, don't you think Kitty would be better off working at the lab again?" Shirley suggested.

"Maybe." Oppie's blue eyes darted away from the question. Perhaps Kitty would be better off with the discipline of a regular job. Maybe Peter, too, would be better off under the care of a paid sitter. But Oppie supposed that the other employees in the blood lab wouldn't welcome back his temperamental wife. Her departure from the job last year had been fraught with conflict and accusations.

When Shirley didn't press him, he let his eyes return

to her. "Thanks for the help. We'll be all right now."

"Do you want me to stay?"

"Nope. I'm here."

But where was Peter now? she wondered. He'd been with her when his papa had come downstairs. But now both he and his big round cookie were gone. Shirley imagined him retracing the route to Hedda's, hungry for more than cookies.

"All right then."

Shirley left with relief, slowly strolling to the Commissary, where she'd pick up groceries for dinner that night. She shopped efficiently, deprived of options by the limited stock on the shelves. Then as she carried her bag of cans and boxed goods outside, she noticed Robert, alone, walking away from his house on Bathtub Row towards the Tech Area. Little Peter, running hard, caught up to him from behind and stopped his father by tugging at his pants leg. Robert bent down to match Peter's height. Shirley watched the father stroke his son's head then turn him around and pat his bottom, sending him home to his mother cat.

♦♦♦♦

Henry the Cat

Jasper emerged from his first three cranky and colicky months as an agreeable baby with ambitions to walk and talk exceptionally early. His valiant attempts to raise himself to his feet, hanging on chair seats for balance, seemed Olympian feats. After each of Jasper's grunts, I'd peek into his diaper to discover more often than not that the sound had punctuated his latest effort to stand, not to digest.

But as much as a mother may love her child, the unvarying replay of challenges that need to be mastered during the process of growth and the repetitive schedule can become tiresome. While Jasper worked with all his might to become a toddler, I escaped the monotony of our days together by reading, and during these lapses in my vigilance, my son sometimes would fall and cry, get frustrated and cry, miss my attention and cry.

"Oh, honey! Come here," and I'd draw him into my arms, contrite. He made the most luscious sounds that I finally thought to record on a portable tape recorder Clifford had bought for a school project. But Jasper wouldn't stay put for long. He would wriggle out of my possession and when he ventured away, continuing to grow and develop, I'd read a few more pages.

"What'd you do today, Pauli?" Clifford often asked when he got home.

Perhaps another mother would have narrated each minute increment of accomplishment noted while she watched her son and played with him, described the most recent eating habits, patterns of sleep, teething activity. And maybe I was cheating Clifford when I'd compact all of this into a terse reply: "Nothing much."

During my many walks around the neighborhood, pushing Jasper ahead of me in his stroller, I saw no evidence of any other babies on our street or any of those nearby. In fact there were no traces, even, of young children—no parked tricycles, no sandboxes, no squalling protests at nap time. What a barren part of town we lived in, I thought, wondering how the species would ever be perpetuated in Winter Hill, as our neighborhood in Somerville was called.

Every day, though, we did encounter Henry, a Siamese cat who always seemed to be looking for opportunities to socialize. Henry would bound out of the bushes and pad along beside us as I traveled the city streets with the stroller, pausing to decide whether to turn left or right at the corners, wishing that there were some way other than a change of direction to introduce novelty into these walks. From our earliest strolls with Henry, he heeded my lead, stopping at the corners while I deliberated which way to turn or in the middle of a block to retrieve Jasper's squishy rubber toy.

Because Henry's entrance never occurred at the same place twice, I didn't know where he lived. Surely an expensive Siamese couldn't be a stray. Yet the cat seemed to be seeking a family to endear itself to, and I, who'd never owned a pet except for short-lived turtles and goldfish, was beginning to look for Henry each day, to actually perk up when he fell into step with Jasper and me.

"Look who's here," I'd say to Jasper.

Soon I was greeting Henry with brief updates: Jasper has a cold; Clifford has parents' night tonight so it'll be a long day. Of my two mute companions, Henry was the more communicative (though presumably Jasper, of the "superior" species, would eventually overtake him), maintaining eye contact while I spoke to him and cocking his head meaningfully in reply to my news bulletins. Once Jasper's pacifier had fallen from the stroller without me noticing it, and Henry trotted back and stood beside it, marking the spot for me.

"Thank you, Henry," I said, and then, "Jasper, can you thank Henry?"

The old lurking loneliness had begun to keep company with me, a shadowy otherness that depleted all light and hope from the space we shared. The five extra pounds that had stayed with me since Jasper's birth had increased to eight. Unaware of my weight gain, Clifford discouraged me from punishing myself with a hunger diet. I'd discovered a packaged cookie that provided me with pleasure when I'd run out of hunches for the crossword puzzle and my enthusiasm for whatever novel I was reading had waned. The orange-brownie variety, so chewy and tinged with the brightness of orange essence, could always revive my declining spirits at least for a time.

Now Henry was having a similar effect on me. I looked forward to our daily meetings. I'd go out with Jasper even in the needling rainfalls that had deterred me in the past from our usual mid-morning walk.

Why did I call the cat "Henry"? The name had been the first that came into my mind. I trusted that the free association must have deep, archetypal significance.

"Henry, I'm thinking that it's time to go back to work." Henry replied with a protracted blink. "I know, I pledged to stay home with Jasper for six months. But I feel so strangely…useless."

Henry averted his attentive gaze and lowered his head.

"Please! You don't have to remind me of all those perfect mothers, like my own, who stayed home full-time. But things were different then. Women were respected for dedicating themselves to their families." That's it, I told myself. What I'm doing no longer seems to have much worth in the eyes of the world. But couldn't I give myself an attitude makeover? Weren't my own feelings about what I was doing what mattered, after all?

"Thank you, Henry, for listening."

Later in the afternoon while Jasper napped, I luxuriated in a warm bath, washed my hair, and redressed for the rest of the day in a long black skirt and a white silk shirt with exaggerated lapels, an outfit I'd worn when Clifford and I used to go out to dinner. I had to stab my earring wires forcibly through the piercings that for a while now had been undisturbed. I even put on a pair of shoes with enough of a heel that I felt almost statuesque. As soon as Jasper stirred from his nap I started playing some of my favorite albums. With my son positioned in my arms like a dance partner, I whirled about the room, through the doorway, and then around the dining room table, trying so hard to muster up enough energy to power me through those sluggish late-afternoon hours.

But soon Jasper, possibly suffering from motion sickness after our lively jaunt around the dance floor, whimpered in distress and then spit up on my white silk blouse. At that same moment the doorbell rang, and I so longed for adult conversation that I set Jasper down on his back on the floor and hurried down the stairs to the outside door.

"Is this your cat?" I didn't recognize the man standing at the door but did recognize Henry, captive in his arms and looking like the slaughter for this evening's supper. Before I could assert that Henry was *not* my cat, the man said, "I see you walking with him. You oughtta keep him on a leash, y'know? This here animal just pulled all the stuffing outta the cushion on my porch-swing."

"Sorry," I said, forgetting to disclaim responsibility for the antics of a cat that didn't belong to me.

The man thrust Henry towards me. "Keep him inside. Or else teach him that he ain't a dog."

I suppressed my impulse to offer to pay for the man's wrecked cushion, even knowing that without explaining to him that Henry wasn't mine, I must seem stingy or ill-mannered. But I received Henry's body like a football pass and pressed him against my chest. Unusually motionless for such a curious animal, Henry roused himself long enough to lap up one stroke of the spit-up curdling on my silk shirt.

"Thank you!" I called out pointlessly to my departing neighbor. After all, he had afforded me a brief distraction and a moment of adult company. I stopped short of suggesting that he come back some time for tea.

"Come on up with me, you bad boy," I said to Henry. As I leaned down to place him on the floor, I noticed a scattering of cat hairs on my blouse. Within just a few minutes, my stylish garment had been transformed into a work shirt bearing evidence of my role as a caretaker.

"Henry..." I began, then realized that he had no control over his shedding. "I don't suppose you dance?"

As if in reply, Henry headed towards the open door and soundlessly descended the stairs. I couldn't interpret his wish to leave as anything but a rejection, even as I told myself that he obviously was an outdoor cat. "Henry, don't go." Of course, since he wasn't capable of pushing on the latch on the downstairs door and letting himself out, Henry seemed to oblige me.

"I'll get you some milk." Not until I poured some low-fat milk into a bowl, which I placed on the floor, did the errant cat come back inside my apartment.

I transferred Jasper from the carpet to his little seat that allowed him to look upward and keep watch on the adult world.

"Maybe I'll join you, I said to Henry. While the cat fed himself the bowl of milk in small splashes, I poured myself a glass of wine from the bottle Clifford and I had opened at least two weeks ago. Our stay-at-home, candle-lit dinner had concluded with both of us, drowsy from wine and sleep deficiency, dropping into bed.

After finishing his milk, Henry rested for a short time beside Jasper, in constant peril from the baby's flailing hands. "OK, Henry," I finally told him. "You can go now." He must have understood me because he immediately went to the door and streamed as smoothly and quickly as liquid down the stairs, then out the front door that I ran down to open for him.

Perhaps it was the promise of milk that lured Henry to my house most afternoons. I'd hear his humanlike voice coming from the front porch and go down to let him in. Since during our morning walks I already would have presented him with any new developments on the home front, I had little to report to Henry but sometimes informed him of how long Jasper had napped that day, what I might cook for dinner, and most importantly, what I was thinking. This terribly one-way relationship left me with the stigma of self-centeredness. How could I possibly inquire about Henry's life when I knew that no answer would be forthcoming? Now and then I managed to offer a feeble statement of empathy or observation: You're quite the explorer, Henry. Do you know that? What keeps you going? You don't seem to eat much.

While the cat gradually consumed his pool of milk, I sipped wine from an opaque mug, just in case Jasper grew to have a photographic memory that could be imprinted with dozens of images of his mother getting drunk. I learned that if I provided Henry with a large enough portion of milk, by the time he finished it and was ready to rest, Clifford would be due home soon. I assaulted my husband with a full-hearted welcome when he arrived, my genuine pleasure at seeing him exaggerated by the rush of alcohol that energized my mind while subduing my tired body.

"Teacher of the year!" I greeted Clifford, hugging him tightly, as if he'd just come home from war.

"Mother of the year," he replied, inadvertently reminding me of my neglected son, who was fortunately amused with as little as the shadow of his hand or the circle of each snap on his stretchy suit. Now the addition of his father to the present company so stimulated Jasper that he started to choke on his own outcries.

"Baby, baby!" Clifford dropped his tote bags full of books and seized Jasper out of his seat, rapidly patting his pliant little back. "Are you all right, my boy?"

As the urgency of Jasper's need passed, I recalled that my mug, wherever I'd left it, still contained a swallow or two of Vouvray, my new favorite wine. The bottle of this particular brand was more yellow than green, suggestive of sunny fields and summer fruits.

I wanted to tell my husband that I'd been drinking wine lately, maybe hoping for assurance that this form of adult relaxation was really very acceptable. But soon Clifford was telling me all about the standardized testing being conducted that week at his school. I was fairly sure that I wouldn't be able to tolerate much more detail about his day without the dulling effect of the wine, so I edged into the kitchen, reached for my mug, all the while saying, "Uh-huh, uh-huh. I'm listening." I wasn't exactly craving the alcohol but the sharp, rusty grab as it washed down my throat instantly calmed me, even before the wine could have had any effect on my brain. Had I become psychologically addicted, and so soon?

As Clifford related a story about one of his students who'd misread the test-taking directions—"It was sad, but kind of funny, too," he said—I experimented with substitutions in the family portrait we'd thought to get taken soon, creating an ever-changing trinity: Clifford and I, seated, with Jasper in my lap metamorphosed into Jasper, me, and a bottle of wine, then finally into me, Jasper in my lap, and Henry in an unnatural, upright posture next to my chair.

On our next morning walk, I said very frankly, "You

might as well know, Henry, that I've instituted a cocktail hour. I'm sure you've already noticed my afternoon glass of wine, but I don't want you to think that I'm…hiding anything. And anyway, I've heard that a glass or two of wine every day is good for your heart. Except that I think that might be true only of red wine," I told myself.

My declaration didn't cause Henry to flee, and in fact he came around that afternoon. "What'll it be?" I asked, serving him his triple of milk then helping myself to a transparent tumbler half-full of Merlot before returning to the living room. I joggled Jasper's seat, for the moment regaling him with my complete attention slightly diffused by the wine.

The autumn air had begun to breathe cold during our morning walks. I tucked a small fleece blanket around Jasper—kissing each of his so-soft cheeks and his nose. "My bunny boy!" I buttoned my jacket up to my neck. Here and there the multi-colored houses— painted in unlikely combinations like kiwi green and coral, or staid ivory with lavender trim—electrically charged the gray days that soon were ruined by rain. Continuous, bullying rain. Pushing a stroller while holding an umbrella required stronger arms than mine. I wouldn't have minded getting wet—and the stroller had a canopy that sheltered Jasper—but the plump slugs that materialized on the sidewalks on those rainy days and the spongy sensation of accidentally squashing them repulsed me. I didn't know why Boston and not Philly should be stricken with this pestilence or why this neighborhood had almost exclusive local rights to the glistening, wormy critters who were as slow as the hours between waking and Clifford's return home. Maybe all of the walkout basements on the side of the hill attracted them, the possibility of getting inside without having to climb any stairs.

Still I did my best to get out for at least a brief walk around the block even on those rainy days, feeling obligated by the unspoken understanding between Henry and me. He was unbothered by the rain, which beaded on the surface of his fur. I wondered if Henry would be as reliable a companion once winter broke, and the hardships of cold, snow, and ice challenged the ease with which he toured the neighborhood.

So I asked him. "Henry, do you come out in the winter?" My question reminded me that I hadn't a clue as to where Henry lived.

"I have a really warm bunting thing that I got for Jasper. It covers everything but his face. I'm not so sure though that we'll be out every day."

Then, sticking to the subject of our future contact, I said, "Of course, you can always come by the apartment." I added, "I mean, I'd really *like* it if you did."

Just as well, I thought at that moment, that the neighborhood was always abandoned during the day. No one around to witness me talking to a cat.

"We humans, Henry, don't always do so well in the cold without a nice fur coat like yours."

But Henry had fallen behind and was no longer in

his customary place beside me. I turned around to see him standing at the edge of the sidewalk, tense with readiness to exit, his back arched as if he were about to leap off of a ten-foot-high wall. I later realized that the long, guttural utterance that sounded deep inside him must have been his goodbye to Jasper and me.

Had I betrayed Henry by my admission that I was a seasonal walker and might not be as available come winter? Although he seemed to make no demands on me, I wondered now if he wanted something other than our me-centered relationship. Maybe in the end, Henry had been burdened by the role of my confessor. I could all along have been directing my comments to Jasper instead, but I wanted to preserve my child's illusion that I was the all-knowing parent, leading him fearlessly towards a certain future, rather than the wobbly woman I'd become, who couldn't see past her afternoon nap.

◆◆◆◆

Necktie Jobs

Early in November, I turned thirty-four. Having a birthday at a time of year often tinged with an unmistakable sadness made the process of getting older seem slightly tragic. Even the vibrant sky—now that the rainy season had passed—couldn't disguise the ominous suggestion that we were heading somewhere lifeless and cold. Could it be winter? My mood, easily influenced by variations in the weather, led me to project ahead to Jasper as an adult, his childhood ended too soon.

My outings with him were becoming fewer since I now had to dress him in extra layers of clothing, mittens, a hat. The convenience of changing his diaper on the back seat of my car had spoiled me; now I worried that the exposure to even a moment of cold might hurt my baby in ways I couldn't guess. So we stayed in more and more, Jasper and I, without Henry, who had either found another family to attach himself to or discovered satisfaction in the indoor life.

If I pounced on Clifford each day when he arrived home, he didn't seem to mind my eager greeting. "How's my little family?" he always asked.

"The littlest little, he's just fine. But me, I'm hankering for some conversation with a big person." I took Clifford's backpack from him and flung it into a corner as well as I could fling such a significant weight. Then I hurried him out of his coat and tossed it over the banister. Clifford, I knew, would have much preferred to hang his coat up promptly and stow his backpack away under the desk, its designated place.

"Tell me about your day," I said.

I could tell that Clifford's mind was still at the doorway, not yet adjusted to a new location despite my effort to rush him through this transition.

"My day…it was good," he said, seeming uncertain about how much detail I expected from him. By now he should have anticipated my investigative interest in the particulars of his work day, especially the updates on faculty feuds, skirmishes, and romances. I'd met one or two of the other teachers at Clifford's school but felt most familiar with those who'd been allowed to blossom in my imagination into soap-opera characters. I'd endowed the seventh grade English teacher with the qualities of a male lead: a handsome face and curvaceous muscles. If I ever were to meet any of the cast in the flesh, my other-world would surely be destroyed.

"Did Cindy ever explain the bandage?"

"No, not yet."

"Why doesn't anyone just come out and ask her?"

Clifford shrugged. "Where's Jasper?"

"Right around the corner."

I went into the dining room and wrenched a plastic fork out of Jasper's unyielding fist, a dangerous plaything that apparently had kept him quiet and occupied for the last ten minutes or so. The edge of the dining-room table must now have been within his reach. Jasper laughed melodically as I drove his walker-on-wheels into the next room and over to Clifford.

"There he is! How's my boy?"

Jasper's steps, assisted by the walker, strained across the rough terrain of the Berber carpet. Not only did its coarse texture impede the roll of the wheels, but the fibers had been snagged—by dog paws, most likely—making the surface of the carpet even more raggedy. Since Jasper's desire to travel closer to his dad was thwarted by the carpet, Clifford reached forward and lifted him out of the walker.

"Daddy's home. I've been thinking of you all day. Yes I have."

How childish I felt, competing with my own son for Clifford's attention. I still hadn't glimpsed more than one or two of my neighbors and was beginning to suspect that all of the homes on our street were part of a stage set, expertly painted facades with no depth and no occupants. And whereas Henry had seemed to favor me over Jasper, Clifford seemed to prefer Jasper's company to mine. I had to remind myself that my husband's day had been congested with people—students, teachers, administrators—and that what he most longed for after work was a wordless ether in which he could simply exist. Trading sweet sounds with Jasper was a lot closer to that state than was detailing the tedium of relationships among his coworkers.

I sneaked into the kitchen and sipped from my secret mug of wine. I never drank more than one cup, or at least not much more. The anaesthetic calm that it produced allowed me to return to the living room and sit peaceably with Clifford and Jasper, soothed rather than threatened by their exchange of shapeless squeals and coos. Usually by that time of day I had thought about what we'd eat for dinner and had assembled the ingredients, maybe even completed whatever soaking, slicing, and chopping was needed. If not, I was far too limp and dreamy after my dose of wine to be able to manage such tasks with any competence. My role of meal-maker bothered me, since as a woman I felt type-cast. But though Clifford was more than willing to cook, food preparation fit into my daily time structure more obviously than it did into his.

"Oh!" Clifford lowered Jasper back into the walker. "There was some news today."

"What is it?"

"Rob is going to be the new assistant principal."

"Rob? You mean Rob the Phys. Ed. teacher?"

"That's the Rob."

"But he's…a gym teacher! How can he suddenly be

146

assistant principal? Will he organize the whole school as if it's one big gym class…uniforms, whistle blows?"

"No, Pauline, he's licensed as a school administrator."

Jasper had maneuvered his vehicle towards me and was bent over, chewing on a mouthful of my pants with his four front teeth. I coaxed the fabric away from him and substituted it with one of my knuckles.

"How'd he do that?"

"Took some courses. Took a test."

I remembered that last year Clifford had told me how one of the teachers on his team had been promoted to assistant principal at a school in a suburb south of Boston. Everyone seemed to be moving on, except maybe Mr. Kaiser, who'd been teaching at Clifford's school for nearly forty years. Mr. Kaiser. Few of the teachers seemed to know his first name.

Clifford leaned his head to rest on the back of the couch as if unable to support its weight himself. Then he closed his eyes, putting an end to our conversation. Or so he thought.

"Cliff, could *you* take a course, take a test?"

Clifford's imitation of sleep didn't convince me. "Could *you* take that same test?" I went on to continue the discussion without his participation. "What happens to teachers as they get old? I mean, except for Mr. Kaiser, aren't all of the teachers at your school fairly young? So where are the others, the older teachers? Did they all get bumped up to administrative positions? Or fall into a hole? Do you ever think about that?"

Still asleep, or pretending to be, Clifford didn't respond.

I gently withdrew my finger from the grasp of Jasper's teeth and towed him behind me into the kitchen. The packaged whole chicken that I removed from the refrigerator bore a disturbing resemblance to Jasper in his baby bathtub. Although I was developing a bit of an aversion towards meat, we were eating chicken more and more frequently. To prepare a healthy, vegetarian main course for dinner would have required too much effort at a time of day when I was normally spent. Broiling a slab of meat, or even sautéing it with some vegetables, was so much easier. And since chicken was the cheapest meat sold, except for liver—home to all the toxins roaming through whatever animal—it had become our number-one dinner entrée.

Little hands were tugging at my pants with impressive force. "What's baby want?" A summer of conversing with a cat had primed me for one-sided discussions with my son and, as when I'd spoken with Henry, I learned to interpret the minuscule movements of Jasper's eyes, his mouth, and the changes in his posture. Jasper, of course, didn't have an expressive tail as Henry did, which made him more difficult to read.

"Are you hungry, my boy? And you're being so patient."

Soon, sitting with Jasper in my lap while I spoon-fed him puréed carrots, I watched Clifford, still on the couch, in the exact same position as before and genuinely napping. That day he was wearing his red knit vest, one of the many vests I'd bought for him. To me a vest made any man more attractive. Clifford kindly obliged me and often dressed in vests. I almost couldn't think of an instance in which he hadn't been willing to accommodate my wishes, and now he was probably agonizing over whether or not he should rethink his career. During dinner I would undo any damage I'd done.

But when we sat down to eat, before I could begin to mollify him, Clifford said, "Pauline, I don't want to ever have to do anything just for money."

I nodded, assuming that he'd explain this statement.

"I mean, I really like my job. I know I don't make big money, but it's not bad. And I have my summers free." Clifford had set his fork down and was speaking with animation as if trying to win me over to his side. "I get good benefits, too."

"Oh Cliff, you don't have to apologize for your job. I was just wondering where all of the teachers vanish as they age." But instantly I thought of ancient, archetypal school teachers addressing their students across an ocean of several generations. Always women. What happened to the men?

"I don't know. I haven't been around long enough. Maybe they end up going into business, cashing in their pensions and buying fried-chicken franchises."

Already this was one of our longer conversations. Once Jasper had been put to bed each night and we had the chance to spend time together, we were most often overcome with fatigue and overstimulation in Clifford's case, fatigue and understimulation in mine.

"You know what I always say. There's nothing like a good teacher or a good nurse," I said, hoping to cheer him up with a dictum that, through experience, I had come to believe.

But Clifford sounded dispirited when he said, "I should've become a nurse. People who are dying get attached to their nurses and leave them their estates."

"I don't think so."

Surely it wasn't my bland response, but something inside him that revived his fire as dramatically as methane alcohol. "But even if I were a nurse and one of my patients willed me a lot of money, I'd probably just give it away. I'd rather be poor and happy than be rich."

"What makes you think that people with money are always unhappy?" Much as I wanted to atone for my earlier insensitivity, Clifford's faulty logic bothered me.

"I don't ever want to wear a necktie to work!"

"So would you even work if you didn't have to?"

"Of course!" Clifford seemed truly offended that I'd questioned his work ethic.

"You have some gravy on your collar."

"What?" His fingers crawled up one side of the red vest towards his collar.

"And see, if you'd been wearing a necktie, you'd have gravy on your necktie, too. Then we'd have to get it dry-cleaned. I hate dry-cleaning," I said, as if Clifford hadn't endured my many diatribes against the dry-cleaning chemical perchloroethylene.

"No, really." Frustration was coloring the rims of his

ears bright pink. I'd never seen him express himself with such passion.

"Stick to your principles, Clifford. No one is asking you to do otherwise."

The topic of work had reminded me that I wasn't contributing at all to our family income. In the pediatrician's waiting room and in the youth room at the library, I'd read article after article about women whose full-time careers flourished even as they raised two children—the number of children never varied—and meanwhile behaved as exemplary wives and even daughters to their aging parents. Could it be that all of that exertion, beyond a certain point, became energizing rather than exhausting? Clifford had insisted that I stay at home with Jasper for as long as I thought necessary. I wanted to be sure that he had a clear "other" to attach to rather than a cast of caretakers and babysitters. Yet I'd noticed Clifford scrutinizing receipts and credit-card statements, discreetly monitoring my budget.

He was slumping in his chair now, defeated. When I heard Jasper's after-dinner tummy grunts, I started to get up but then decided to delay the next diaper change. I feared that if I left Clifford alone, he might strangle himself with a necktie though I was fairly confident that he wouldn't know where in the apartment to find one.

"Wasn't there a man who retired last year who'd been teaching in one of the schools for fifty years?" I asked. But Clifford was mummified, apparently unable to speak or to move.

The next day I first swished aside the clothes in our bedroom closet and then groped through stacks of towels on a bathroom shelf in my quest to find the neckties that I almost could remember putting away somewhere when we'd moved in. I looked everywhere, even in the most improbable places, like in the drawer with all of the files that we needed for taxes. Finally, in between Clifford's set of white hospital sheets that we never used, I discovered his few, all terribly outdated ties inside a wrapping of tissue paper. One tie was as wide as his chest and a couple of others were as thin as shoelaces. Style-wise they must have spanned at least three decades. I imagined them displayed artistically, each the centerpiece of its own exhibit in a necktie museum. Visitors could learn about the evolution of tie styles by reading the text posted on the wall.

In order to prove my support for Clifford's refusal to enslave himself to money—and in acknowledgment of the necktie as a symbol of surrender to the job—I considered throwing away all of his ties or, even more dramatically, burning them, a necktie fire emitting fumes of fine silk mingled with polyester. But sometimes, maybe once each year, Clifford was confronted with an occasion that required him to wear a tie—a faculty awards ceremony or a family wedding.

So after all, I replaced Clifford's collection of ties in that slice of space between the white fitted sheet and the white top sheet, where he was unlikely ever to find it.

♦♦♦♦.

152

Necktie Party

I believe your people actually want to want to build a bomb I believe. They want to build a bomb. Enrico Fermi, an Italian transplant to Chicago and then to Los Alamos, viewed the making of the monstrosity as an act of patriotic duty—obligatory war service, same as marching across a field with a gun in hand. Yet he couldn't match the demon gleams in the eyes of those scientist soldiers.

I believe your people actually want to build a bomb, he said to Robert Oppenheimer.

Yes, they do.

Oppie couldn't suppress a smile expressing pride in his work crew. But just the previous week, he'd flown to San Francisco to consult with a psychiatrist, wondering what he could do to protect his men from the consuming stress that had been eating away the edges of their sanity.

"What else is there to do there? Besides work?" Dr.

Sterman had asked.

"We've developed quite a community, Doctor. There's the *Daily Bulletin*—that's our newspaper—and we have a radio station, KRS. We put on plays, have parties, dancing. Plenty of romance."

In addition to the armchairs occupied by Drs. Sterman and Oppenheimer, four others, similar but not identical, were placed thoughtfully in the room. The Persian rug, its dyes as dark and deep as nights in the desert, reached almost to the walls.

Dr. Sterman appeared to be writing down everything that Oppie said. For all Oppie knew, the psychiatrist was colluding with the government and would be passing along every word of their meeting to Security.

"That's all good," said Sterman when he'd finished taking notes. "That's what they need."

"But something else, something more..." Oppie was about to conclude that this meeting was a waste of time. Had he chosen the wrong psychiatrist to consult or was there, sadly, nothing he could do to forestall the psychic collapse of his entire team?

He ended the meeting early, excusing himself to attend another—a fictitious—meeting that he made sound real by specifying its time and its purpose, neither of which Dr. Sterman was likely to try to verify. The men shook hands. The sky had taken on a blue moodiness, drooping down and conveying the immensity of its weight onto Oppie's shoulders, a crushing rock of responsibility. He was back in the air at 1am, knowing that in the lab at that hour, the intensity of the day's work had not abated.

They were all working long hours. Whether their bed pillows were vacant in the mornings when their wives awoke or at night when the wives went to sleep, they weren't at home much. The Army siren shrilly summoned them out of sleep at seven in the morning, allowing them exactly one hour before they were expected to begin work at eight. Army time-management experts had computed the amount of time necessary to wash, dress, brush, and eat, even down to the number of brushstrokes recommended by dentists and how long the prescribed toothbrushing should take.

Now that the top-ranked scientists had migrated to Los Alamos from their respective labs, now that the organizational chart ghost-written by Isidor Rabi linked them all laterally and up and down, now that they were willing to sacrifice sleep and song and family, they didn't have enough plutonium or uranium$_{235}$ for experimentation. Not enough for trials along the way. Instead they had to pose a number of "what ifs," their hypothetical plotlines played out on paper, calculations related to weights and amounts and time. Deprived of the satisfying gala of small explosions, they had to settle for pencil scratchings on pages of a pad.

Each of them pursued his own small piece of the puzzle. Oppie could only shake his head, drawing on his nineteenth cigarette of the day. Now that they finally were centralized all in one place, they had to be split apart like the atoms in their experiments.

Hardworking atoms, constantly in motion at the lab.

These days it wasn't uncommon for whoever was first on the spot, usually Oppie himself, to discover that he wasn't the first to arrive after all. A disorderly arrangement of cots would be heaving with the deep breathing and snores of men who'd passed the hours before dawn either in the lab or else hunched over the most recent calculations—physicists, chemists, engineers, all equalized by the sleep they could no longer resist. Though Oppie hated to invade the sacredness of rest, he couldn't risk an unscheduled visit from General Groves in the midst of these men napping.

"Eight o'clock!" he crowed loud enough to be heard over the soundtracks of their dreams. Harold Agnew flipped himself over like a pancake. Dick Glazer buried himself further under the Army-issue blanket. No one woke, though.

"Eight o'clock! Work time!"

"Is it ever *not* work time?" Seth Neddermeyer complained from his cot, his eyes glued shut with sticky discharge.

"This pajama party wasn't my idea," Oppie said. "I'd rather have you at home in bed with your wives," he said even as he was aware that the pressure to work all night had been passed on by him from the general, who had long ago begun the countdown that would culminate in the dropping of the first bomb. But why sleep over at the lab when the walk home from the Tech Area couldn't be longer than ten minutes for any of these men?

"My wife?" Agnew had propped himself up with his arms though his eyes remained shut. "Who's that?"

The innumerable hours in the lab had strained many a marriage on the Hill. When the men did make it home, their brains were basking in the day's successes and re-playing each failure, needing to figure out what had gone wrong. None of the particulars of their work could be shared with their wives by order of the Army. "Lucky us," Elsie McMillan had said during the early months. "For once we don't have to listen to a lecture with our meals."

Ever talk to a man who's thinking about something else, something that matters, while the two of you dis-cuss the most piddling news of the day because that's as much of his brain as he can spare? You're getting the fat, the throwaway bones, while the meat's being saved for—what else but the bomb.

Meanwhile you're all starved for oxygen at that alti-tude, for one good deep breath.

Dick Glazer, thin and brittle as an autumn twig, struggled out of his cot and yawned. If any of the oth-ers, the bodies lying in their beds like skeletons in a graveyard, had noticed that Glazer had stealthily entered the lab close to dawn, they weren't asking him why he'd come there to work for just half an hour and then to retire with the rest of them. "Night," Glazer had said along with the others even though he'd already slept at home one shift, from 10pm to 4. Waking to a starry sky

157

looming at his window, a vacant bed across the room, Glazer had dressed sloppily and sped over to the Tech Area. The padlocks on the doors to the stock rooms had been hacksawed, he knew from scant gossip overheard at work, though by now they must have been replaced. The most likely culprit—Richard Feynman was not only good at cracking combination locks but had the humor of a prankster.

Outsmarting Security had become a popular sport at Los Alamos—along with quarreling at home. Oppie hadn't mentioned these forms of recreation to Dr. Sterman, nor had he told him about the regularly scheduled baseball games. Scientists in red hats and the Army in green competing with a fierceness that few recognized as a displaced will to win the war. Every pitcher's face that the batter targeted with a hard-hit line drive was a German soldier. The war had brought out the sadist in even the mildest of men. Hatred of the Nazis kept the men's batting averages high.

Robert Wilson, after double-time in his lab, went home at dawn to a dark room with all the shades drawn.

Harold Agnew went home at dawn and found the rooms dark, the shades down.

It was as if the bomb had exploded in each of their homes, and marriage was its first casualty. Silence, a cloud of dense, miasmic silence engulfed them all in pairs. "Hans stopped talking about his work," Rose Bethe said. "We just stopped talking." When at last the couples were nested together in their homes, the men wanted only to be back at the lab, working to rescue the war victims sooner, more of them. They could only—but could not really—imagine the human preys' hiding places: wells deep with water, toilet holes.

Even Oppie, who used to sit in an armchair, a cigarette active in each hand as he reduced international chaos to rhetorical formulas, was now a patriot with specific political views. Whether or not because he was a Jew, he clearly saw Hitler as the enemy: a warehouse fire sure to spread through the neighborhood. A man who would rule the world, modeling it after a private-membership club.

But such danger was distant. Through the mass-produced streets of Los Alamos prowled a gang of little children. Their mothers, awash in an excess of hours, trusted that their children were safe inside the houses with them. One day on the mesa could not be distinguished from the rest. So the mothers would relive a day when all was well, when their children were playing right under their watch, when a stirring of contentment traveled from house to house like a plague.

Whoever got the bomb first, they all knew, would win the war, but how to hurry the production of uranium$_{235}$ and plutonium? There's only so fast you can go, only so much of the precious stuff that the government alchemists could conjure. Though Oppie nudged Groves, who nudged his people in Oak Ridge and Hanford, the atoms weren't to be rushed.

Once a mastermind of ideas, now an effective administrator, Oppie had to work his men hard but was ideologically incapable of turning them into slaves. Still, slaves they were. Up too late, headaches, backaches from bending over pinpoints of matter. Too tired, too revved up to sleep. Aspirin and sleeping pills kept them going while their wives could not be sustained even by the abundant beauty surrounding them.

"He's different. Quieter. I almost don't know him anymore."

If only they could have listened to the endless chatter inside their husbands' skulls.

Whoever got the bomb first would win the war. Not with the bomb, but with the threat of the bomb, the ghastly specter of how deadly war had become. I believe your men want to build a bomb, Fermi said, and Oppie gravely nodded, knowing, as did his men, that whoever got to the finish line first would win the war. The pressure to get there clouded the sky, weighed on the rooftops and on the shoulders of those faced with the ever-changing deadline—finish the bomb for the sake of the wretched who were hunted, then shot on the spot; finish it before the possible subjugation of the world to a despot.

The five-o'clock siren meant to signal the end of each work day sounded like a call to arms, a plaintive wartime wail. Who could have put aside his notepad, gotten up off his stool and walked out of the lab at the behest of that one protracted note?

But come weekends they gathered, most often at Fuller Lodge. The men came as they were, the usual jeans and cowboy boots, the customary furrowed faces engraved with worry. The women paid more attention to their party attire and took out dresses they would otherwise have no occasion to wear. Now and then someone would suggest a theme: come as your secret fantasy; dress for a tropical luau. And word would circulate, as the usually discreet, tight-mouthed citizens shared the not-secret news.

One week Beverly Agnew printed out invitations on the office mimeograph machine, instructing the men to "wear a necktie if you have one." The ladies were to wear their very nicest dresses. Friday night and the "necktie party," as everyone was calling it, were just days away.

The pulse of time like a metronome never paused or altered its pace. The men, perhaps, glanced too often at their watches, knowing that this night would end, that the square dancing, the drinking and the laughter would end. They might each sneak fifteen minutes alone behind the Lodge, sipping fruity punch and listening to the sage silence of the mountains before returning to the frenzy of the dance floor.

The phonograph amplified the same old dance tunes, while young Michnovicz played the accordion and Rabi, if he were in town, beat on makeshift drums fashioned out of empty chemical containers and lids. Up there so high, approaching God, the dizzy bliss brought on by drink kept them recklessly content. Alcohol, atomic energy: the two powers they could never quite control.

Very late, the dancers and drinkers began to leave

Fuller Lodge, their flashlights casting pathways of surreal moon. Better to go home than back to the lab, where drunkenness could lead to miscalculations or breakage. Certainly the alcohol gave them no better insight into a war being strategized far far away from their own make-believe world. Would any of the scientists have worked so hard if he'd grasped that the bomb-child could kill whole cities and their future offspring? And that if Germany surrendered before work on the bomb was done, it would be dumped on Japan instead?

Whoever gets this first—

♦♦♦♦

Locked In

The community of Los Alamos was surrounded by a fence. Within that fence, the Tech Area, where all of the research labs and offices were located, was outlined with a security fence, and within that fence was another. To be admitted, a person had to show a badge—a white, blue, or orange badge, color-coded according to how much access that person was given once inside. So the scientists were enclosed within walls within walls, the mountain wall, as well, implying that even out there, once you escaped, there would always be another barrier to surmount, another wall to climb.

What to do? Where to go?

Perhaps the most impenetrable walls were those around the scientists' brains. A world of discovery thrived inside each of their heads. Certainly most of their wives hadn't found a way in through those walls, though some of the men, in defiance of General Groves' ban on marital confidentiality, passed along state secrets on the hiking trails of the Jemez Mountains.

"Let's stop there. Over there," Jane said to Bob, hefting the metal bucket serving as a picnic basket.

"Not yet."

"Oh but Bob, I'm hungry."

Bob scanned the mountain ahead of and behind them. With his arm around her waist, he guided Jane farther along on the trail as her insistence on stopping to picnic quieted to nothing more than the audible rumblings of her stomach. Jane could tell that Bob had something on his mind and was about to reveal it to her. Up here, the thin air was already saturated with secrets.

Again Bob scanned the area all around them. "Jane, there's been a breakthrough. It's encouraging."

"Really? What is it?"

If the early stars seemed to be spies, if the trees seemed to conceal lurking traitors, Bob reminded himself of the power of imagination, to which he was witness every day at the lab. He sat down on a rock, indicating another rock nearby where Jane could sit across from him. She didn't entirely understand the new development that Bob began to explain. And though she didn't admit so to him, she found his account of subatomic frolics rather boring. Someone else, perhaps, could have offered a more poetic description, an action-packed metaphor—maybe Oppie himself, the poet-physicist—but Bob's overdeveloped aptitude as a scientist had been nurtured at the cost of his more verbal side.

The fullness of that nearing bomb blast,

gestating within its hard metal womb, wrote Oppie one night, pausing before the next stanza. A war between lyricism and accuracy crossed the right and left halves of his brain.

Where is the distant eye that perceives our own galactic commotion

As a future star-speck light years away?

Oppie's office had a lock on the door. So after passage through the sequence of security checks, he had still to reach into his pocket, littered with the grit of sand that found its way everywhere, take the key, insert it into the lock and turn it. All of his desk drawers were guarded with locks, too. The cabinet where he kept his coat on cooler days was also equipped with a lock. On General Groves' periodic visits to Los Alamos, when he arrived in Oppenheimer's office, first thing he'd do was walk from lock to lock, test each drawer and door to make sure that it didn't budge. As a matter of habit, Oppenheimer had learned to lock his coat up in the closet. Otherwise, he'd never remember to do so on those days when the general was in town.

"I'd like to read you something," Oppenheimer said to General Groves after the general had yanked on every handle and knob in the room. *"The fullness of that nearing bomb blast..."*

One of Oppenheimer's many languages, Groves supposed. That many-tongued man of letters.

"...gestating within its hard metal womb. Where is the distant eye that perceives our own galactic commotion as a future star-

speck light years away?"

The general just now recognized the words as poetry. Had his head-man lost his head? General Groves shut his dropped jaw. He thought of how to avoid reacting like an ignorant literary critic. "Oppenheimer, when in God's name are you finding time to write poetry?" he demanded.

Oppenheimer, smiling, said, "I'm a night writer," as he replaced the pages in a folder on his desk.

The general nodded, pacing, nodding while he paced, nodding. What had he come here for? Oppenheimer had a way of knocking him off-center, causing Groves to pat his pockets, trying to figure out what he'd forgotten. Of course he visited Los Alamos regularly, but never without a purpose, never just to look around even though he looked around, at the doors, drawers, locked, at the art prints on Oppenheimer's walls. How small this office was. How could Oppenheimer stand the confinement? The general couldn't possibly guess that just about the only times his Scientific Director was caged inside this small space was when he, the general, was in town and they needed a private place to meet, somewhere with a door that could be shut and locked, a window that could be veiled with a shade.

"I hear you flew to California last week," Groves growled.

"Yes, I did. Meetings. And I checked back with that headshrinker."

Groves spent a moment appraising the size of Oppenheimer's head. "Listen here, Oppenheimer. If you're not going to be careful about your safety, then I'll just have to keep reminding you. No airplanes. No driving farther than a few miles."

And if those few miles were on a road well-away from traffic, Oppenheimer should be accompanied by a body guard. And he should take special care to drive safely. Or if for some reason his driving might be compromised, he should arrange for a chauffeur.

When Oppie arrived home that night, protected only by whatever angels heaven could spare, the responsibility for his wellbeing was wordlessly transferred from those angels to the military police assigned watch over his house. Kitty often complained about the loss of privacy. She'd peer out of the front second-floor window and watch the man who was being paid to watch her. But never once during her vigil did she witness him misbehave in any way or disrespect her property—spit in the dirt or tamp a cigarette butt out in her yard.

She soon recovered from her indignation at having to show a badge at the door of her own home; the man on duty could easily be persuaded to babysit her son. So Peter would sit on the ground at his ankles as he stood guard, a military playmate always smiling at the boy and tweaking his cheeks but never abandoning his post.

Meanwhile Kitty would hop into her petite pick-up truck and pound down the road leading to Santa Fe. Where to go? Everyone's trips into town were limited to a certain number each month, but Kitty flouted the restriction and drove down the mountain, truck's tank half-full of gas, her own tank half-lacking the liquor that would stabilize her mood. *"Don't sit under the apple tree with anyone else but me, with anyone else but me, with anyone else but me,"* she sang, feeling the fences topple and the loops of barbed wire fall away. So what if she was seen in town too often by the locals? For now they seemed to have lost interest in the mysterious project on the top of the hill.

But once in town, what to do?

"Dorothy, wanna grab a bite and a beer?" she'd asked Dorothy McKibbin on East Palace, forgetting that Dorothy was on duty. But somehow Dorothy always found someone else to accompany Kitty to La Fonda or the corner coffee shop, knowing that consent to spend time with the First Lady of LA was considered a favor, one she'd have to repay.

Some of Kitty's luncheon companions didn't make it through to the end of the meal. Dr. Oppie's wife could be as abrasive as the desert sand. Most often she'd complain about her last lunch-mate, and whatever woman was sitting across from her could predict that she herself would be the subject of Kitty's next grievance session. But Kitty usually paid the bill after staring cross-eyed at the total.

"Need a ride back?" she might offer. Extending a visit with Kitty never appealed to her guests, nor did driving up the mountain with a woman who'd been drinking all afternoon.

Back through the main gate, crossing the boundary of the fence, heckled by the thorns of barbed wire around the Tech Area, past one security guard, she'd finally flash her badge to the very military man who was playing peekaboo with little Peter. Often, though, she'd forget her badge, and the guard, even knowing her by face and name, would have to ask one of the neighbors to vouch for her.

What to do?

Not just the scientists' side of town was short on entertainment. Among the Army green, talk of what fun they'd have if they were elsewhere substituted for actual recreational thrills. Trained, as soldiers, to adapt to the worst conditions of war, some of the GIs would head out on hunting expeditions, shooting at antelopes with sub-machine guns. Overkill was a trend up on the hill, where seven thousand fire extinguishers were on-call for unintended explosions.

The men played baseball, the Army against the scientists, while the women, on the sidelines, cheered their teams on. Short a shortstop? Maybe bring in someone from town, one of those brawny outta-workers seen hunched over the lunch counter. But the baseball diamond was forbidden to outsiders. Instead that extra outfielder, with a powerful but imprecise throwing arm, would have to do. Inning one, Army up at bat. Used to combat, the lineup was confident about the game. "We're gonna humble those wobbly-oggling lab boys," they'd say, forgetting that most days, those "wobbly-oggling lab

169

boys" were their allies.

When had the world shrunken, become so small? Only the span of sky suggested a reality beyond the containment of so many fences, regulations, and rules.

Lena Wisniak was, she liked to think, a reasonable woman. She allowed her closest neighbors an occasional noisy night, didn't count cents when the dinner bill was split, and Lena never spoke spitefully of anyone without just cause.

"I don't, do I?" she asked her husband, Carl.

"You don't."

"No really, do I?"

"You don't, Lena. What's this about?"

"That little yapping poodle that I'm ready to rip the stuffing out of."

Carl, though a visionary scientist, was a literal man and assumed that his wife was complaining about a toy dog. "Let's just throw it away, then, if you don't like it." Lena, he knew, counted at least five children in her fantasy family; while they were in this transitional home, he was hoping that every kind of substitute would satisfy her maternal urges. So before they'd set out from Cal Tech, he'd tucked a stowaway teddy bear, stuffed mongoose, and even a lifelike baby doll among the clothes in her suitcase.

"This is a real live dog I'm talking about, Carl. If you were ever home, you'd hear it, too, yapping away every five minutes."

"A *real* dog..."

During the dark hours, the large window at the back side of their house became a portal into somewhere deeper than the night. A man, looking at the glass, could see through himself. Carl turned on his heel, away from the disturbing inside-outside reflection that he didn't think could be him.

"It belongs to that nurse two doors down," Lena said. "Do you know who I mean?"

How could he not know? There were only so many faces that they all saw each day, repeatedly, the same faces to blame for not being someone else. The lack of turnover or expansion among the population left them all so sick of each other, of the same lame jokes, the same anecdotes told over cocktails.

"How long have we been here?" Lena asked Carl now. "It's been about, what? Five years?" She heard a buzzing generator somewhere, or perhaps a horde of flies.

"Lena, you must know that we haven't even been here two years yet."

She slumped as if struck by a gunshot. "Do we even know, Carl, if the world is still out there? Do we know for sure exactly where we are?"

No one, when recruited by Oppenheimer or his staff or the Army operation, could be given a specific location for his new home. Not an address, not a project name. Even the radio station had no call numbers, a ghostly vocalization drilling through the mountain air. Groves was amazed, when he saw the first edition of the town's plain-named newspaper, the *Daily Bulletin*, that he'd ever approved this potential indiscretion. As always when Groves doubted his own actions, the face of Robert Oppenheimer appeared in his thoughts, most prominently those blue eyes that could bore through you.

On her way to the infirmary one morning, Nurse Donnelly heard a curse hurled out a neighboring window. Something about a dog. Is someone talking to me? she wondered. Then she heard her little Mimi's bark, and a curse again.

As Nurse Donnelly continued on to the infirmary, Lena Wisniak packed an overnight bag. She packed the cotton calico nightgown that she loved, and her furry slippers, selecting what she imagined she'd need for a stay at a spa. In the uncertain light of early morning, she walked, carrying her bag, three-quarters of the way across town. An aerial view would have established that she didn't take the most direct route, avoiding the Commissary, perhaps, the windy exchange of news that took place at the checkout.

She had never been inside the infirmary. She saw now, through a doorway into the hallway linking the examination rooms, the staff doctors and nurses costumed in white coats over their jeans, busy treating lesser malaises and petty medical complaints. Lena had read up on one or two in one of the books boxed in the social room awaiting the creation of a library. She'd memorized the symptoms she planned to present, a combination of aches and twinges that should suggest an ailment serious enough to get her checked in overnight.

172

Lucky that she'd only quarreled with Nurse Donnelly facelessly through the window. If her neighbor ended up taking care of her here at the infirmary, she would probably not associate this frail, ailing Lena with the angry voice that had attacked her on the street because of her dog.

Lena viewed the walls and ceiling of the waiting room as if they were painted over with frescoes. This was one of the few remaining places she'd never been yet in the years that she'd lived in Los Alamos, where Carl was always working, working, or thinking about work.

He wouldn't be home for hours. Lena had left him a note: *Needed a change of scene. Be back probably in a day or two.*

◆◆◆◆

Locked Out

Our honeymoon hadn't really counted as a vacation. For me it was more like a period in the recovery room after surgery, a chance to recuperate from the shock of our wedding ceremony before commencing my new life as a married woman. True, I'd tremendously enjoyed the museum at Los Alamos, but during most of our time in New Mexico I'd been working hard to comprehend that every morning into eternity, I'd be waking up next to the same man.

So I could say in all honesty to Clifford, "I haven't gone on a vacation in four years!"

Since he didn't disagree, I had to conclude that, like me, he didn't think of our honeymoon as a vacation. But not until I more directly said, "I want to go on a vacation!" did he suggest that we spend a weekend in Montreal.

"How perfect!" I said, my words vibrating along with Jasper riding up and down in my arms. Though he was on his way to two years old, I hadn't quit the habit of jouncing him rhythmically when I held him, a sure pre-scription for settling his stomach and quieting him down during his infant era.

"It's only about a five-hour drive," Clifford said, as if he'd recently researched the trip.

"*But*...we can pretend that we're in faraway Europe!"

"All on one tank of gas!"

Neither of us had to point out that a motor trip to a nearby city would be much easier on our finances than would the vacation that we might have planned had we not had to work within realistic limitations. Ever since the subject of necktie jobs had tyrannized our chicken dinner that night, both of us had been suffering from a low-level anguish about money, Clifford because he worried that he wasn't earning enough, and me because I wasn't earning any at all.

Traveling with Jasper would be an experiment, much more ambitious than driving him to the grocery store or even venturing out on a day trip with him. We consid-ered asking my parents to come stay with him while we were away or else asking Clifford's parents, who'd visited their newest grandson last year, to fly back to Boston from Minnesota. In the end, though, neither of us wanted to be apart from the baby for an entire weekend.

Heading north to Canada meant entering a more wintry weather zone. I subtracted five degrees from the Boston temperature and then wondered if even my heaviest coat would be adequate. Since Jasper could be expected to need a clean outfit every hour or so, I brought nearly all of his stretchy suits with us. Clifford was more than willing to pack for himself, but to prevent grossly mismatched tops and bottoms or rumpled shirts, I chose to pack for him as well.

He came into our bedroom and saw the many piles of clothes. "I guess we should be heading south this time of year," he said.

Clifford had gone to the barber in preparation for our trip. Once his very fine hair was trimmed even as little as half an inch, his head looked much smaller and his ears much larger. I'd never before known him to get his hair cut without prompting from me. Whenever I pointed this out to him, he'd retaliate by saying, "What do you think I did all those years before I met you, Pauline?"

I had theories about this but didn't share them with him.

Besides our bulky clothing, I brought provisions to meet every need Jasper might have or mishap that might befall him—fever, injury, excessive hunger or thirst. We had so much baggage that one of our neighbors asked if we were moving out.

"No, just going away for the weekend."

"Really?" she asked as she incredulously inventoried the jam-packed trunk and back seat.

While Clifford drove through several states, I napped, the well-earned rest of the family packer, and hoped that my husband wouldn't take a wrong turn. Now and then I'd rise to the surface and glimpse the glorious Vermont scenery—seemingly green even in winter—mountainous and free of billboards. Whenever

I glanced back at Jasper, he was either asleep or happily inspecting his fingers. Somewhere still in Vermont I sensed the car stopping and opened my eyes.

"We've got to get that diaper changed!" Clifford declared with great zeal. I noticed his stainless steel thermos, which had been filled to the brim with enough coffee to keep him awake throughout the trip, lying uncapped near the gas pedal, already empty.

We stopped at a family-type restaurant just off one of the highway exits. None of the tables inside, however, was occupied by families: overweight men with tiny cups of coffee coddled in their large hands, a young couple joined at the mouth, and a uniformed waitress whose shift must just have ended.

"I'll do it," Clifford offered, carrying Jasper and his fancy diaper bag into the men's room. Meanwhile I dozed, sitting upright in one of the booths. Nearly two years of parenting had left me with a serious sleep deficit. Maybe instead of opting for a rousing weekend in a big city I should be going to a cabin in the middle of the woods and sleeping for two days.

At the Canadian border, we were subjected to the usual questioning about the purpose of our trip, where we lived, where we'd been born. When Clifford answered, "Minnesota," I was reminded of an earlier period of his life I knew almost nothing about.

"May I see some identification?"

I didn't remember being asked to identify myself on the way into Canada in the past, only on the way out to qualify for reentry into the U.S. The customs official read our drivers' licenses and then excused himself to confer with another blue-jacketed man. Neither Clifford nor I spoke during the man's absence, as if we might be overheard by a wiretap.

The customs official returned, but instead of giving us back our licenses he said, "And the baby...do you have identification for her?"

"It's a boy," Clifford told him, and the man nodded.

"He's just a baby," I said. "He's not old enough to drive."

"A birth certificate," he said politely.

Just as I was about to explain that the document was locked away at the bank in a safety-deposit box, Clifford reached into his shoulder bag on the floor behind him and withdrew a business-size envelope that contained, to my bounteous delight, a copy of our son's birth certificate.

"Clifford!" I snuggled up against his coat sleeve, newly smitten by his organizational abilities.

The man barely scanned the document. "Oh, but this is a photocopy."

With unfortunate timing, Jasper began to cry, making himself more conspicuous.

"Please pull over," our inquisitor instructed us, pointing to the parking area beside the Customs building.

Obediently Clifford drove into the parking lot, his face more grim than I'd ever seen it. "Let's just turn around, Pauline," he said. "We can spend the weekend in

Vermont instead."

My drowsy glimpses of Vermont while in transit had left me with the impression of the perfect landscape. But at such short notice I didn't think I could adapt to a vacation in such a pastoral setting after the urbane, metropolitan street scenes I'd been imagining. And anyway, I wasn't ready to give in to this authoritarian official, especially when we hadn't even been informed of why we were being doubted.

"Let's just get on with this," I said.

"Remember, we didn't actually make a hotel reservation, so we wouldn't lose anything by changing our plans."

As I hoisted Jasper up out of his car seat I was surprised, as I'd been so often lately, by his mass and weight. Our baby was developing into a little boy.

"Clifford...Why do you always have to be so—" I was about to say "submissive" but revised my word choice and said "...adaptable? Let's stick this out a little longer."

"But look." He was able to gesture much more extravagantly than I because he wasn't carrying the baby. "We could be tied up here for hours. And who knows what they'll dig up!"

"Cliff, we haven't done anything wrong."

"Who knows, Pauline? Maybe they'll discover some problem with our documents." Still, Clifford marched bravely inside and forgot to hold the door open behind him for me. About ten other cars were parked in the same lot as ours, yet when we entered the small, one-story building, I didn't see any other detainees. Perhaps they were all huddled in a holding cell, awaiting news of their fates.

The same official who had directed us to the building was now stationed behind the counter. He asked us to approach and questioned us again about the purpose of our trip to Montreal, where we'd each been born, our dates of birth, and our place of residence. Then he nodded, as if we'd passed an exam.

"The baby, what is his full name?"

I now detected a light French accent, which made the customs official far less intimidating and far more, well, romantic.

"Jasper Black Halloway," Clifford said with as much sincerity as if he were reciting the Boy Scout pledge.

Again the man nodded. He riffled through some papers then returned our drivers' licenses and the questionable birth certificate to us. "Enjoy your trip," he said.

"So…we can go?" Clifford asked.

"Bonjour."

"We're in!" I whispered into Jasper's ear, half-covered with the cuff of his pastel hat. Meanwhile Clifford was lavishly thanking the official. I pulled him by his cold hand away from the counter and towards the door.

"We got lucky, didn't we?" he said, but I couldn't agree.

Because Clifford had been so traumatized by our encounter at Customs, I offered to fill in as driver until we reached the heart of the city, where we traded places again. I was out of practice battling traffic since Clifford always drove. He could sit patiently through three cycles of a traffic light without advancing as much as an inch. In the same situation I became surly, blaming the other drivers, the city planners, even Clifford and Jasper if they were in the car with me.

Our hotel, recommended by one of Clifford's colleagues as both charming and affordable, transported us back to the early nineteen-hundreds and reinforced the illusion that we had jetted to Europe for the weekend. In the morning, the first real day of our vacation, I could see blemishes on the high ceiling and the walls that revealed our hostess's true age but didn't detract from the old girl's classic beauty and old-world elegance.

Jasper's speech consisted of only single words and a small number of useful phrases—"me want more" and "no nap." But he was an English hearer, if not speaker, and so the surround of French and its unfamiliar cadence baffled him at first and then made him cry. He must have felt the way stroke victims feel when suddenly they can't understand what anyone is saying.

I felt similarly disoriented, not by the language—thanks to my long-dormant high-school French—but by the cultural quirks that resulted in irregular business hours. For instance, the Musée Juste Poure Rire, a museum dedicated to jokes and laughter, was closed for the season, we learned from a hand-printed sign posted on the door.

"What season?"

Clifford shrugged.

Next we went to a gallery that featured contemporary Canadian artists. A sign on the gallery door informed us that the gallery was closed on weekends. This near-lockdown was reminiscent of our visit to Albuquerque.

Le Vue Omni-Theatre, where I hoped that Jasper would be fascinated more than terrified by his first movie, would be offering films in English much later that day, but no sooner. So far we'd reparked the car three times. What to do with our one full day of vacation and a splurge of Canadian money?

Although we'd agreed not to base the day's itinerary solely on Jasper's limited tastes, we finally ended up at the science center on the river, a place designed for children. Jasper was too young to manipulate the moving parts on the hands-on exhibits or even to grasp the simplest cause-and-effect demonstrations. But he was getting heavier every minute. And there at least they had a changing table in the bathroom; by then his sodden diaper was sagging halfway to his ankles. When finally we let him loose, we stood by while he toddled over the expanse of uninterrupted carpet. Clifford and I leaned against an exhibit on animal camouflage titled "Peekaboo" and emptied ourselves with hurricane sighs.

"What'll we do tomorrow?" I asked

"We have to start back around noon. Once we get packed and eat, there won't be a lot of time to do anything."

"Do you think we'll find a place that's open for breakfast?"

"I don't know. Maybe breakfast season is past."

Clifford giggled and grinned, quite nearly reproducing the face of that sweet, guileless boy in the *My School Year* book. I just then noticed that he'd added one of his vests—my aphrodisiac—to the thought-out outfits that I'd packed for him. With Jasper sharing our room and with such a compressed schedule, I hadn't even fleetingly thought of this weekend as a romantic getaway. But now I ribboned my arms around him and nestled my cheek against his arm.

"Jasper!" he shouted, lunging away from me.

I turned to see our little boy tugging on a cord running underneath a table, about to disconnect the electricity powering one exhibit and possibly the entire museum. Clifford deftly snatched Jasper away, unwrapping his plump sausage fingers from the cord and abducting him from that perilous moment.

Rather than feel grateful, Jasper, outraged, cried.

"Why are there dangling wires in a place designed for kids?" I demanded.

The rescue had wilted my Clifford. He passed Jasper to me and smoothed his own hair, his pants. "I don't think they were dangling at first. Our little electrical engineer here was working at that wire for a while before we spotted him."

We. How like Clifford to share credit for his heroism after our lapse in vigilance.

The rest of the day played out like any day at home: dinner, an hour of lounging around, then the sequence of bedtime rituals concluding with the sleepiest boy in the world protesting his destiny.

Without intending to, all three of us slept late the next morning. The abundant folds of drapery covering the windows blocked out the morning light. After reading the clock, I said, "Nine o'clock? Did we just doze?"

"Nine o'clock in the *morning*," Clifford corrected me, whisking one panel of ten-ton fabric aside to expose a diamond-bright day.

We'd slept so long that I swore Jasper had grown an inch overnight, entombed in our antique room removed from the rest of the city. As we emerged onto the street, I felt as if we were tunneling through centuries to arrive at the present time and place.

The next steps back into normal existence were far less jarring. Instead of the wistful reentry into Winter Hill I would have predicted, a sensation of comfort seeped through me like warm milk as we turned into our ghost-town street with its three-layered houses.

Jasper had been lulled into a profound state of sleep by the long highway drive. "Let's leave him here while we bring all of our stuff in," Clifford suggested.

We each loaded up with as much cargo as we could bear—several straps crossing each shoulder, bags stuffed under our arms—then waddled up the stairwell to the second-floor. Clifford, who'd arrived ahead of me, crowded to one side and made space for me in front of the entrance to our apartment, but I stopped at the edge of the top step with my two hundred pounds of freight, waiting for him to unlock the door.

After a long freeze-frame during which neither of us spoke or moved, I said, "Come on, Clifford. I'm developing spinal curvature even as we stand here."

"Don't you have your keys?"

"No."

"But you *always* have your keys."

"What about you? How did you get the car to start without a key?"

"Well I have *that* key, but it won't open this door." Clifford slouched forward, shedding all of his gear onto the floor. "Who has the spare?"

"But where's your key?" I asked.

"I took it off the ring." And anticipating a scolding from me, he said, "I know, it doesn't make sense. I just thought it was one less key to lose."

"Must be off-season here on Hilltop Street."

"Or else the wrong day of the week."

While Reena, our upstairs neighbor, would have been the more likely keeper of our spare key, being a stable, mature woman with maternal tendencies, she worked at countless jobs and was so rarely home that I'd entrusted the key instead to the herd of young men who lived below us. The five of them, all packed into a three-bedroom apartment, were both polite and strangely silent. At least one of them was almost always home.

"I'll go," I told Clifford, who harbored a non-specific

185

prejudice against these young men.

Remembering that Jasper was stranded in the car, I peeked out the front doorway to make sure he was still asleep. Then I knocked on the boys' apartment door and heard the footfalls of what sounded like a four-hundred-pound creature.

"Hi there." I couldn't remember his name, and I was pretty sure that he'd forgotten mine since he didn't use it.

"I bet you want your key," he said, precluding any neighborly pleasantries. Maybe he'd overheard me talking with Clifford outside our door. Had I been unreasonably harsh with my husband? I wondered now.

"Yes, thanks…Phillip, is it?"

He neither confirmed nor denied his name. I watched him go into the kitchen and open a drawer, from which he took my key. I marveled that he had so efficiently located the key in such a messy apartment.

"Here you go. You're lucky I was home," he said with an edge of moral righteousness.

"Yes…lucky. Thanks again."

I climbed back upstairs and found Clifford gone but his whole load of our belongings heaped on the floor. Once inside our apartment, I looked out the window and saw him—his back arched catlike and his legs athletically flexed as he took our last load out of the car, easing Jasper out of his dreams and back to the numbing routine that he so loved.

◆◆◆◆

Calculating Women

The first meeting, attended by about twelve of the women, was hosted by Ruth Marshak in her living room. As usual, her husband was at work in the lab, and since Ruth had no children, all business discussed among them that night was guaranteed to remain confidential.

Ruth hosted the second meeting as well. Encouraged by how much had been accomplished at the first, she could afford to embellish this one with refreshments: lemonade and cookies (some batches burned crisp by her damned Black Beauty, others underbaked but at least rescued from immolation). The meeting was threatening to become more of a social gathering than an activists' work session when Ruth stood up, underdone cookie in hand, and announced, "Tonight we'll make the list, as we agreed." Her statement curtailed most of the friendly conversation, the delicate, butterfly-like flitting from here to there. Every woman in the room, silenced, now looked at Ruth, their unofficial leader.

"And then we'll go over the list with Oppie."

"Shouldn't we start with Dorothy? Robert's so busy, you know."

"Don't we count?" Bernice Bode half-asked, half-challenged.

"That's right. Can't make a bomb without our husbands. Can't have our husbands without us," Ruth quipped as if this weren't the first time she'd spoken these same words.

In fact, some of the women were thinking that this terse defense of their right to full citizenship might make a catchy slogan. And suddenly an epidemic of outrage left every woman at the meeting brimming with wrath. How dare those brutes in uniform try to order us around! Who do they think we are? More of their bottom-feeding privates?

Enrico Fermi had surprised his wife Laura at dinnertime that same evening with an earlier-than-usual homecoming. Laura had surprised him with an empty table. "I wouldn't have thought to expect you this soon. I usually just have a sandwich at around five."

"Where are you off to?" he asked just as she was leaving for Ruth's house.

"Book group." Clever cover-up. Laura had lied. After all, the men were withholding so much from their wives these days.

As she strolled the short distance to Ruth's house, Laura traveled farther, in fantasy, to the pond behind their property in Illinois, the evening walks, the sweet-talk she

188

and Enrico used to exchange like the sticky kisses she'd taste later, after their lips had separated. Why had they come here to this sterile, sand-floored mesa?

That evening, after the meeting, Ruth folded the women's list of demands into sixteenths and tucked it into her bra. Her husband would never find it there. Even side by side under the blankets, they lay estranged from each other, the bomb between them.

All fourteen women who'd been at Ruth's that night went to bed with a secret.

And in the morning, Ruth retrieved the folded list from her bra, the paper dewy from a slight night sweat moistening her skin. Oppie was never hard to track down. As a matter of policy he tried to make himself accessible to everyone connected with the project. His model of democratic rule was the ever-present guide whose head was visible above the masses. He never interfered with the Town Council or forced an agenda on any of the numerous committees that thrived like live organisms up on the Hill.

Ruth spotted him outside the Commissary. "Good morning, Robert."

"Yes it is," he said.

She mustered her charm and her dimpled smile. "Robert, I'm wondering if I might have a word with you some time. A sit-down word. In private."

He didn't hesitate in the least, didn't consult a date book laden with appointments, or a secretarial gate-keeper. "I'm all yours. What are you doing this afternoon, say around three?"

Ruth would need to rehearse and then to smooth out the creases in the one document created to support their cause. Before the appointment, she freshened her face, changed into a cleaner pair of jeans, and coaxed her curls around her finger. She knew she had to look her best. The beckoning bomb, after all, was a compelling rival. The men just couldn't stop chasing her.

When Ruth arrived at Oppie's office door, he was on the phone and simultaneously drawing a chart with rectangles and connecting lines. Had he remembered their appointment? In any case, he briskly concluded his phone conversation, wiped the papers aside, and cleared the second chair in his office of papers and books.

She couldn't wait. Before she'd even settled her bottom on the chair, she blurted out, "Robert, the women are awfully unhappy." Bottom down now. "We're like war widows. Always alone, and even when the men are home, they can't talk."

Oppie heard her words spoken in his own Kitty's voice. He'd heard all these grievances before on his own home front. His head bobbed up and down, up and down. Of course they missed a good dry cleaner's and a laundry service, too. He already knew of the incident that Ruth related to him now concerning a pot of diapers boiling over on the stove.

"She could've burned her place down!" Ruth went on to aggrandize her argument. "Or the whole row of homes there. She could've burned the whole town to the ground!"

"We wouldn't want that," Oppie had to admit. Those old Black Beauties, the imperfect gas stoves installed in most Los Alamos homes, were reportedly impossible to operate. His own household was equipped with a superior model, so while he could commiserate on principle, he'd never experienced the burnt meat loaf or singed eyebrows.

"You do have the beauty parlor," Oppie reminded Ruth.

"Is that all you think it takes? Doll us up and we'll be happy?"

Oppie began squirming in his seat and finally stood and started to walk across the small office and back, across and back, but purposefully, Ruth noted, as if he were actually going somewhere. Then he turned to face her. Oppie had yet to meet a woman who couldn't be won with his blue, blue eyes.

Ruth handed him the list, which of course she'd removed from the sacristy of her cleavage before the meeting. Oppie scanned the demands numbered from one to eleven: more organized schooling for the children, a more reasonable work load for the husbands...laundry service...housecleaning help...He stopped mid-list. What would that psychiatrist, Dr. Sterman, have to say about this? Perhaps nothing very useful, but another trip to California wouldn't hurt.

"Let me think on this, Ruth. General Groves will have to be brought in on it, too." General Groves, who reigned from the detachment of Washington, D.C., had been the one to recommend that a beauty parlor be opened. However, he was less liberal in his willingness to enact other people's ideas.

"Well, he didn't say no," Ruth reported back to her committee.

"Did he look at the list?"

"Is he going to try to influence the general?"

"We'll just have to see," she said.

The advice of the psychiatrist this time seemed to Oppie worth his fee. Put the women to work, he suggested. And pay them. Certainly help was needed everywhere on the growing compound.

Ruth expected that she'd have to meet with Robert again. To prod him. But immediately upon his return from San Francisco, he contacted her and asked her to come by his office. He'd been in touch with General Groves just that morning, keeping secret his recent trip further west. The general wanted to treat the women's requests as an outright rebellion against the state and to employ heavy-handed tactics of suppression. So Oppie had quickly gotten him off the phone, making excuses.

While Ruth and Oppie met in his office, nine of the women lurked outside, each pretending to be busy with something that would explain her presence. Like tracking a cloud overhead, or tallying the number of pedestrians coming through that intersection. Then when Ruth came out of the office, the nine women converged in a bevy of breathlessness and questions.

"We're getting jobs!" Ruth told them.

A round of applause belied the disappointment of some of the women, who'd rather be pampered more than be put to work. Marion Marcus, for instance, had started to teach her five-year old girl, Sandi, to read. Marion would rather tutor her own child than dust the shelves at the Commissary or sterilize medical apparatus at the infirmary. Should she confess her unwillingness to work?

While they were congregated conspicuously at that crossroads, other women, walking by, latched onto the group. The need for secrecy had passed; everyone was welcome to celebrate the news along with the committee members, even those who were unhappy with the outcome of their protest. From inside his office, Oppie heard the applause. If he waited long enough, General Groves would call him. Most often it was the general who initiated contact between them, the general who was willing to chase after his Scientific Director because, more often than not, it was the general who wanted something from Oppenheimer, not the other way around. This time, though, Oppenheimer dialed General Groves' direct number. But General Groves had just dialed Oppenheimer's direct number, and the two calls collided.

"Busy," said Oppie.

"Busy," said Groves.

Both men redialed at the same moment and again the repetitive tone sounded in their ears. So both hung up, and Oppie directed his mind to another matter. As so often lately, he allowed his mental space to be populated by atoms. Plutonium atoms, each as spirited as a puppy. When the phone rang, Oppie waited a moment before answering it, letting the atoms settle into stillness.

The general was calling to inquire about the status of "the women's mutiny," as he called it.

"Let's put them to work. I've been figuring in what areas we need help. For one thing, Bethe can use—"

"Halt!" the general ordered his officer. "Oppenheimer, I can't have you spending your time finagling with the Ladies' Auxiliary. This is war time! You just leave it to me."

And so, at their next meeting, Oppie told Ruth that the general himself would like to speak with her, and Ruth began primping right there, fluffing up her hair, pinching her cheeks to bring color to them—as if General Groves were waiting in the anteroom. A day later, she heard from Colonel Nichols, calling to schedule the promised meeting with the general.

On the day of the appointment, her inner wrist as she sculpted her hair for the loud-mouth general gave off more than a suggestion of *Les Nuits Romantiques*, the perfume that until now she'd had no occasion to wear in Los Alamos. Ruth had heard herself described as "handsome," a handsome woman with a straight nose and shapely lips, even if they were quite thin. She'd never longed to be a beauty, but now, as she prepared to meet the round, mustached military man she'd seen striding through town with the right of ownership, she concentrated on her appearance contrary to the fundamental goals of the women's campaign: to be valued for their intelligence, and to be respected as equal to the men.

Groves noticed how lovely she looked, but he didn't like the implication that the price of his support was a dose of perfume and a pretty painted smile. He therefore greeted Ruth with a gruff "hello" and a manly handshake.

"Mrs. Marshak, let's see if you and I can't agree on some useful work for the women who want it."

"Yes and—"

"Dr. Bethe in the Theoretical Division needs more calculators."

"And you want us to—"

"No, see, he's already got mechanical calculators. They're not as helpful as he hoped they'd be, so what he needs now…"

"…is—"

"—human calculators, that's what he needs. You women to work on computations and to operate adding machines."

"I see."

Groves willed himself not to interrupt her this time, but apparently she had nothing more to say. With his hands gripping the edge of his desk, leaning forward, he said to Ruth, "This is important work. *Very* important."

Now Ruth leaned forward, too, shortening the distance between their faces. "And, General Groves, what about a laundry service?"

The general slammed backwards. "That too, that too."

"And, General Groves—"

"A school, a library…why don't you women get working on these yourselves? The Army will step in when you need us."

Ruth rose, wanting to terminate the meeting before she might lose any of her gains and before her curls might start to droop. She offered her hand to the general so he could either kiss it or shake it, as he pleased.

And so a number of women were placed in the Theoretical Division, where already Mary Frankl, Mici Teller, and Jean Bacher were employed. Early on, the theorists had boasted a surge of progress; they didn't need any supplies as did the divisions relying on actual matter, on lab equipment that had to be ordered, constructed, shipped, and paid for. But eventually the work of the theorists had slowed down, hampered by the necessity of constant calculations, long, intricate calculations that lasted for pages and days.

For three months the women were trained to use calculators. Too bad Bethe couldn't teach them to add the figures in his head, as he did. Most of the new positions were to be three-eighths time, according to the Army's structure of jobs.

But the factory-like atmosphere of the Tech Area was depressing to some of the women. They'd earned their victory. They'd rather capitalize now on the general's suggestion that they set up the institutions still missing from the mesa—schools, churches, libraries ("How about a massage parlor?" one of the wives proposed)—and serve as volunteer staff themselves, a necessity thanks to the stretched Army budget.

Soon one of the committee's dearest wishes was fulfilled. Backed by the organizational savvy of Dorothy McKibbin, the wives established a maid service that employed Indian women from neighboring towns. An Army vehicle would transport these women to the mesa and then home at the end of their working days. Each morning, a vicious competition ensued among all the wives with dusty houses and dirty laundry. They'd swarm the entrance to the housing office, from where the maids were dispatched, when the van pulled up. These *mujeras criadas* had never known such celebrity, nor had they ever seen the claws and fangs of the white woman.

"But what about me?" big-bellied Edna Scofield complained to Dorothy one afternoon. "I'm too sick to get up that early and fight my way up the list."

At a glance, Dorothy estimated that Edna was by now about five months pregnant. Far enough along that she should have gotten past the morning woozies.

"Have they gotten any saltines in at the Commissary?" she suggested, even knowing that Edna hadn't been asking for advice about her diet. Dorothy had listened to the same complaint from many others, those who, because they were pregnant or had jobs, had lost the advantage of showing up at the housing office so they, too, could woo the maids when the van arrived.

Finally a caste-system was instituted, favoring pregnant women and mothers above all. And women, too, who were ill. Was it any wonder that expectant mothers ranked so high on the list? Turned out many of the wives were discovering that they were pregnant.

◆◆◆◆

Labor Force

Every year, the new spring opened up ahead like a frontier, unspoiled and grassy. It was the season of second chances: my second chance to be kinder to Clifford, more appreciative of the privileged life I took for granted. When Jasper and I went on our slow, wobbly walks, I pointed out to him the unfolding early blooms, the birds, returned from winter and tentatively poking at the thawing ground.

One day as I was unharnessing him from his car seat, I saw a woman about my age walk by. So rarely did I see anyone out on the streets that I yanked myself out of the car to say "hi" to her. She slowed down and, unwilling to let her get away, I began my seduction with an uninteresting comment about the weather. "Ready for spring?"

"What are you doing in there, in your car?" she asked, venturing a few steps towards me.

"Oh…" I dove back into the car and easily lifted

Jasper, now unhitched, out of his seat, holding him up like a just-caught fish so the woman could see him. With that, she ran over to us and cried out, "A baby! Oh he's so cute!"

Jasper rewarded her with a smile.

"Do you live around here?" I asked.

She pointed to the house across the street. "Thatta way. On Sunset Road," a street she could have reached most directly by cutting through someone's yard. "Just renting," she added.

"Me too."

"Really?"

I was tempted to tell her that marriage and motherhood weren't enough to qualify a person for homeownership, that money for a downpayment didn't come easy. But I'd been purposely avoiding any thoughts related to our finances—or more exactly, our poverty. So instead I changed the subject.

"You must have just moved. I haven't seen you before."

She laughed, crossing the first threshold on the way to becoming friends. "This very day, in fact." She looked around as if she'd just landed. "So where is everybody?"

Jasper was squirming forcefully, wanting to be put down. "Don! Don!" he cried out. I could either try to talk with this woman while chasing my toddler up and down the street or else invite her inside, where Jasper's travels could be contained.

"Want to come in?"

Again she looked around, almost as if she thought we were being watched. "Sure. Yeah." Her hair, artificially black, was separated into clumps held fast with rubber bands. Her hybrid eyes—somewhere between brown and green—offered no clues as to what her natural hair color might be.

Once inside we settled in the living room, furnished only with a couch, one arm chair, and a bulky table, all too heavy for Jasper to tip over or slide out of place. The room was saved from looking like a warehouse by the cantaloupe-colored walls we'd painted at our own expense.

"That's Jasper," I said, and only then realized that we hadn't told each other our names.

"And I'm Pauline."

"I'm Lilac."

As soon as she'd introduced herself, I decided that I may have misjudged this woman and shouldn't have let her get as close to me as the inside of my house. I didn't think that I could be friends with someone I had to call Lilac, unless she really had been the victim of a parent who'd stuck her with this whimsical name. But if that were the case, wouldn't she by now have come up with an alternative or a nickname for herself?

"My given name is Vivian, but somewhere along the way I decided that it didn't suit me."

"And how did you come up with 'Lilac'?"

Lilac was nodding, as if in anticipation of this familiar question. "Well, I was sitting in the most comfortable chair in the world, right next to an open window. I was running through names in my head without reacting. I must have gotten a whiff of the lilacs that were in bloom outside. I've always *loved* lilacs."

I decided to test our brand-new friendship. "But loving them isn't quite the same as wanting to share a name with them."

Lilac laughed, suggesting that she wasn't overly sensitive, though I was soon to discover that she laughed at nearly everything. "OK, so call me 'Viv' if you want. Actually, I've been thinking about 'Viva.'"

Never in a lifetime would I have thought to change my name, an inescapable link to my parents, much like my DNA or my belly button, the remnant umbilical cord. Already I was beginning to admire this woman's independence and audacity.

"Lilac's fine," I said.

Had Jasper and I been alone, his goal that afternoon would have been to elude me as he staked out new territory. But on the rare occasion of a guest in our home, he was instead trying to earn as much of my attention as he could, if not by proximity and noise, then by injuring himself—falling, banging into the corners of tables—and so requiring emergency care from me.

"He's a busy little guy," Lilac observed.

"Yes he is. So Lilac, do you live alone?"

This was as close as I dared come to asking her if she was married. Even if I were to presume that she was heterosexual, I understood that marriage wasn't the ultimate endpoint that all roads led to. While I wholeheartedly supported the concepts of commitment and cultivated love, I hadn't been able to entirely dissociate marriage from the repellant images of bridal magazines, shopping carts, and TV in bed. On the other hand, the popular images attached to motherhood weren't nearly as offensive to me; they were, however, unattainable—the radiant smiles, tranquil naps. In my reality as a mother, I always was attempting to break free of repetition, isolation, and the uselessness of language.

But Jasper was becoming more articulate, suddenly able to explain all of his mystery urges and needs that had previously kept me guessing. "Maw mook, mama!" he demanded. The utterance of the mother-word in his little voice always, without exception, persuaded me to obey him.

"More milk," I translated for Lilac as I got up to fetch my master his drink.

Jasper's preference for cow's milk over my own had accelerated the weaning process that I'd intended to draw out over months. Even if he liked the taste of cow's milk better than breast milk, how could he so willingly give up those languid hours of fulfillment in my arms?

"Don't you nurse him?" Lilac asked, following me into the kitchenette, and suddenly I felt as if I were under investigation by the Department of Social Services.

"Yes!" I nearly shouted, hiding Jasper's orange sippie cup behind my back.

Lilac began pacing with her head down until finally she returned to the living room. From there she called out, "Nope, not married. I moved here to get away from the damnation of a bad seven-year relationship."

"I'm sorry." I handed Jasper his cup, which he immediately pitched across the room into the back of the chair. "Sorry," I said again, this time because I had to remove myself from our conversation in order to retrieve the cup just as Jasper had planned.

"It's OK," Lilac said. She was curling one stubby lock of her hair around a finger, winding it so tight that I expected it to rip off of her scalp.

"Your choice?"

"Well…yes and no. I chose to leave, but this wasn't the ending I was hoping for."

I nodded and was relieved when Lilac released her torqued lock of hair. "Now I'd like him dead."

I'd read the oven-front clock when I was in the kitchen getting Jasper's milk; Clifford would be home within half an hour. I decided that she'd have to leave at once if I were to avert a meeting between the two of them. I wasn't being miserly with my new acquaintance since Clifford wasn't the type to crowd anyone out of a three-way friendship. But Lilac was my first prospective friend since marriage and motherhood had muddled my identity. I didn't want her to think of me as being too married, too much like those images that were so distasteful to me. Better that she get to know me completely independently of my husband.

"Listen, Lilac, I have to give Jasper a bath."

"Do you want me to wait down here?"

I was encouraged that she didn't show any scorn for my domestic chores. "Except then I have to feed him." I was going out of my way not to refer to my husband or to his imminent arrival, not to present myself as one-half of a marital unit.

"Oh. So I'd better leave."

I never would have figured Lilac for a hand-shaker, but she extended her hand, took hold of mine and pumped it up and down. Afterwards I wrote down my phone number for her but purposely avoided asking for hers. This would be a test of sorts. As much as I was hungry for friendship, I didn't want to be friends with someone who wasn't willing to seek me out.

I watched Lilac continue along Hilltop in the direction she'd originally been headed. As she neared the corner, Clifford was just getting out of his car in the nearest parking space, at the end of the block. Strangers to each other, unknowingly connected by me, they passed without as much as a sidelong glance; apparently my cosmic print was very faint.

For the next two days I tried to relate the phone's infrequent rings, as well as its more typical silence, to the likelihood that Lilac would call. I was reluctant to take Jasper for a walk in case I'd miss Lilac's call while we were out promenading through the neighborhood, though I didn't mind missing the wrong numbers or marketing calls. Somehow during our hour-long visit, I hadn't asked Lilac what she did, whether she was employed and, if so, what her hours were.

Now that Jasper was learning to talk, he was both a more engaging companion and a more complex one—observant, intelligent, and stubborn, as I'd discerned even during his pre-verbal days. My baby was solidifying into a real person. Even his appearance, which during infancy had fluctuated between resemblance to Clifford and to me, was beginning to stabilize. Jasper undeniably looked more like his dad with flavorings of Clifford's father. After toting him around in utero for all those months, I felt somewhat resentful, and yet his leanings towards my personality traits evened the score.

Two days after I'd met Lilac, the phone rang in the evening. I was convinced that the call was from her and so actually was disappointed to hear Alia's voice. "Where you been?" Normally we spoke on the phone at least once a week.

"Oh, probably in the exact same chair I was in when you last spoke with me. And probably wearing the exact same clothes," I said. Alia was the one person to whom I could confess my boredom without being judged as a mother who didn't love her son. But since she had no children of her own and the very idea of giving birth appalled her, her sympathy was suspect.

"So when you going back to work?" she asked.

"I don't know. Soon, I guess. I'm not looking forward to a job search, though."

Never in my life had I felt as worthless, wicked, and unclean as during those times when I was in the market for a job.

"Be sure to get dressed every day. And don't let your hair get greasy. Those are the sure signs that job rejection is getting to you."

"Alia, I'm so glad you called. But I have to go now."

This had been the shortest phone conversation in the history of our friendship, and I knew that I should offer an explanation for why I was terminating the call so soon. But how could I tell Alia that I wanted her off the phone so the line wouldn't be busy if Lilac called? Alia was a blood-thick friend, a soul sister. She, however, lived hours away, and my yearning for a friend-in-the-flesh was very strong.

"I just...I'm expecting a phone call."

But once I hung up, the phone didn't ring for the rest of the night. Meanwhile I mentioned to Clifford that I thought I might be ready to get a job.

"Great!" he said with electrified enthusiasm that couldn't disguise the underlying financial worry. But had my husband overestimated my earning power?

"Clifford, you know that I'm not a surgeon. Or even a professor."

His laughter smelled of the piquant lemon sauce I'd made to dress up our daily chicken. "Maid's wages would feel like a fortune right now."

How could we be in such a state of peril? I usually bought store-brand groceries. I'd made a habit of turning off the lights whenever I left a room. And even though I hadn't quite returned to the size-six figure I maintained before getting pregnant, I'd managed not to buy any new clothes. My pants were rarely zipped up all the way. Frequently I wore my maternity shirts over them. Not acquiring new, size-eight clothes was only partly a measure of thrift. Disbelieving, as I did, that my body had been permanently enlarged by childbirth, I was waiting to revert to my former physical self.

Just as I was about to escort Jasper up to his room, his face formed into a pout that I recognized from photos as mine. Clifford, too, detected this fleeting resemblance.

"Did you see that, Pauli? He looked exactly like you! Exactly."

And then the resemblance passed.

"Let me put him to bed," Clifford said. "I'll read him a story."

As Jasper unsteadily scaled the stairs in front of his father, I poured myself a belated cocktail. I hadn't been observing my happy-hour tradition as regularly for a while. Perhaps just being able to open the windows had cured me of my feeling of being trapped. But now I was preparing to look at the classifieds from last Sunday's paper. Few things caused me the severe anxiety that seeking employment did: being evaluated, compared, and finally chosen or rejected. Yet work had lately become more desirable to me than it had been before—a way out of the undifferentiated hours at home—even though looking ahead to the ache of missing Jasper had instilled in me a terror of what it might feel like to lose him in a more permanent way.

When Clifford came back downstairs, he was still speaking in the sing-song voice he adopted when talking to our son. "Whatcha doing there, Missus?"

I folded up the classified pages printed with vitals of all the jobs that weren't mine.

"You know, Clifford, that if I get a job, we're going to have to pay someone to take care of Jasper while we're both at work."

Clifford nodded thoughtfully, and I could tell that he'd failed to factor this expense into the respite from poverty he foresaw once I got a job. "You mean like a babysitter?"

"I wouldn't call it that. Someone who's competent and experienced. Or it could be a daycare center."

He cringed but promptly tried to convert his expression of displeasure into a smile. "Still, we'll end up ahead, right? I mean, you must make more than someone who plays with Jasper for hours and waits for him to wake up from naps."

Clifford seemed confused when I responded, not to his faith in my value on the job market but to his dismissive summary of what child care entailed. "Is that what you think I do all day?"

He bounded up out of his chair and squished himself into the narrow vacancy beside me on the couch. "No, not you, sweetie. You do so much more when you're home with him."

"You mean like...clean?" I swept my arm through the air cluttered with dust motes and cobweb wisps. At least the room had been stripped of small, sharp, and breakable objects to make it baby-safe, so there was much less stuff in it than there would have been otherwise. "Or could you mean those tasty dinners I prepare every night?" I wasn't reacting only to Clifford, but to my own misgivings about how well I was performing in my role as parent. Since I was devoting myself full-time to being a mother, who else could I blame if Jasper grew up to be less than perfect?

"Anyway, Pauline, this is about more than money or how big a salary you can earn. It's about…your personal satisfaction with what you're doing." Clifford began stroking my back from the top of my head all the way down to my tailbone. Perhaps he was hoping to sedate me and spare us both a battle. Soon I was in a state of stuporous bliss, removed from the troubled past and future, and Clifford's cushy shoulder was the only place I wanted to be.

Not until the next day did I finish reading the classifieds. While I did come upon jobs that I was qualified for and even some that attracted me, there was no overlap between the two categories. I read the most recent draft of my resumé, which had magically appeared on the kitchen counter the month before. At the time I'd wondered if Clifford was embarking on a campaign to nudge me towards work and I could expect other such hints.

Revising my outdated resumé proved much less stressful without an application deadline for a specific job. I worked on it while Jasper napped; I felt uplifted by this new goal that forced me into the world outside of my own circumscribed existence. Later, after my burst of productivity, I thought I was entitled to a walk around the neighborhood with Jasper. Spring was still romancing me with its aphrodisiac fragrances and glorious light at all times of day. The simple act of treading, step-by-step, over the ground, taking in the glimmering air, being charged by the powerful yet gentle light seemed at once so earthly and so sublime.

Jasper no longer accepted captivity in a stroller; instead he'd toddle along in front of me, stooping to examine plain stones and scuttling bugs, then labor to stand back up again. Our excruciatingly slow progress strained my patience until I thought to pay attention to the mixture of smells in the air—earth and wind and light—and how both cool and warm the breeze could be. If I let myself transcend the tedium of the moment, I could gauge the insignificance of every bother on my list, including the necessity of getting a job.

Jasper was first to spot her across the street. "Mama, look, Mama." Lilac was flying wildly on a porch swing, riding it back and forth while holding a tall glass of iced tea in her hand. Certainly she wasn't doing anything that would prevent her from making a phone call, and I hesitated to speak to her. Maybe our time together had been a one-shot affair more than the basis for a friendship. But Jasper had shouted so loud that Lilac heard him, even in the midst of her flight.

"Oh hi!" she said, letting the swing gradually lose its momentum. I wondered if she remembered my name—admittedly less memorable than hers. "I was hoping I'd bump into you again."

"You should've called then." Could Lilac sense from my forced casual delivery that I'd been desperately hoping for her call?

"I should've gotten your number."

I wasn't sure whether this lapse in her memory was better or worse than a lack of interest in calling me. Rather than remind her that I had, in fact, given her my number, I cut across the grass and stepped up onto the porch.

"Swing included in the rent?" I asked.

She very seriously told me that yes, all of the tenants were welcome to use the swing. What had happened to the woman who laughed at everything?

By now the swing had come to rest, and I climbed on board with Jasper in my lap. Lilac's black hair had been tousled by her ride through the air. For once Jasper submitted willingly to my restraining embrace, squealing with pleasure as we arced forward and back, the contrived breeze creating enough of a thrill to keep him satisfied. With such an adorable boy in my possession, I felt as if I were sitting across the table from Lilac with a delectable pastry that was mine, not hers, and that I couldn't share.

"How's the new place?" I asked, peeking in through a front window each time I passed it.

"I could use more space, you know?"

"How many people live in this building?"

At our next backswing, Lilac pushed off the porch floor with her foot, launching the swing into a crooked flight pattern. "I'm not sure. I've seen three different people in and out so far." After a pause she said, "This isn't the building where I live. I live over there," pointing to a square, very plain house across the street. "I'm just borrowing the swing."

If Alia or another friend I'd known for a while had said this, I would have appreciated her talent for mischief. Not knowing Lilac that well, though, I couldn't be sure that she didn't have some type of social disorder or a problem with boundaries. But I chose to give her the benefit of the doubt, motivated by my desperate need for a friend.

"I see. Then I guess I'm borrowing it, too."

I hoped that the occupants of the house were more generous in their reactions to trespass than the neighbor who had rung my doorbell and thrust the vagrant Henry into my arms.

Lilac enclosed my hand in hers—large enough to fit around mine, and noticeably hot even though she'd just been holding a glass of iced tea. Perhaps she had a fever; maybe she was even contagious. When she did the same to Jasper's hand, the thought that she was passing along unwanted germs signaled from my brain to my feet, which I used to touch ground, and I evacuated the swing mid-flight.

"It was nice to see you again," I said, half-meaning it. Then I reminded her that she probably had my number somewhere, but I didn't offer to give it to her again.

Jasper and I resumed our movement down the street. He was able to spot the very smallest elements of the sidewalk ecosystem—every critter and every seed—leading me to hope he hadn't inherited my extreme near-sightedness.

"Do you like that woman? Do you like Lilac?" I asked, seeking a second opinion. I'd taken to talking with Jasper in the same way I used to talk with Henry. Often I was awarded an actual response though it was always more crude than the eloquent replies I'd attributed to the cat.

"I like the swing!" For as long as I'd be acquainted with Lilac, Jasper would surely associate her with that one fast ride on the stolen swing.

"I guess I don't have to decide yet whether or not I want to get to know her." And maybe eventually I'd even decide to like her. After all, people could grow to like each other. My reservations about a lifetime with Clifford had vanished. I'd gone from being chafed by his constant company to missing him during the workday when he was gone.

But now that I'd stopped faulting my husband for not being taller and having straighter teeth, our relationship was stuck in the mud of a higher road. The drain of parenting a young child and the financial overload of raising a family made our life together feel complicated and hard. Despite my thrift, we owned kitchen utensils that I'd never seemed to need before, as well as life insurance and a retirement fund. Were these needs real, and if so, where had they been earlier?

I couldn't imagine a more Spartan lifestyle than the one implied by the abandoned caves at Bandolier National Park. I remembered the row of tiny inlets carved in the mountainside, and the barren interiors of the caves. Maybe the solution to our money problem wasn't to earn more income but to reduce our costs, to reconsider some of our expenditures.

And yet I definitely had to get a job. I wanted but didn't want to work, in the same way I'd wanted but not wanted to marry Clifford. Perhaps this was my affliction, to always feel both sides equally. And while this might make me a fine mediator or an objective reporter, in the personal realm, the tendency left me forever unable to commit myself to one path or the other.

♦♦♦♦

Forced Labor

After several weeks of editing my resumé, reading want ads, checking job listings, and opening my ears to atmospheric inklings about who was hiring, I still hadn't applied for a single job. None of the openings I'd found were quite right for me. But the bigger obstacle to getting a job was that I wasn't really ready to start working again, now that I was a mother and knew that while I filled out client intake forms or attended professional workshops, my little boy would be waiting for me to reappear. Clifford urged me on without really understanding what it would be like for me, this separation from the child I'd been fused with for almost two years.

"He's not dying. Just going to daycare."

"Just?"

Clifford suggested that we enroll Jasper in daycare as soon as possible rather than wait for my employment to begin. "That way, you'll have more of a transition. You can even pick him up early some days, or maybe visit him there."

Not a bad idea, I conceded. Once again I was touched by my husband's generous nature. Despite his chronic worry about our shortage of money, if paying for full-time child care while I was at home doing nothing that resulted in income might assuage my uneasiness, then he was all for it.

"But…when did we decide on a daycare center instead of hiring someone to stay home with Jasper?"

Clifford's eyebrows rose nearly to his hairline. "Think about it," he said. "Compare the costs of paying one person to look after one kid to paying two people to look after ten."

"Plus administrative costs and overhead." Had he forgotten that, of the two of us, I was the more practical one? "And anyway, whoever said that this is only about money? I mean, this is our *son!*"

Clifford shriveled at my implied accusation and could say only, "Of course."

I would miss my boy, his breath in my face when he screamed—that uncorrupted wind of small fury. His grip on my sleeve, my pants leg, assuring himself that I was still there, permanent and columnar as the Colossus. I would miss him.

That week, in the classified section of the neighborhood newspaper, I found out about a position that sounded like the exact duplicate of the one I'd left in Philadelphia. Here was a job I was indisputably qualified for. But, I asked myself, did I really want to be doing the very same thing I'd been doing before? Wasn't I supposed to be learning, changing, aspiring to elevate myself above what I used to be?

From the living room, Jasper ordered me to come see a bug he'd discovered, which turned out to be a whole accumulation of dead bugs in the window casement. Did I need any proof other than him that I had grown? The responsibility of parenting, as common as it was, would probably be the most epic achievement of my lifetime.

Jasper had been a planned baby. Like so many other women, I claimed to have known instinctively that I was pregnant. But pregnancy brought with it certain early symptoms: a corkscrew tightening behind the belly, a watercolor nausea soaking into the most minute gestures and neutral thoughts. And anyone trying to get pregnant is on the lookout for just such telltale signs.

Now, as I prepared to entrust my baby to someone else, I didn't feel the subtle changes in my body until one day when I realized my period was overdue. My entire worldview changed, its mosaic pieces rearranged, some replaced with others. I was already doubting my ability to adapt, to jump tracks from grieving my perceived loss of one child to welcoming the addition of another. Clifford, I supposed, would react in monetary terms: another mouth to feed, another delay in my return to the work force. I felt like a Welfare mother, with Clifford cast as the government, pushing pushing pushing me to get a job and stop having babies. But of course he, too, the father of our child-to-be, had been as much a cause of this pregnancy as I had.

I had an urge to call Alia. But telling her first, before Clifford, seemed a breach of my marital vows. I would have liked to rehearse with Henry, my latest confidante, but I hadn't seen him in months. I even considered practicing my delivery of this news to Jasper. But he was old enough to understand what I'd say, at least literally; what if all the reservations I was sure to express lodged in his brain, to be reviewed in later years when he was better able to comprehend them?

That same day, after Clifford had led Jasper to sleep with a bedtime story, he asked me, "Any new job prospects?"

I reviewed the assortment of money-saving ideas I'd been hatching over the past several weeks. "You know, Cliffie, we *really* don't need two cars. In fact, having two is wasteful."

He rocked his head side to side, considering this proposal, and then opened one of the kitchen cupboards and began browsing the selection of snack food. Since we'd just eaten a complete meal—one of my more ambitious menus—I couldn't understand why he was hungry so soon.

"Clifford, if you're still hungry, have more dinner. There's plenty left."

He came over and hugged me, as if having chosen me over the potato chips. "Nah. Save you a night of cooking."

My Clifford. I'd never known anyone else whose first reaction was from someone else's point of view. I took his head in my hands and slowly, as slowly as I could, moved my face towards his so that the kiss that clinched our gradual approach seemed long awaited, the conclusion of years of anticipation.

But during the gleaming moment afterwards, when our faceted eyes matched up as we gazed at each other, I became positive that he was about to ask me again about a job. So I disengaged my eyes from his, wiggled out of his embrace, and said, "You're not the only one who doesn't want to have to wear a necktie."

His amusement soon changed into confusion, leading me to think he'd forgotten the memorable conversation that to me had seemed like a milestone in our marriage. A spike of anger made me blurt out, despite the script I'd written for myself, "I'm pregnant. The most work anyone can get out of me is about eight months' worth."

"Pregnant?"

Did I imagine a musical score begin to dazzle the routine evening? Was my husband headed for an epileptic seizure or was he experiencing paroxysms of joy?

"Clifford? Are you all right?"

His rapture surrounded me, jolted through me, a sizzle of excitement that until then I hadn't allowed myself to feel. He ejected me from his arms, thrust them straight up towards a heaven beyond our second-floor ceiling, and exclaimed, "Hallelujah! We're having a baby!"

The chill of melancholy autumn air coming in

through the window couldn't dampen our elation. I pursued Clifford, who was now managing athletic leaps around the apartment, and when I overtook him, squeezed him with the might of my whole self. His muscly body offered itself to me with a surface softness. He was half the baby rooted within me.

Once Clifford's mood had quieted and he lay down on the couch to recover from so much delight, I phoned Alia to tell her my news.

"Didn't you just have a baby, what, a couple of years ago?"

"I did. And he's already walking and talking and…"

"Really?"

Alia's picture of Jasper was probably months and months behind time. We hadn't seen her for as long, and not being a mother herself, she couldn't accurately project his growth and development since then.

"So when are you coming up?" I asked her.

"I was just about to ask when I can come up."

"Oh I'm here. I'm very much here," though any day the tide of nausea would be knocking me flat if this pregnancy was like my last. Except that this time I had a two-year old to take care of while I was retching up the runny nothing in my gut. "But why don't you wait until the nausea sets in," I said, thinking that I could use her as a respite worker.

"I don't get it. Wouldn't you want me to visit *before* you're out of commission?"

Not a mother. Wouldn't understand. And neither

would Lilac, unless she had a child named Poppy hidden away in her horticultural past. None of my friends, in fact, were parents. But all of the mothers I met seemed to be of a different species than I was. We might say "hi" to each other at the grocery store and even sit on the same bench in the play park across from the school, but none of these mothers had ever come near to touring a homeless shelter nor, I suspected, did they want to.

Alia agreed to be on-call. I predicted that I'd be summoning her to Boston within two weeks, so she should gas up her car and mark the page in the road atlas. Meanwhile, weeks after I'd given up on Lilac, she called me one late-morning and suggested that we go shopping together. "I'll drive," she offered.

"No, let me. It's easier than transferring the car seat."

"What's that?" She quickly answered her own question. "Right. The kid."

Although Lilac was the newcomer to town, or at least to the neighborhood, she acted as the director of our outing, telling me where to turn, when to slow down. She even told me, "Go now," as soon as a traffic light changed to green.

"I know," I told her. "It's universal," and then I recalled that even though Lilac laughed a lot, we weren't on the same humor frequency.

Our first stop turned out to be Pennywise, a thrift store run by two women dressed like investment brokers. "Oh, *this* kind of shopping," I said with pleasure.

"What? You don't like thrift stores?"

"Vivian," I said, my animosity driven by hormones, "you don't even know me." And right there, in front of this single, childless woman with the flamboyant name and black hair and ankle-high turquoise boots, I began sorting through the baby-clothes bin. The pristine kimonos, only fitting for about three days before they were outgrown, looked brand new. One or two were stained faintly with spit-up.

Lilac prowled around the store without touching anything, as if she had the power to locate the choicest items completely by sight. Eventually she arrived at my little corner smelling of freshness and confectionery pastels, where I was still digging through baby clothes and Jasper, in his stroller, was resisting sleep.

"That'll never fit your boy," she said in reference to a blue stretchy suit printed with sleepytime clouds that I was holding up by its small shoulders.

"It's not for him. I'm pregnant."

I'd concluded that Lilac and I weren't destined to become real friends, so I no longer cared what she might think about my pregnancy. By then I'd not only confirmed my condition with two home-pregnancy tests, but received the more official word after an appointment with my doctor.

The enthusiasm with which Lilac sprang over to me and strangled me in a hug was so extreme that at first I thought she was a vigilante from a population control organization, attacking me. "That's fan*tas*tic!" she proclaimed.

Still, she remained a wish more than a friend, a contrast to the closeness I'd so enjoyed with Alia. Like Henry, she gradually disappeared from my life, but I didn't miss her as I missed my intelligent cat friend.

Just days later I was wakened by a rush of nausea so severe that it had to have been caused by chemical weaponry, I thought. I reached for my bedside phone and let Alia know that I was ready for her visit, trying during our brief conversation to disguise the stomach-sick sensation coloring my skin green, I was sure without needing to look in a mirror. I dragged myself like a prehistoric reptile into the kitchen and pulled the largest mixing bowl I owned out of a bottom cupboard. This I placed right beside me in bed so that when I was overcome with the urge to throw up, I had only to roll onto my side and let my head drop.

Although I was seriously seasick throughout Alia's visit, we spent most of my awake time together. She sat on the mattress near me while we played card games. The picture cards somehow provoked my vertigo so we switched to Scrabble with its sedate letter tiles.

"Those jacks," she said. "Real heartbreakers. Look at the way they've sent you into a dither."

"It's not just them," I answered flatly.

"The kings? The queens? Their parents! Who do you think they got it from?"

Just the presence of another—a more functional—adult kept Jasper happy. When he did fuss or scream, Alia responded promptly and, during that week, learned to distinguish between the hungry cry, the frustrated cry, the feeling-neglected cry. She became fluent in Jasper's developing dialect. She even acquired a new skill—changing a diaper.

Alia and Clifford were barely acquainted. I'd met him not long before he relocated to Boston, so though the two had met, Alia knew my husband mostly from my narratives about him and from the long list of doubts I'd confided to her. Now suddenly they'd been plunged into circumstantial cohabitation.

"He's really nice," Alia said to me on about the second day of her visit.

"What did you think? That I'd marry someone who wasn't?"

Her eyes narrowed as if she were remembering back ages ago to another era of history. "No. But I'm remembering some of the things you said about him. Your criticisms."

As if in punishment for my past, a shudder of nausea quivered through me, compelling me to turn towards my bowl. One empty heave and I was through. Alia stood and adjusted the blinds to save me from the slices of light aimed right at my eyes. She picked up my empty water glass, probably intending to refill it. My ailment was bringing out the nurse in her, her maternal side. Jasper had so taken to Alia that I was worrying whether a two-year attachment to me could compete with his infatuation with my friend.

That week of her visit, Clifford, who was used to

being overwhelmed by my welcome in the evening, had to shout from the front hall to announce that he was home. Then when none of us went to greet him—I, of course, was unable to be upright, and Jasper was usually affixed to Alia—he'd advance further into the apartment until he found us, always assembled in the bedroom, no doubt resembling a deathbed scene painted in earthy tones of dark, blood, gray. He was not, while our guest was with us, the celebrity he normally was at five o'clock, when both Jasper and I would have welcomed even the parcel-delivery man with all our hearts.

I was swimming in a primeval jelly, upside down. Even love for my dear son became meaningless as sickness and starvation abused my body and preoccupied my mind. At most I could eat a hard-boiled egg or a mouthful of dry cereal, but then usually I gave back what little I'd eaten in a gush of saliva embittered with bile.

Of course Alia couldn't stay for the duration of my misnamed morning-sickness; once she'd departed, I was faced with two months more of round-the-clock nausea. Instead of gaining weight as the baby inside me enlarged from the size of a seed to the size of a walnut and then an orange, I was losing an average of a pound a week. But even after reading the results of my weigh-in at each appointment, my midwife showed no alarm.

During my pregnancy, Jasper was introduced to television. Until then he'd sneaked peeks of night-time dramas and talk shows, but I'd deliberately denied him the littlest glimpse of any children's programming, not wanting to deal with his likely clamor for more. I tried getting him interested in radio, but he kept looking around for the presence of the voice's owner and finally succumbed to tears, haunted by the disembodied commentators and singers.

Once I'd been stricken with mother-sickness, as I renamed it, and Alia had come and gone, I resorted to television as a substitute for my company. Jasper—and I, as well—was happy to sit passively in front of ours, perpetually charmed by its charismatic offerings. I was astounded at how effective a method of child-control the big box was. Jasper bounced up and down with merriment whenever I turned it on. I could watch with him or nap; he was indifferent to the status of my consciousness if the TV was on.

Clifford continued to enter the apartment cheerily each night, even knowing that there was no dinner awaiting him, not even a feeble chorus of "hello." Only a flattened wife on her back in bed and a son glutted with electronic input, with commercial jingles and unrealistic ideas of family and country. A master of self-control, Clifford was able to tolerate his hunger until he'd gone to the grocery store—taking the protesting, television-addicted Jasper with him—minced onion, boiled pasta and produced a dull but filling meal for himself. Miraculously Jasper would already have eaten by then. He had become a prodigy in the kitchen, following my directions to fetch this and that, get his plastic bowl, so that together we staved off starvation. After Clifford had eaten, he'd put Jasper to bed—quite late, so he'd sleep later in the morning. My husband had no time for me.

This arrangement suited me since the effort of being social made me sick. Our routine had drastically changed; we seemed to have been removed from our ho-hum middle-class life and transported to a prison camp. But I knew from experience that this phase of pregnancy would end. Last time it had ended abruptly on the last day of my first trimester, and from then on I had loved being pregnant.

Apparently Clifford had been plotting during those first months while I was bedridden. So when I finally rose from my crumpled self to become a ripe woman aglow with health and fertility, he had me sit at the dining room table, cleared of the ruins of our meal, and he said, "I'm all signed up for a graduate program beginning this fall."

"What?"

"It's an education degree with a concentration in school administration. I'll take classes at night, part-time, and I'll get credit for some of my work experience in the field. Then, when I'm done, I can be a school principal."

The salad bowl had been overlooked, and as I studied its surface slicked with oil, the intricate wilting of the lettuce, I realized how much I missed during the vacant hours when I was home with Jasper. "Why are you doing this?" I asked Clifford, and then said, "You didn't even discuss it with me."

But he was still on the upbeat from delivering his news bulletin, as if my negative response hadn't yet sunk in. I pictured him in the noose of a necktie behind a boxy oak desk in a school office.

"You know how it is. At first I thought I'd just look over the information. Then I thought I'd apply, without any commitment to actually doing it. But then I started…wanting it to happen. I didn't say anything because I was worried that I might not be accepted. And now…"

And now I'd be mothering a two-year old and a new baby, suspended in the airlessness of long days alone while my husband went to work and then, in the evenings, to graduate school. Meanwhile Alia had been around for most of a week, leaving me with a tease of what it felt like to have a close friend nearby. I exhaled a sigh so vast that I had no breath left in me and had to gasp to revive myself.

"Pauline?"

"I'm fine," I said with a red edge of anger. And I was fine. I could zoom in and savor the richness of detail of the vegetables in my salad or the fissured skin on my son's small fingers. I could back away and take in more earth, air and light, more of the world beyond my little cubicle. After all, I was pregnant, an exalted state of being in which I became, up until the great day, a small god of sorts.

Three months into my pregnancy, the nausea

abruptly ended. However, as the year warmed towards summer, I realized that my last months, the time of deathly fatigue and impossible sleeping postures, of panting up even the slightest inclines, would coincide with the brutality of high temperatures and humidity. I could easily remember my first pregnancy, which also had peaked in summer, and the dense, palpable air lying too close beside me in bed.

Already I felt oppressed by weather that to everyone else was perfect. The only relief I could find was inside my air-conditioned car while I was in transit. If I'd had any friends, I might have invited them to a dinner party in the back seat.

Still I chose to walk to my appointments with my midwife, her office a mile and a half away. I'd diagonally cross the small park on the top of the hill that our neighborhood was named for. Farther along the way, the gangly trees planted along the green belt were shyly showing off their quiet, white blossoms. I scheduled my appointments at a time of day when Jasper not only permitted me to strap him into his stroller but fell asleep during the ride. I wished I could have used the time to catch up on sleep, but though Margaret, my midwife, encouraged the participation of siblings in preparation for a new baby, I wanted to give this child my exclusive attention, equal to all that we'd given Jasper even before he was born.

Margaret Hurley had trained her receptionist to treat each patient like a royal guest. That training had included the cultivation of a hushed voice that evoked associations of lullabies, a peaceful nursery, and a dream mother, all at once. "Oh, isn't he splendid?" she said of napping Jasper. Pat wheeled the stroller forward and back a few times and then ushered me to the scale, where she doubled as a quasi medical assistant, weighing me and measuring my blood pressure. "Wonderful," she sang in a voice so sublimely soothing that I believed she might be an angel in human form.

Pat kept an eye on Jasper while I submitted to a routine exam inside one of the floral, rock-a-bye rooms. "You're getting big," Margaret said, a rather obvious observation, I thought, for someone in her profession. I may have fallen asleep during the two minutes when she was manually examining me inside and out, but I instantly came awake when Margaret, armed with a stethoscope, said matter-of-factly, "I'm not getting a heartbeat," and my own, I'm sure, stopped too.

Margaret rolled out the ultrasound machine and deftly unveiled my body, lubricated the transducer, and began voyaging across the expanse of my distended womb, watching the underground on the screen. She nodded, pressed down on a button, and then I heard the amplification of a rapid lifebeat.

"There it is," she declared, the first tinge of emotion in her voice. Margaret's evenness in the pit of this little crisis had probably kept me from panicking, I realized now.

"What was that about?" I wanted to know.

She shrugged. "Hard to say. Looks like your baby's cuddling pretty close to herself. And maybe she turned." A previous ultrasound had revealed that my baby was a girl. Clifford would have rather not known in advance the gender of our child, but I wanted to add some specificity to my fantasies.

Then, somewhat casually, Margaret told me that the baby was small and that I'd have to be monitored more closely. "I'd like you in here every week," she said.

At each appointment, as I left whichever of the flowery rooms I'd been in, I belatedly wondered at the scent of flowers, which couldn't have been coming from the wallpaper. But from where then? Margaret herself? She seemed as elemental as the blue sky and the rain and the ancient dirt. I looked forward to delivering the baby right there, in one of those rooms. For a while, I'd thought of giving birth at home, an improvement over the institutional setting that had dominated Jasper's birth. Margaret had cautioned me, though, that any emergencies that came up would have to be handled at the hospital; in fact, at the least indication of extraordinary leanings, she would call for an ambulance and have me moved to Brigham and Women's, where every conceivable piece of medical apparatus would be a reach away.

As I rolled Jasper in his stroller homeward to the promise of snack food and eventually more TV, I imagined that we'd switched places and that my growing boy was pushing me, compressed into the seat of the stroller, up the hill.

"Mama, do I have to give my food with my sister?"

Jasper asked me one day soon after.

"You mean share?"

He nodded.

I was slouched in an armchair in the living room, too inert to stand up and go turn on the window fan. Although Clifford and I had informed Jasper again and again that I would be having a baby, that he could see how it was getting big inside me, that it was a girl, none of our explanations seemed to approach reality for him. He absorbed these fantastic prophesies as if they were part of a tale being read to him at bedtime. But now, finally, he was starting to understand, and his first reaction was a fear of having to give up some of his ravioli and frozen peas.

"No, of course not, dear boy. We'll have enough food for everyone." Was my son aware, as I was, that we were really talking about love and only secondarily about food? He seemed satisfied with my answer, and in fact slowed his hand-to-mouth intake of crackers, assured that he didn't need to stock up for a famine ahead.

The bold, warrior summer seemed to be everywhere at once: inside my lungs, clogging up my breathing, close against my skin and beyond, insistently infinite, so there was nowhere left to go, nowhere to imagine. Sometimes Jasper, unbothered by the scorching summer, would pound on my belly, trying to activate me but only receiving my wrath. The television was on constantly, assaulting us with random programming at a volume that irritated me but seemed to boost Jasper's energy.

"Nap time," I'd announce just two hours into the morning. I was more than ready for a nap. Jasper was not.

Clifford called to check in now and then during the day. I always felt as though he was calling from halfway around the world, from a culture as different from mine as it could possibly be. My single two-year-old seemed equivalent in disruptive potential to Clifford's entire school building full of early adolescents.

"Why don't you take Jasper to the park?' he suggested on a day so humid that my vision was bleared with sweat collecting along the rims of my eyes.

"Because I'm tired, and it's hot. Plus I've had this pain in my side all morning."

"What kind of pain?"

"The kind that hurts."

"No, really, Pauline, don't you think you should phone Margaret?"

Clifford's alarm prompted me to call Margaret's office as soon as I'd hung up with him. When Pat said, "She's with a patient. Is this an emergency?" I instantly answered, "No," convincing myself that I had no cause to worry. But once I explained why I was calling, Pat asked me to hold and soon returned to the phone, saying, "Can you come in now, dear?" She added, "Don't drive yourself, though."

I groaned in answer to her question and acknowledgment of her advice. Only twice in my life had I taken a cab, once as a child with my mother on a shopping excursion and once when I was stranded late at night somewhere near West Philly. My memories were of a smell not quite like smoke, of seats not quite leather, of furtive drivers remote and menacing at the same time. I chose one of the dozen or so companies listed and was told, when I explained that I needed to get to a medical office right away, "We'll do our best, but this ain't no ambulance service."

The cab driver sounded exactly like the dispatcher, making me wonder if this were a one-man operation. Not until I'd pressed through the clinging air into the strange space of the back seat did I remember Jasper's car seat. But I was frightened and in a rush and knew that this driver wasn't going to enforce the car-seat law. In fact, he acted as if conveying a dilapidated pregnant woman and a hyper-verbal boy recapping hours of TV shows was pretty normal for him. "Please forgive me," I mouthed to an anonymous deity or legislator as I bound myself, my son, and my unborn baby all within the safety of my arms.

I overtipped the driver, incapable of waiting in the heat for my change. I'm sure that if he'd known in advance I'd be such a generous tipper, he would have behaved a little more kindly to me, perhaps opened the door and helped me up onto the curb or remarked on how cute my son was.

Margaret and Pat nearly jumped me as I entered the waiting room, where one placid woman stared ahead, a magazine in her lap. They hurried me into an exam room and then Pat spirited Jasper away with her cultish

235

voice. "Let's take a look," Margaret said, standing by attentively as I took off my underpants. First she applied her stethoscope to different places on my body and listened to my inner murmurings. Next her latex fingers probed inside of me, her face, meanwhile, betraying nothing of her findings. Finally Margaret rolled out the ultrasound machine and positioned it, I noticed, so the screen faced away from me. What irregularity did she expect to discover?

"Having some cramping, you said?"

"Cramping? No, I wouldn't call it that. It feels more like a gas pain. I just figured…" But I hadn't really thought it out.

Margaret breathed in enough air to supply her with oxygen for at least five minutes. She switched off the ultrasound machine and said, "I want to transfer you to the hospital."

"The hospital?" My due date was three weeks into the future, and though I knew that such predictions were far from exact, I didn't think that this change of plans was based on a miscalculation.

Margaret leaned out into the reception area and instructed Pat to call an ambulance.

"An ambulance?" I struggled against my front-end bulk to sit up. My heart was a bird I'd swallowed, its wings beating futilely inside my throat.

"Pauline, your baby isn't getting enough oxygen. We have to get in there."

"You mean—"

"We've got to deliver her right away."

Jasper incongruously laughed. He crouched just beyond the doorway, dangling a cloth clown by one arm. "This clown is so so happy," he squealed.

"What about Jasper?" I asked in a small voice coming from my most powerless self.

"He can ride along with you in the ambulance. I'll meet you at the hospital."

"Clifford!" I suddenly remembered.

"Pat will get a hold of him."

In a strobed sequence of movements, Margaret shut down the ultrasound and slid it away. I waited for her to switch the lights back on but then realized that they'd been on all along in the dreary cave that the room had become.

◆◆◆◆

Force of Nature

Clifford told me later that Pat had phoned the school and directed the administrative assistant to summon him from whatever meeting he was attending, books he was inventorying, or catalogue he was ordering from. He arrived at the hospital only a minute or two after me, just in time to receive Jasper—who assumed that the ambulance ride was a spectacle organized for him—in his arms. Either Pat had sufficiently briefed Clifford over the phone or he was too stunned to question me about what was happening.

"I love you!" he declared in plain hearing of every other waiting room pacer and the emergency staff as I was driven away on a gurney. But by then everyone around me—the attendants, Jasper—and everyone else in my life had receded until only my baby and I existed in the misty throb surrounding us. She, whom I had talked to, dreamed into being while she multiplied into a mass of cells. Now we were inside each other, close but far, an amplified breath, thunderous, whisper-soft.

"Stay with me," I breathed, and I thought I heard her say, "I'm here, Mama. I'm with you." But her voice was somehow unformed, as her body still must be, with gaps and scratches that made her sound so very old and knowing, as if perhaps she'd been born at least once before.

The shot of pitocin couldn't hurt me in my faraway fear. The cramps, though, that it gradually induced were horribly uncomfortable. Had labor tortured me so the first time? I was being sliced and folded, sliced and folded. "Stay with me, Mama," I almost heard.

Margaret, a hush among the drone of doctors, came over and touched me on the shoulder with a delicacy that registered even against a field of overbearing pain. "How are you doing?" she asked quietly, as if she didn't know.

I couldn't spare the effort of answering. "My baby…" I could get no further than those two constipated words.

"She's hanging in there."

A web of wires and tubes radiated out from my belly, the kind of equipment I couldn't dissociate from a medical tragedy. Which of us, though, was in peril, or was it both of us? Again I managed to speak the same phrase. "My baby…" Margaret said nothing, so I asked my question again with only my agonized eyes.

"Sweetheart," she said, "you've forgotten. This is what labor feels like. If you really can't handle it, you tell me

239

and one of the doctors will give you something."

Clifford reappeared in the room without Jasper. I was too possessed with worry and dread to ask where our son was. Just as Clifford arrived at my bedside, a killing contraction wracked me at my center, and I let out a howl from some primitive place within me.

"Pauline?" My husband seemed not to recognize me. Margaret urged him to help me up and then to lead me in laps around the room, unusually large for a hospital room and cluttered with excesses of equipment. Margaret explained to Clifford that the two birthing suites were always reserved well in advance and therefore unavailable in emergency situations.

"Emergency…" he repeated listlessly, and Margaret nodded.

"All right then, Woman, let's get walking," Clifford said to me as he prodded me in the back.

I seized his arm and twisted it cruelly, passing on the pain of another contraction that couldn't possibly have been caused by anyone as small as my girl. Deep inside me, she was on her heroic journey out of the safe soup of blood and love and water, into the fluorescent blare of light and the indifferent beeping of machines. Clifford was supporting my weight and urging me forward. But when I bent over with a piggish grunt, he looked to Margaret, ready to surrender me to her.

"They're coming pretty fast one after another," she said, as if I needed her to tell me that. "Let's get you back in bed for another check."

Getting me back in bed turned out to be an athletic feat for the two of them even as I yielded to their control. New-baby-girl went with me. "Mama's baby. Mama's girl." My endearments were interrupted by the savagery of more muscle clutch. Each scream, her shouts, were expressed in my muscles as she courageously plowed through the tunnel towards this awful, garish light.

The bright fluorescent bulbs and white linens on the bed coolly peaked in snow caps at my feet. "Into the stirrups," Margaret directed me, though she had to manually position my feet and insert my heels into the openings.

"Isn't this happening too fast?" Too fast, Clifford asked. And she, Margaret spread my legs farther apart, and with her gloved hand examined me and I could see her becoming quicker. She ordered the lights turned off then switched on a small lamp somewhere. Somewhere. Even daylight vanished from the windows.

"Remember your breathing," Clifford told me.

I felt the room split in two by my jagged scream.

Clifford peeked. "Her whole head is already out!"

But Margaret knew, and with her silken voice spoke to me and to the baby. She would not allow the beeping monitors to prevail over the peace and order we had planned.

Clifford was with the baby now, not with me. His eyes wouldn't leave her. "She's so small," he murmured. Is she too small? he asked I thought. As in one slippery stream she came shooting out of me. He was beaming, or no, upset. One of the nurses hustled the baby away to a table, where she was syringed clean and fitted with a skull cap. "What's her Apgar?" another nurse asked the one who was handling my girl. Two two two two. The curve of her cheek—all that I could see of her since she'd been swaddled in flannel—wasn't fair wasn't pink, but a stormy purple.

"Why aren't they bringing her over?" I said to Clifford, and as if she'd overheard my question, the nurse cradled our baby in her arms and brought her, small as a doll, to me.

Finally I thought to ask Clifford, "Where's Jasper?"

"Plan C."

We had no Plan C.

His co-worker, Phyllis, was on the job, which we'd known might happen. Our neighbor Reena was often unreachable. We'd meant to, in the last weeks before the birth, come up with a more reliable person to entrust Jasper to while we were at the hospital.

In answer to my unspoken question, Clifford said, "Phillip."

"Who the hell is Phillip?" I snapped.

"Our downstairs neighbor."

Our new baby shifted with the swell of rage that inflated my chest. "You left our son with that…big boy?"

"We gave him our house key."

"What does that have to do with it?"

The encircling nurses were fleeing from our marital

242

fray. Margaret, though, came closer, came right up to us and deftly took the baby away from me. Had I already been deemed a bad mother for my outbreak of temper?

"I have to take her now. She's slightly hypoxic, but I wanted to sneak a quick cuddle in there for you."

"Hypoxic?" Clifford and I asked in unison.

The baby had already been handed over to a swift nurse who was carrying her out of the room. A buzzing undertone that must have been audible all this time became suddenly loud and took over the room like a monster bee.

"Is she all right?" I asked Margaret, about to weep. My girl's off-color skin. Her tiny, tiny fingers. "Why is this happening?"

"It's not anything new. It's why she wasn't developing. We're going to hook her up to oxygen, sort of let her catch up."

Now the messy sobs overcame me. Clifford, even as he reached a strong arm around me, was less someone to lean on than a partner in misery.

Her birth was to have taken place in Margaret's office. I'd chosen the most soothing classical music to greet her. My parents, not quite back from a Caribbean getaway, were to have driven up and served as our domestic staff, relieving us of all of our roles except for mother and father. Summer was, sadly, to have been ending.

We hadn't finalized our choice of a name for the baby, and our short list was about twenty items long.

Still brimming with tears, I said through my nose, "Let's name her Sonia," the name we'd discarded when Jasper had turned out to be a boy.

"Sonia…huh." The name hadn't been one of our semi-semi-finalists, but I knew that Clifford wanted to stay clear of conflict and would probably agree, just then, to any name I suggested.

Then came another nurse, walking too briskly, sparks glinting in her eyes. She whispered a sibilant message to Margaret that we couldn't hear.

"What's going on?" Clifford asked anyone in the room.

Margaret marched over to us quietly on her rubbery soles and said, "Your baby had a seizure."

Simultaneously Clifford and I reached for each other and held on tight. As our little huddle began to quake, I realized that now Clifford was crying. What else to do but join him in that turbulent grief?

We asked, or didn't ask more questions, then or later. Time seemed a broken-down machine in need of repair. Together Clifford and I moved on to another hospital room, he on foot, I in a wheelchair, as if what had been lost in this drama was my ability to walk.

As soon as I'd been relocated in a bed, Clifford said to me, "Sonia is a nice name," pronouncing it with a generic international accent.

The phone on the table next to my bed rang. Dangerously, I feared. More bad news? But who knew yet of our ordeal, of the turn our lives had taken? The caller had to be someone as remote as a telemarketer.

"Don't answer it!" I warned as Clifford picked up the receiver.

"Yeah, thanks for calling. I don't know. There may be a problem..." This possibility, until formed into words, was near and looming but somehow abstract. "We're not sure. I don't know how much the doctors even know yet...Yeah...OK, thanks, Phyllis."

I'd forgotten about her. Of course she knew. Clifford had called her first, before he'd had to improvise the questionable Plan C. Right away, the phone rang again.

"Hi, Turtle...Yeah, thanks...I don't know yet. I appreciate the call, but Pauline is just getting settled in her room...No, it's OK...Thanks. Bye."

Turtle, the most popular teacher at Clifford's school, would have heard from Phyllis that we were in the hospital. We should call our parents, I thought, before they heard our news from someone else. They would want to know, to know that their grandchild had been born, that her birth was close to a month early, that she'd been deprived of adequate oxygen for who-knows-how-long, that she was encased in a medical tent now, watched over by mindless, heartless machines, that I was feeling responsible, that my body had erred, that I was apprehensive about how disabled she might be, about my ability to mother her, my resistance to love. Our parents would want to know how drastically our world had changed in just a few hours.

"Stop answering that phone!" I ordered Clifford.

He smiled. "She's really cute."

This man who belittled the bother of a flat tire, a bad job interview, a twenty-dollar bill misplaced…surely he wasn't going to apply that same optimism to the possible brain damage of our child. I would have attacked him with the worst words I knew if Margaret hadn't entered the room just then, harmonizing with the white, bright and blue hospital color scheme, a calmer version of pale, her presence the physical equivalent of her sedative voice. She dragged one of the visitor's chairs closer to the bed.

"So," she said, "let's talk about what just happened and what it all means."

We waited through her silence, figuring that right now she should be doing all the talking.

"Your daughter wasn't growing as much as we'd want her to. I told you that, Pauline, when I started noticing it last month. Why does a baby in utero not grow?"

Clifford started to attempt an answer. "I imagine if she's not—" but Margaret interrupted him, apparently not having expected us to actually respond.

"Not enough nutrients, not enough oxygen…"

Inwardly I groaned since delivery of these essentials had been up to me.

Then, to me, "There's no blame to be assigned here. You ate well, you rested, you exercised."

"But what about those months when I couldn't keep anything down?"

Margaret waved away this concern with one ethereal hand. "Not a big deal. Look how your boy turned out after the same kind of start."

"So, will she be OK?" Clifford asked.

Margaret breathed in the longest, deepest inhalation I'd ever witnessed, a reverse sigh. "I don't know, Clifford. The fact that she was born hypoxic along with a seizure right away makes me pretty sure that there's some CP."

"CP?" we both asked at once.

"Cerebral palsy—"

"She won't be able to walk or talk?" My hard-beating heart had expanded and was crowding up into my head.

"Pauline, let's not rush to any conclusions. We can't say yet how much brain damage she may have suffered."

"Brain damage!" Clifford, already the protective father, reacted as if to an insult or a slur against her character.

"Can't you take a picture of her brain?" I wanted to know.

"We could. But that won't really tell us what we want to know. Listen, you two…" She placed one of her hands translucently on one of each of ours. "This isn't a progressive condition. It won't get any worse. You're just going to have to take it day by day, month by month, and get a feel for what your daughter's limitations may be."

"Sonia," I said. Then, "That's her name. Sonia."

"It's beautiful. But what happened to…Celeste, was it?"

What had happened to the classical music and the pink light bulbs, to the nearness of family, a future in

247

which my flawless children moved fluidly through all the phases of their ordinary lives? What had happened to the smooth ride over what I now understood was, in fact, treacherous territory? Sooner or later we'd all hit a bump or career out of a pothole.

Fortunately Clifford would be at home for the next several weeks. It seemed to require both of us to pick Sonia up out of her bed, to sponge bathe her sometimes gnarled body, and certainly to change her diaper. We handled her as cautiously as if she were a breakable piece of pottery or a lovely mushroom prone to crumble. At the same time, we were scrutinizing her for signs of abnormality. Time and time again I interpreted her startle reflex—that exaggerated movement typical of infants—as a spasm. Clifford was more inclined to assume the best unless bullied towards a gloomier outlook. I peered into her eyes and through to her deepest being. My dear girl, the victim of biologic circumstance.

"You're lucky. It's as mild as they come," our pediatrician told us. We didn't feel at all lucky, though. Sonia's disability was beginning to resolve into a slight but noticeable curling and stiffening of her limbs and savage sounding cries that she released only after a visible effort. We were to watch her for seizures, as if I could distinguish those normal, arrhythmic baby flailings from signs of a malfunctioning brain.

Meanwhile Jasper was existing in an unsupervised wrinkle in our routine. Sometimes he seemed ecstatic with his unprecedented freedom and would spin through the apartment like a dervish, seeming to possess four arms and as many legs. Once we found him out on the first-floor porch. When Clifford asked him how long he'd been there, Jasper answered with a haphazard sense of time characteristic of his age. "Two days, I think."

Other times he'd tail us, grabbing and whimpering, obviously feeling deserted and envious of his little, slightly disfigured sister, the culprit who had masterminded the takeover of his home. So for a while, he'd put all of his projects aside, including his recurrent schemes to open every mystery box in the closets, to flip every switch. Even when Sonia slept, her primary pastime, Clifford and I were worn out from the last interval of hyper-concerned parenting and trying to work up the stamina needed to deal with the next.

"Play with *me*!" Jasper would say.

I tried to explain to him that his sister was sick but only succeeded in frightening myself. Jasper clearly disbelieved me, and my increasingly graphic explanations made it impossible for me to deny her condition.

But like most babies, Sonia had superbly soft skin and a purity of heart. I asked Clifford, "Do you think she's in pain or suffering in any way?"

His lips extruded during a moment of thought. "Nah. She looks pretty happy to me." And certainly she was getting more attention and love than most newborns. She could trust that when she hollered out of hunger, she'd be nursed; her lover's gaze into my eyes never wandered. When she was sleeping, one irregular breath broadcast through the monitor brought Clifford and me racing to make sure she was all right.

One afternoon, a miserably humid afternoon, I sat on the couch in serene union with Sonia as she nursed. The boys had gone out on "an adventure," as Clifford deceptively described the series of errands they were running. Sonia's small, unthreatening fist was beating against my chest above the breast. A spill of milk welled out of her mouth as she stopped sucking to gurgle at me. I bent my neck and gave her a full-lipped kiss on her forehead. And then it happened. A swell of affection, like a voyage beyond the gravitational field of normal emotions, and suddenly I loved this daughter of mine, loved her thoroughly and without reservation, loved her not because I felt badly for her, but just because she was who she was. She was Sonia, my child, and I loved her simply for that.

After that transformative moment, her care became less fraught with worry and guilt for me. I even began to coach Clifford. "She'll be fine, with or without the blanket."

He glared at me as if I were a criminally unfit mother.

"No, really," I promised. And when her head flung backwards as he was burping her, "It's OK. Just remember that babies' neck muscles aren't very strong."

Finally I could afford to renew my relationship with Jasper, who seemed extraordinarily big to me now, "not a big boy, but not a little boy anymore," as I told him.

He'd become suddenly rough—a two-fisted puncher, a twist-pincher—but I suspected that this aggression was more related to his wish to control our family politics than to his age or nature. He'd disguise his bruising intentions towards his sister by squeezing her too hard when he hugged her or by pounding her dropped rattle back into her possession, almost always making her cry from the blunt force into her tummy.

Since Clifford was around, we'd all four make the trip to the different doctors involved in Sonia's care. Margaret was mostly out of the picture now that I'd had my post-delivery checkup. Instead of her, a team of white-coated doctors hovered about Sonia every two weeks, at first, until our appointments were distributed among the lot of them. Usually now, when we went to the neurologist's office at the hospital, a resident examined Sonia, and afterwards Dr. Trahan himself would give her a cursory exam but rely on his protégé's notes to answer our many questions. His more expert exams, though, confirmed that already muscle tightness was evident in Sonia's limbs, and some degree of spasms.

"What about some kind of brace?" Clifford asked. "Would that help straighten her out?"

Neither he nor I had dared to do much research on Sonia's condition, especially since we hadn't yet received a hard-edged diagnosis. So I wondered whether his idea of braces was based on medical reality or just an outlandish layman's fancy.

"It's too soon to think about anything like that," the

doctor told us.

Clifford persisted. "But isn't she more...plastic now?"

"Remember, it's not that her bones are misshapen. Her muscles are tight, stiff, and prone to spasms. Braces or splints, when used, help to counteract some of the muscle rigidity."

During our consultation with Dr. Trahan, Jasper journeyed around the small room, tried to scale anything climbable, meanwhile chattering to us, to himself, an exemplary child-in-motion in contrast to his sister, small and taut on the vast flatness of the examination table. The intern had asked, "Has she rolled over at all?" and I remembered Jasper's triumph when he had flipped himself over, the first step in his conquest of matter and energy.

"Is she suffering?" I blurted out. Clifford pulled me, the tormented mother, into an embrace.

Dr. Trahan seemed confused. "Suffering? I don't suppose so," he said as if no one had ever asked him this before. As if he'd never pondered the question anywhere in his human heart or mind. "Is she raising her head?"

"She *is!*" Clifford reported hopefully.

Dr. Trahan added to the half page of notes that documented that day's visit. Maybe we should find another doctor, one who wasn't limited to discussions about symptoms and behaviors.

"Can I have my sticker now?" Jasper asked, used to doctors' visits concluding with happy stickers that he'd apply to his car seat on the way home. But we ignored him, ignored his plea. "I want to *go* now!"

I was wrapping Sonia back up in the white receiving blanket with gay blue buds printed cheerily across the flannel. Outside the artificial chill of Dr. Trahan's practice, the morning already was unpleasantly hot. But I wanted my daughter to feel, in a very tangible way, that she was surrounded with love.

In keeping with our usual choreography, Clifford snatched Jasper and carried him out of the room. I followed with Sonia. On the way out, Clifford paused at the check-out counter, begging for stickers. The receptionist scrounged through her drawers and found a button and a loose stick of gum, which she offered to Jasper.

"No gum!" I said sternly.

"Of course not," she croaked, as if she'd only been joking.

Too exhausted to explain to Jasper that the neurologist wasn't accustomed to treating children in the same abundance as a pediatrician or even a dentist, I promised him that we'd buy some stickers. His relentless inquisition—"We buy stickers? We going to the toy store? When we buy stickers, Mama?"—continued all the way to the parking garage, on the thru-city highway, and then through local traffic until we got to what ever after that day was designated as "the sticker store."

Had anyone been watching us as we came out of the store with our precious purchase—three sheets of giddy, glitter-encrusted stickers—we would have been perceived as an average family out on a frivolous mission. What that observer wouldn't have been able to see was Sonia's limbs within the swaddling blanket, our increasing neglect of Jasper, the impending change in Clifford's schedule, my panic at this change, the lowering of the sky, encroachment of the city, and my aloneness, even in the midst of my beloved three.

◆◆◆◆

Natural Selection

Jasper was too young to realize that he'd been cheated of the advance buildup that we normally would have given him for his approaching birthday. Had Sonia been born closer to her due date, the two kids' birthdays would have been separated by less than two months. Now, however, they were perilously close, and probably Jasper was doomed always to have the second, anticlimactic family celebration. Certainly that first year, the occasion of his third birthday was obscured by Sonia's arrival and our panic about her health.

But our neglect may have worked in Jasper's favor. Even though his birthday hadn't been heralded with a day-by-day countdown or anything like plans for a party that would include the kid-acquaintances we had collected here and there, on the day before it I did buy every existing party accessory—bright plates and matching napkins, hats, pin the nose on the rocket, noisemakers, a birthday candle shaped like a three, and even party favors, though our guest list didn't extend beyond the four of us.

Jasper didn't actually grasp the concept of birthdays. What he did quickly figure out, though, was that the next day was to be a day dedicated to him, that we'd eat his favorite foods, play the games that he liked, and most importantly, acknowledge his existence. For several weeks he'd been viciously fighting for the attention of his parents: clawing at my skin, yanking Clifford's pant legs with disturbing strength. Now, unrelated to anything he'd done himself, he was suddenly to be lavished with more attention on one day than he'd received in total during recent weeks.

On Jasper's birthday, Clifford asked, "Do you think we should try explaining to him what's going on?"

"But I have. Once, anyway."

Then suddenly our son came crashing into Clifford's legs. Jasper wouldn't permit any conversation between Clifford and me, or any interactions that excluded him.

"I wonder how he'll feel about a group diaper change," Clifford said as he was being pummeled.

"You're right," I said. "He's probably expecting that today since it's his birthday. Sonia will have to go without nourishment and sanitation."

Unprepared, having no film for the camera, we couldn't document the occasion and later use the photos as evidence that we had, indeed, honored Jasper's birthday that year when I learned that being a parent wasn't a guarantee of happiness, that the pain of life's tribulations was, naturally, in proportion to the love at stake.

Every protective maternal urge I felt was thwarted by helplessness. At night, during that transit between wakefulness and sleep, I'd automatically replay the pregnancy, the stages of concern that Margaret had expressed, and of course the premature delivery, the dramatic birth. Whether I was seeking some possibility of control that I'd let go by or else justification for self-blame, I'd review, over and over, the timeline of the pregnancy and birth, as if I could have changed anything. As if now, discovering some such lost opportunity, I could reverse or revise the monumental history that had preceded this very moment. As much as I knew it was destructive to continually look back, I couldn't bear to look ahead.

Clifford would be starting back to work at the end of August, and his graduate classes began two weeks later. Because of all that had happened since he'd decided to get a degree, I thought that he'd reconsider this ambition, hoped that he would. Even were he to be home every night, I was overwhelmed by the prospect of those whole days without him, now with two kids, one of them soon to present me with trials that my previous experience as a parent hadn't prepared me for. But I couldn't ask Clifford to postpone his plans since, after all, I still believed that our conversation over chicken about advancement and promotion in the schools had driven him to sacrifice himself. Clifford didn't really want to become a student again; he was trying to be a dutiful husband and father.

"I'm going to miss you around here," was the closest I could come to begging him to drop out of the graduate program before it had even begun.

"And I'm going to miss all of you," he said, gently tugging on Sonia's big toe and activating an elastic spasm of her leg muscles. "Oh! Sorry," he told Sonia, or maybe me. I strained to detect a deeper regret implied by his words—an apology that he was forsaking me at this crucial time, and maybe, I thought, he was even suggesting a broader sorrow for the continual sadness we would now have to endure. A whole childhood marked by limitations and exclusions, the stares at her mangled speech, her labored movement, the teasing. I would much rather have been the victim myself of such meanness than have my own child troubled by it.

Then Clifford swiveled on his sit-bones and directly faced me and aligned his gaze with mine. "Pauline, how 'bout we put the little guy in daycare? We were talking about doing that before…before Sonia was born."

I shook my head side to side. "Yes, but that was because I was going to go back to work."

"Well, but isn't this"—his gesture vaguely encompassed the living room and both kids—"just as good a reason to go ahead with the arrangement?"

"Except that, if I'm not working, how can we afford it?" I asked.

As always, I was conscious of the white noise of anger in the background. Someone else, perhaps, would have thanked such an indulgent spouse, one ready to put the mental health of his wife before budgetary problems. I, however, resented Clifford's easy reorganization of priorities, leaving me to be the sensible one, burdened by how to balance our increasing expenses with a single salary that had increased only by a negligible cost-of-living raise. I imagined that he was thinking ahead to the fabulous riches that would come our way once he was a public-school principal.

The first to go were the meals that elevated us above hunting-and-gathering status. Diverting Jasper long enough to chop an onion now was as challenging as napping. Having both him and Sonia accounted for at the same time was such a rare achievement that I didn't want to waste it on petty meal prep. No, if Jasper was enthralled by his educational TV friends and Sonia was dozing, I fit myself into the corner embrace of the couch and slept. Baths were a pleasure that I saved for nighttime, when I'd fall asleep in a froth of lather, my head surrounded with clouds of steam.

Cooking for Jasper was manageable, especially since he liked the most uncomplicated dishes—nothing with multiple ingredients or even sauces or anything that involved much preparation. Plain noodles with butter. Boiled chicken. Peanut butter on bread. Cherry tomatoes. Slices of apple. My own diet had changed considerably. I'd become a snacker—crackers and cheese, nuts and raisins, yogurt. All healthy choices, I told myself, but in such small quantities they never satisfied my appetite. My snacking became more frequent and the sizes of the servings grew until I was constantly eating. Remnant baby fat at first camouflaged my gradual weight gain. The only eating I did all day that resembled a meal was in the evening, when both Jasper and Sonia were in bed. I'd resorted to canned and frozen foods. Sometimes I ate baked beans right out of the can, bypassing any dishes that would need to be washed.

Clifford would have to fend for himself on those nights when he came home late, usually all four nights during the week since he had classes on two and claimed that he'd never get his course work done at home on the other two.

As his semester went by, he came home increasingly later. Often I'd be semi-conscious when he arrived and greet him from somewhere in my delirium. While he was supercharged by trends in educational philosophy and debate on the topic with his peers, I was switched off, unwired, and good only for my parts. Maybe if I'd been in a nightgown and in bed, Clifford would have recognized my fatigue and readiness for sleep.

On weekends he reserved some time to himself to work on his assignments. One Saturday I handed him a few photos I'd taken of the kids that week.

"I took these," I told him, "to keep you up to date on what they look like."

When I saw Clifford's mad eyes, I tried to soften my sarcasm by saying, "You know how quickly kids change when they're this young."

"Look, I know this is hard on you, but I'm doing it for all of us. Don't you think I'd rather be home with my family than out grinding my brain?"

I didn't answer. But Sonia crowed at the deep bottom of her range.

"Fix this," Jasper ordered, slamming a plastic dinosaur with moving legs into Clifford's lap. Perhaps I let myself be swayed by my imagination, but I sensed that the kids were on my side. All three of us were feeling forsaken.

"What are you doing for lunch these days?" I suddenly asked, thinking that we rarely had the makings for a sandwich or any leftovers from our lowly dinners.

"Don't worry about me," Clifford said, his eyes leaping away from contact with mine.

"I'm *not* worrying. But I'd like to know."

Clifford stood, crossing to the dining room window. I could still see him, his back towards me, Jasper's broken toy dangling from his hand, but he was beyond the reach of my wrath when he answered, "I've been buying a bite to eat most days."

"At the school cafeteria?"

"Oh no. I don't eat till dinnertime usually." He turned to face me, as if this information could possibly mollify me. "You know Frank's Fine Food?"

"Near Inman Square?"

"That's the place!" he said excitedly, as if we'd just scored in a game show.

"But that's so close to here. You might as well come home to eat and save us some money."

He paced back into the living room with the authority of a trial lawyer. "Oh? And exactly what would I eat here?"

"Same as I do."

"Cereal? Canned ravioli?"

Jasper's eyes became neon-bright, and his smile shined. "I want rabioles!" he said. If he wasn't feeling endangered by the electricity coursing between his father and me, his sister was. In her infant seat down on the floor, out of the range of fire, Sonia squawked and then began to cry.

In one efficient motion, I rose from the couch where I'd been slumped among the softness of the weary cushions. "Well how 'bout this? How 'bout you not only come home to eat, how 'bout you stop on the way and buy some groceries?"

Sonia was howling with feral abandon.

"What are you saying? That I don't do enough? That working all day and going to classes and studying in my spare time is too easy? Do I have to start doing your share of the work, too?"

I was engorged with rage. Both my hands were fisted into fingery rocks. I was breathing no more deeply than my throat. My air pipes and blood vessels were constricted with tension, a huge pulse thumping in my chest.

"Rabioles, *please*," said Jasper, believing that the

magic word would always get him what he wanted.

I shut my eyes, inhaled expansively, and listened to the din of the fury in me. As my breathing deepened, a slow, sedative wave of oxygenated calm circulated through me. When I felt ready to open my eyes again, I saw that the scene had been rearranged: Clifford was standing at the open front doorway holding Sonia, his mouth pressed against her delicate ear. Jasper, in the kitchen, was almost out of sight except for his lower legs, poised on tippytoes atop a stepstool.

I sped to rescue him from a likely accident, grabbing him in my arms. He looked at me. "Rabioles. Mama, I'm hungry."

That night, hardened against the approaching moon hour when I'd have to share a bed with Clifford, I performed all of my nighttime rituals earlier than usual, hoping I'd beat him to the sheets and be asleep when he joined me. Our conversation for the rest of that day had been sparse and neutral. We used Jasper and Sonia as buffers, over-responding to their least utterances, initiating games and story times. Mostly I was coupled with Jasper, and Clifford with Sonia. Doing much trading of partners would have required more communication. Of course he had to pass the baby along to me so she could nurse, and when she was through, each time, I'd either settled her into her bed for a nap or strapped her into her padded throne that rested on the floor. Clifford, when he chose, could pick her up again.

I was still awake when he climbed onto the mattress

and knee-walked in from the edge. But I was facing away from him and could pretend to be asleep by elongating each of my breaths, controlling the rise and fall of my body. The rattling window fan, stationed on a desk chair at the foot of our bed and aimed more at me than at Clifford, spared me the need to produce convincing sound effects.

Clifford bounced on the bed a few times and then, with both hands, rolled me towards him. He either doubted that I was asleep or had decided to brave my anger if he was waking me. "Pauline, let's talk."

I posed as a beached sea nymph, sprawled across the bed with limp limbs and sodden desire. But Clifford wasn't fooled by my unresponsiveness.

"C'mon. This is important."

He was right. And so I gave in to his plea, sat up and became all at once functional. I didn't, though, speak, since Clifford's urgency had suggested he had something to say.

"It's true, I've been so caught up in my own day-to-day that I haven't really noticed that you're…" He was being cautious about his word choice. "I realize that you're treading water. It's too much, with the baby's needs and all."

We hadn't actually established yet just what Sonia needed, or even the severity of her condition. But I didn't correct Clifford, didn't subject him to my red-pencil editing.

"So…even though money's a little tight right now, I

say we put Jasper into nursery school. Maybe just for a couple of mornings a week, anyway."

Suddenly the thought of my son, my firstborn, forfeited to paid workers while I dedicated myself to his sister, displaced my heart to a rancid, dark corner where it had never been.

"I don't know, Cliff."

"It's just for now. Once I'm out of school, I'll be able to earn more money, and eventually you'll be back to work. In the long haul, we'll be fine."

A pesky sty was ripening on the rim of one of his eyes. I couldn't stop staring at it. "I'm not even thinking about the money." I was thinking about the small, glistening growth. "It just doesn't feel right."

He flipped my ponytail behind my shoulder, and he said, "Think of it this way. When he *is* with you, then you'll have more to give him. You won't be so wiped out."

People often told me that I'd make a good lawyer because of my relentless aptitude for logic and my willingness to apply it. But Clifford, more than I, was a master at rationalizing anything. I felt myself yielding to his perspective. He seized the silence and cluttered it with as many more reasons as he could think of to let our little boy undergo the process of socialization much earlier than we'd planned.

Without more nudging from him, the next day I called every daycare center I'd heard mentioned by mothers I'd met in passing. All of those and more, with cutesy, clever names, taken at random from the phone book. Most every place I called had a waiting list that extended into the next decade. Of those that didn't, none could accommodate a part-time child. Jasper would either have to enroll for the full-week program or not at all, I was told firmly by a voice representing the Cedar Center for Children.

"I guess I could pay for all five days but only send him for three," I mused out loud.

"We wouldn't want that," the voice retorted. "It throws off the group dynamics."

Still, I scheduled a visit to the center. If the place turned out to be unacceptable, I had few alternatives, all located at the end of long, highly trafficked commutes. The Cedar Center was my best hope, for sure, so I tried not to think too much about why they had vacancies.

"Who's going to *school*?" I asked my boy again. Ever since he'd received the news about daycare with such gusto, I loved baiting him with this question and his ever-fresh answer, "I am!" And I'd assumed that if he could, he would have remained with me in the small vessel of our home forever.

As I drove sadly to the Cedar Center, my ecstatic son and sleeping daughter in the back seat, I speculated about the center's name. Was it set amidst a grove of cedar trees? Or constructed out of cedar wood, maybe? To pay for such a high-end building material, the tuition would have to be steep. Already my dream of owning our own home where I'd never again have to dread a landlord's unexpected knock on the door was quickly vaporizing.

In fact, the Cedar Center for Children, with its boarding-school name, resembled a shanty more than a pre-school. The distracting colors of paint covering every bit of surface might have served less to entice the kids than to stall the final decay of the wood. About half of the exterior seemed to be fashioned out of plywood, its hefty grain showing through even the thick frosting of friendly hues.

"Hello, welcome." Not the voice on the phone. "I'm Sarah Cedar. And you must be Pauline Black."

"I am. And this is—"

"Jasper, of course." Sarah Cedar indicated no curiosity about Sonia, who therefore remained unintroduced even though she might be a future student.

Who would name a daycare center after herself? I wondered. Of course, Sarah may have named it after a benevolent old grandfather, or her parents may have invested in the business and named it for her, possibly despite her humble protests.

"Jasper, should we go see some of the kids?"

My son's head waggled in agreement. I wasn't sure if Sarah wanted me to join them or was encouraging his independence. "Should I...?"

She must not have heard me as she led Jasper by one hand to the classroom. Sonia stirred in my arms but returned to sleep. Soon I decided that unless I, too, visited the classroom, I wouldn't be able to decide if this place was worthy of my son. So I intuited the way to the room where they'd disappeared, and just as I turned into a corridor plastered with children's artwork, Sarah was, rather briskly, I thought, escorting Jasper ahead of her out into the hall. Immediately she spotted me.

Apparently Jasper had boasted to her of the new velcro-tabbed wrap worn over his cloth diapers. "Didn't Raquel tell you? All of our students must be potty-trained."

Jasper had shown no interest in becoming the "big boy" he was promised he'd be if he learned how to use the toilet. He was downright opposed to the idea, in fact.

"Oh. I don't think Jasper's ready for that."

Sarah Cedar shook her head and half-closed her eyes. "Ma'am, it's never the child who is ready. It's the parent."

I decided not to delve into this topic that surely could never be resolved. Instead I exited with my children and drove on to Kid City, a daycare center with no waiting list though slightly farther from our part of town.

"I wanna go to school," Jasper said ferociously, banging his head against the padded seat back.

"We *are* going to school. Just a different one."

Considering that we showed up without an appointment, the director of Kid City was abundantly gracious and welcoming. She put aside the forms on her desk and invited me to sit.

Right away I asked, "Do you accept boys who wear diapers?"

Jasper buried his face into as much of my lap as

wasn't taken up by Sonia. Given that he'd rejected every opportunity to outgrow the use of diapers, I couldn't imagine why he would feel publicly disgraced. The director, Courtney James, opened a drawer and peeked into a folder then told me, "Yes, we do." I waited for elaboration but concluded that since she hadn't seemed familiar with the policy, she wasn't going to explain the philosophy underlying it.

"Jasper, would you like to meet some of the kids and see the classroom?"

He revealed himself again and, already recovered from his shame, took Courtney's hand and walked with her out of the office.

I counted only about six children in the room. While I understood that small classes meant less competition for the teacher's attention, I wanted to know why most places were full to capacity and Kid City resembled London after the plague. Jasper was quickly drawn into the circle of children listening to the teacher read. He loved being read to. No doubt he would now think of school as a very long storytelling session.

"Should we leave him here and go talk?" Courtney asked me in her quiet voice.

As we left the classroom, a toddler girl was being delivered by a tall man with a beautiful face—high cheekbones, square jaw, and eyes that, though they were brown, suggested undertones of amber and the deep blood-color of a garnet. He was carrying a brown briefcase made of leather. He nodded at me, and I very well may have swooned with Sonia in my arms.

Why are there so few children here? Why is there no waiting list? Why did you have to look up the policy on diaper-wearing? Who was that handsome man? These were the questions that were forming in my mind but that I didn't ask. Because what if the answers were unsatisfactory? What recourse did I have? And after all, I'd observed the class myself, toured the center, read the one-color brochure that Courtney offered me. Last of all, I couldn't imagine that a man as classy as the one I'd not-quite met would have entrusted his daughter (was it his daughter?) to the care of a place with an incompetent staff or an unsafe facility.

Jasper would begin attending the next week. The poor boy must have been baffled by the intensity of our contact during his last full days at home. I felt as if he were going off to war, a farewell melancholy flavoring each "last": the last weekday lunch of grilled cheese, the last nap in his own crib, the last outbreak of boredom. If this passage was so pungently painful for me, how would I tolerate his first day of kindergarten, his graduation from high school, and ultimately his walk out the front door to the street, his wave good-bye to his mournful mother?

He took full advantage of my sudden devotion. "Read!" he directed, bringing me the pamphlet I'd gotten at the museum in Los Alamos on our honeymoon. Jasper had pulled it from the pile of my memorabilia waiting to be preserved in a scrapbook.

The pamphlet contained little text. After reading the museum address and hours, I improvised a description of the work conducted at the labs during the war and of the secret town up on the mesa. That night, Jasper requested that the pamphlet be read for his bedtime story.

"I don't want to go to school," he said when he woke up in the morning. And why should he when he'd been subsumed by his mother for days, even on the weekend, his father lurking off to the side? Meanwhile my insides were being corroded by acid anxiety.

Clifford asked if I'd like him to go with us on Jasper's first morning at school. "I could use a personal day," he said. He then continued to collect his teaching materials for the next day and his notebooks for the evening.

"We'll be fine."

Somehow the impending separation had become so intensely personal that I didn't want anyone else present at the event except for Sonia, of course, who would probably sleep through the whole wretched goodbye even as she clenched and uncoiled.

"Who's going to school?" I asked Jasper one last time en route to Kid City.

"Mama, I don't want to go to school," he told me again, and though I longed for him to choose me over his first social institution, his resistance would make this parting much more difficult for me. I couldn't carry him and Sonia both, but I did hold onto his hand extra tight as I escorted him straight to his classroom. He was cupping his crotch, I noticed.

"Jasper, do you have to go to the bathroom?"

"My diaper, Mama. No diapers at school."

I crouched down to meet him eye to eye. "Sweetheart, at this school you can wear diapers." He didn't look convinced, his forehead puckered in premature folds. "Honest," I said.

"I want to use the potty."

"All right. When you get home."

I'd purposely come early so that Jasper wouldn't feel like an add-on. After he'd inspected the toys and art supplies for ten minutes, accompanied by the reassuring commentary of the lead teacher, Rosemary, other kids began to arrive. I'd seen their names printed above their coat hooks—Damon, Thor, Lovely, Greta—a very nontraditional roster until plain-named Katie arrived with her father, Steve, the handsome man whose face I'd admired during my first visit.

At least he went by the less conventional spelling of his name, "Stephen," I learned when he gave me his business card. "Keep me in mind if you decide to buy or sell property." We'd barely introduced ourselves before he began promoting his professional services to me. Either he was a very aggressive real-estate agent or he was using his job as a ploy to talk with me. I'd always thought of real estate agents as people who hadn't found a niche anywhere else and finally gave up and took the real estate test. But Stephen had the demeanor of a man who'd attended an ivy-league college and had straightaway proceeded into the field of real estate with the same determination that landed some people in medical school to fulfill their lifelong dreams.

"Actually, I just might be in the market soon," I said, hoping that I'd conveyed some ambiguity about my living situation and even marital status, all this within close earshot of my youngest, who was nestled right up against my heartbeat.

Steve wasn't wearing a wedding ring. The woman—of a racial blend I couldn't identify—who picked up Katie that afternoon wasn't wearing one either.

"Hi, are you Katie's mom? I'm Pauline, Jasper's mother," I said, beaming a smile at her. For a brand-new parent at the school, I was behaving rather aggressively.

"No no no," the woman answered with an accent that was equally hard to identify. "I am not her mother. I am the family housekeeper." She spoke with exaggerated slowness as if to compensate for her accent.

Who was I to care whether or not Steve was married when I was married myself? And what was I thinking of, anyway? Any man who had the qualities that I cherished in Clifford—consideration, kindness, humor—would have seemed like the ultimate catch to me. I knew that I would never behave in a way that would jeopardize my marriage.

Still, I could shop around for houses even if I wasn't seriously in the market for one.

◆◆◆◆

Infidelity

The circuitry of hearsay and rumor passed through Berkeley, Washington, and the little town of Los Alamos high up on a mesa. When in California on business, Oppenheimer might hear a different interpretation of the latest tattle that he'd heard back at the lab. Such variations—who'd meant what, or where first contact was reported—were of no consequence to him when they related to personal alliances or career promotions.

But this time, a more official form of gossip caught his ear and contradicted his understanding of human character. No, Rossi Lomanitz could not have continued to be politically active after joining the Radiation Lab at Berkeley. The young man had promised Oppie that, once attached to the Manhattan Project, he'd cease his association with the Communist Party.

Not so, Lieutenant Colonel Lansdale informed Oppenheimer. Lomanitz had committed a certain "indiscretion," which the colonel refused to specify. "Just believe me. It's true," he said. Oppenheimer distrusted the intelligence that had led Lansdale to this conclusion at the same time he mourned a betrayal by his protégé.

"Can't be. We had a pact, which you're saying he disregarded."

"Fact is fact," Lansdale retorted.

Oppenheimer himself was being watched despite the security clearance he'd finally—and with reluctance—been granted. "Here or elsewhere, we'll be following you," warned Pash and Nichols and every other Army patriarch who'd opposed his controversial appointment. At home, Kitty attributed every shadow without a source, every night sound that she couldn't name to the constant surveillance her husband was subject to. As always when she was distraught, Oppie tried to calm her.

"Do you not believe we're being spied on, or do you just not care?" she asked.

He sat down beside her on the bed. "Oh, I believe it. And yes, I care."

So why wasn't he pacing nervously, why wasn't he swiping aside the curtains to catch someone in the act? His wife could see only so far into his heart and mind; sometimes she felt she hardly knew him. Now, as she fiddled with the coverlet over the sheets, she asked herself, What really had happened to that man, the Communist sympathizer, attender of meetings, faculty union activist? Kitty knew her husband well enough to know that he didn't support fads—in fashion or in poli-

275

tics—and that he had to still believe in the socialist principles that he had once upheld.

"I've practically wrapped myself in the damned flag. Those lions need a goat."

*　　　*　　　*

General Groves would later remember that the meeting had occurred in August, 1943. The date, though, he wasn't sure of; he doubted that it mattered. Oppenheimer had requested an appointment with him but was unwilling to disclose in advance what he meant to discuss. "Take your hat off," Groves wanted to say when Oppenheimer entered the general's office. Still, after all the negotiating and haggling between the two men over matters of policy and protocol, the wearing of the porkpie hat peeved Groves more than anything else about his top man. None of the general's tactics thus far had been effective in training Oppenheimer to remove his hat when he came inside. His latest method was to pointedly remove his own hat in greeting when Oppenheimer appeared. First, though, he had to be sure that the hat was on his head since his habit was to lay it on his desk and put it back on whenever he left the room, torn between the etiquette of hats-off-indoors and the wholeness of his uniform.

Groves had never seen Dr. Oppenheimer as serious as he now appeared. He didn't even smoke one cigarette during their brief meeting.

"General, I want to make you aware of a certain fellow. I know he was involved in organizing at FAECT—"

"What's that?"

"Federation of Architects, Engineers, Chemists, and Technicians," Oppenheimer recited, then explained, "The professional union over at Berkeley. He has ties to the party, too."

"The—"

"Communist Party. He's an engineer at Shell. British fellow. Known Russian sympathizer. Not long ago—" Oppenheimer was deliberately vague about the timing since he hadn't reported the incident sooner—"he was trawling around for a go-between to transmit information about...the gadget...to the Russians."

General Groves didn't want to know any more precisely when this transgression had occurred. He was satisfied that Oppenheimer had reported the incident at all, thus bolstering his own defense of his administrator—indispensable by then—against the insistence of others that he was a security risk.

Groves asked the name of this man.

"Ellenton," Oppenheimer told him.

The general fiddled with a sheet of paper, and Oppenheimer recalled Kitty similarly fingering the coverlet on their bed. Groves for a moment seemed almost dreamy. The two men then, with an unspoken consensus, proceeded on to another topic of discussion, an issue related to the restructuring of two of the divisions.

Later that same August while in Berkeley on business, Oppenheimer visited the office of Lieutenant Lyall Johnson, head security officer for the Rad Lab. Here again, he offered up a confession of what he knew about Ellenton, suggesting that this active Soviet-sympathizer be watched. What Oppenheimer didn't tell either Johnson or Groves was that he himself, in fact, had received a message from Ellenton earlier that year via his close friend Haakon Chevalier. He may have hinted to Johnson about this communication—someone sometime somewhere. Then Oppenheimer steered the discussion back to the subject of Lomanitz and what the young man's indiscretions that so concerned the government may or may not have been.

"Come on, Lieutenant. Union organizing isn't exactly subversive activity." In a glance, he took in the mess evident in Johnson's office. "A little organizing might benefit you, if I may say so."

Lieutenant Johnson's eyes suddenly became big and explosive, resembling the expansion of energy in two small bombs inside his head. Unfortunately Oppenheimer, whose intention had been to fish for clues about what the government had against Lomanitz, had so provoked Johnson with his joke that their discussion jumped onto a very different track.

"Oppenheimer, there are some of us who've been against your appointment from the start!" Johnson shouted. Not a very menacing threat, he realized too late, since obviously he and his likeminded colleagues had been overruled. "We've got our eyes on you. There's nothing in the books that says even someone in top management can't be removed."

Oppenheimer frisked his upper body and found his cigarettes—never in the same place twice—in the inside pocket of his sports jacket. He quickly lit one and only then asked Johnson, "Mind if I smoke?"

As soon as Oppenheimer left Johnson's office, the lieutenant was on the phone with his boss, Colonel Pash, who told him to get Oppenheimer back there the next day. Pash was sitting with Johnson in the office when Oppie returned in the morning. An invisible ear listened to the interview, a microphone concealed inside the telephone and attached to a recorder in the next room.

"Cigarette?" Oppenheimer offered from his flattened pack as if he were the host here. Both men refused. The glint of metal adornments on their shirts matched the flash in their eyes.

"Tell me again," Johnson began, "about this Ellenton."

"He's an engineer with the Shell Company."

"That's not what I want to know," Johnson said.

But Pash, in his most unctuous manner, intervened. "Of course, Dr. Oppenheimer, we appreciate your time. And we are most impressed with how you've been running things out there," as if the Manhattan Project were so secretive that he didn't dare refer to it by name. "I'm here to protect you and the project."

Where is the air here? Oppenheimer asked himself. He snuffed out his cigarette and drew in lungfuls of oxygen, then began to cough. "Yes, Colonel, that I know. If I hesitate, it's because I'm trying to sort out the significant from the trivial. I don't want to waste your time with too much detail."

Pash's smile seemed to pain him. "Doctor Oppenheimer, you just tell us everything, and we'll sort out whether it's trivial or not."

"To start with," Johnson barged in, "do you know of any contacts attempted by this Ellenton?"

Oppenheimer realized that this interview was not going to be about Lomanitz at all. Unprepared, he bumbled with some words before saying, "I can tell you that I heard of some approaches."

Johnson: "Who was approached?"

Pash: "Who told you of these?"

Oppenheimer considered both questions and chose to ignore Pash's, rather than Johnson's, question. "I can't remember who or how many were approached. And I can't say for a fact that anyone was approached."

"Who did you hear of this from?"

Haakon Chevalier was one of his closest friends. Oppenheimer would never divulge his name, at least not in these circumstances, faced with two inquisitors eager for both men's downfall. Oppenheimer tried to recall whether, when Chevalier had told him of Ellenton's proposition, he'd even thought of mentioning it to someone not likely to interpret it in the worst possible way, someone like Groves. Now his failure to do so would no doubt be mistaken as an act of withholding, a form of deceit.

So while he still wouldn't say who had broached the idea of collusion with the Soviets those months ago in his Eagle Drive home, he now told them about the incident—that is, as best he could remember. At the time, that evening's exchange had seemed of little importance. He was as likely to remember how many martinis he'd mixed for his guests as the order of events or a verbatim transcript of who had said what.

They had been munching on chips (or had it been pretzels?). The women—Kitty and Barbara Chevalier (there had been no others, he was nearly certain)—had remained in the living room when Oppie went into the kitchen to mix more martinis since the drinks were dwindling (or was that the first round produced for his guests?). Haakon followed his friend into the kitchen, and there, while Oppie shook the gin with chunks of ice and emptied it into the martini glasses at just the right moment—cold enough, but not yet diluted (of this particular, Oppie could be sure)—Haakon told him about a conversation he'd had with George Ellenton, no better than an acquaintance of both Oppie's and his. Ellenton, speaking on behalf of a certain diplomat, had inquired about Oppie's willingness to pass on scientific information to this Soviet diplomat at the consulate in San Francisco.

Oppie had answered Haakon, "That would be (is) treason! (I refuse)," maybe even evincing anger that his friend (or George Ellenton, whom he barely knew) would expect cooperation from him in such a subversive matter.

Just a tinge of vermouth.

Haakon, who Oppie referred to throughout the narrative as "this man," hadn't pressed further (though he may have revealed that two others were being asked for the same form of cooperation). The drinks were cold, were strong, froze the bones and dulled the brain. Neither of the men referred to this part of their conversation again (even if, inwardly, Oppie kept hearing the audacious question and experiencing a recurrence of righteous outrage).

Eventually, when all four of them present that night were questioned—Oppie, Chevalier, and the wives—the discrepancies in their accounts of what had occurred aroused the distrust of their questioners. Who was concealing what? And why?

*   *   *

Meanwhile Ted Hall, the youngest scientist at Los Alamos, was working side by side in the lab with name-brand physicists and chemists, privy to the late-breaking news from inside the atom. But as the junior-most member of the team, he was the one they'd ask to reach that pencil there, rinse off the lens, will you, Ted? While still working at Los Alamos, Hall went home to New York, walked into the Soviet consulate and volunteered to supply information about the bomb to the Russian government.

Another infidel, Klaus Fuchs, was transferred to Los Alamos in 1944 from Columbia University, where he'd been assigned to the Manhattan Project. By then Fuchs had crossed more national borders than a vagrant wind: Germany to England, England to Canada, Canada to

Scotland, back to England again.

Fuchs was a quiet one, his co-workers noticed, intent on his work in Bethe's division. Fuchs' specialty was gaseous diffusion, applied to the process of implosion at the core of the bomb. He was quiet, more than quiet, and pale, so he seemed to have withdrawn into himself, taking his pigment and his voice along with him. Poor soul, poor soul, they called him. Kind soul, he'd drive Richard Feynman to the sanatorium in Albuquerque to visit his ailing wife. Fuchs' car coughed and sputtered; its blue paint had flaked away, baring spans of corrosion. After each of Feynman's visits, which for all he knew might be his last, Klaus Fuchs' eyes were full of the sadness that Feynman couldn't bear to feel. Instead he'd rummage in the glove box; read scraps from atlas pages out loud, mimicking Klaus's German accent; discuss his scheme to catch General Groves wearing a skirt; describe how he planned to sneak hot peppers into the vat of stew at the next meeting of minds over dinner.

Fuchs was neither evil nor vengeful. The bomb belonged to the world, he believed. From 1945 on, he smuggled specifics about the bomb out of the country and into the Soviet Union. This was not his first betrayal; Fuchs had been conveying intelligence to the Soviets while working on atomic bomb research in Great Britain.

And while Fuchs and Hall were playing traitors, Oppenheimer was being interviewed by every Army officer convinced that he was not to be trusted. "What else, what else can you tell me?" he was asked again and again. Even the color of Barbara Chevalier's dress seemed to fascinate Oppie's interrogators. All of the poems that he could have composed! About injustice, persecution, martyrdom. But Oppie wrote none of these.

He allowed one of the general's lackeys to accompany him on his next trip to Berkeley, the purpose of the man's presence being to oversee Oppenheimer's safety, not to spy on him. Groves, however, implied that this escort would report back to him if he observed anything out of the ordinary, anything that might link Oppenheimer with espionage.

Then towards the end of 1944, the U.S. government learned that the Germans' attempt to produce an atomic bomb had failed. At Los Alamos, the effort was intensified. The scientists found more hours in the day; they strained their brains towards ever more distant boundaries. Oppie smoked more, ate less.

Still Pash watched him, and the haunting incident wafted after Oppenheimer like a ghost. Pash was never quite satisfied with the truthfulness of Oppenheimer's account or the authenticity of his patriotism. Neither did he appreciate the quality of the darkness at night in the Jemez Mountains, its density, the grim silence.

◆◆◆◆

Nuclear Family

As tired as I was, rather than go to bed I'd sat out on the porch, where the season and the hour intersected in a truly magnificent evening. The air was like a poem, each breath one of its wise, rhymed lines.

Then suddenly, I couldn't be sure, but I thought I heard a gunshot. A noise with edges so clean that the silence after it contained no trace of memory. I'd never heard a gun fired except on TV. A moment later, a flurry of dispute erupted up the street—shouts, screeches, and what had to be threats, in a language I didn't know.

I lunged inside, ran back along the hall to the kids' room and cracked open the door to make sure that they were asleep and not wounded. Just being inside the apartment no longer felt quite safe enough. I belly-crawled across the living room to the couch, wary of the windows that would make a target out of me. My urge to call Clifford instantly left me when I remembered that he was in class, inaccessible.

Since no further shots had been fired, I crept over to a front window and raised myself up, eyes just above the sill, to get a view of the brawl. For the first time in a while, I'd see some of my neighbors. I had to boost myself up higher than I wanted to, taking the chance of being shot, to see far enough up the block. Instead of a group of individual neighbors out on the sidewalk, I saw a conglomeration of them, each attached to another by some vicious act. They were scratching and punching each other, pulling at each other's hair.

Surely we didn't belong in this neighborhood where people were either invisible or violent. I didn't know what the fight was about. They could have been battling out the issue of affordable health care or pay equity for women, but more likely someone had borrowed someone else's weed whacker and forgotten to return it.

We may have been the only young family living on the block. Now that there were four of us, we felt more like a family to me than a set of parents with a child. Sonia was young enough that her presence wasn't very imposing, and Clifford was rarely home. Still, each night the four of us went to sleep within the same walls. Though Clifford often expressed regret about missing so much of his children's development, he continued to come home no earlier than nine o'clock, and often later.

One morning after Sonia and I had delivered Jasper to Kid City, where Steve and I had progressed a micro-inch in our flirtation, I strapped Sonia into the stroller and set out for a walk around the neighborhood. Rarely had I taken her out in the months before her brother started school; those simple, pleasurable outings that I used to go on with Jasper would be much more complicated once I had to keep him in tow and prevent him from wandering off while I pushed Sonia in her stroller.

After two corner-turns we were on the street where Lilac lived. I couldn't remember which house was hers. I'd seen her only once since Sonia was born. Perhaps by now she was Viva. She was still the closest I had to a friend within three hundred miles even if our life circumstances clashed.

Though Sonia was sleeping, I spoke quietly to her about Lilac, describing her distinctive style of fashion, her intensely black hair, her almost childish gusto and love of fun. "Maybe, who knows, we'll run into her," I said.

Then, in front of a gray house with a wraparound porch and a hanging swing, I stopped. I remembered that swing and Lilac's way of riding it as if it were an amusement-park ride. And I then remembered that Lilac didn't actually live in the gray house, but in the brown house across from it, the brown house with an orange door.

"I'm pretty sure she lives there," I told sleeping Sonia. Of course, even if my memory were correct, I had no reason to expect that Lilac would coincidentally appear just then. I stood in front of the house for a minute, all the while scooting the stroller forward an arm's length and back. I could have gone to the door and figured which of the three bells was hers, but my enthusiasm for Lilac was too mild to prompt that much action.

"Let's keep going," I said.

The early October air seemed summer-like, hot and smothering, but the light, amber rays of melancholy sent from beyond the sky were reminiscent of autumn. Soon this humid spell would be over, as would the golden days, the warmth. I thought ahead to a long winter lock-up with the two kids, the elongated nights that began before dinner. Clifford's late homecomings meant that I put Jasper and Sonia to bed every night. Even a friend as incompatible as Lilac would help to displace the gray spook of loneliness that seemed always to be at my side.

Soon I began walking again and turned twice, back onto Hilltop Street. Just after I passed a gray double-decker at the other end of the street from mine, I sensed movement on a human scale behind me and spun around to catch the phantom disappearance of someone who had gone inside from out on the porch. I pulled the stroller backwards until I was even with the door through which one of my neighbors had so recently vanished, and I waited, supposing that the person might soon return onto the porch. A white resin chair paired with a foldable table made of varnished wood indicated that someone at least had thoughts of sitting outside.

"Be right back," I told Sonia, and then I climbed the gray stairs and placed myself in front of the door. Only the screen door was closed, so I could see into the living room dominated by a large television set that was off at the moment but surrounded by an audience of chairs and a sofa, all organized into a semi-circle.

"Hello!" I called through the screen.

The depths of the apartment concealed the approach of an elderly woman who seemed to materialize suddenly on the other side of the screen from me.

"Hello, dear," she said as if she knew me. She was in possession of a pair of wood-handled garden shears, which she may have armed herself with before coming to the door.

"Hi. I'm Pauline Black. I live down the street." I pointed, as if she needed this gesture to understand my meaning.

"How nice. Welcome to the neighborhood." Her words were shaped by an Irish accent.

"No, actually I've lived here for a while. But I never see anyone outside when I walk my children." Again I pointed, this time to Sonia, as I explained, "I have a son, too, who's in school now."

"That's lovely, dear." The pruning shears were still poised with the blades upward. Apparently I hadn't sufficiently convinced her of my harmlessness.

"Anyway, I thought I saw you going into your apartment, and…"

She rescued me from a sentence I didn't know how to end. "Well now, I'd invite you in, but your little one there looks deep in sleep. Why don't we have some iced tea out on the porch?" She looked at the shears and finally explained, "I was just giving my shrubs out there a wee bit of a trim. Used to be you'd find me in the garden every morning. I'm eighty-seven, you know. Some days all I'm fit for is sitting on that sofa in there," she lamented.

"I feel the same, especially on these hot days, and I'm only thirty-four."

She smiled an Irish smile. "Sit down there now, Pauline, did you say your name is?"

"Yes. And yours is…"

"Bitty. For Elizabeth. I'll go get us something cold to drink and another chair."

"Let me help with the chair."

"No, you sit right there and keep both your eyes on your precious one. This neighborhood isn't as safe as I'd like it to be. Not as safe as it once was."

"How long have you lived here?"

"It's been fifty-four years this last spring. Longer than your lifetime, isn't it? My mortgage is paid off but the taxes keep me poor just the same."

Bitty brought out a side chair from her living room and, on the second trip, two glasses of iced tea.

"So where is everyone?" I asked after a long swallow.

Bitty drank in tiny sips that reminded me of going downstairs one step at a time, right foot always leading. "My daughter Edna is at work. It's just the two of us."

"No, I mean in the neighborhood. All of the houses seem abandoned."

Bitty leaned towards me and spoke confidentially. "Darlin,' I wouldn't be surprised if they're all flat on their backs sleeping off whatever it is they do all night."

At eighty-seven, Bitty was entitled to some antiquated assumptions about city dwellers. "So you're Irish, huh?"

"As sure as up is up and down is down I am. I come here when I was just sixteen and I've still got the accent. I was paid to look after other people's children and didn't have my own until I was thirty-three."

Sonia stretched and cramped and then began to bellow.

"Your girl here's a little princess, if you don't mind me saying so. You don't want to let her make a habit of crying to get her way. Is she your first, dear?"

At eighty-seven, she was also entitled to an imperfect short-term memory.

"No. I also have a three-year old son, Jasper."

"The boys are lovers, aren't they, compared to the girls?"

Sonia's back arced, thrusting her into the straps. "She's got cerebral palsy," I told Bitty, who reached for my hand with hers, unnaturally cold from holding her iced tea.

"I promise you, dear, that the Lord doesn't give us anything that we can't handle."

I'd finished my drink, Sonia was restless, and a theological discussion was threatening—three reasons for me to say goodbye and walk the baby back home.

I deliberately stayed awake later than usual that night so I could report to Clifford when he got home, "I met one of our neighbors."

He didn't, I could tell, appreciate the extent of my isolation and the social promise of even an old woman. "She's Irish," I said. "I mean, she actually grew up in Ireland."

"Well there's a guy in my ed. seminar from Brazil. That's pretty exotic, huh?"

I hadn't mentioned anything to Clifford about Steve or that I'd suggested I might want to look at some houses. With Clifford's overly busy days, he just didn't understand how badly I needed companionship.

Except that the next evening, he told me that his parents would be flying in for a long weekend. "You get along pretty well with my mom, don't you? They'll keep you company when I'm not here and give you a break from the kids."

Clifford managed to be available so the four of us could meet his parents at the airport. We conducted our preliminary visiting in the vicinity of baggage claim. Both of the suitcases that the Halloways heaved off the treadmill loop had built-in wheels. Clifford and I each dragged one of them behind us as if they were the family pets. Once in the parking garage, we had to divide into two smaller groups; only both of our cars together could accommodate all six of us. Clifford's mother, Gail, wavered between loyalty to her son and kindred connection with another woman, finally choosing to ride with Clifford and the kids, leaving Dave and me to improvise a conversation that reflected both our familial tie and our total unfamiliarity with each other. When he asked me what kind of work I did, I told him, "I'm making sure that your grandchildren grow into decent people."

We got to the apartment first. Dave tested the integrity of our lock by yanking at the knob before I opened the door. "I used to live around here...well, many years ago," he said.

"I know. In Medford."

"Oh. Clifford told you," he said, though Dave himself had told me so during an earlier conversation, at our wedding, I thought. When I heard Clifford leading his part of the group up the stairs, I felt relieved. Yet Dave and Gail had flown all the way to Boston to provide me with some company. How, then, was I going to withstand a week alone with them while their son was working and going to classes?

"Pauline, what are you doing to keep your mind alive?" Clifford's mother asked me within ten minutes of their arrival. "Are you in a book group or maybe taking a class?"

"No," I admitted, waiting for Clifford to jump in and explain that I was the primary caretaker for the children. As Gail's eyes roved across the utterly plain walls, I didn't doubt that she wondered why, if I was home all day, I couldn't at least decorate our home so it looked less like a monastery.

When she and Dave witnessed one of Sonia's spasms for the first time, he smiled agreeably and she said forcefully to Clifford and me, "Don't let the doctors bully you into a diagnosis. I'll bet this is a stage that Sonia can overcome."

"Mom!"

Dave interrupted to ask Clifford where we'd like to eat. He guessed that we didn't dine out much because of the kids and said that they would love to treat us. All we knew of the local restaurants were their names, either from ads or drive-by fantasies. To spare ourselves having to form another convoy, we agreed to walk to a place on the nearby main street.

Gail kept Jasper busy with pencil-and-paper activities throughout the meal; in fact, she prodded his intellect through two years of development during that hour at the restaurant. By the time Dave paid the bill, Jasper could count all the way to twenty and say "hello" in two new languages.

I left Sonia with the Halloways when I took Jasper to school in the morning but promised that they could come with me to pick him up. The arrangement allowed me a more relaxed interaction with Steve than usual. He seemed to have sole custody of little Katie. He brought her to school every day, though she was picked up by their housekeeper. Bringing the Halloways with me at the end of the school day wouldn't infringe on my morning tryst with Steve. We lingered in the corridor after all the other parents had dashed off to revel in their free time. Mostly the two of us talked about my real-estate prospects, with a variation on the standard

ABC song in the background.

"I came across a new listing today that I thought you'd want to jump on. Except that it's way down in Weymouth."

"That's a ways—" I started to say, "from Clifford's job" but caught myself in time. "—from where I want to be."

"The less you can afford, the farther out you must go," he said with a comedic delivery. At the same time, the line sounded like something preachy from a sermon.

Truthfully, I was tiring of this topic of conversation even though I valued its safety. And after all, it was a subject preferable to the analysis of children's needs and behavior, a subject popular among the mothers. I hoped that the telltale flush that warmed my cheeks when I talked with Steve would fade during the ride home.

When I walked through the door of our apartment, I saw that the living room had been tidied, vacuumed, and dusted. The bed linens that Gail and Dave had slept in on the sofa bed were folded and stacked in rectangles of decreasing size. Flowers of unreal colors in a vase that didn't belong to me glamorized the room.

The next morning, Gail led me on a shopping trip. She selected and paid for kitchen gadgets, indestructible versions of the flimsy, rusting peelers and slicers that filled my drawers.

"Do you have one of these?" she asked. "For making lemon twists?" Gail hadn't yet discovered that the extent of my cooking these days was cheese omelets—and those only on the nights when I had any motivation.

Then, unhooking a stainless steel sieve from the store wall, "They don't offer lifetime guarantees unless the product's going to last."

"Or else they're betting that people will be too busy to spend time trying to collect a refund."

"What?" Gail asked, innocent of my cynical outlook.

"Nothing."

And while we stocked up on paraphernalia that I wished I could return for cash, Dave stayed home with the kids, four of them since Jasper now counted as three boys in one.

"Shouldn't we get back soon? Dave has probably had enough by now."

"That man has changed more diapers than I," Gail told me.

When we arrived home with the ingredients for my kitchen makeover, Dave was singing to both kids. I didn't know the song, but it sounded like a dated popular tune from the forties.

Gail said to me, "Don't you just love his voice? If he hadn't become an engineer, he could've been a singer."

I was prepared to disguise my dereliction in the kitchen by forcing myself to cook decent meals during their stay. But Gail forbade me to take on the duties of chef that week. She replaced me at the stove and, if I came anywhere near, would shoo me away, assuming that I still remembered how to relax.

Even minus Clifford, this much of our extended

family felt enormous and somewhat tribal. With this new distribution of labor, I questioned how I'd been able to cope these last two years. Again I recalled those peephole entrances to the caves at Bandolier Park. Though they might separate to sleep in smaller groupings, the entire community operated as one clan; loneliness was non-existent, I was sure, except possibly as a symptom of mental illness. Even in nearby Los Alamos years later, though the residents weren't related by blood, they were held together by secrets and by the assigned heroism that would save the world. Nothing that they ever did could become ordinary. Those sad-eyed parties, flavored with fun but still philosophically downcast, reminded me of a joy ride that ends with car and passengers crashing into a tree.

Once Gail and Dave returned to Minnesota, our four-person household would feel lacking to me, almost unnaturally small. This didn't seem to be the way that children should be raised, in isolated units, boxed within walls. Would my tight little knot of a family be enough, now that the supporting players had come to seem so essential?

On the last day of my in-laws' visit, Clifford coaxed us all into a small circle in the living room, and I could tell that some sort of announcement was about to be made. Were they moving east? Was Clifford dropping out of school?

"Mom and Dad want to help out by making the down payment on a house for us."

Clifford's lustrous eyes harmonized with his glowing skin. Anyone else would have read his face as ecstatic; I, however, knew my husband, and that a certain amount of anguish would accompany acceptance of such a substantial gift.

"Oh! That's...the best news I could imagine!" And I meant it.

"We're very grateful for the opportunity," Clifford said, as if he'd practiced the words.

"Isn't it great?" Gail said, as if she might like to be thanked again.

"It really is. Thank you. Thank you both." I stood up to hug Gail, who heeded my cue and stood up herself to surround me with a flaccid hug. Dave, though, remained in his seat.

"Don't rush into anything. Buy something you really like, a house that will have good resale value."

When had they discussed this? I couldn't recall a single minute when Clifford had been alone with his parents. Had they been meeting out on the porch in the middle of the night?

I asked him later, when we were getting into bed, "When did all this get decided?"

"Pauline, no one meant to leave you out of the discussion. They only just told me."

"No, Clifford, that's not why I'm asking. It's just that we've all been stuffed into this apartment every night, and—"

"Exactly! We need more space."

"That's not what I was saying. But never mind. And I agree. We need more space."

I knew that Clifford was debating the matter with himself more than with me. Not that he wouldn't have liked more and bigger rooms, a yard, an end to the powerlessness that went along with renting. But he likely was humiliated by his parents' offer and the recurrent doubt that he wasn't making enough to provide for his family.

I couldn't buy a house without consulting Clifford, so I would have to either find a new real-estate agent or use Steve's services to do some general research on what was available. Somehow I didn't consider telling Clifford about Steve; maintaining a buffer of secrecy around him was the biggest part of the thrill for me.

In the morning, after driving Clifford's parents to the airport, I came home and cried from the neck up, and soon the rest of my body was overtaken by sobs. I would miss the round-the-clock company, but more than that, I would miss my mother-in-law, whom I'd gotten to know this time more deeply than the surface of her face powder and sweater sets.

Sonia, in her little seat down near sea-level, was alert and cooing. I picked her up and carried her in my arms down the block. Bitty was in her garden, where all of the perennials and shrubs had been cut back drastically into other-planetary life forms. Her garden had been ready for winter last time I'd been at her house, so I wondered why she was armed now with her pruning shears. She wasn't wearing a coat, not even a cardigan over her thin white blouse.

"Bitty, cover up! It's too cold to be out here in your shirtsleeves."

"Hello, dear."

Her smile was so consistent, her teeth so uniform, that I concluded she must wear dentures. And why wouldn't she? I couldn't imagine anyone's teeth enduring eighty-seven years' worth of grinding and chomping.

"I don't feel the cold," she said. "Can you believe it, with this thin skin of mine?" Bitty began studying her arm as if it were a laboratory specimen. "You'll see. When you get old, your skin gets so thin you can see right through it and watch the blue blood flow in your veins." She laughed. "Now don't be worrying about it quite yet, dear. It'll be years before you look like me, and by then you just might not even give a darn."

"What are you doing out here, anyway?" I asked her.

"Why, I'm remembering, dear. Remembering how nice the garden looked with all the flowers. And it wasn't that long ago now, was it?"

"I guess not." Except that the brief time since then encompassed Sonia's entire life so far.

"Princess is awake, I see."

Sonia smiled through a brief spasm, revealing her glistening gums. Bitty flicked Sonia under the chin with the calloused tip of her finger, launching my girl into another spasm. "Well I'm not so sure she likes me now," Bitty said. "And why should she? I'm a lifetime older than her."

Then leaning in and speaking to Sonia, "Don't give up on me too soon. I just might be the angel that will watch over you from Heaven."

Through with courting Sonia, Bitty said to me, "Here, dear," passing the pruning shears to me. "I've been meaning to give these to you. Maybe next spring you'll get outside more, fix up your yard." She added, "I have another pair."

I accepted the shears, careful not to endanger Sonia with their dull beak that still could cut her. "Thanks. Not a bad idea." I didn't tell Bitty that I'd probably be moving away from Hilltop Street by next spring.

When I got home, the apartment smelled of Gail's soap or cologne or whatever the fragrance was that tailed her from room to room. Not a flowery scent, not overly cheery, but clean and pleasant like her.

Once she'd stopped insisting that Sonia *was* fine, she had proven herself to be an astute and sympathetic observer of our situation. "You two may have to work extra hard for a while. Or who knows, maybe…maybe it'll all come together very soon." Her eyes were locked in a trance, a philosophical seizure of thought that lasted close to a full minute.

Then she'd looked at me and said, "Tragedy can bring people together, so they say." She paused. "But it can just as well drive them apart, you know."

◆◆◆◆

Family Secrets

Sonia's hair was growing and thickening as fast as the weeds in our unkempt yard. Even with the genetic input of two brunettes and with a dark-haired brother, our daughter was a blonde. No one who paused to admire her or talk baby-talk to her suspected that she was afflicted with a medical problem. Her slightly twisted limbs and her jerky torso were bound in a bunting since winter had begun. Bundled up, her body out of sight, she seemed like any other infant. But I knew of the abnormality underneath her layers, and of the fear masked by my motherly smile.

"We thought Katie might have a wandering eye, but then it turned out that they were wrong." Steve was obviously trying to offer me the possibility of hope, but like so many others, he didn't know what he was talking about. Rather than pursue this line of thought, I said to him, "We….you mean—?"

"Esther and me. My ex-wife. We divorced soon after

Katie was born."

At last I'd learned the marital history of my new friend. Until now he'd never mentioned a wife, and I'd started to think that Katie was the product of his seed and a surrogate mother.

Jasper yanked on Sonia's wrapping, a tactic he knew would distract me enough to end my conversation. Though my son had become an avid pre-schooler, he didn't care to linger in the transitional phases between school and home. So I told Steve, "I've got to go."

"Oh." I let myself be detained by as little as this. "Are you free to look at a house some time in the next couple of days? It's a beauty. I thought of you right away during the walk-through."

I thought I heard my shirt rip at the seam as Jasper once again protested my dallying. "Sure. How 'bout... Friday? Does that work for you?"

With a magician's sleight of hand he made a black date book appear, bulging with inserts paper-clipped to its pages. Just as deftly, he flipped to the current week's calendar. "Friday at...say, ten?"

I wanted to suggest that we leave together from the school, but such a visible exit had too much potential for scandal. By Friday, I figured, I could decide whether or not to tell Clifford about the appointment and how much I'd reveal to Steve about my circumstances, though I was on the verge of a sluggish realization that he never asked about me, my marital status, or anything at all personal. And I did wear a wedding ring; I suddenly grasped how one-sided this whimsical romance really was.

By Thursday night I still hadn't told Clifford about the first stop in my house-hunting saga. The attraction of my imaginary relationship with Steve, I was coming to understand, depended on its secrecy, an insight that suggested I wasn't in danger of actually breaching my marital vows.

Clifford, though, in a much more confessional mode than I, almost couldn't wait to get through our lean greetings to tell me, "I met someone today."

He reminded me of a school boy telling his mother about a new friend he'd made on the first day of school. "Oh?"

"We talked forever about this one reading assignment. It turns out we both have an interest in subject-based remedial reading."

Suddenly my illicit association with Steve seemed both more hurtful and more justified. Here I was, anchored at home with two small children, sealed inside our second-floor roost while my husband was out in the world, nourishing his intellect and making friends, or entertaining thoughts of having an affair, for all I knew.

"Would it be OK if I invited Steve over for dinner some weekend?" My brain short-circuited, unable to understand how Clifford could have crossed over into my private inner domain.

"How do you know Steve?"

"He's in one of my seminars. Administrative Ethics."

The shapely temptress reeking of feminine musk metamorphosed into a balding man in a shirt and tie.

"Do you know Steve?" Clifford asked me, bitten by my contagious confusion.

"Different Steve," I said, then, "So Cliffie has a friend!"

As long as I'd known Clifford, his only friends were figures from his past: high school buddies, a college roommate, another teacher from his first professional job. I gathered that he'd either outgrown the need for friends or else hadn't met any suitable matches since taking up with me.

"I mean, I know we don't get enough time together, the four of us, but maybe it'd do us all some good to bring in an outsider. Know what I mean?"

I nodded silently, remembering the boon that Gale and Dave's visit had been to our flagging family spirit. Out of the dark elsewhere in the apartment, a yelp rose and faded like a shooting star against the everness of the night sky. But Sonia's outcry hadn't upset her own sleep, I learned after checking in on her.

The next morning I had to get her up so we could take Jasper to school on time. Before I jostled Sonia awake, I lay my hand on her forehead, feeling for a fever since she had slept so deeply and so long. She was only as warm as any baby, blanketed with a weightless cover, afloat in impressionistic dreams.

What did she feel like inside? Was she aware of being different? "I'm so so sorry, Sonia," I sniveled into the velvety nape of her neck. Then I peeled the cover back, rolled her over so that when she opened her eyes, I was filling the frame of her view. "Good morning, sweetest. What's this?" I asked her, noticing an edge of tooth butting through her gum. "Are you getting your first tooth? And you haven't complained once!"

If I hadn't had to bring Jasper to and from his school, I never would have combed my hair and I probably would never have gotten dressed. Or rather I would have slept in my clothes and not bothered to change, then, in the mornings.

Since I always set out Jasper's clothes for the next day on the chair in his room, he was able to dress himself while I got Sonia ready. The length of her hair lately meant that I'd had to add brushing it to her morning toiletries. That Friday when I carried her through the hall and into the kitchen, I discovered my son eating spoonfuls of sugar from the sugar bowl.

"It's sweet!" he said in a high-voltage voice.

"Jasper! It's sugar! You're not supposed to eat that."

"It's good, Mama," he explained.

The effort required to translate the concept of nutrition into the concrete language of a three-year old was just too much. So I simply confiscated the sugar bowl and made him eat a bowl of unsweetened cereal.

"But it's not sweet, Mama."

"Jasper, not everything has to be sweet, you know."

Leaving the house—loading myself up with snacks and a diaper bag, then locking the door—and getting the kids situated in the car was a complex, multi-step operation, something like a military maneuver, that would never become easy. At such moments I marveled that my mother had cared for four children, and never mind the O'Connors, a family with nine children that lived up the street from me when I was a child. Of course, my kids were both so young, both in need of constant attention from me. What some might consider the perfect spacing sometimes seemed very crowded to me. Fortunately Jasper's desire for independence spurred him to walk out to the curb by himself then scale the back seat to his own boy-size seat, though that same independence sometimes resulted in less favorable outcomes, like eating sugar for breakfast.

"Mama loves Daddy?" he asked as I buckled him into his seat.

I paused, not so much to decide whether or not I loved Clifford as to ponder why our son was asking this question. Perhaps he was much more sensitive to the bristling between his parents than I'd suspected, or perhaps he was clairvoyant and saw ahead to some trouble that was to come. I gave him the most minimal answer possible, "Yes," and entrusted him to the taut straps that would substitute for my arms during the ride.

Steve was late bringing Katie to school, so I had to loiter for fifteen minutes after parting with Jasper. I viewed the gallery of student art in the main hall. I listened to the shadows of songs coming from behind closed classroom doors. And all the while I spoke into

Sonia's tender ear, whispering commentary about the school and the teachers, a confession of my nervousness about the day's outing with Steve. She was a good listener, less fidgety than her brother and, I imagined, graced with an abundance of moral tolerance, able to take in what I said without judgment.

"Sorry." If Steve was flustered, he was still impeccably groomed. He excused his lateness with a tale of misplaced documents and a frenzied search. Katie seemed unwilling to say goodbye to him, so Steve went with her into the classroom and sat for a while against a wall. I peeked in at him through the narrow vertical window in the door. Sitting squarely upright, listening intently to the teacher, he could have been attending a real-estate seminar. Soon he sneaked out of the room, and he told me how to get to the property we were going to see.

Since Sonia didn't speak, she couldn't ask me where we were going, but I filled her in. "We're going to look at a house. A house!" She couldn't ask, either, what her mother was doing with this tall, handsome man, a question I had asked myself repeatedly without getting any closer to an answer.

As I drove step by step through Steve's directions, my thoughts about him were increasingly displaced by thoughts about the house, by disbelief that I could be considering a home in an indescribably beautiful setting, an urban enclave where birdsong adorned the earthy quiet, where the trees rose protectively against the rest of the city like older brothers.

I checked once, twice, and again to make sure that the house I'd parked in front of corresponded to the address given to me by Steve. Before I'd even ventured inside, I was ready to make an offer at the top of our affordability range. A small house but with the semblance of space and possibility. Here I had no doubts that I could excel as a thinker, a writer, anything I might choose. Steve hadn't arrived yet. Again I read the address, this time wondering if I'd transcribed it incorrectly. Then his car pulled up behind mine.

Throughout my tour of the house, Steve acted with more animation than he'd ever shown at the school. He seemed authentically excited about the double-paned glass, the skylight above the stairway, the cedar closet in the cellar. "Look at this," he said, folding and unfolding a hingeless closet door. "I think the original owner was a woodworker." His enthusiasm made me realize that his interest in me really was only as a potential client. I could never dazzle him the way this house did.

At the conclusion of the tour, we ended up in the dining room. On the table were copies of the sheet describing the house. I took one to show Clifford, and as I glanced at it, I noted the list price, nearly double what we could possibly afford.

"Steve, I thought I told you my price range."

He nodded thoughtfully. "Pauline, let me tell you something. I've been doing this a while, and people always, always think they can afford much less than they can."

I couldn't decide if he was unintelligent or just in-sensitive. Obviously, we would never qualify for a mort-gage so far beyond our means.

The house smelled like the American southwest, like sun and mountain rock and desert. The air inside its spacious rooms felt as boundless as a wide-open sky. Like Steve, the place was beautiful but unattainable. But would I actually want to live in a home with its own im-posing culture, a home that would overshadow my deco-rative influence? For that matter, what would I possibly want with Steve? He was utterly handsome, but other-wise nondescript—the perfect screen on which to pro-ject a fantasy affair.

Was something lacking in my marriage? I asked my-self. Did I need more attention or was I mad at Clifford because he was rarely home?

"Let's look at the yard," Steve suggested. As I fol-lowed my leader through a sliding glass door out onto a deck, then down onto a lawn that had been intimidated into perfection—all the while rocking Sonia to keep her sleeping or soothed—he explained, "Of course the property includes much more land than the yard. This is as much as they've landscaped. There's point-nine-oh of an acre altogether. A pretty package."

As was he.

"There are paths through this wooded area." He turned to verify, for the first time, that I was still with him. "Come on, let's take a walk."

Steve swatted aside the graceful, drooping arms of the smaller trees, remembering not to release them until I'd passed. The path wound and waned, but he seemed to know the way and was apparently unconcerned that his glossy black dress shoes would lose their luster as we tromped through an interval of underbrush. So purposeful and brisk was our walk through the woods that when he stopped abruptly, stated, "OK, let's turn back," I thought Steve might be covering up some unexpected disaster ahead—a mass grave or sign of land mines.

Back in the precisely landscaped yard, he stopped again and waited for me. While I stood sloppily, shifting legs, rocking Sonia, Steve positioned himself in front of me and looked directly into my into my eyes unblinkingly. "Pauline, wouldn't you want your husband to see a sweetheart like this before you reject it?"

For a moment I thought he was referring to himself, not to the house. Then I found the flaw: an asymmetry in his eyes, one slightly smaller than the other. At the same time, I read in those asymmetrical eyes a purely professional interest in me. With such clarity I would no longer be able to sustain my imaginary love life. But as I turned away from him, planning to return through the house to my car, Steve captured my hand and brought it to his lips, then kissed the inside of my wrist. So lightly that he could deny the kiss had ever happened.

"I gotta go," I said.

At home I scrubbed the site of the kiss with soap and a nailbrush, my inflamed skin drawing more attention to the spot than any trace of his scent would have. I decided to take a mid-day shower, a rarity, setting Sonia's seat solidly on the bathroom floor and then, with frequent peeks through the stall door, watched her vanish amid spumes of steam. I washed off the aftermath of Steve's cologne and the distinctive smell of the house that I could never afford even though Clifford, who would drink sour milk without noticing it was rancid, would be unlikely to detect any clues as to how I'd spent my morning.

Soon after I'd showered, my legs began to prickle with an itch that I couldn't resist. I raked my nails over my ankles and shins, vandalizing myself with scratch marks.

"What did you do? Wrestle a cat?" Clifford asked that night.

I didn't know what he was talking about but still felt accused.

"Looks like poison ivy," he said.

And then I looked down at my legs and realized that the itching had progressed into a rash, a redness around the bloody scratch marks that were evidence of my lack of self-control.

"Maybe," I said.

When he stepped towards me and surrounded me with his arms, I caught a whiff of an unfamiliar smell. Somehow I couldn't dissociate it from my afternoon shower, my trek in the woods, and so irrationally began to worry that Clifford, too, would notice the smell and my guilt along with it.

Later, though, while he was working on a lesson plan, I put my face right up against the wool herringbone sleeve of the sports jacket he wore nearly every day. Yes. There it was. A smokey, barroom residue trapped among the tweedy fibers. I sniffed again. Definitely smoke. I leapt towards anger, furious that my husband was out drinking—regardless of who his drinking partner might be—while I was devoting days and nights without a break to the care of our children.

"Been to a bar lately?" I asked bluntly.

Clifford continued with his teaching preparation but, without raising his eyes, said, "Not unless by 'bar' you mean 'library.'"

I snorted noisily and crossed my arms in front of my chest in what I meant as a posture of defiance. Finally Clifford looked up, the whites of his eyes bloodshot.

"What?" he asked.

"I know smoke when I smell it. And I know that smoking isn't allowed in libraries."

He gazed away at some distant thought, nodding. "You're right about that. Then, once he'd created an alibi, his eyes returned to me. "Sometimes I stand around outside with some of the other grad students. Some of them smoke."

"I see. Well, if you have time to stand around talking, I wonder why you can't come home earlier."

"Pauline, this is between classes."

"But you only have one class a night."

Clifford nodded again. "I mean during class break."

I unfolded my arms though they remained rigid, and I stomped down the hall to our room. I would have slammed the door to emphasize my anger but I didn't want to wake the kids.

Later in the night, though, the kids woke me. Jasper, nose to my nose as he struck me in the arm, was saying, "Mama, wake up. Wake up." The feral cry that had infiltrated my sleep was more audible now.

Jasper had been promoted to a regular twin bed that allowed late-night escapes. "Sunny needs you," he said.

I shot out of bed, stumbling as I freed one foot from a skein of sheets, and followed Jasper back to his room. Sonia was crying hard. I picked her up. Overhead, the footsteps of my upstairs neighbor, who'd probably just been wakened, crossed the floor. Sonia didn't feel feverish. She wasn't bleeding or gagging. But she was hungry. I lowered myself into the rocker in her room and began to nurse her.

"Mama, Sunny's sick."

"No, not sick, my boy. Just hungry."

Never before since early infancy had Sonia woken up this time of night. She was bigger now, and her voice had gotten louder. No wonder Jasper had perceived this as an emergency.

"Thank you for coming to get Mama," I said.

Jasper reached up to the switch on the floor lamp, turned it on, then dumped a milk crate full of blocks onto the floor.

"Uh-uh. This isn't play time, Jasper."

But he was extremely awake, and though he put the blocks away, I couldn't force him to fall back to sleep. Once Sonia was done nursing, I suggested to Jasper that we go out onto the porch and look at the stars. As we formed a small caravan and began journeying up the hall, I suddenly realized that Clifford wasn't with us. I had become so used to his absence that only belatedly did I remember he had to be somewhere in the apartment. But he had slept through the disturbance. I consoled myself with the thought that had Sonia's distress been caused by a peril greater than hunger, and had I been away, Jasper would have made sure that his dad woke up.

Where the hallway widened into the living room, I came to a stop. There on the couch was my husband, sleeping in his clothes, one arm dangling down over the edge of the front cushion. All that he needed to complete this picture of debauchery was a drained vodka bottle lying cast-off on the carpet.

"I be'er wake Daddy."

"No." I grabbed Jasper's shoulder so roughly that I hurt him, and in reaction he punched me. "Sorry, honey. But let's let Daddy sleep."

The longer Clifford slept, the more justified my resentment would be. And anyway, angry as I was, I didn't want to have to attempt being civil to him in front of the kids. Especially not at two in the morning.

Jasper opened the door to our porch and surged outside, the most unlikely place he would have thought of being at this hour. The darkness that he scanned, slack-jawed, was somehow different from the darkness at five o'clock on a winter evening when we arrived home from the grocery store. For one thing, it seemed to be inhabited by no living creatures. Even in our neighborhood, where I never saw anyone out and about, I could usually hear telescoped coughs and shouts, see cars passing by. And the moon! That night, it was so large that it seemed to have cruised light years towards us, the only souls awake on our side of the globe.

I crouched down, holding Sonia close to me in one arm, and with my other hand took Jasper's wrist and motioned his hand up and down, waving. "Hello, moon."

He repeated, "Hello, moon." When I let go of his hand, he continued to wave and to chant "Hello, moon" into the night like a prayer.

Though Jasper wasn't complaining, I knew that I should get him and his sister back inside before they became glazed with frost. The cold was still and fragile, made of porcelain but of a piece with that greater dimension—the darkness, the stars, the sky.

And then, as we stood in the still night, so still that the slightest sigh of wind felt like a shifting of planets, a sudden flare of light striped the sky. "Mama?" No, not a light, but an interruption of the luminary moon, a streak of shadow crossing its even surface of light. I would have doubted what I'd seen, but Jasper had seen it too.

"What is it, Mama?"

"I don't know, honey. Looks like a witch just flew across the moon."

The suggestion frightened him. Jasper turned and wrapped his arms around my legs, burrowing into the old sweatsuit I slept in.

"Oh, honey, I'm just kidding. There's no witch."

Cautiously he exposed one of his eyes and had a look again at the cold, dark night. "Mama, I want to go to bed."

But first I wanted to dispel the fear I'd caused. "Y'know, Jasper. I think we just saw an electric rocket."

Now he fully emerged from hiding and boldly faced the moon. "Where is it, Mama?"

"It's far away. Those electric rockets travel *very* fast."

"Yeah!" I could sense that he was grinning, though I couldn't see his rounded teeth, his unbearably pink, bulging cheeks. "I want to see it again."

I started for the door back into the apartment, guiding Jasper ahead of me. "It's gone now. But maybe there'll be other electric rockets."

As we crossed, chilled and brittle, into the living room, Clifford was just raising himself to a sitting position on the couch. If the cries of his child couldn't wake him, nor the bustle of Jasper coming to get me, the stealth of icy night air entering our apartment through the porch door could.

"Daddy!" Jasper rushed over to Clifford, assaulting him with a head-on hug. "We saw a 'lectric rocket!"

Then he moved away to turn on the overhead light.

Clifford asked a question with his eyes: an electric rocket? But the peripheral glint of something shiny led my eyes away from Clifford to the floor. There, at his feet, was a half-full, or half-empty, pack of cigarettes. He saw that I'd spotted them and fast snatched the pack off the floor, sliding it under one of the pillows on the couch. Clifford was watching Jasper now to see if he, too, had spied the cigarettes, I think.

"An electric rocket, yes," I said, seemingly including him in our night adventure but really barricading him, with this invention, from the truth.

◆◆◆◆

Boom Town

Late one night, or very early one morning, Jim Nolan's bedside phone rang. He picked the receiver up after
the first ring and, through the muffle of crusty breathing and half-sleepy voices, realized that the two other
doctors at the Los Alamos hospital had picked up their
bedside phones as well. All three were connected by the
same number, a party line that allowed them to be
reached when finally, after long hours at the hospital,
they arrived home.

Their incoming calls were distinguished by the number of rings assigned to each of the three extensions.
But when at 4:30am, Dr. Nolan heard that first ring, he
remembered nothing beyond the boundaries of his
dreams, not the whole carefully engineered system that
required them to wait and count the rings. All three—
Nolan and Barnett and Hempelman—hung up at once,
thinking that one of the others had taken the call.

Out in the dark, a young man reluctantly set down

the receiver of a borrowed phone.

"Too bad, Sir, but one call is all I can give you," he was told.

"I don't know what happened. The call got picked up. I heard voices."

"Too bad."

Renssler decided not to argue. The guard's uniform, the same uniform that had indicated to Renssler that the man would have access to a phone, discouraged him from challenging the policy that dictated civilian use of phones. With the Army behind him, the guard would win any dispute.

Hardly anyone in Los Alamos had a phone. As a security strategy to limit the possibility of leaks, this was a necessary deprivation. Only those who might need to be reached in emergencies related to their professions were assigned phones—electricians, plumbers, and doctors among them. Renssler realized that the most efficient route to Dr. Nolan was the street leading to his house rather than a search for another phone.

So unassisted by streetlights, Rennsler trotted through town towards the doctor's home. In his head, the swell of his wife's screams filled him to the hard bone of his skull. This would be their first. He'd never before heard such an agonized vocalization from a human, and only once from a young buck shot on a hunting expedition. He'd been trained to time the contractions; they were now six minutes apart. This fact more than the gut punches she suffered as her body was transformed into an escape route sent Eve Renssler into a panic. "It's time for the doctor. Jim, call him quick. Call Dr. Nolan."

Renssler pounded on the door of the doctor's home, one of those belonging to a Ranch School faculty member in the past. A wee light was turned on in a house down the street. Not wanting to wake anyone but the doctor, Renssler refrained from knocking anymore; instead he turned the knob, found the door unlocked, and entered after opening it just enough so he could fit through.

The darkness within the house was much less decipherable than the black opacity outside on that starless night. Renssler pawed at the air before him. Nature, even city streets, were more predictable than the furniture arrangement inside someone else's home. All clear at shoulder height, but an ottoman got him in the shin. Renssler suppressed his outburst of pain, limping along until his knee was caught on the corner of a regal, upholstered chair. "Dr. Nolan!" he wanted to call out. But the house was asleep; the town was asleep, except perhaps for the percolating mind cells of the somnolent scientists.

Renssler's next step led him into a collision with the Nolans' piano. When he reached to feel the shape of the obstacle, his hands landed percussively on the keyboard —a dissonant, random chord. Right away he heard stirrings upstairs, skittering voices. Better to declare himself, he decided, before the doctor or his wife came charging down the stairs armed with a shotgun.

"Doctor! It's Jim Renssler. Evie, she's about to pop!"

The doctor came charging down the stairs armed with his black-leather bag, still somewhat asleep but narrowly focused, too, like a ray gun. "Where is she? Outside?"

Renssler wondered why a doctor would even imagine that a woman contorted from labor, hurting, shouting, grunting, could walk across town and stand waiting outside. "Well no, she's at home."

"Of course." Nolan was waking up now. "Be back down in a minute."

And when he returned in clothes, the two hurried over to the Rensslers' home. Before the night ended, Dr. Nolan had delivered Christianna Martin Rennsler, all six pounds, eleven ounces of her.

*   *   *

The first year that the Manhattan Project occupied Los Alamos, eighty babies were born. During the next year the birth rate escalated. In the still of the siesta hour, late afternoons, a polyphonic squall could be heard throughout the town. Again then, late at night, a chorus of infants wailing for milk agitated the atoms in the lab. Huddles of new mothers and their babies soon were formalized into play groups.

The upsurge in population maddened General Groves. "What do these people think this is? A laboratory school?"

Oppie was amused, especially since his own Kitty

was expecting. "You know, Leslie, there's not a lot to do in this town. So we try to work with what we've got, which means—"

Groves trampled over the reference to sex that was soon to come. "We've got to stop it. Or at least slow it down."

"How many troops do you think that'll take?"

Groves ignored the question and managed not to ignite. "If you recall, we were originally projecting a town of six hundred or so. Instead we've ended up with thousands. I'm not prepared to expand the place—build more or bigger houses—just to accommodate this over-run of babies. Can't we schedule more dances, maybe some late-night church services?"

"Still, Leslie, at the end of the night, everyone ends up at home…in bed." Except some of the scientists, he almost added, who end up back at work.

"But if we tire them out. Make it so they're out as soon as their heads hit the pillows."

"Wouldn't it be easier to dose the food with saltpeter?"

No more jokes, Oppie told himself, ready to apply his administrative skills to the problem at hand, which was curiously an inversion of the plutonium prob-lem—how to speed up production. He knew he'd do best to ask around; his strength as director was that he was a great synthesizer of other people's ideas.

But as soon as Groves was out of the office, the idea of trying to enforce a lower birth rate seemed ridicu-lous. Oppie wasn't going to embarrass himself by poll-ing his people about how they thought this could best be achieved. The general couldn't be cured of the delusion that military decree was the ultimate authority. His plan for reducing the number of births in town would include bedroom wiretaps and round-the-clock surveillance with the spy-eyes of cameras.

Just how big a problem was the outbreak of babies? That afternoon, Oppie left the Tech Area and strolled towards the hospital, drawing in the spicy autumn air along with each drag of his cigarette. When he was still a block away, he thought he heard the bleating of newborns. The closer Oppie came to the hospital, the louder the crying and the more babies he imagined in the crate-like cradles built according to Army specs by the same work crew that had positioned the studs in place and faced them with plywood.

At least a dozen mothers walking their babies in buggies passed him before he reached the entrance to the hospital. Perhaps if General Groves hadn't made such an issue of the birth rate, Oppie wouldn't have noticed what was now beginning to seem so visible to him: the overflow of babies (many of them firstborns), newborns, infants, their puling cries, the everywhere smell of souring milk, clouds of baby powder, the narrowing of aisles in the hospital nursery. The nurse overseeing the new litter that day was too flustered to spare Oppie much time.

"I could use another two of me," she told him, circulating from one bed to the next. "And pretty soon we're going to have to put these sweet things in bunk-cribs, though I don't know how I'll reach those on top."

Oppie scanned the rows of lookalike babies. Then he noticed in the window a cluster of fathers' faces looking in. When Oppie left the hospital he went around back and saw that these men were elevated by wooden boxes so they could see in through the window.

Hysterectomies? Vasectomies? Mandated by military decree? What a rebellion that would inspire! Oppie could probably be more effective by reasoning with the laboratory staff. These practical men would appreciate the burden placed on the town by a burgeoning population—the thinning out of rations, the insufficiency of housing. And he was not oblivious to the powerful influence he had. Not only now at the lab, among the scientists, but since the very start of his career when his dark, wiry hair had spiked up from his scalp like a desert cactus. The women had liked him; they'd been slain by his smarts and by knowing the Oppie wasn't just straight lines and sharp angles. He had the poet's heart and eyes.

Back at Berkeley, back when many of the men at the lab had been graduate students absorbing the wisdom of their elders, Oppenheimer had been a campus celebrity. His classes filled at once, sometimes with repeat students, many of them young women who went as far as hunger strikes if denied enrollment in a course taught by this superstar of science. Serber, one of those former graduate students himself, was accustomed to following Oppie's directions exactly. If Oppie told him, "No babies," Serber would no doubt comply.

But instead of issuing an order, Oppie found Serber in the lab and asked him to lunch. The menu at the mess hall changed every day; still it was as predictable as any restaurant menu. That was fine with Serber, who would order Sloppy Joes every time he ate there, whatever the other choices. Meat was scarce, but scraps were easier to come by.

Serber chewed as slowly as he spoke, allowing Oppie ample time to formulate his question. A juicy stream of tomato sauce dribbled down from the corner of Serber's mouth and off the edge of his jaw.

"So the question is how do I make my case without seeming to stick my nose where it doesn't belong—in other people's bedrooms?"

Serber giggled, still chewing. If such an oblique reference to intimacies between husband and wife embarrassed Serber so, perhaps he wasn't the right man to ask. Oppie couldn't imagine his lunch companion taking off his pants and slipping under the covers with Charlotte, an assertive and to-the-point kind of woman.

So Serber surprised him when he said, "If FDR can approve condoms to keep the military clean, why can't he sanction them as a method of birth control? At least for us here at work on this military project."

Not a bad idea. Condoms, diaphragms, they were all illegal, but exceptions could be made at the executive level. Oppie would have to take the matter up with Groves. He stood up, patted Serber on the shoulder, and walked out of Fuller Lodge without a word, leaving his colleague to eat alone. Oppie hadn't ordered any lunch, Serber realized. No wonder he was so thin.

Not a bad idea. Still, Oppie would solicit another suggestion or two. He noticed Phil Morrison walking away from the Tech Area. A different boss might have lambasted his underling for taking off from his job in the middle of the day. But Morrison appeared weary, wrinkled and unshaven. He'd probably been camped out at the lab for at least two days straight, and after a while, even the finest of minds just shut down.

"Morrison!"

By nature, Oppie wasn't much of a shouter. The distinction between when he was speaking and when he was thinking was not so clear to him. Sometimes he waited for answers to questions he'd only thought, not actually spoken out loud. And when he did talk, his voice was sketchy, like bad radio reception.

So he had to call after Morrison four times before the sleepy scientist heard him and stopped so Oppie could come near.

Oppie waved his hands in front of the fixed eyes of the young physicist. "Are you there, Phil?"

Morrison grinned. "I'm here, Docco. But I'm dreaming on my feet."

Oppie reached around him and rested his arm across Morrison's shoulders. "I like that in a man." They began to walk in step, Oppie in the role of guide though they were heading towards Morrison's destination.

"I got one for you." This is how he always intro-

327

duced mathematical puzzlers to Morrison. These puzzlers were a tradition shared by the two men dating back to Morrison's days as a grad student at Berkeley.

"If I can solve it with half a brain, I will."

Oppie looked down at the muddy ground as the two men continued to walk. "This here's a little different. Goes like this: how do we slow down the birth rate in this town?"

"You're not thinking of forced sterilization or abortions, are you?" Morrison asked, aghast as he envisioned his wife, Emily, laid out on an operating table.

"No, but I'm sure that Groves is."

Oppie could talk frankly about this with Morrison, once his student, in a way he couldn't with Fermi or Bethe, imported thinkers from different cultures. Acknowledged international brains. But perhaps, Oppie thought, when Morrison gave only a blank reply, he should broach the topic with someone more objective. One of the single men.

During the next weeks, he and the general continued to bicker back and forth about how to influence the ever-rising birth rate. When the two next met, Groves proposed reducing the supply of milk and diapers as a deterrent to future pregnancies.

"What? That's got to be a violation of basic human rights," Oppie said with disgust. Careful not to speak the words aloud, he inwardly chanted a verse that had lately become popular around town:

The General's in a stew
He trusted you and you
He thought you'd be scientific
Instead you're just prolific
And what is he to do?

♦♦♦♦

Little Boy and Fat Man

Lately a hard rock of anger had been pressing against my ribs up near my heart. Lately I felt as if I couldn't swallow without clearing the way with a scream. My chest was clenched too tightly to allow me to cry, to ride a tide of tears to a distant place undiscoverable by anyone but me. I felt less like a mother than like a driver and a cook. Jasper had to be transported to and from school each day. Maybe some other kid at Kid City lived near us and I could have arranged a carpool with his family, but I wasn't on familiar terms with any of the parents except for Steve. My other main responsibility as a driver—in addition to fetching groceries, returning books to the library, and getting the car repaired and inspected—was to go with Sonia to the increasing number of medical appointments that seemed to define her life. I didn't feel much like a maid since the apartment was chronically untidy and unclean.

Jasper had stopped asking me where Clifford was.

Instead of reacting to his father's reentry into the family on weekends with overt excitement, Jasper barely acknowledged him; Clifford might as well have been an invisible visitor from the hereafter. In his own little-boy way, Jasper was mad at his father, I thought. Maybe I had prejudiced him, but wasn't such animosity within the range of emotions that a healthy child should learn to recognize?

Clifford could tell that Jasper was shunning him. One Saturday morning, as if he were launching a crusade to win back his boy, he said, "Jasper, why don't you and I go out into the woods looking for bugs? And maybe for lunch, we'll get some pizza."

"Yeah!" my fickle son answered at once.

"And while you boys are eating lunch out, Mom'll have a can of dry tuna and some carrot sticks."

"Yeah!" Jasper shouted again.

"Look, Pauline, it'll give you some time to be alone with Sonia."

"Which I already have every morning when Jasper is in school, and which you could do without spending money on pizza."

He inexplicably nodded in agreement. I couldn't bring myself to point out that Clifford's diet as of late had reshaped his body, thickened his waist. And with his exercise now limited to walking from the car to school, to class, to the apartment and then back again, he was softening and spreading.

Neither he nor Jasper was put off by inches of snow

and the frozen ground, both surely inhospitable to insects. "He's just going to be disappointed," I said to Clifford, who answered, "We'll see. It's pretty warm today. Maybe we'll find something hiding under a rock."

Jasper had gathered some bug-hunting equipment from his room: a toy butterfly net, a plastic-framed magnifying glass, and a screened-in bug house that allowed him to kidnap the creepers and crawlers then hold them captive and scrutinize their lives. Next he dragged his vinyl backpack from the hall-closet floor and emptied it of its usual contents—his latest favorite book; a figure of Frankenstein with moving limbs; a bunch of stickers (the currency of the very young); and my blue bandana, which somehow Jasper had claimed as his.

"Aren't you going to put your things away?" I asked, rather than told him.

"Not now, Mama. We going to get some bugs and pizza." He repacked his bag for the morning safari.

"Where are you taking him?" I asked Clifford.

"Probably out near the Fellsway."

"When will you be back?" I was thinking about my son frozen through to his marrow.

"Don't worry about his nap time. Maybe we'll have a little snooze in the car." And with that, they were gone.

I'd laid Sonia on her back on a play mat on the living-room floor, where she was stiffly reaching, stretching and emitting a sustained drone that showed off her lung capacity. I lay down on my side next to her and with one finger stroked the top of her wrist. For now we were just monitoring her. Every doctor we'd consulted had agreed that no intervention existed that would change the course of her condition. The more encouraging doctors would then say, "She could have a very mild case. We just have to keep our eyes open these first few years and see how she does." Physical therapy, speech therapy, seizure medication—these were possible treatments up ahead. Meanwhile I'd seen Clifford poring over descriptions of coverage in health insurance brochures. Sonia would be a most expensive child.

I rolled over onto my other side then pushed to my feet and crossed to the front window. Until some new snow fell, we were doomed to the remains of aging banks tainted with car exhaustion and urban pollution. Still, if I stayed inside any longer, I expected to transmute into a piece of furniture or a sedentary life form, like a barnacle or a fungus.

"We're going out into the cold!" I announced to Sonia. I then patiently dressed her in several layers, buttoning the tiny buttons of her sweater, snapping the tab at the neck of her jacket, stuffing her clasped hands into thumbless baby mittens. I didn't even bother to zip my own jacket; instead I pressed Sonia close against my body for warmth.

Bitty's door had a knocker on it, but I'd learned that she was hard of hearing and might not respond without five or six brass beats. When she still hadn't appeared after number nine, I started to feel mild despair and ransacked the cloudy sky with my eyes. Never once had I

333

come to visit Bitty when she wasn't home. Though she did venture out to the grocery store or for occasional medical appointments—"Those shots of B-12 are keeping me heart beating"—an eighty-seven year old woman was most often resting in her customary chair, especially during winter. Bitty was a rock, a mountain, the fixed ocean shore.

Her absence puzzled me even more when a car as long as an ocean liner pulled up in front of her house and only Bitty's daughter got out. I'd never met Edna but had seen photos of her in Bitty's living room— Edna by herself, Edna and Bitty, Edna and her brother, John.

"Is everything all right?" I called out to Edna as she hauled a bag of groceries out of the back seat.

"Who're *you*?" she responded in a mannish voice.

"Oh, sorry. I'm Pauline. I live up the street. Your mother must have mentioned me."

Her lower jaw slid forward as she shrugged.

"Oh. Well, where is she?"

Edna was having trouble closing the car door with the hefty parcel in her arms. But I was sure she'd succeed in the time it would take me to climb down from the porch, so I stayed put.

"Mother's off to spend the afternoon with John." After a violent kick, the car door shut so forcefully that the vehicle shook. "My brother."

Edna didn't invite me in. Just as well, since I would have hesitated to try to socialize with a stranger, an irritable stranger at that. I held the storm door open for her while she unlocked the door, and then as she continued further into the house, I offered a feeble "goodbye."

No Bitty. No Clifford, no Jasper, no friends. Sonia's delicate breath paused to shape a haze just beyond her lips. The grimy drifts of snow were littered here and there with snack wrappers or takeout coffee lids. This time of winter, the only consolation to be found was the increasing daylight hours. Though the days were cold, often drab, and slicked with ice, they offered reprieve from the colder, more menacing nights that resembled post-nuclear landscapes: forlorn and vacant, the consequence of human sin.

A wash of tears for a moment brought perfect focus to my vision. When I blinked, I felt the wet trickle down both cheeks. "Oh, my poor child. What lies ahead for all of us?"

Sonia granted me a smile, her new tooth almost fully emerged. The only way out of my sorrow about the hardship she seemed bound for was to go deeper, to search beneath the surface, to ponder questions about life's purpose and the lessons we're meant to learn. Maybe Sonia was blessed by having limits on the headlong pursuit of the prizes we all so desired. Maybe she could be content after all. I noticed, as we entered our heated home, that her blissful reaction to the warmth was no less acute than Jasper's pleasure when he balanced a megalopolis of blocks.

Once I put her in her crib to nap, her eyes remained

open in an unblinking, meditative trance. She didn't seem ready to sleep, but neither did she fuss or cry.

In the dining room, the jigsaw puzzle I'd been working on in my rare free, wakeful minutes was scattered over the table. I sat down in front of it but couldn't seem to sort the colors and jittery edges into any meaningful perceptions. So I plunked myself down on the couch and covered myself with my jacket, still chilled from outside. I had just barely crossed the line into sleep when the clomp-clomp of my returning troops filled the hollow of the stairwell.

"Mama, look! We found feathers and fur!"

I struggled up out of my nap, my bones too rigid, my muscles too limp. "You hit the jackpot, didn't you?" Inside his little bug cage, Jasper had stashed a clump of animal fur and a large, plain gray feather.

"No bugs?"

"No. They hiding from the cold."

"I see."

After hanging his jacket up, Clifford came into the living room, the embodiment of happiness. His morning with Jasper had transformed him from an eye-strained, studying hunchback into a proud papa, the same man who had so lovingly rocked Jasper in his arms soon after he'd slithered out of me at the hospital.

All at once I saw him from a different angle. Clifford hadn't been avoiding the rest of us, hadn't been avoiding his household duties. He really did miss us.

"Are you still smoking?" I asked him in an undertone

so Jasper wouldn't hear.

"What?" His forehead folded up into a pleated hand-fan.

"You know it's bad for you. And it's money we can't afford."

He stamped off into the kitchen. I could feel a margin of hostility around me as dangerous as fire. Only Sonia, who had no choice, would be able to stand my company in the state I was in.

I closed myself in my bedroom and called Alia, who didn't answer her phone. Then I called my mother. But before I could talk to her I had to get past my father the watchdog, and I had to control the wellspring of tears ready to gush while he talked to me about his plan to convert the garage into a workshop. I didn't ask a single question, not wanting to prolong his explanation. Finally he said, "I'll put your mother on," and then, as if an afterthought, he asked me, "How are those grandkids of mine?"

"They're fine. We're all fine," I lied.

My mother took over the call. "What's wrong, Pauline?" assuming that only a major tragedy would compel me to talk with her at any time other than Sunday morning when they called me each week between ten and eleven.

"Nothing, Mom. I'm just—" and then the dam inside my chest gave out. "It's been a bad day. Bad week." Bad year, I wanted to add.

"Are the kids all right?"

Sniffing in the tears, I said, "They're fine. I just, I feel so lonely."

"Lonely," she repeated, as if trying to remember what the word meant. "But you have two lovely children. And a husband who loves you."

I felt exactly as I had when I was a child and she'd scolded me for eating more than the two cookies I was allowed. "I guess" was my weak reply. Maybe I was expecting too much from Clifford. Was it his fault that I was lonely?

I couldn't let her hear me weep. I couldn't try to explain that I was grieving over every little thing, every hurt that had ever injured me or seemed to me unjust. "I have to go, Mom." I was sure that she could tell from my voice that I was crying.

"All right, dear. But think about what I said."

About three seconds after I hung up, the phone rang. Much too soon for my mother to have instructed Sylvia to call her morose younger sister.

"Howard and I just got back from a long weekend in the city. Mom kept the kids. It was *fab*ulous."

I was as full as a sodden sponge. But somehow my voice managed to find a way through the mucous and congestion and tears. "Sylvia, I can't talk now. I'm... bathing Sonia."

"Oh. Then why did you answer the phone?"

"Goodbye," I whispered amid a slush of sobs. Once my nasal passages drained, I felt empty and gutted. If only Clifford would hear me crying and come in to comfort me, assure me with his glib optimism that the world wasn't the bleak, uncaring ghost town that it seemed. I so wanted to be enfolded in his body padded with the new fat rounding his belly.

Even if he couldn't hear me, I could hear him, them. Little boy and fat man.

"You're right, Jasper. You are getting bigger."

"I'm a big boy now, Daddy."

"Let's bring your snack to the table. Not a big boy yet. But not a baby anymore."

"Sunny is a baby, Dad."

"That's right. And you're a little boy."

Once I'd spent all my tears, I got through the rest of the day without anyone asking me what was wrong—as if I could even answer. Then after the kids were in bed, our clumsy nighttime conversation commenced. As he did so often lately, Clifford took an extra blanket from the hall closet and began to fashion a bed for himself on the couch.

"I gotta get up early tomorrow. This way I won't disturb you."

Didn't Clifford understand yet that a woman with two very young children was unlikely to sleep in past six o'clock? I turned and started off for our bedroom.

"You don't have to leave, Pauli. I can fall asleep with the light on in here," he explained as if I weren't familiar with his sleeping habits after four years of marriage.

With my back still towards him, I answered, "It's all right. I think I'll read in bed for a while."

I knew, as I was sure he did too, that his recent practice of sleeping on the couch wasn't merely a matter of convenience but represented the growing separation between us. We were both going to bed earlier and, more often than not, in different beds.

In the morning, after being awake for only ten minutes or so, Jasper asked me, "Is Daddy going to work today?"

"No. Today is Sunday. But Daddy will find somewhere to go just to get out of the house."

During the instant when I realized I'd said something I shouldn't have, Jasper started to cry. I tried to correct my mistake with false explanations. Daddy likes to be outside. Daddy is an explorer. Daddy doesn't like to leave you. Daddy misses us when he's gone.

"Daddy does fun things with me!" Jasper said in protest.

I took in his statement with envy, remembering the time when I could have said the same.

◆◆◆◆

Paradox

There, encircled by mountains, buffered by woods and sheltered by the big sky, one could feel that beauty was enough. Beauty and serenity. That sanctuary of nature might inspire one to believe in great, limitless possibilities—that you could conquer, you could fly. Or inspire one to believe that simply this was enough.

Perhaps Robert Oppenheimer experienced such certainty during his visits to the region as a boy and then as a young man. However, by the time even the earliest of the scientists arrived, the setting was spoiled by construction. Digging and machinery, stacks of building material, engineers with clipboards, and debris. Except for the remnants of the boys' school that had homesteaded the land, this was a town erected all at once, mass construction to establish laboratories, housing, medical facilities, a storefront, recreational halls, dining places, all at a pace that couldn't equal the rate of death resulting from the war and couldn't even approach the speed with which the first dropped bomb was to demolish the city of Hiroshima.

A paradox, that such a flurry of construction—buildings built, the town colonized—marked the start of an undertaking that was to culminate in buildings toppled, pulverized, bodies burnt and disfigured if not included in the considerable death count.

Think of the Greeks, the Romans, the Aztecs, civilizations that surged forward because of the knowledge accrued during the time each of them flourished. Objective knowledge based on observation. Manipulation of known facts. And finally, knowledge obtained indirectly through theoretical conjecture. These are the civilizations that developed mathematical thought, that erected architectural wonders, and that advanced ideological standards such as democracy and heroism. A chain-reaction of thought, one idea spawning another spawning another until the sequence of so many vanquished unknowns resulted in a new view of the universe.

So, too, with the fizzlers and the stinkers at Los Alamos. In such a short span of time, they reached their destination, leaving stepping stones of knowledge along the way. But what a paradox, that this accumulation of knowledge was aimed towards one end: the swift and sudden annihilation of a place that had grown very gradually over the years.

Even at the start, when multiple hypotheses—conflicting, competing, compatible—had yet to be explored, confirmed or disproven, the unanimous understanding was that the bomb would be based on the mechanism of fission—the chain reaction of one split atom releasing neutrons that split another atom and so on, an inconceivable thrust of energy released from the intra-atomic bonds. So each tiddlybit of uranium or plutonium was broken down, divided in two. The process of fission was investigated and then refined during the creation of the bomb.

Sometimes generating new ideas requires the disintegration of old beliefs or the dismantling of prior outlooks. Sometimes, paradoxically, assembling smaller truths into new understandings is founded on the taking apart of things.

In order to plan and predict, endless calculations had to be made, and for this purpose, calculators were purchased. Some of them, less expensive, proved to be so slow that they were virtually discarded. How much, how fast, how far? Many of these required highly-trained scientists to articulate what had to be figured, and to execute the complex calculations. But certain computations could be relegated to trained laypersons, mostly wives of some of the men.

Another paradox. Each of the calculations utilized by the Theoretical Division could fit on a page or two. Yet the scale of the explosion, once the bomb was finally detonated, could not even be contained within those square units of Hiroshima that were hit. The force, the heat, the radiation resonated beyond that time and place. Airborne ash, contaminants, and gamma rays overtook Japanese citizens miles and years away; the next, unborn generation was already sentenced to telltale genetic alterations.

Numerous staff were paid to handle the challenge of how to hide a bomb. How to hide it from the carpenters and electricians who were permitted to trespass on that sanctified property. How to hide it from the population of Santa Fe, who had to have noticed a sudden increase of traffic, unfamiliar faces around town, uphill shuttles heading for the vicinity of that boarding school for boys. Imagine the novelty of trains gliding into the Lamy train station with as many as six arrivals at a time. Usually most of the seats on that line were empty, but despite talk over the years, the line had not been canceled.

Try to keep secret a huge blast as bright as the brightest star. Ultimately the atomic bombs activated as weapons against Japan became one of the most public phenomena known to everyone in the industrial world. Even the Trinity test bomb wasn't as secret as the Army would have liked. Ranchers miles away could sense the epileptic trembling underneath their feet. The utmost in secrecy was maintained throughout the planning of a blinding, screaming freak that could never be concealed.

Imagine creating such a beast! Not only for the purpose of waging and then winning a war, but of offering up the dull but volatile capsule as a threat to any who would escalate the fighting. This, at least, was what some among the scientists had in mind while insulated in their labs: that they would brandish this hideous bomb, and peace—an uplifting and permanent peace—would overlay the earth. Was this not the most striking paradox associated with the scientific work at Los Alamos—producing the ultimate weapon of war in order to promote peace?

Robert Oppenheimer's role in the development of the bomb is best characterized as a facilitator, a man who could provoke then comprehend others' discoveries, who integrated the insular work of individual thinkers at Los Alamos into a combination so much more than the sum of the parts. So what if it wasn't his own thunderbolt of insight, his own calculations or conjecture that formed the core of the bomb. His leadership took the project where no other person may have found a path, and at a pace thought implausible by those in the know. As many of those directly involved in Project Y—both science and military personnel—said, no one else could have effectively managed what Oppenheimer did.

What a tragic paradox that, after those years of patriotic dedication, his true belief in the rightness of weaponry as a deterrent to war, the man was judged to be a traitor. Many different sets of eyes viewed Oppenheimer's security file: General Groves, Colonel Pash, Lewis Strauss—government advisor and the arch villain in Oppie's life who resolutely toiled to oust him from his place of esteem. When it suited the American agenda, possible misdeeds in Robert's past were over-looked or tolerated; when the context changed, how-ever, those same "indiscretions" were interpreted in the worst possible light and deemed unpardonable.

The resources of nature—the givens such as matter and energy and complexities of structure—were bor-rowed to bomb the enemy into submission. Did nature have any choice? She gave herself unconditionally, en-dured adoring gazes at her gorgeous views—tourists hanging over the rails at overlooks, riders on rafts on the river tilting back their heads so to see the superb sunset.

How could the same matter that comprised the variegated mountains, the jewel stars, the vapor that dif-fracted light into coral hues be coerced to perform in the guise of those first bombs, Little Boy and Fat Man?

◆◆◆◆

Beauties and the Bomb

Phil Morrison entered Oppie's office quietly, not wanting to disturb the great thinker who was hunched over some diagrams on a table with his back to the door. But Oppie was expecting him, Phil knew, and once inside the office he publicized his arrival with an artificial cough.

Oppie didn't turn around but said, "Have a sit-down, Phil."

Books were stacked on the desk, and Oppie was thinking so deeply, too deeply. Phil wondered if he should start talking just yet, not wanting to waste the scarce time of the director of the lab. Yet Oppie always let his men know that he was unconditionally available to anyone anyhow associated with the project.

And after all, Phil reminded himself, Oppie was the one who had asked for this meeting, not Phil. Not Phil, even though he was tempted to broach the subjects of worms in the water, of rusty water, of the shortage of water since none of the grievances initiated at lower levels had gone anywhere.

Oppie whirled around, as agile as a dancer, Phil thought. He'd seen the big boss dancing at the late end of the parties powered by lab alcohol. Oppie was tall, but too thin. He carried his weight effortlessly and he moved elastically, so the hinges at his joints seem to bend both ways.

"What's on your mind, Phil?" asked Oppie. Phil understood from the question that he must be scowling. "What's on your mind?" Oppie asked him again, and Phil took the question as an invitation to complain.

"Look, Docco," young Phil began, "the bachelors here can put up with a lot of discomfort that the others can't. They're too far removed from their mothers and haven't been pampered yet by wives."

Oppie mused to himself that he'd never existed in that gap between the love of one woman and the next. Morrison noted the professor's pensive absence, the almost visible brain throb from thinking too hard about a mere introductory statement.

"Docco?"

Oppie blinked away the gossamer images of women. "I'm here." He'd become used to having to assure people of his mental presence. "Go on."

"The water supply…"

Oppie knew all about it, and nodded.

"The worms. Do you have them over on Bathtub Row? I suppose they serve a purpose—distract us from the rust that comes and goes. Mostly comes." Morrison had forgotten that he'd been summoned by Oppie. He'd persuaded the boss, as well as himself, that the agenda was his.

"'Course," Morrison continued, "I suppose we should be grateful on the days when we're getting water at all. But does that mean we'd be expected to go along with roadkill circulating through the pipes because at least we're getting water?" By now Morrison was standing, a vertical surge of outrage lifting him up off his seat.

Oppie smiled softly. "Oh yes. I've got one of the coveted tubs, but I share my bubble baths with a whole spaghetti-full of those same worms. By the time I drain them free and they show up at your place, they should be gardenia-scented. I use Kitty's bubble bath, you know."

Oppie could do that. Defuse every angry bomb inside his men, curtail the countdowns. He wasn't an arguer. He was an agreeer. And once he agreed, any argument you'd been preparing to lay on the table simply fell apart.

"Let's walk," Oppie said, leading his former student out of the office and across the splintery floor—a mimicker of their footfalls—to the outside door. The two men had to tightrope-walk along a length of narrow plywood meant to bridge the outside door with dryer ground beyond the small moat of rain-puddle. Morrison had let his brown oxfords become slathered in mud, the leather soaking in the moisture until it was swollen. The finished surface, mostly concealed by mud, had begun to peel. Morrison figured he might just as well let them be beaten into uselessness before replacing them with a pair of the cowboy boots worn by so many Los Alamites. He'd seen the nosey toe of Oppie's boots thrust forward below the cuff of his work pants. Today, though, Oppie was wearing what must have once been his dress shoes. For this meeting with me? Morrison wondered, remembering then that he should let Oppie get to the point.

An aroma dominating the damp air could have been a whiff of coming winter. But it could just as well have been a stirring of springs past, that provocative scent that comes with the thaw. When Phil had first come to Los Alamos, the desert edges were softening, melting into summer. The dry heat made play time out of work time. Windows were up at the lab, and friendly breezes enticed the men to look up from their work, if not to take a break outside, still discussing the grand-scale tinkering that occupied them.

"What have you been hearing about Teller's work?" Oppie asked. "Are a lot of the others agreeing with him?"

The question was not what Morrison had been expecting. What have you been hearing about my extra-marital love affair? he was prepared to hear. Because consensus had established that there was, indeed, another woman, and now everyone was speculating about who she might be. Did Oppie know that the sport of trying to name her had become as interesting to some of the men as their experiments in the lab?

Morrison had to get his head back on straight before he could answer. Oppie was asking about the other bomb, the big bomb that appealed to those who wanted to produce the most potent weaponry they could rather than invent a menacing god whose very existence would compel the warriors to lay down their swords and live in peace. Teller, especially, was pushing hard for the hydrogen bomb.

"Most everyone," Phil replied, "whether they're with him or not, believes that first things should come first. They think he's getting ahead of himself, going for the bigger when the big is still in the making. You know?"

"And what about you, Phil?"

Oppie always personalized his concerns about the work. What do you think, Jim? Can we handle this, Tom? And most of the men believed that his curiosity about their opinions was genuine. Certainly Phil did.

And yet he wanted to say, "What do I think? I have to vote for Priscilla. Someone on the Hill, definitely, because though you travel elsewhere, it's not one place that you keep returning to. It's someone close." Should he also confide that a worthy minority favored the California-girl theory?

"Docco, after these months with Division C, I'm over my head in implosion, and so I'd welcome the change. But I know that's not what you're asking me... I don't think that Teller's drive in that direction is detracting any from the other work. Maybe it even advances what we're doing by providing another point of reference. But if you were to tell me that you're redirecting a good part of our team to work on the super bomb, and then only because it's bigger, deadlier, I'd have to vote against you."

Oppie's head bobbled in a nod. Back at Berkeley, he had frequently consulted his grad students about pending physics problems even though they were less trained than he and their intelligence was less practiced. Still, Phil was surprised that in this different setting, with higher stakes, his former professor would seek out the opinions of his staff. Line them up, and more than half of the rank and file would have attested to the man's congeniality and his democratic methods of leadership. The rest of them, though, would have charged Oppie with being an intellectual snob inclined to disparagement. Morrison understood that both perceptions were true, that a personality as complicated as Oppie's could encompass contradictory tendencies in a paradoxical whole.

The men narrowed again into single file so they could dryly cross the puddled ground. Morrison noted that his boss directed him to go first. His charm, his insincerity. Within another minute or two, Oppie was leading again. Perhaps the magic of being two men at once explained how Oppie had become the object of so many women's desire. Who was the latest of his requited loves? Morrison's wife had scolded him for succumbing to such frivolous speculation, but Morrison argued that, given the shortage of entertainment here on the Hill, it should be considered a sport, no less wholesome than the betting pools organized around the behavior of atoms.

Oppie teetered on one of the dry islands until Morrison, distracted by his own thoughts, could catch up. "Maybe I just make those boundaries between the bombs a little less penetrable, limit the drain on personnel. Think that'll do it?"

Oppie spit-slicked his wiry hair and blindly straightened the knot of his tie as if he were readying for a date. Who is she? Morrison wondered.

"I'd say so. What else can you do? You don't want to risk alienating Teller by releasing him from the project."

"No." Oppie generously responded to the comment as if it were new to him, when of course he'd often considered the situation from this point of view.

Shirley Barnett was gracefully hurdling the small pools of lingering rainfall that defied many of the residents' notions of what a desert should be, navigating the messy desert terrain with her glamorous high-heeled shoes. Another week or so and she'd be in boots. She glanced sideways at the two men and ripened into a visible blush. Is it her? The pediatrician's wife was newly wed and probably still in love with her Henry. Yet she worked on the project herself, was always in and out of rooms ruled by the professor. And from what Morrison had observed over the years, Oppie's appeal to women was often more powerful than their commitment to marriage.

"All right then, Phil."

Morrison observed that Oppie was trailing Shirley with his eyes. Or in fairness, he might be admiring the mountains that never became ordinary. Like Oppie, the mountains were statuesque and slightly aloof. You couldn't but look up to them. And though they were ever-present and conspicuously imposing—in that way like Oppie, too—one always experienced them as existing at a distance. Unreachable.

Oppie lifted his hat in farewell and soon was skimming across the muck He's going after her, Morrison thought. But his assumption was almost immediately proven wrong by a sudden turn that took Oppie in the direction of Fuller Lodge rather than in pursuit of Shirley Barnett.

Morrison stopped and watched his former professor, wondering how he could manage to maintain such a margin of secrecy around his love life in this fish bowl. Did his wife know? Everyone agreed that Kitty was crazy about her man. And she didn't seem the type to share her toys. Bossy, rude, demanding. But Oppie, whether or not he loved her with all his heart, was generally thought to be a responsible husband, attentive to his wife. As attentive as one could be when working eighty hours a week.

Seth Neddermeyer had guessed that Oppie's latest beauty had to be in California. Why else so many trips out of state? "What do you mean? Cal Tech, Berkeley, his family home," retorted Harold Agnew, who was betting on a beauty here, on-site. Someone right under their noses. Teller had grunted, rejecting not just Agnew's opinion but the whole busybody sport.

The men didn't resent Oppie for his talent of winning women's hearts. No, in fact many of them were a little in love with the man themselves. So it wasn't impossible to imagine what about him attracted so many women. But what kind of woman could earn his affection in return?

That was the question that powered the betting pools as well as all the individual speculation. Jean Tatlock, acknowledged by most as his true love, was certainly an achieving kind of woman. A psychiatrist, a party activist, a singer with a contralto range. Oppie liked his women smart and with a backbone. But Jean had demurred whenever he had talked about marriage. And later, she had taken her own life. One way or another, she'd remained out of reach.

Kitty had that same strength and spirit, but didn't Oppie see in her the meanness that everyone else so disliked? Morrison couldn't blame the man for seeking escape beyond his own bedroom. Who could she be?

"Phil! Phil!"

Suddenly Morrison's view was filled with the up-close face of Faye Granger.

"Did Emily tell you? I'm having some people over Friday late. The Wilsons, the Bethes, and I'm hoping you two can come. Just a small gathering."

Morrison hoisted himself up on tippytoes to see over her head. There it was, the porkpie hat. He stepped to one side and tried to see around Faye's trim but fluctuating body in motion. "As I said, just a few of us. Drinks. Maybe Bob will play the comb." Finally she stopped her chatter and turned to locate the object of Phil's attention.

"What'cha looking at, Phil? Are you keeping an eye on your Emily?" Faye teased with a twinkle in her eye.

"No, it's not that," Phil answered, as serious as a schoolmaster. He took one giant step to the right now, but the hat, the man, had edged out of sight. Oppie seemed to have found his way into a hideaway where his mystery mistress may have awaited him.

"Friday. OK," he said at last, still hoping for a glimpse of the faceless beauty, wondering who she was.

"Oh—don't tell anyone," Faye said. "About Friday, I mean, though it's practically impossible to keep anything secret in this town."

Phil continued to stare past her at the invisible destination of Doctor O.

♦♦♦♦

Letters from Arline

K CO DTGCVKPI GCUA. FQPV PGGF QZAIGP HQT PQY.

EQWIJKPI JCU UWDUKFGF. K RCUU JQWTU CPF HQWTU

UNGGRKPI KP VJG UWP.

Dick Feynman glanced, just glanced, at the letter from his wife. He wasn't alone; an official from Security was studying the letter over his shoulder.

"What's this about?" asked the big, brawny man with shiny buttons.

Feynman shrugged, feigning innocence. "I don't know any more than you." To decode the letter, he'd need paper and a pencil. For now, the only certainty he could derive from the letter was that he missed his wife. Consumptive, she was living an existence parallel to his in a sanatorium near Albuquerque. At least she was closer to him than she would have been had he left her at her previous sanatorium outside of Princeton, where they'd lived until he'd been recruited to work on the bomb.

He was the brightest of the bright and could easily have cracked his wife's code in just a few minutes, an impish young man who applied his humor even to matters of national security. However, without turning around to read the face of the security rep, Feynman knew for sure that this other wasn't in the least amused by Arline's verbal antics.

When Feynman couldn't, or wouldn't, translate the letter, Briggs grew an inch in height after straightening his spine. "I'll have to ask you to hand that over," but in fact he seized the letter before Feynman could voluntarily give it to him.

*　　　*　　　*

Dearest Richard,

I'm terribly uncomfortable writing to you, knowing as I do that your mail will be censored. It's as if someone has bored a hole through our bedroom wall and an eyeball is now watching us. Nkwo htta I htiknfo ouy veeyr ayd, on, veeyr imnuet.

Briggs crumpled the page, smoothed it out again. He had to decide whether to outright confiscate the letter or present it to Feynman and attempt, once again, to extort the meaning of these indecipherable passages. "...*your mail will be censored.*" Feynman well knew, as probably did his wife, that all references to censorship were forbidden.

Quite suddenly Briggs called to mind his nine-year-old son. Was that why Richard Feynman seemed so familiar to him—his silliness of a boy? And yet Briggs had been advised repeatedly that all of the scientists working in the Tech Area represented the most intelligent minds in the world. So this Feynman, this man of mischief, must be a genius like all the rest.

Briggs staked out the entrance to the "T," figuring that his prey would soon enough emerge for a break or, eventually, to go home. Finally at 5pm, the officer accosted a sleepwalking Feynman as the latter passed through the third and last security fence. Briggs waved the latest letter in front of Feynman's dazed face, shouting, "She used the word 'censorship.' You know that's not allowed. I'm sure she does, too, but you'd better remind her."

*   *   *

My dear Arline,

Did I tell you? I sleep with your picture under my pillow. It's not the same as having you near, my dearest, but still it gives me some comfort.

Fuchs has promised me another ride next week. He's been a pal. It ain't easy, though, to spend all that time alone with him. He's so quiet. He even thinks quietly.

I'm asked to remind you not to mention "censorship" in your letters…

Feynman's letter was being read by a lowly private whose duties included standing watch here, there, checking badges, snooping on correspondence in and out of Los Alamos. He'd been trained to look out for certain trigger words and phrases, "censorship" among them. The most recent letter from Feynman to his wife was removed from the outgoing mail freight and later that day delivered to Briggs along with all of the other intercepted letters.

"Whatcha got there?" Briggs asked.

"Somebody's writing about the censorship here."

As he received the unsealed envelope, Briggs noted the return address—identical on every letter dispatched from the compound. Not that, but the giveaway curlicued letters suggested that the letter-writer was Feynman.

"Let me see."

He grabbed the envelope, raided it as if he were ripping it open, and went right to the verboten word underlined in red. Censorship. Briggs didn't bother to read anything beyond that one word. As his hand began to wad up into a fist, the letter became more creased. A beastly growl sounded in Briggs' gut.

His office was just outside the forbidden city of the Tech Area. Briggs marched through the layers of security, unnecessarily flashing his badge at each, marching on to the building where he knew Feynman worked. Briggs had the guard at the door go get Feynman for him.

Before Briggs spoke a word, he brandished the letter right in front of Feynman's face, assuming that Feynman would understand what this gesture meant, why Briggs was there, why he was turning red around the edges.

"Afternoon, Officer."

"Feynman…"

"It's actually *Doctor* Feynman."

Those damned advanced degrees, Briggs thought. Left you expecting these lab monkeys to pull stethoscopes out of their shirts.

Briggs removed the letter from the envelope and pointed to the contraband word. "What do you have to say about this?"

Feynman stared at the paper. "It's underlined in red."

A gravel of cackle and gasp came out of Briggs' mouth. Wasn't this young man supposed to be bright? Wasn't he supposed to be beyond making obvious statements? "And why do you think that is?"

Feynman appeared thoughtful. "Do they make 'em in any other colors? Red is most likely the easiest to get, especially during wartime."

Briggs' hand, now fully fisted, mangled the paper even more into a rumple of wrinkles.

"You know that any reference to censorship is forbidden. It suggests…that we have something to hide."

"Which we do."

"But we don't want to advertise it."

"All right, Sir, but you told me to tell her not to use the word 'censorship,' which I can't do without referring to the word."

Briggs stiffened then sagged. He folded the letter in

half and put it in his pants pocket. "I did tell you to do that, didn't I?" Feynman nodded. "Well, your letter's unreadable now. Write another, will you?"

Again Feynman nodded.

Two days later, the same scene replayed in Briggs' office when the young private entered with a handful of letters to be challenged.

"What do you have there?" Briggs asked.

"A few references to place. A slip of the pen. And again..." He took a letter out of an envelope, unfolded the letter and pointed. "Censorship."

For a moment Briggs closed his eyes. He'd forgotten to alert the censors to make an exception in this case. "I'll take that."

With less swagger this time, Briggs presented the intercepted letter to Feynman, mumbling something close to an apology. "Can you write it one more time? I promise we'll be done with it then."

"Can't I just send this copy?" Feynman asked him.

"No. No, that wouldn't do. It's one thing to let the offensive word through, but to have it underlined in red... Sorry, Doctor Feynman."

Arline missed his letters, which normally arrived daily. Now two days had passed—two days corresponding to the two confiscated letters—without a word from her husband. She knew that he slaved long days in the lab, but until this interruption, he'd fit in a letter to her each day.

Dearest dearest Richard,

Are you out there?

J'k xmspice ufbr zmv'pf zfgoe icmb dyqrjtf. Ysc zmv upplgoe omx ujri y hso rp wpss ffye?

Kz jbqu u-syzq egelu jpml epme. Ricz fbtf kf mo zfbsctr, omx, yob bpf rfjmgoe nc ufbr j kvqu cbr nmsc.

From my heart,

Arline

Meetings between Briggs and Feynman by now had become frequent, almost routine. Each meeting was preceded by the delivery of a bundle of impounded letters by the military lackey, one from Feynman or his wife invariably among them. This time the entire coded passage had been underlined as if Briggs could have missed the written gobbledegook that made up nearly all of the letter.

The normally pleasant Feynman expelled a breath of annoyance when he found Briggs waiting for him at the entrance to the lab after having the young scientist called away from his very urgent work. "What is it this time, Briggs?" he asked. "Did I forget to dot an 'i' or cross a 't'? Was my wife's latest letter written in Russian, unbeknownst to her?"

Briggs lowered his head in submissive shame, not even trying to deflect the near-insults to his department's performance. He couldn't possibly justify this slapstick procedure that had required the busy physicist to rewrite the same letter several times. Briggs had to concede that all of the scientists in the lab were indeed occupied and striving towards a significant end. Sometimes, though, he resented the holiness of their work and how they were treated like agents of God. They weren't the only ones putting in long hours and going without the comforts of home.

"I thought you promised that I wouldn't have to re-write that damned letter again."

"You don't. It's something else."

Feynman struck his forehead with the heel of his hand when really he wanted to strike Briggs.

"Your wife's last letter. It's mostly in code."

Feynman shook his head. "If my letters telling her not to do that can't get through…"

"I know. Dr. Feynman… I've been told that you visit your wife regularly."

"When I can get a ride."

"Any visits planned for the near future?"

"It just so happens that Klaus Fuchs has offered to give me a ride this Sunday coming."

Briggs nodded, almost as if he'd expected this answer. "OK then, why don't you just give her the message in person?"

"The 'no censorship' message, you mean?"

"Exactly." Briggs had never felt so embarrassed in all the years of his career.

*   *   *

Dear Arline,

Good news. I've got a ride this weekend. I'll keep this letter

364

short. They've been grabbing all of my letters to you, quibbling over words. Anyway, I'll talk about the censorship issue when I see you.

Yours,

R

Briggs summoned a lesser officer, a man he barely knew. When the officer arrived in Briggs' office, Briggs surreptitiously slipped an envelope into his hand.

"Take this," he told him, "over to the lab. Give it to Feynman. Richard Feynman."

The officer couldn't decide if this assignment was important or not. In either case, he had no choice but to obey it. And since he'd never been inside the Tech Area, the errand offered just a little thrill. But the officer didn't get far into the laboratory labyrinth. Even in his uniform and with a security badge colored in a mid-level hue clipped onto his pocket, he was asked to step aside and wait while Dr. Feynman was informed that someone wished to see him.

Not recognizing the officer, Feynman was ambushed by yet another rejected letter. "No need to refer to the subject of censorship since you'll be discussing it with her so soon." The officer paused to remember what else Briggs had instructed him to say. "Your visit is just two days away. You're being requested not to write to your wife until after you've seen her."

"Requested?"

"Yes, Sir."

"My wife, you see, is ill. A letter every day from me is important to her health. She's alone there." Feynman felt a dribbling behind his eyes and a tightness in his throat. At the same time, he saw before him a soldier—a stranger to him and quite young. Feynman deep-breathed his way to calm and jerked his shoulders back, military style.

"Private, since this is a request, not an order…" And then, so like himself, he circled the soldier, sprang out from behind the erect figure with his thumbs in his ears, danced around and returned to the lab.

*   *   *

Dear Arline,

JVYY FRR LBH FBBA. AB FRPERGF ORGJRRA HF.

Yours,

R

♦♦♦♦

Notes to Clifford

The note was on the mirror of the medicine cabinet, held in place by the chrome rim around the edge of the door. Clifford had written it with a red felt-tip marker, but now the steam lingering after his shower had dampened the letters and made them run.

No class tonight but arranged to be part of a study group for my seminar. Tell the little guy head up, knees high. He'll know what I mean.

No signoff "with love," no "x"'s and "o"'s to remind me that even if he was never home, even if he didn't use my name in the note, he hadn't forgotten his fondness for me.

"Head up, knees high," I told Jasper as I shook him out of sleep.

"What, Mama?"

"Head up, knees high," I repeated, and this time he asked, "Mama, what you are saying?"

Clifford could have told me about his study group

the night before, when the silence had expanded all the way to the walls and was pressing against the window glass, trying to escape from itself through lapses in the outdated frames. No doubt he'd decided, as I had so many times in recent weeks, that any words we might introduce into that gap between us would only serve as a contrast and emphasize how little we were talking to each other.

That day, Sonia had two medical appointments, both of them routine, that had to be crowded between picking up her brother at school and nap time. While I was driving, I ripped off bites of a sandwich to feed to Jasper, passing them on like a mother bird. Sonia had eaten some cereal before we'd left home.

After consulting with the pediatrician and the neurologist, who both concurred that still nothing needed to be done, I decided that I'd wasted that much of the day. All of the driving, preparing a portable meal for Jasper, waiting in waiting rooms, only to be told nothing new. Jasper had lasted through the appointments thanks to the incentive of some new stickers. I, though, had no such reward to lure me onward.

As soon as I put Jasper and Sonia down for their naps, I got into bed myself even though I wasn't tired enough to fall asleep. In fact our compressed schedule that day had invigorated me more than fatigued me. Before burying myself beneath the blankets, I got back up, scrawled a note to Clifford in case I forgot to at night and inserted it between the bathroom mirror and its frame, as he had.

Cliff, nothing new from the docs. Neither of them. But they need their revenue, don't they? Tuna salad in fridge.

I hesitated after writing the note, unsure whether to sign my name or not. Obviously the message was from me so to do so seemed unnecessarily formal. On the other hand, the namelessness of our written communications felt more impersonal than intimate to me, given the tension between us. Finally I forced myself to close with just one "x" and one "o," no more than I'd allot to my Aunt Risa, who I never saw.

Throughout the rest of the day, whenever I went into the bathroom, I was startled by the piece of paper secured on the mirror, one corner flopped over. The note seemed to represent Clifford himself, his corporeal presence.

*   *   *

The next day's note from Clifford was lying on the dining room table, undifferentiated from the sprawl of other papers covering the surface.

Better that she be seen regularly by the doctors. Isn't that what preventive care is about?

An ambiguous scribble at the bottom of the page might have been a "C" for Clifford or else an "o" without its mate.

I began to compose a reply on the same piece of paper but then reminded myself that this wasn't some faraway acquaintance I was writing to. Most likely I'd see Clifford that night.

But at ten o'clock, when he still hadn't come home, I wrote to him on the back of a grocery store receipt.

The gas meter is iced over. The gas company has asked that we clear it off.

I couldn't remember if Clifford had a class that night or was doing research for a paper. Or maybe he was out socializing with some of the other graduate students. That I had managed to write such a tame message was something of a feat.

"Mama, does Daddy still live here?" Jasper asked in the morning.

"Of course he does, baby. Do you think he'd move out without saying goodbye to you?"

Fortunately Jasper seemed innocent of the menacing potential of my question, but as soon as I'd spoken it I wished that the censor in me had been more alert. "What I mean is that daddies don't just one day move out." Yet again I had to amend my still-ominous suggestion. "Daddy is at work and school a lot. That's why you don't see him."

"Can we have pizza for lunch?"

Without any overture, Sonia began to cry forcefully,

and I rushed over to her and picked her up out of her seat. All of my hugs and kisses did nothing to allay whatever was bothering her. "What is it, baby? What is it?" I kept asking, even knowing that I'd never get an answer.

"Sunny is *very* sick, Mama." Jasper's diagnosis accelerated me towards a state of hysteria.

Even last year, before he'd started graduate school, Clifford would have been inaccessible at this time of day, entombed in his classroom. And I knew I could have left a message for him at the school office. Still, I let myself feel bitterly alone. Was this an emergency? A new and normal phase in her development? Hurrying off to the hospital would only scare me more. Reverting to the child inside me, I picked up the phone and then scrounged around with one hand until I found the number I was looking for.

"Hi, Gail," I said when she answered.

"Who is this?"

I suddenly feared that I may have idealized my mother-in-law. But when I identified myself, she melted into loving warmth. "I'm so sorry, Pauline. I just didn't recognize your voice. I have a head cold and my ears are blocked."

"Oh, too bad."

We didn't stick with the subject of her head cold for too long since Sonia was screaming quite close to the mouthpiece of the phone.

"Good Lord, someone sounds unhappy!"

"I don't know what to do, Gail." I was well into an elaborate analysis of why this might be something serious and why it just as well might not be when she interrupted me.

"How about we apply the wait-a-day rule."

"A day? But what if this is something..." I almost couldn't say it. "...life-threatening?"

"Wait now, let me explain. Most problems turn out to be nothing, or close to it. They get better, they pass. You have to assume that nothing is really wrong."

"But Sonia has a medical condition. It's a little different, don't you think?" I wanted to hang up. Time seemed to have quickened and each moment could cost Sonia's life. "Gail, I have to go."

"And just where are you going?"

"I have to take her...somewhere." And then I did hang up. I would apologize to Gail later, once this episode had reached its resolution.

A trip to the emergency room would be far too frightening for me. So I decided to pay an unexpected visit to the pediatrician, thankful that this crisis was occurring during regular office hours.

"Get your coat on, Jasper."

"But Mama, I'm hungry."

"Not now."

While my two children thrashed and squalled, I propelled us all out to the car, underfed and underdressed. As an afterthought once the kids were buckled in, I went back upstairs and left a note for Clifford, just in case Sonia had to be hospitalized and we didn't return by nighttime.

Had an emergency. Going to Feder's office and then...?

Sonia was seen right away by the doctor, mostly, I suspected, because the receptionist couldn't bear to listen to her bellowing. "Tummy ache" was Dr. Feder's verdict. By massaging Sonia's stomach with long, firm strokes, she rubbed away enough of the discomfort that Sonia quieted down and then fell asleep. Jasper earned three wintry stickers of snowpeople showing more acrobatic agility than Olympian gymnasts.

Clifford came home at dinnertime that night and discovered the note within minutes of his arrival. "Pauline, what's this about the doctor?" he asked with high-pitched concern.

"Oh. I was going to tell you," but instead I let him know that I wanted to go to a meeting of a book club I'd seen advertised at the library.

"So...is everything all right?"

"False alarm," I said and then thought that I really should call Gail and acknowledge the wisdom of her advice, which I'd ignored.

Clifford was a fetal bundle in blankets, sleeping on the couch when I got home from the library. Once the group had disbanded, I stood outside in the parking lot talking with Maya, an Indian woman who must have been wishing for friends as much as I since the temperature that night was in the low teens; both of us seemed willing to risk frostbite and gangrene for a few moments of social conversation.

*   *   *

Jasper insisted you'd promised him three cookies for dessert, but I couldn't find any cookies in the house. Be prepared. He's mad at you, Mom.

*   *   *

Even if we had cookies, I never would have promised him three. Two has always been the limit. Don't let that boy lead you around by the nose.

*   *   *

To my surprise, given my low expectations of prospective friends, Maya called me two days after we'd met and asked if I'd like to have dinner with her. I then had to confess to her that I had two young kids, a biographical fact that I'd purposely omitted. Maya was some years younger than I and single. What interest would she possibly have in an older, married woman encumbered with children? Despite this slight alteration of my life story when we'd traded phone numbers written in the margins of library bookmarks, I didn't think I'd hear from her. And after my failed friendship with Lilac and my inert flirtation with Steve, whom I barely spoke with anymore, self-doubt prevented me from initiating any new relationships. Bitty was the exception. Almost always home and craving human contact other than with her daughter and her doctor, she was both available and willing.

"You will bring your children, then. I am going to cook an Indian meal for you."

What Maya meant by a meal was a full five-course feast accessorized with multiple condiments. Jasper ate three full rounds of the naan, a baked bread, but nothing else.

"You have read all of Proust?" Maya asked me as soon as we sat down. Apparently since we'd met at a book club she assumed that we would be linked by a shared literary zeal. Maya, however, was much more of a reader than I had ever been, I quickly learned.

*   *   *

Where are you? I called the hospital to see if any of you had been admitted. Should I be calling the jail?

*   *   *

Sorry about last night. We had dinner with a new friend. First good meal I've had in months!

After all, the last note was unnecessary. Clifford showed up precisely at five o'clock. He was actually skipping a study group to be with us.

"You know that this is all leading to a better job, more income, an easier life for us, right?" he asked.

I wasn't sure that we'd make it to that fabled day but didn't say anything. I imagined that our absence the night before had made him realize what he would feel like if he lost us, or any one of us. He kept picking Sonia up and kissing her little cheeks and continuously mussing Jasper's hair. "How's it going, big boy?" he asked at least twenty times.

But the next morning Clifford must have left the house at five o'clock. I purposely set the alarm for six, but when I walked drowsily out of my room and into the living room, I found evidence of my husband but not the man himself: his folded bed linens piled on the couch, a plate of breakfast crumbs in the sink, and a note on the dining room table.

*   *   *

So good to be home last night. Have class and research to-night. Maybe just one class next semester?

*   *   *

Sonia stood herself up today! She was crawling around and I left the room for a moment. Then when I turned back, there she was, almost upright and leaning on the coffee table.

*   *   *

Damn, wish I'd been there. Won't our hands be full with two of them on their feet!

*   *   *

You must mean won't my hands be full. Your hands are pretty empty when it comes to the kids.

*   *   *

Your last note sounded outright hostile. What's going on?

*   *   *

Do you really have to ask?

*   *   *

The notes between us never seemed to be thrown away or recycled. Instead they accumulated into a chronicle of our marriage strewn across all the surfaces of our lives.

♦♦♦♦

Part II

The King and the Crock of Fire

If the Manhattan Project were a myth, Robert Oppenheimer would be one of the gods, ordering around his thousands of subjects. He would be known as a wise god, but not the god of wisdom because of the folly of the great fire he'd brought into the world. The bomb would be fire, but a fire unlike the kind kindled with a flint. This fire would be intensely hot, a moral heat that would seem to be the natural consequence of human failing. An unstoppable fire. A warning. An end.

The Oppenheimer god would confer with his fellow gods in their intangible dominion. None of them could advise him, though; they could not comprehend this unpredictable power that he must control, now that it was out of its theoretical lockup. In this myth, Oppenheimer would be a troubled god, a god with a heart, a heavy heart. He alone had to reckon with this daunting fire that was almost a god itself. He must rule the world.

He observed, from his perch, both the clerics and the scientists, thinking that surely someone among them could be called in to offer counsel. He watched for a woman or a man who demonstrated a superior under-standing of the earth and its rickety revolutions round and round. But as he watched, the clerics began to re-semble the scientists, the scientists to look like the cler-ics. And the Oppenheimer god would realize that all knowledge was one.

Perhaps after all he would be a king. If the Manhat-tan Project were a myth, Robert Oppenheimer would be a king with great power but also with limits on his power. He would be advised by the finest thinkers in the land. One would wear eyeglasses crookedly across his nose. Several would have escaped unsafe futures in neighboring sovereignties. Perhaps among those advi-sors would be one with treason in his heart. A dissenting son, a surly prince who played Beethoven on the piano late at night.

Was this king responsible for the creation of the fire? No, perhaps it would have arrived in plain packag-ing, sent by the gods to test not the king, but the whole of his empire. How would his people handle such an invincible force? The gods watched to see if the greedy warriors would master the fire for their own selfish ends, the conquest of territory, or if instead, all of the king's subjects, and indeed the king himself, would humble themselves before the fire.

The king would be troubled. Late at night, witnessed by only the queen—always jealous of the problems of state that engaged him—he would pace their huge bed-chamber. His queen would want to comfort him with drops of an intoxicating elixir. She would warm his bed for him.

One morning the king summoned one of his advisors. Though Serber had served as an assistant to the king when he was just a prince governing one piece of the kingdom, he had advanced along with the king to become a royal confidante.

"The fire," began the king. "If only we could put it back in the box."

"Send it back to the gods?" Serber asked incredulously. "Imagine their fury at having such a gift returned."

The two, without an idea between them, called for another advisor, Bethe, and eventually those three called for a fourth. And this process of consulting ever-another advisor continued until at last they called in the great one, Niels Bohr.

His proposal was not unlike one that the king had been considering himself but had been dismissed by all who heard it. "Let us share this great devouring fire with the world," he said. "Let not one of the gods, nor any single mortal sovereignty, make claim to its potential to destroy all others."

"Yes," agreed the king, "for if no one of us has this advantage, the fire will never be used by any nation against another. I think," he said, "the only hope for our future safety lies in a collaboration based on confidence and good faith with the other peoples of the world."

The gods watched the king in this myth in which the bomb became fire, though the fire might as well have been tears for all the sorrow it caused, the grief. They observed the king wringing his hands, sick with the onus of ultimate power. The king coughed. He coughed again and the edges of his nostrils began to turn blue. This sin. This sin.

Or if the Manhattan Project were a myth, perhaps the bomb would be a god, a wrathful god that could choose to demolish all of its mortal playthings. A god of light, of fire, of darkness.

And all the day, the king would wash his hands in advance of the blood on them. His kingdom would become increasingly hot from the fire and from the threat of the fire. Everywhere around them. Up above.

The royal scholars, day and night, would dissect this fire that was different from any other fire they'd known. They analyzed the mechanics of the fire, discovered its fuel source and quantified its illimitable vigor but could not stop it from burning. The fire had a voice. The king could hear it: *I am the atomic bomb. I am an international disaster.*

He plugged his ears with beeswax. But still the king could hear the voice of the fire that now came from within.

We are the bomb. Sun fire, night dark.

This sin. This sin.

♦♦♦♦

Why Rabi Refused

Back when personnel were being recruited for the Manhattan Project, Robert Oppenheimer had repeatedly asked Isidor Rabi to move to Los Alamos and serve as Associate Director. Each time, Rabi refused, sometimes citing a particular reason for declining, other times listing his whole body of objections not just to his own involvement, but to the project itself.

For one thing, Rabi believed that the work on radar he was doing at MIT was more essential to the war effort than was inventing a bomb that was unlikely ever to be used.

"I'm telling you, Izzy, you're lacking in foresight," Oppie said.

Rabi simply shrugged.

Then and again later, he expressed his opposition to scientists becoming commissioned officers in the Army. He wasn't alone in this point of view. The mass resistance to Groves' mad dream of a band of scientist warriors had finally driven Oppenheimer to negotiate a deal:

he himself would become an Army man and the others would follow later, a compromise that never came to pass. Still, the incongruity of conducting scientific research within a military culture repelled Rabi. He'd prefer to work as a scholar in an academic setting. In Cambridge, Massachusetts, a community hosting two of the country's top universities, study and inquiry were more genteel sports.

His wife had her own reasons for not wanting to leave the idyllic city where they lived. Helen Rabi had her women's hiking on Tuesdays and her school committees and MIT wives.

She cleared her husband's plate of eggs before he'd finished the last bite or so. "Izzy, can you actually see us up there in the mountains, the girls reading from government-issue primers in some pioneer school?"

"The mountains, the fresh air, going to school with the children of the elite?"

Rabi suspected that Helen had already prejudiced their two daughters against the move, depicting for them a backward western town offering no advantages whatsoever. If his wife thought that he was arguing in favor of moving to Los Alamos, she was wrong. Rabi only wanted to be thorough in his consideration of Oppie's offer and not just reject it out of hand. Though Oppie's elder by a handful of years, Rabi had been his student after veering away from a career as a chemist. He respected his former professor, but Rabi had misgivings about Oppie's competence as an administrator. This was not a man he would have cast as an organizer or leader.

Rabi excused himself from the table. Because his wife opposed a move to Los Alamos, he couldn't really rehearse his speeches to Oppie in front of her; she was too sympathetic to his objections. Better to talk to himself in an empty room—the study, made narrower by the bookshelves built into two opposite walls. Here Rabi could pace back and forth, back and forth with barely enough room to turn around at either end.

"Is this," he began aloud, "what it's all been heading towards? Three centuries of physics culminating in a weapon that would devour all space and time?" His question, nearly shouted to himself, rattled the glass in the window frames. Outside, the slanting trees shuddered. A veil of cloud, in passing, blocked out the sun.

When finally Rabi expressed this most eloquent of all of his objections to Robert Oppenheimer in person, perhaps his voice was not as loud, perhaps his heart was not pounding in his throat, and perhaps the sky stayed clear and blue. But he presented himself as a man who could not be swayed. And rather than try to change his mind, Oppie convinced him to come out for the opening sessions and to serve as an advisor throughout the development of the atomic bomb.

After the news that the Germans had made no serious progress in producing a bomb, work at Los Alamos, rather than slowing down, intensified. "Make war to end war"—a toast, a prayer, a slogan that might have been engraved over the innermost entrance to the "T."

Then the next year, when the Germans surrendered, many of the scientists at Los Alamos—as citizens—saw no purpose in continuing their work there. The Nazi swastika, iconic target of the bomb, had been the symbol of the enemy. Certainly the Japanese weren't themselves working on a bomb as far as anyone knew. But as researchers, the scientists couldn't tear themselves away from the addictive thrill of success. The news that the bomb might now be used against Japan met both with excitement—that their project, so close to completion, would continue—and with horror—that the commander-in-chief was determined to find a victim for the country's newest military device—if not the Germans, then the Japanese.

Informal discourses on the politics of the bomb took place throughout the work day. A pause, a foot up on a stool, an elbow on a knee. An oral editorial delivered with eyes on the instrument in hand, or a stream of gibberish while passing through one section of the lab to another. Dick Glazer pointed out, "Americans could be killed by the bomb!" then returned to his calculations.

"How so?"

"He means Americans overseas, in Japan."

"Who's to say one day the Russians won't drop one on us?"

All at once, the legendary battle with the Axis began to look more like what it actually was: a wartime exchange

388

of violence between two masses of men, each reaching into their big bags of strategy and routing around for the most powerful of them all. The atom bomb was the most incontestable, the ace of all weapons.

"It's still just a threat, right? We're just redirecting our threat to another part of the world."

Robert Wilson set down his pencil and stared off into the cosmic distance. "But a threat isn't a threat unless it's backed with the true intention of carrying it out." Could he see the speckles of atoms in dust motes, in the plasterboard of the far wall that finally stopped his gaze? "I'm telling you, Roosevelt is ready to drop this thing if need be."

"So maybe that's not bad. If it ends the war…"

At least three men looked up from their work to glare at Bethe, then to go after him like attack dogs.

"Our business isn't to demolish the enemy," Morrison said.

"Right. We're scientists, not soldiers. Aren't we meant to make the peril of war more real…in the hopes of making war obsolete?"

"Why did we refuse to become Army officers?"

"Let's not be naïve."

Dick Glazer added, as he passed by, "Who do you think issues our paychecks?"

Teller, off in the superbomb chamber of his brain, if present would have said, "You are worrying about whether or not this bomb will be used? I am worrying how can we make a bigger, better bomb to assure our victory."

The night was starry with far sparkles of incinerating matter. Up in the Jemez Mountains, beneath a cloudless sky, those who were out for an evening stroll felt that they could reach up and touch the glitter light years away. The muted fire of the stars at the edge of the galaxy seemed not only safe but beautiful, like an artist's exhibit in a gallery. Even those men of science, while enraptured by the night sky, weren't mindful of the gaseous emission that, up close, could burn off their hands, ravage their world.

Robert Wilson kept one eye always on the stars, the sky, and on world events beyond the lab. Often when he walked into his home, Jane mistook the fixity of his eyes as a sign of brainwash. "What have they done to you, Bob?"

At this, he shook himself free of his ruminations. Wilson and his wife had preserved the health of their marriage with conversations that, while not referring to the details of what transpired in the lab, addressed the moral themes that hovered nonspecifically above the men at their stations and like gray clouds above the pillows cushioning their heads at night.

"The work's not slowing down at all," he told his wife.

She nodded. "The Army's invested a lot in this project."

"But Jane, they've dropped their guns. The enemy has surrendered!"

Even though Los Alamos residents, insulated by a buffer of uniformed security, learned of current events two beats after the rest of the world, Wilson and his wife by now knew about the downfall of the Nazis. He looked straight into her eyes. Jane was still trying to compose a reply to her husband's outcry when he said, "The worst is over. We shouldn't need to flaunt our achievement by blasting half the world into ashes." And yet already the search for a test site was underway.

Now more than ever Robert Wilson opposed the actual use of the bomb. More than ever he viewed its mere existence as a message to humankind, an appalling image of the risks of advanced reasoning. He could hear a disembodied voice of judgment proclaiming, "I put before you this day two choices..." For a while now, Jane had been acting as the other voice in her husband's head.

"Bob, maybe a theoretical threat has no meaning. Not in a war that's already left so many dead." She almost could see the soul writhing inside the cage of his bones.

The best she could do, she'd long ago decided, was to balance his airy preoccupations with the earthiness of bread. Tonight she would simmer a couple of chunks of stew meat in a gravy of clear broth. Fresh vegetables were scarce, but Jane had acquired two potatoes and a turnip. Though not contributing any color to the meal, these tubers helped to root Bob Wilson in the ground, to keep him from levitating up into an ethereal zone of constant unrest and turmoil.

That night throughout dinner he was quiet. Jane

knew her husband well enough not to try to lure him away from his thoughts. So as they chewed through the meal, the muscly meat, the roots sodden in thin gravy, she too traveled away in her mind, revisiting the sharp-edged seasons in Princeton, the honey-hot summers, the wistfulness of autumn, a world before war, or between wars. Before the mouse had gotten into the house, that troublemaker—nuclear power—that they were forbidden to speak of at home even as it lurked in the streets of Los Alamos and just inside their doors.

Jane swallowed a mouthful of chewed-up meat and felt it, gristly as a fist, making its way down her esophagus into her stomach.

"Good dinner," her husband said just then, reaching out from the fog that churned behind his eyes and in the space around his brain.

"Thank you," she said, and then let him be.

A sensitive man, her husband. A moral man carved out of the hardest rock of unwavering principle. She accepted his brooding silences, his ongoing judgments—loved him for them, in fact. He abhorred war as passionately as he revered science.

Wilson shoved his chair backwards and stood up. "I've got an idea!"

Every day he generated ideas. That was his work, his calling. But Jane could tell that this idea was somehow different from his electromagnetic brainstorms at the lab.

"I'll bring everyone together. Call a meeting. "Course I'll have to clear it with Oppie first."

To Wilson, the man who had first proposed a town council up on the Hill and had then been active in it, a meeting was a natural forum for thinking through the dilemma he was sure others shared with him. Let them all voice their opinions in an orderly way and then together reconcile the opposing tugs on their shirtsleeves. He was lately pacing from room to room of his small home. Had the Army anticipated how many miles he would cover, surely his floor would have been built with a material that could have endured that much traffic instead of plywood.

"The Impact of the Gadget on Civilization" convened one evening in Wilson's lab. The turnout pleased him, though he knew that the attitudes of those attending ranged from indignation—their goal was to make the world safer, not to destroy it—to resignation to resolve—after all of their work so far, why reverse the go-ahead for the bomb? Feynman, shadow-dark and flattened against the wall, wasn't his affable self since the death of Arline—the woman whom he'd recognized as his mate from the instant he first saw her.

Oppie attended the gathering reluctantly. The swell of sentiment against continuing work on a weapon in this new context of war had worried him. Some of his men were poised on the boundary of indecision, either believing in both sides of the debate or in neither. From his chair on the end of the third haphazard row of seats, Oppie read the faces he knew so well by now, then measured the roar of protest. He listened. Coughed.

Listened.

Finally he stood up and spoke, and by the end of his brief preamble had commandeered everyone's attention. He purposely stayed at his chair rather than presume to talk from the front of the room. He concluded his number one argument with a question: "How can the people of the world possibly appreciate the threat posed by the gadget without ever witnessing its effects directly?"

For the first time since he'd begun to speak, he looked around him at the audience of physicists, chemists, mathematicians.

Number two. "I see before me," he began, "an assemblage of the finest minds in science." Oppie coughed to rid his throat of a gurgle. "Dedicated workers, toiling into the night, giving up family time, sleep time in order to get the job done. What I do not see before me is a decision-making political body. I do not see a legislature whose job it is to decide whether or not to drop this bomb, or when, or on whom. Certainly we can have our say"—"we," he said, as if they all were in concurrence—"but we are *not* entitled to the final word."

Wilson was seated on a lab stool at the front of the room with one arm cocked on the edge of a table. He watched now as the determination and doubt on his colleagues' faces softened into compliance. Oppie's persuasiveness could not be explained merely by his gift of reason and an intimidating intelligence; many experienced his charm as irresistible as witchcraft.

With no one presently addressing the group, a diffuse mumble-buzz broke loose. But an orderly mumble-buzz, unlike the wildfire of words that Wilson had had to shout against to get the meeting underway. He tried to overhear what the men were saying now, wondering whether his own position on what to do with the bomb might have gained support.

But the various conversations blended into one long sheepish bleating of complacency.

Soon the scientists started to leave the lab. For an almost imperceptible instant Oppie, as he strolled alone back to his house, recalled his friend Rabi's dire forecast. And now the project had become exactly what Rabi had feared—a horrific war machine based on the evolution of scientific thought.

Still in the lab, Wilson grabbed Morrison by the sleeve. Morrison answered the unasked question: "It's inevitable, Bob. And anyway, we shouldn't pretend to be owners of the bomb."

All of the earlier protest among the scientists—at Los Alamos and beyond—quickly lost its steam. A proposed letter to Roosevelt became a thwarted dream. For once, Edward Teller spoke up in support of Oppie, his intellectual foe, saying, "The things we are working on are so terrible that no amount of protesting or fiddling with politics will save our souls."

◆◆◆◆

Searching for a Site

He walked an ordinary walk, fingering an old coin in his pocket. Oppie had ridden his horse Tandy some miles away from the compound, his first foray into the wasteland surrounding Los Alamos in many months. One of the features that had finally persuaded the original search committee to choose the boys' school up in the Jemez Mountains was the amount of uninhabited frontier nearby that was large enough for a serious explosion.

He walked unceremoniously across the petrified rock no differently than he walked from his house to the Tech Area or home again, always with the coin in his pocket and a dried plum pit, too, soon to be worn smooth by his worrying touch. During his first spring in Los Alamos, on a hike through the woods, he had found the pit, far removed from the juicy fruit that someone once had eaten. The coin, a souvenir of his student days in Göttingen, was now useless to him as currency.

He scanned all of the land in sight, flat spans among

intervals of mountains, and tried to figure out where the center might be. Visualizing the spectacle of an atomic explosion—its shape and dimensions—was a mental exercise that even he couldn't do. Nor could he envision the big bang with which the universe had been born.

"Let's go, Tandy," he ordered, back up on his horse, spurring the old animal onward with his boot heels. Oppie was shaken by a seizure of coughing, its rhythm conflicting with the gait of his horse; so he was propelled downward by the force of his cough just when the horse was bouncing him upward in the saddle. During the next lull in his lungs he lit a cigarette. Smoking always seemed to quell the cough.

The spring mud had mushed up around Tandy's hooves. But the quarter-ton Army truck recruited for a more distant search expedition some weeks later plowed through the muck, its momentum more than the sucking mud could oppose. Oppenheimer sat in the passenger side by the window, smoking. Kenneth Bainbridge, a Harvard physicist, was driving the truck. Three Army officers followed in another truck, one of them Los Alamos security officer Captain Peer de Silva.

They were looking for the perfect place to conduct the test explosion, an ideal that most of the search team believed existed. It would have to be fairly flat and far away from concentrations of people. But it had to be close enough to Los Alamos that all of the men and equipment needed at the test site could be transported in less than a day. The two trucks stopped. Oppenheimer, Bainbridge, de Silva, and Major W.A. Stevens got out and crouched in a circle around topographic maps laid out on the ground. They ruled out many an expanse of land that satisfied some, but not all, of the criteria they'd agreed on.

"But after all," Oppenheimer reminded them, "these are only maps. The most objective representations of this remarkable country. What can't be measured, and certainly not drafted in two dimensions, is the epic scale of the land. This is history we're engineering. History on the grandest scale."

Bainbridge glanced at Oppenheimer, trying to decide if the great man was joking. His own perspective on the search was utterly pragmatic. His job was to develop the site once it was chosen, and as they traveled around central and southern New Mexico, even crossing the state line, he kept in mind his projected design. Though Bainbridge had heard that Oppenheimer, the bohemian scientist, had been tamed and become an effective administrator, he detected the ghost of the onetime eccentric.

They rode through the back country, bumpety-upping over the uneven terrain. The officers talked about Roosevelt's death and the war. In the lead truck, Oppenheimer and Bainbridge spoke to each other in no more than terse phrases, rags of thought. Bainbridge was assessing the land they passed through while Oppenheimer was rationalizing to himself the need for a field test. Groves had argued against the waste of precious plutonium, but ultimately Oppenheimer and Kistiakowsky, the explosives expert, had convinced him that the outcome of all their years of work was far too speculative to skip over a test run.

"Imagine," Oppenheimer said to Bainbridge, then stopped to cough away the tickle in his lungs. "Dropping this monstrosity without being sure that it would even work. And meanwhile the world is watching." He would have much preferred not to drop the bomb at all. Ever since Niels Bohr had agreed with his notion of world cooperation regarding the bomb, Oppenheimer was more than ever against the actual use of nuclear weapons though he didn't let his men know how he felt.

Bainbridge turned in his seat to look at the man, or more exactly at the profile of the man, just recently changed back from purple to pale. "You must have some idea of what to expect. Yes?"

Oppenheimer's finger, calloused from so many burns, tapped the inch of ash off his cigarette. "It's relative, Bainbridge. Even once the gadget's tested, there's no telling that the actual detonation will be a repeat performance." He assumed that he could speak freely out here in this nowhere spot. "The post-test bomb could be a dud."

That night, the stars overspread their sleep in the bed of the truck. A spew of tobacco smoke rose like a spook above their eyes. Once the last cigarette had been extinguished, the aftermath of coughing shook the truck, metal against bone.

"Lights out," one of the officers said in jest.

But Oppie, swaddled up to the neck in his sleeping bag, wanted to talk about his years as a student in Göttingen. The all-night seminars. Thirty people crammed into one room. A gutsy beer river running through it. Perhaps the overarching sky that this moment had in common with that past had set off this reminiscence.

Suddenly Bainbridge shushed him. "What's that?"

In the desert silence, they could hear the braying of a mule.

"This won't do," Bainbridge said. "Too close."

So they slept though the night, then in the morning moved on to another region. En route, an unseasonable snowstorm came at them, trapping one of their vehicles in a bunker of snow. The officers' truck had been packed by the prescient military with two snow shovels, unloaded now to dig out the other, larger truck, snub-front in a drift, tires sunken in slushy shoals. Despite his thin body and raggedy cough, Oppenheimer manned one of the shovels with tremendous speed and freed the left front tire. They didn't let the snow deter them from carrying on with their mission as planned, though to avoid further such incidents, they took an alternate, less direct route to San Luis and Estrella.

The next day, they drove around a former coal region surrounding Star Lake. Narrow trails led them past vacant ranches that had surrendered to the desert climate—dry earth, antagonistic winds. When one of the trucks balked, when mechanical breakdown put an end to the expedition, all of the men crowded into the other truck and headed back to Los Alamos.

"We don't have to turn back, you know," Oppenheimer suggested, the taint of tobacco on his breath. "We might just as well keep going."

"I don't think so," one of the officers said.

Bainbridge had heard of Oppenheimer's romance with the rugged, undeveloped desert. He noted the wistful glimmer, a dying spark, a dampening ember in those too-blue eyes and said, "We'll be back, Bob."

But not soon enough to satisfy Oppie's need. The New Mexico landscape had imprinted itself on his heart; long, hard days of work had strengthened the attachment. And then he thought of how defiled this landscape would be by the toxic blowup that would shatter each particle of sand, ignite the skyline, razzle the rock under their feet, loosen the teeth of anyone within twenty miles.

When Kitty saw her husband come into the house, head down and dejected, she assumed that he was discouraged about the search for a site. Even she, who knew him so well, couldn't correctly diagnose his condition as the heartbreak of parting with the open country. She offered him the drink in her hand.

"No. But thanks." Instead he lit a cigarette. Kitty snuggled up close to him on the couch, she reeking of vodka, he of nicotine.

"Have any other prospects lined up?" asked Kitty, sipping her drink.

He nodded, ever hopeful. But when he turned to face his wife, he noticed her watery eyes, her mouth misshapen. She seemed to have an old sock in her head where her brain used to be.

Trying to find the perfect test site reminded Oppie of his lifelong quest for the ideal woman. One had this about her; another had that. He had yet to find one woman who had it all. Not since Jean. But then Jean had lacked the desire to marry him; at least she had until he was already wed. He loved Kitty's pluck. Her punch. When he'd married her, though, he hadn't anticipated having to rescue her so often from liquor and the scorn of others.

"Not much in the mood to talk now. I'm tired, Kitty. I must have shoveled a ton of snow out there."

She squeezed the bicep barely bulging beneath his sleeve. "So I can tell. What else can you do with those arms, mister?"

Oppie untangled himself from her embrace and got up off the couch. "I've got to get some rest. We'll be going out on another expedition. If not tomorrow, then soon."

But Oppie knew that he wouldn't be included in the next trips. His administrative duties now, as the project was nearing its peak, demanded more of him than even before, and any trysts he might have with the she-wilderness would have to be postponed.

But he kept track of the search, checking in regularly with Bainbridge, poring over maps with him, discussing the sites that Bainbridge had viewed first-hand but that Oppenheimer could only vicariously enjoy. When Bainbridge described the surveillance conducted from a C-45 plane, the aerial views of the countryside, the reduction of hundreds of miles to a bird's eye view of the western United States, Oppie craved escape from the confines of his office, the whir of overwrought minds and the slickety-boom of military staccato. That unkempt ranch where he and his brother Frank used to spend summers as young men now beckoned him like a luxury hotel. He missed the Spartan existence, missed the croaking desert breath, missed Frank, a physicist himself; when the two brothers did meet, they talked about childhood, the decrepit ranch, and subatomic wonders.

Inside the Tech Area, the fizzlers and stinkers were getting excited about the climactic experiment, the near finale of all these years of work. Each seemed to the others like a war monger motivated by a zest for killing. Not so. "Make war to end war!" was their creed.

Oppie was hush-hush about the search process. He walked around the lab just as he would have roamed the lonely desert that he had so loved since his youth. Stroking the coin or the plum pit. He deflected the questions fired at him like gunshots: "Will we commute back and forth?" "Who'll be stationed there?" "Will the surrounding area be evacuated first?" Meanwhile the grooves in the plum pit were smoothing into no more than surface texture.

"Nothing to report yet," Oppie told them.

Yet his men disbelieved him. They sensed that they were outside the same security wall that until now had enclosed them. Some of them sent Serber in to ply their leader with more questions. If Oppie would confide in any of them, Serber was the man. But nothing.

"Nothing," he confirmed when his colleagues paused from their work and surrounded him with their need to know. Serber shrugged. "For real." Yet the men disbelieved him, too.

Oppie himself had begun to probe Bainbridge with the same curiosity exhibited by his men. When Bainbridge returned from one of his scouting missions, Oppenheimer greeted him the very instant he lowered himself from the truck and set foot on the ground. And if Oppenheimer learned that Bainbridge had been on the phone for more than a few minutes, he'd find an excuse for seeking him out and asking if he had any news.

Most often Bainbridge would sum up the latest exploratory outing with the words "outta reach," meaning that the potential site was either too far away to lug all of the materials and equipment they'd need to set up an outpost, or it was reached via too hazardous a trip—too many ups and downs or inadequate roads to get there. Oppie refrained from asking for a lyrical description of the scenery, a list of the succulents growing there and which reptiles had been seen skittering across the desert floor. Missing out on those forays into the open country pained him, locked as he was in his box of an office. His blue eyes saddened like the dark-blue twilight sky.

Phil Morrison noted how the big boss had been moping about, his porkpie-hatted head drooping to one side as if needing to rest on his own shoulder. Not surprising that his mind, so overloaded with science and politics, would be hard to hold upright. But what else? Spurned by a lover? Who could she be? Morrison still had no clues. Late at night those nights, Oppie was visibly working—at the lab or else in his office with the door ajar.

So who was his latest beauty? Who could she be? Morrison thought through all of the virtuous wives, the affianced female workers, single women, widows…no, not Dorothy. This woman would have to be elusive, beyond reach. Unknowable.

And then Morrison experienced the jolt of realization. The bomb! Among all Oppie's lovers, she was, perhaps, his most captivating love.

But now his time with her was coming to an end.

Finally, late in that summer of 1945, when every other possibility had been deemed "outta reach," what remained was a ninety-mile length of land in the central part of the state, three hundred miles south of Los Alamos. The sandy sprawl was open to battering winds, subject to a scarcity of water and hell-high temperatures in the summer.

Oppie decided that the project deserved a name. Unable to sleep those nights, he'd been reading John Donne's *Holy Sonnets*. "…Batter my heart, three-personed God…" Soon he began referring to the site

405

and to the test to be conducted there as "Trinity."

Bainbridge, more oriented to logistics than to literature, eventually wrote a memo to Oppenheimer that began, *At present, there are too many designations.* To support his point he listed several-of the names referring to the field test: A, Project T, S-45. *I would like to see the project, for simplicity, called Project T.*

But before the government had ever schemed its trespass against nature, before Oppie had attached the lofty name of Trinity to the area of desert chosen for the site, the place had been both known and named. That swath of land that had proven so treacherous to bands of pioneers was referred to by locals as *la Jornada del Muerto*— the Journey of Death.

♦♦♦♦

House Hunting

I waved high and wide, hoping that Clifford would see me among all of the cross-traffic at the Pine Woods strip mall, set amidst auto repair and parts shops with no pine trees in sight. He pulled in behind my car, where a discussion about whether to park his car more permanently or to transfer both kids' car seats from my car to his ensued. Since neither of us wanted to go through the tedium of unbuckling two sets of straps and buckling them again, Clifford backed away into a space under a linden tree at the side of the lot. By the time we would return and separate into our two cars again, the roof of his car would be slathered with wet leaves, dead leaves. The last sign of the season change before we were all driven inside of ourselves by winter.

I left my keys in the ignition but got in on the passenger side. Throughout our marriage, Clifford had continued in the role of family driver. Once we'd become parents, though, the leisure I'd enjoyed as a passenger had been replaced by the necessity of vigilantly safeguarding our two children and keeping them entertained.

"Hold on, kids, here we go!"

Jasper laughed merrily at Clifford's announcement, as if we weren't about to merge into sedentary suburban traffic. We could have rendez-voused at the real-estate office where we were headed, somewhere between Clifford's school and our apartment, but he'd offered to meet me more than halfway since I wasn't familiar with the neighborhood. "I'd come all the way home and get you," he'd explained, "but then we wouldn't make it to our appointment on time."

"I can't wait to meet this Frances, real-estate agent extraordinaire," I said.

With an overabundance of real-estate offices in the greater metropolitan area, each of them home base to dozens of men and women who'd ended up there after changing careers and dozens of others who'd entered the work force directly with newly earned licenses, I still didn't understand why we had to travel so far. Supposedly this Frances was a real-estate agent unlike any other. She was especially renowned for her negotiating skills, comparable to those of the average elder statesman.

"But with her own clients, she's not at all pushy"— pushiness being the germ that contaminated most agents. "No high-pressure tactics," Clifford had told me. "She really wants to see people in the house that's right for them."

Clifford referred to "the house" as if there were only

one house meant for us. Like the one perfect love. I flashed to a memory of my father instructing me when I was barely an adolescent that there was no such thing as a soul-mate and that I could build a relationship with many of the men I'd meet during my life. At the time I'd wondered how my mother could have settled for such an unromantic spouse. Now, though, I wondered if my father might have some useful advice that would cure my own ailing marriage. The tension that had been developing between Clifford and me combined the awkwardness of a first date with the boredom of a bad date. Talking to each other was an effort, yet the silences were excruciating. And still we were going ahead to look at houses.

Apparently this rave recommendation of Frances had come from just one source, Tim the Social Studies teacher. The condo that Frances had helped him buy was uniquely suited to him even though, as Clifford described it, it was indistinguishable from hundreds of others being built on any tract of land with hospitable zoning laws.

Jasper sprang out of the car after unbuckling himself, and we hustled Sonia into her stroller. At two years she was finally able to stand and venture a few steps forward, but she was prone to fall, and we wouldn't be able to keep picking her up and standing her back up again during our meeting.

As soon as we stepped into the lobby, we were greeted by Frances, an overweight woman with princess blond curls. "What lovely children!" she gushed.

Frances could have been either younger or older than she looked. At a glance her colorful hair and smooth skin deceived one into thinking she was just at the cusp of middle age. A more sustained appraisal of her, however, suggested hair-coloring and a foundation of liquid skin concealing her own.

We relocated to a conference room meant to accommodate many more people than just the five of us. Jasper immediately began climbing on the stacks of chairs. Frances asked, "So what are you looking for?" I let Clifford answer while I answered inwardly with images of the ideal marriage, a blissful home life and a satisfying job. Frances sat across from us, listening intently as she looked alternately into Clifford's eyes and mine. Occasionally she'd reach out to tousle Jasper's hair or lean over the table to admire Sonia. By the time I returned from my romp in the best of all possible worlds, Clifford had supplied Frances with a summary of the features we needed in a house. We sat silently then while she transposed the information from our interview onto a checklist and client profile.

Later, while I prepared a most ordinary dinner, Clifford raked leaves in the front yard of our apartment building, a chore not expected of mere renters. I guessed that he'd chosen to volunteer his services as a means of escaping the close quarters indoors. I could hear Jasper's whoops as he leapt into the peaked piles of leaves, then Sonia, inside the apartment, echoing him.

The evening was near enough to dark that I could signal Clifford by turning our living room light rapidly on and off. When he and Jasper pushed through the front door, Sonia began the arduous journey towards them in her walker.

"Hey, Sissy," Clifford called then lifted her out of her seat and high, high up towards the ceiling. Though this ride to the sky delighted her, she accepted the return to her walker and trailed after her faster brother and father into the dining room. Sonia rarely demanded more attention than she was given. Because of the challenges of mobility, she spent much of the day in her walker and didn't seem to want to be removed or to get past the metal surround that barricaded her from the rest of us.

Meal times, the forced contact, were lately accompanied by wine for Clifford and me. Only the contrived relaxation brought on by alcohol could ease those stretches of taut silence between us. Since he didn't work during the summer, he'd signed up for two classes but was now taking a semester off. He hadn't said so outright, but this concession was an attempt to heal what had become a serious alienation between us. We had to fix our marriage. And yet because of the estrangement that had developed between us, time together had become intolerable, especially at night after the kids were in bed.

"I can't tell you how good it is to be eating real food again for dinner," Clifford said, forking green beans into his mouth.

"Same for me."

His increasing presence at home had allowed me to cook actual meals. For Clifford and me, this upgrade in our culinary standards was long overdue; for Jasper, it was a cause for displeasure. He yearned for the reinstitution of meals-in-a can, for soft, bland, fatty foods overloaded with salt and sugar.

"Mama, I want macaronis and tzeeze," he begged.

"Not tonight," Clifford said, then distracted Jasper by asking, "Do you want to hear about the spider I found in my desk drawer today?"

"Yeah!" And Sonia, too, piped in with a malformed version of her brother's response.

Neither Clifford nor I had explicitly suggested last year that we put on pause our plan to buy a house. We simply had done nothing other than accept a weighty check from his parents. "Tell them to hold off," I'd said. "We don't know yet exactly how much we'll need." The tens of thousands of dollars, however, remained in our checking account earning almost no interest, and I suspected that Clifford didn't want his parents to know that we were traveling over such a rough road. When he'd talk with them on the phone, I'd hear evasive statements like, "Nothing yet. We're still looking." Meanwhile I had sewn the plainest curtains for the downstairs windows, figuring that this apartment might be my home for longer than I'd thought.

Just a few days earlier Clifford had said, "How 'bout we set up a meeting with a real estate agent, at least get our feet wet?" and then told me about Frances. Before I could answer, he added, "I like the curtains. Nice touch."

"Mama, nice." Jasper might not have noticed the curtains if Clifford hadn't commented on them. He gathered one of the panels hung across the lone dining room window and tugged at it.

"No, honey." I rushed over to release the fabric from his fist.

"Aw, come on, Pauli. We can give fake names." Clifford had been in the kitchen, checking for evidence of the mice infestation I'd heard coming from behind the walls. He mistook my words to Jasper as an answer to his suggestion.

Rather than explain the misunderstanding, I just said, "Sure. You set something up with Frances."

At our second appointment with her, Frances's hair was several shades closer on the color wheel to orange than before. She presented us with a printout of every property for sale in the county. These were arranged according to increasing price but hadn't been sorted into categories. So we scanned through listings of storefronts and warehouses along with listings of studio apartments and small houses we might have liked if they hadn't been situated an hour-plus drive away from the school where Clifford taught.

"Don't expect to find more than a few that really excite you," she told us, and I wondered if this warning was an example of her lack of pushiness. The listings together with her gloomy prediction left me already discouraged about our prospects. I stopped looking at the pages as Clifford continued to flip through them.

"Whoa, Pauline, look at this one!"

Frances put on the reading glasses suspended from her neck by a jeweled chain and began nodding. She jotted down a note in our file.

The house in question was a very narrow structure that appeared to have been cosmetically boosted with terra cotta lawn ornaments and an expensive mail box at the curb. I wondered what about it had so appealed to Clifford. He'd stopped turning the pages, as if we'd arrived at our final destination.

So I took over the job. "What else?"

"There's a cute ranch coming up. Two bathrooms, and in your price range."

Eventually Frances had to leaf back through the listings and point out this ranch house, so perfect for us that we'd passed it by. I shook my head. "No." When we got to the houses priced above $250,000, I stopped.

"Keep going," Clifford prodded me.

"Are you expecting a promotion, Cliff?" I asked, and immediately realized that I'd dared into dangerous territory.

"*That's* not going to happen until I get an advanced degree."

I joined my hands in my lap and bowed my head contritely. Neither Clifford nor I said any more, and Frances, apparently adept at navigating marital tiffs, reached for the big black binder then shut it and stood up grandly.

"We've got some houses to see!" she exclaimed, and Sonia mimicked her with a broad guttural vibrato.

As we walked through each of the four houses on our shortlist, I tried to imagine coexisting with Clifford within those walls. While all of the houses were larger than our apartment, as soon as I inserted us into them, they felt crowded. But I didn't have to make excuses. They all presented more objective problems that offset all of their plusses. The narrow house that Clifford had liked was, underneath a superficial makeover, in need of significant work. Quite like our marriage, I thought. Frances must have sensed my skepticism. "The price is right. It'll leave you the money you'll need to be able to fix things up."

"It's not that…" I said.

She seemed to expect me to elaborate, but I was unwilling to discuss my broken-down marriage with her. That night, though, once Jasper and Sonia were not only in bed, but sleeping, I dragged a chair from the dining room to inches away from Clifford in the tapestry armchair where he liked to read. He didn't look up from his book right away, and I could tell he was deliberating how to present himself before he faced me.

Wisely, he chose the safest route—silence—leaving the setting of the tone to me. "Clifford, I've been thinking…"

He nodded and, while continuing to look at me,

deftly inserted the bookmark on the cushion beside him into his book, understanding that we were about to embark on a substantial conversation.

"Buying a house now…" I hoped that he'd jump in and rescue me from the gravity of the subject I was introducing. Instead he widened his eyes and nodded again to show that he was listening. Only a direct question was likely to get him talking now. "Do you think it makes sense? I mean, because of the way things are between us?"

Still Clifford said nothing. I couldn't imagine that he didn't know what I meant, so I waited.

At last he said, "Maybe…maybe it's exactly what we need, Pauline. Maybe it'll bring us together, give us more space, and something…something to be excited about."

"But, isn't that like when a couple has a baby to try to save their marriage? I wouldn't want to be that baby."

"Fortunately, a house you can sell."

"I don't know. The way I see it, home ownership will bring with it a whole new set of stresses. You know, added expenses, rooms to paint, home maintenance."

"So say we get a house in good condition."

The very idea that the fate of our marriage depended on choosing just the right house, one harboring no flaws or mechanical flukes, seemed no better than gambling that our situation would get better by pure chance.

"Or…how about this?" he said. "We keep looking for a while, see what that feels like, and decide from there."

I remembered how, when we'd been stopped at the Canadian border on our way into Montreal, I'd wanted to persist and Clifford had wanted to turn back. But now, when the blockade ahead of us was posed by a troubled marriage, our roles were reversed. I peered into my husband's eyes, wanting to detect even a grudging spark that might grow into a more genial warmth.

I was about to capitulate when he said, "I feel some sense of obligation to Frances. You know?"

"What?" I yelled.

"I'm just kidding!"

"Could we please, please go with someone who isn't so far away?"

Clifford set his book on the floor and took my hands as if about to propose marriage. "We don't have to go with anyone. The weekend's coming up. What do you say we take ourselves to some open houses?"

I remembered why I'd married this man. "OK." The shortage of adult companionship in my life left me easily seduced by the chance to spend an afternoon with another grown-up, even if we'd be trudging around looking at real estate.

Late Saturday night, Clifford went out to buy the Sunday paper. He looked as if he were preparing a lesson in real estate for his seventh graders, the real estate section and a city map unfolded on the floor near a fresh pad of paper. Together we composed a list of our top-ten most likely prospects, and then Clifford charted out a course—locating each address on the map and determining the order in which we'd visit them. Since we wanted to get an early start, we packed sandwiches and snacks before going to bed.

"We're goin' a-house-hunting," Clifford told the kids in the morning.

Jasper was disappointed when he found no guns or other weapons among our provisions. "This is a different kind of hunting," I explained.

The first two houses on our tour taught us that camera angles could misrepresent a small home with a yard the size of a blanket as a majestic dwelling on a never-ending lot. We knew that we couldn't afford a large house, but we wanted one where we could take more than four sequential steps without encountering a fence or a wall.

Clifford said, "What do they think, that once they trick you into coming here you'll just give in and buy it?"

By the fifth house Sonia was bawling miserably, as if expressing, for all of us, disgust with the gouges in the wallboard, the water-stained ceilings, and plastic doors. I appeased her with some crackers.

"We've got to use our imaginations," Clifford said. "See these places repainted, full of our own furniture, transformed by your excellent taste."

"Clifford, please. There's nothing to be enthusiastic about in any of the houses we've seen. If you need me to tell you that…"

He reached into the pocket of the diaper bag and filched a cracker.

"Those are for the kids," I scolded.

"You know, you manage to find a problem with just about everything," he accused. "You do know that about yourself, don't you?"

My skin must have flushed with deep-colored shame. Clifford had never offered this observation before, not as a helpful insight and certainly not as an insult. I looked at Jasper finding flavor and texture in a plain cracker. I worried that, once hearing his father's remark, he might forever perceive me differently.

"More crackers, Mama," he said, and Sonia seconded his request with a wail.

Then a warm, fleshy hand settled on my forearm. A familiar soap scent gathered then dispersed.

"Are you stepping out on me?"

I turned around. "Hi, Frances." But Clifford saved me from being the one to have to "break up" with her.

"We're just having a look around," he said. "And also…" He paused. "Your office is too far away to make sense for us." He wrapped his arm around Frances's shoulders. "Even for the chance to work with an agent who comes so highly recommended."

Sonia screamed. Frances melted. I remembered how charming my husband could be.

"All right, darling." She actually stroked Clifford's cheek with a slightly amorous touch. "Ron Martinez is your man, then. His office is out your way, and he leaves no customer unsatisfied."

I think I might have blushed.

Once we held no commercial value for Frances, she willingly relinquished us and rejoined the clients she'd brought to the open house.

"Breaking up is hard to do," Clifford said as we left the room, and then the house, and the neighborhood.

Not until we arrived at the sixth address on our list did I believe that I might ever find a house that I'd desire enough to give away hundreds of thousands of dollars to be able to own. This one, a bungalow style painted in coral and aqua, was small but tantalizing, like a vacation island. I wasn't sure that Clifford was having the same reaction as I was because within our first minute inside, he'd come upon someone he knew. So while Sonia and Jasper and I traipsed from dream room to dream room, Clifford stayed behind in the turquoise-accented living room and talked with his acquaintance.

The current owner was, if not an artist, someone gifted with a flair for home decoration. I loved not only the floor plan and the color schemes, but the furniture. Even the decor of the kid's room, its vibrant blues and ceiling mural implying that parenting could be glamorous and fun, made me want to step into this family's life.

When we returned to the living room, I plunked myself into a soft chair and proceeded to sulk, quite willing to sacrifice my public image in order to wrest Clifford away from whoever this other house-shopper was.

Finally Jasper's "Daddy, let's go" distracted Clifford from his conversation. He suddenly seemed to see us, as if he'd forgotten that we'd all arrived together and what we were doing in this house.

"Oh. This is Richie," he said to us all, and though Clifford didn't identify any of us by name, Richie offered a broad "How're you doing?" He seemed pleasant enough, not a man who could justifiably be vilified, and so I blamed Clifford instead.

"Richie was in graduate school with me. He'll be finishing up this summer," Clifford added wistfully. Patting Jasper's head, he said, "Let's go, then."

"Don't you want to look at the house?"

"Oh, right. But I don't want to keep you waiting."

"Take a quick look, anyway," Richie suggested. I couldn't believe that we needed mediation for such a minor issue. At the same time, I appreciated Richie's generosity, considering we might become rival bidders on the house.

I slowly, slowly herded the kids out to the car while Clifford had his look around.

The heat of old anger sizzled just under my skin. Our little day trip, the picnic lunch and the quest for property had uplifted my spirit for less than an entire afternoon. I wanted Clifford to see the house, but I wanted him to get back to the car and drive us home. When he did step out onto the front porch, he was smiling. For the first time, the possibility that he might like the house became vexing and posed something of a predicament. I worried that, faced with a wonderful house, neither of us would have the willpower to resist buying it.

"Is this the house we've been looking for or what?" he asked as he got into the car. Again the notion of a one-and-only unnerved me. "It'll be hard to keep an open mind at houses number seven through ten."

"Let's just go home."

"Pauline, are you really that sure? Do you want to make an offer?"

"No, no." Sonia followed with a repetition of "no no no." "It's not that," I said. "I just want to go home."

By the time we returned to our apartment, Clifford had withdrawn into a place as private and unreachable as the hole where I'd landed.

◆◆◆◆

The Effects of

The children stand watching, as impressionable as new snow. They stand watching, witnesses to war—the screams of the father, the mother's defense, the galactic flash of blue. They are paralyzed but soon can run, can find a place to hide.

A warning darkness. Then heat. Then light.

There is a girl. "Where is mama?" she whines. No one will speak of it. Of what? She misses her mother. Meanwhile Father follows his compelling thirst. He is drinking up the river. The cool, soothing water is poisoned with hate.

Now the children are hiding away behind a midden of ash. Their limbs are heavy with the blame that both have assigned themselves. *It is me!* each shrieks within the small prison of his body. *This has happened because of me.* The older brother steps out of hiding, prepared to accept his sentence.

Who am I? he cries to the sky, which is now his enemy. The sun will forever be mistaken as that once-only chaos of light that could have been seen from another planet. From that far away, you could have heard the yelling that keeps the kids awake.

Such a change they must live with now, the rapid rupture of their families, dividing and dividing after each battle that they can hear even tucked into their beds, supposedly asleep. The house trembles with each outburst, the radiating anger that will feed their own fury as teens, when they will beat at the sides of buildings, scrawl their names on the bricks in letters larger than the years they have lived so far.

Dividing and dividing. Atoms of uranium. Needles of glass. Splinters of a window embedded in her skull. Will she only have one parent from now on? Which parent? Will she have to choose?

The girl's dark dress is blanched with a stripe-like pattern on the side where the explosion was. The lashes on both her eyes have been singed off. She cries out, "Okaasan!" even though her mother is right beside her, even holding her hand. It is as if the bomb has eradicated everything she once knew, once remembered.

The memory of breakfast dishes clattering in the sink as they are washed, rinsed, and set in the rack to dry. The clink of a soup bowl, the drone of a plane.

Parents who get divorced may justify the choice by arguing that it can't possibly be healthier for children to live with a mother and father who are embattled over matters ranging from domestic decisions to political opinions. For these moms and dads, staying together for the sake of the children would never result in a peaceful home. "We'll stay together" but with so much anger and disdain between them, the very air in the house will become combustible.

So their bodies are covered with burns.

Down to the bone. Gathering bones gathering bones. The city is still burning the next day. Instead of going to school, the children migrate to the fields. The earth is glowing and they dig with charred sticks so they can see the fire underground.

How hungry they are, still hungry at night in the shacks slapped together to provide shelter from their fear. Each person is given a ration of two rice balls. With it, perhaps, a sip of clean water. "This isn't how Mummy feeds us," the boy tells his dad.

I'm doing the best I can, the father thinks. Two homes where before there was one. His skin hangs from him in tatters.

Survivors of the Hiroshima blast and their offspring were monitored for genetic abnormalities. Numerous studies have confirmed that children of divorce experience significantly more mental health problems than children from families not fractured by divorce. It is hard to look at them, these children, these faces— melted, plasticized. Blood is leaking from their ears. Such grotesque rearrangement of the human form seems to bear no relation to the outcomes that had been

425

computed in advance by the scientists at Los Alamos.

*　　　*　　　*

In theory, a bomb could be created that would forever put an end to war.

In theory, the mere threat of such a weapon would work as effectively as the weapon itself.

In theory, the predictive numbers, the equations, would never move off the page.

In theory, physicists, chemists, mathematicians and engineers could spend years helping to produce a bomb and experience fulfillment and pride.

In theory, love may be the most indomitable force experienced by humankind, the most indestructible.

In theory, love will outlast us all.

♦♦♦♦

Fission or Fusion?

There it was. A small explosion of light. Then when I tilted the ring at a different angle, another burst of white, bright. A star-shower of effervescence.

"Look, Sonia, it's a diamond."

But she was reaching for the much less interesting contents of our safety-deposit box—the birth certificates, marriage license, a letter from my father that I wouldn't have wanted to lose in a fire.

"Here, sweets." I offered her my keys, a percussive wonder that she never tired of playing with.

I slid the ring onto my finger, where it stopped at the thin wedding band.

Neither Clifford nor I would have cared much about an engagement ring, much less been able to afford one. But after he'd revealed to Gail that we planned to get married, she had given him the ring in a small manila envelope without any explanation. Later, when he'd opened it at home and then called her, she told him the ring had belonged to her mother. Since Clifford was an only child, he was the uncontested heir to all of Gail's valuable hand-me-downs.

Now Sonia, usually so complacent, was straining to get down and walk in the three-by-five-foot cubicle, a baby-safe haven I decided after a glance, and so I set her down on her feet and she crumpled down onto the steadier base of her bottom.

Clifford's grandmother must have had large hands and thick fingers because the ring had been reduced several sizes in order to fit me. I'd almost never worn it, embarrassed by the ostentation of such a visible piece of expensive jewelry. Twice we'd borrowed it from the bank box and I'd self-consciously put it on when we went to a New Year's party and to Clifford's cousin's wedding.

But during the early months of our engagement, I'd worn the ring every day. Its glitter suggested glamour, promise, laughter. Each time I'd look at the twinkling stone, a little giggle would ripple through me, and I understood the worth of diamonds apart from their rarity.

Now in this stark cell the sparkle reminded me of the first flicker of a diabolical bomb blast. The ring felt slightly too small, as if it were insisting that I pay more attention to my marriage. In fact I'd gained a few pounds since the ring had been sized to fit me.

When Clifford asked me later what I'd done that day, I listed all of my mundane errands but omitted my trip to the bank. Trying on the ring had triggered all kinds of reactions in me, among them a film clip in my head of throwing my diamond at Clifford's face and leaving him forever. Though the action was rather extreme, I thought of it as just another of the melodramatic fantasies that I was sure everyone had: shoving your best friend off a cliff when mad at her, or overdosing on pills as an expression of extreme exhaustion with life. But the ring had also reminded me of those sweet, succulent moments with Clifford that affected me now like a favorite song even if, at the time, I'd been unable to appreciate them. Maybe I would look back even on this phase of our marriage with some nostalgia.

Our renewed effort to find a house officially ended when we'd let the adorable bungalow go. No other house would ever surpass it, and since we weren't going to bid on it, the quest was over. Yet we didn't actually discuss this decision. Again our history was being shaped by what we didn't do more than by what we did.

Our inconsequential conversation, like bad dialogue in a screen play, lacked any depth and did nothing to advance our relationship.

"You left your lunch on the kitchen counter this morning. I guess you know by now," I said to Clifford.

"Yes, and I ate the school lunch, first time in I don't know how long. And guess what? The food's improved. It was actually half-decent."

Before we lost momentum, I quickly asked, "What did you have?"

"Oh. Well I'm not sure what it was. But it tasted

good." Then to the kids, "Maybe worms in goo sauce!"

They laughed full-heartedly, innocent of the family tragedy nearing its climax in the same room.

"OK, but don't expect anything that special for dinner," I said. Again the kids laughed. Not that long ago, this same discussion would have seemed amusing. Now it felt like a substitute for authentic communication.

Our fragile nighttime routine dictated that we alternate which kid each of us readied for bed. So I'd bathe Jasper one night and dress him in his pajamas while Clifford tended to Sonia; then the next night we'd swap. Afterwards I'd read them a story and Clifford would wash the dinner dishes and clean up after me in the kitchen. Those were the moments when I wished for a house. A house with enough rooms that I could manage to avoid sharing the same space with my husband as the evening tapered into night. Jasper's many questions about why Clifford was sleeping on the couch had driven him back to our bedroom. My habit of staying up too late, a genetic tendency evident in both my parents, was clashing with a desire to go to sleep early and be deeply unconscious when Clifford joined me in the bedroom.

"Pauline?" he'd call into the room in a thin whisper before he entered. I'd clench my arms and my legs and even stop breathing so I'd be less likely to move. It's a wonder that Clifford never supposed I might be dead. When I didn't answer, he'd know that he could safely enter with no danger of being entrapped in a conversation with me.

One afternoon, I got a phone call from Frances. "Just want to see how you're making out. Did you call Ron Martinez?"

"No, we haven't done anything about houses since the day we saw you."

"Pauline, everyone gets scared and thinks they can't afford it. But trust me, you can."

I had to restrain myself from telling her that Clifford and I were not getting along and that our marriage was in jeopardy. For Frances, a near stranger, to be the first person to learn of this didn't seem right, though I longed to hear myself say the words, to get advice, to unblock the dam holding back my tears. And who better to bare myself to than this ambiguously middle-aged woman with an ample chest to lean on and a certainty about everything, at least within the realm of real estate?

The more logical person to serve as my confidant was Alia. During the past months, we'd spoken to each other at increasingly longer intervals. She'd been dating a man who, after seven months, she still hadn't found anything wrong with. I assumed that my backbreaking load of troubles—worries about Sonia, budgetary imbalances, a collapsing marriage—were now not only outside the domain of her experience but flavored by a far different mood than anything she was contending with. Still I knew that she would rally her supportive forces and supply me with, at very least, consolation, no matter how alien my problems were to her.

"What's wrong? I can hear in your voice that something's wrong," she said first thing when I called her.

"It's…" I allowed my tears to speak for me.

"Oh, honey. Tell me."

Unable to reverse the current, I tried to answer again while taking in wet breaths.

"What happened to the old lady on your street?"

"She's…still there. Sometimes…we have tea, but she's so old that I'm afraid all of my problems will crack her bones."

"Nah. She's probably thrilled with the company, whatever form it takes." Alia must have suddenly remembered that I'd called *her* to help me out of my desperation. "Really, Pauline, tell me what's going on."

Now that I could breathe again with only a stammering sob here and there, I tried to summarize my multiple miseries. "I think…there's the always stuff, worrying about Sonia and about money. And of course I still have no friends up here." I quickly inserted, "Except for Bitty, but we can't try on each other's clothes or talk about our favorite songs."

"Well, you *could*. But go on."

"I guess I could get by with just those things troubling me, but on top of it all, Clifford and I, my marriage…just isn't doing well at all."

"Uh-oh. I've been wondering about that."

After a long talk that ended coincidentally at the same time as the kids' naps, I was no closer to knowing what I should do but understood that I had to decide

432

whether to rededicate myself to my marriage and hope that the relationship would improve or else propose a separation. Alia carefully avoided stating any opinions about which option I should choose, but she did convince me that muddling in a state of indecisiveness would only prolong my suffering.

Before heeding Sonia's calls or attending to Jasper, who could get out of bed by himself, I opened a can of salmon and ate all six ounces of it. I didn't fret over the drips of oil absorbed by my shirt because finally I was going to start to focus on what was really important. I was done teetering on my small square-inch of indecision and was about to step off onto one side or the other.

"Are you drooling?" Clifford asked me at dinner that night.

"What?"

I saw that he was looking at the oil stains on my shirt front. From the salmon. I didn't answer him.

"Pauline, I was thinking… Maybe this would be a good time for my parents to come for a visit. You like my mom…"

"I like her. That doesn't mean that I want to have to make the house presentable, put everything else on hold—"

"Like what?"

He had come dangerously close to suggesting that I had nothing of importance in my life. But snapping back at him wouldn't bring me any nearer to figuring out what I had to do.

"I'm in the middle of something," I said evasively.

When Sonia slapped her hand in a heap of scrambled eggs on her high-chair tray, I hoped that our conversation had been derailed. But Clifford efficiently grabbed a hand towel, wiped off her buttery fingers, and reshaped her supper into a rounded peak.

"Middle of what?"

"An idea I've been playing around with."

"Oh? What is it?" he pressed.

When had he become so interested in me? I stood up and lifted Sonia away from her supper prematurely, then took her off to her room to begin getting her ready for bed. This slight tampering with her schedule allowed me a way out, and I knew that my darling girl would never stage even the meekest of tantrums. "I'll sneak you some crackers once you're in bed," I promised into her ear.

"I'm going out," I announced upon my return to the dinner table.

"Oh? Where?" Clifford asked.

"To Cuppa, I guess." Or maybe to the library. When I hadn't been able to keep up with the pace of my book group, my developing friendship with Maya had ended, as had all of my other Boston friendships.

"Do you have a date?"

"Do you have a date, Mama?" Jasper repeated before feeding himself a shovelful of peas. He'd begun to make his peace with healthy food again, or at least in its more

434

innocuous forms, such as buttered peas.

"Not a date." I'd moved to the closet and was putting on my denim jacket, knowing that the car keys were still in its pocket from my last outing. "Be back in about an hour," I called as I began to descend the musty stairwell. Since Clifford normally washed the dinner dishes, my unplanned departure wasn't going to create an unfair overload of work for him.

A night out! I lowered the driver's side window and let in the edgy night air. After I'd driven no more than a block or so, I remembered that I'd never smuggled any crackers into Sonia's room. Abruptly I applied the brakes, as if I'd just spied a deer in the road before me. Then I pulled over alongside the curb.

I'd promised her. Had she understood what I'd said, and worse, was she lying serenely on her back in bed, trusting that a delivery of crackers would soon be arriving? I had to go home and honor my promise to her. And yet, after my rather defiant exit, I wasn't certain that I'd be able to escape as successfully a second time. Clifford would have had time to produce a roadblock.

"Forgive me, Sonia," I whispered to my distant girl. "When I get home…"

And after ordering a cup of decaffeinated coffee, after staring for an hour into its liquid depths, and after tuning in and out of conversations between pairs of customers nearby, I returned home and lay two saltine crackers on the mattress, beside her resting head. Clifford was asleep, and I was no closer to a decision. So rarely did I spend any time by myself that I was unaccustomed to thinking—or at least to thinking very hard. My first session had barely prepared me for the sensation of being alone.

Three days later I reenacted the same dinnertime scenario: a groping conversation with Clifford interspersed with managerial directives to the kids, a vague reference to an idea that had been on my mind, a sudden excuse-me from the table and flight from the house. Again I sat by myself overlooking the still waters of a cupful of decaffeinated coffee. Already I felt more capable of meditating on my thoughts. I understood that I couldn't stay married while experiencing such corrosive doubt, doubt beyond the little whisper of reservation that I'd heard since the very beginning of my marriage. But neither could I end my marriage just to quiet those doubts. I would have to commit myself to being either with or without Clifford. No more standing astride the line with one foot on either side.

"Is anyone sitting here?"

I looked up from my coffee to hazel eyes and a dimple on one side of an easy smile. I smiled back, ready to benefit from the kindness of a stranger.

"No," I said, expecting that he'd sit down. Instead he dragged the unoccupied chair across from me over to the next table and sat down with his friends.

And right then I felt very much alone. Even if I'd been piled high with my two children, even sitting full-familied at the dinner table I would have felt that same deep-down loneliness. The question that I now had to answer was would I be more alone if I quit my marriage or if I stayed with Clifford? And what would be best for the kids? To feel their family wrenched apart or to live according to an uninspiring model of love?

I pondered the consequences of both choices as I sipped towards an empty cup. Together, apart. Together, apart. The party at the next table slurped and snorted and shrilled while I toiled away at my momentous decision.

* * *

"Bitty, what should I do?" I so needed wise counsel that, after dropping Jasper off at school the next morning, I had driven directly to Bitty's rather than park at home and walk five houses up the street.

"Well I don't know. Are you going to tell me any more than that?"

I set Sonia on the carpet, where she half-walked, half-crawled over to Slug, Bitty's dog.

"I think I have to leave my husband. I don't know…"

"And where would you go, dear?"

I dropped down onto the couch. This was a question that I hadn't even considered. Where *would* I go? And if we could barely get by with one home, how ever would we afford two?

"How about a nice cup of tea then?" Bitty offered. "There's many an affair of state that's been decided over a cup of tea." She started off to the kitchen.

"No thanks, Bitty. I think I'll go."

"Well now didn't you just get here, dear?"

Sonia had begun to yell, attempting to rouse Slug, who was indifferent to her advances. Finally the dog got up and resettled on a section of the carpet farther away from her.

"Come on, Sonia. Sorry, Bitty, I have to get home. I have to think." After picking Sonia up I headed for the door.

"All right, dear. But maybe it's not thinking that's going to lead you to a decision. Maybe instead of thinking, you should be praying."

"Thanks, Bitty," and I left. I didn't think of this as a spiritual matter.

Appealing for divine intervention might have seemed like a reasonable last resort except that I hadn't spoken anything like a prayer in so long, and hadn't examined my beliefs about the universe and human purpose in as long. I hated to be an opportunist, begging for a miracle only now when I so needed help.

I hugged Sonia close to me, heartbeat against heartbeat, and shut my eyes. Together or apart? I pictured myself living in a room somewhere with discolored white walls, a sagging ceiling and shared bathroom, the kids and I clinging together on one twin mattress. But I wasn't going to stay with Clifford just because of money.

Together or apart? Does love really vanish? Or is it always there, tunneling underground and then resurfacing over time? How could I know that if we stuck with it for another six months, our road ahead wouldn't become smoother, the scenery more picturesque?

Sonia had fallen asleep in my arms. Her spasmodic wakefulness had slowed into the regular breathing of a napping child. My poor dear, already unfairly handicapped by a medical condition that would make her life a swim upstream. Could I really punish her for my own vain attempt to form a family?

Together or apart?

Clifford and I were as mismatched as were our wedding rings. When we'd gone shopping for them, he had wanted a wide gold band. From yards away, one could be sure that he was married. I, though, had picked an unobtrusive but unique rose-gold band, one of a heap of rings at a store that sold estate jewelry. The narrow band very quietly advertised that I was a married woman.

"Come on. Our rings should match," Clifford had complained. But such a brazen symbol of our union as his flashy gold band would surely aggravate my persistent doubts. "And anyway, do you really want to be stuck with someone else's karma?"

But the saleswoman promptly said, "Many people include family wedding rings in their estate auctions. It doesn't mean that the person who owned the ring got divorced."

Clifford disputed her argument. "As far as I've ever heard, people go to the grave wearing their wedding rings."

I teamed up with the saleswoman. "Maybe not everyone is as sentimental as you are."

"And some people, years later when they have more money, buy more expensive rings," the saleswoman added.

So we'd purchased our dissimilar rings.

I'd believed that Clifford's invariable confidence in positive outcomes and his aversion to conflict would complement my readiness to find the worm in the apple and rinse it down the drain. Opposites attract, so they say. Of course anyone who believed that similarity is the basis of compatibility would have foreseen the ruin of our relationship. By now I was tired of entrusting my future to his style of indiscriminate optimism. At very least, I needed a rest.

When would I drop this bomb on Clifford? We hadn't had any conversations about separating, hadn't once even formed the possibility into words. As far as I knew, I'd decided this alone, inside myself, between contractions of my heart. Yet I couldn't imagine that such thoughts hadn't occurred to Clifford or that he hadn't suspected my drift in that direction. Still, the idea of separating was likely to seem sudden to him. Sudden and damaging.

And how could I ever tell my children?

I waited in bed for Clifford, knowing that he'd never expect me to be awake and so might almost be startled by any movement on my side of the mattress. As soon as he'd laid down on his back with a long, decompressing sigh, I let my hand travel over to his and took hold of his fingers. His skin was dry like an unwatered plant, as raspy as sand.

He didn't turn towards me, didn't speak, didn't return my hand hug but lay immobile as a corpse.

"I think it's time," I said. When I'd last spoken this phrase, just before Jasper's birth, Clifford had raced into a state of frantic overfunctioning. He'd seized my small pre-packed overnight bag and hustled me out to the car, nearly lifting me off the ground in his effort to be helpful.

"What? I don't know what you mean," he said now.

"Things are just so bad between us." I shifted onto my side, facing him, still with his hand in mine. "Don't you think we'd be better off separating?"

And then his inert, unreactive body came alive and acquired the ability to speak. "No, Pauline. I don't." Clifford wrested his hand free and grunted up into a sitting position. "You don't really think it's gotten *that* bad, do you?"

To my relief he didn't allow me to answer. "I've been thinking a lot lately about something that Peter said. The guy who goes from school to school and fixes all the electronics. He was talking about his neighbors. I wasn't really listening until he said, 'What does it mean if you can't get along with even one person in a close relationship?'"

"Yeah, so?"

"Well, if you and I can't get along, just the two of

us—"

"But maybe that's because we're not right for each other."

Clifford yanked his hand out of my grasp and catapulted out of bed. "Don't say that! Maybe I'm not right for you, but I know that you're right for me!"

Such an impassioned confession of feeling wasn't typical of Clifford. Then his voice materialized in the darkness again, in the corner of the room near the door. In just a few seconds he had decided not to fight. "Fine. But you can tell the kids."

"Clifford. I know you're mad, but don't you think we should tell them together?"

"Why? I'm not going to pretend that I've had anything to do with this…road wreck!" His voice had migrated away from the door, near but far at the same time. While I was still thinking how best to respond, Clifford said, "I stopped smoking. I dropped out of school. I've done everything that you wanted!"

His breathing sounded forced, like a handsaw working through wood. I couldn't tell if he was crying or angry. Then I heard a sharp intake of air, a wet, weepy gasp for composure.

"Clifford…Clifford, don't you think I want things to go well between us?"

"Honestly, I don't know." Another pause. "One person. Just one person! Not even *one* person," he added incredulously.

I could sense him approaching the bed. When he

next spoke, all of the tears seemed to have been wrung out of him. "It's fine. It'll be fine." I wasn't sure whether he was referring to our marriage or the separation: together, apart. His voice was fading. He seemed on the brink of sleep, willing to agree to anything just to be able to snuggle under the covers and float to wherever his dreams might carry him.

We agreed that when we told the kids, we wouldn't present the separation as a permanent change. After all, we might reunite, and if we didn't, we'd know better then what to say.

"A *trial* separation," I said.

"Kind of like a test bomb."

Probably exhausted from so much emotion, he sank down onto the bed. Again I sought his touch. But I couldn't find him. My fingers scrabbled, lost, across the sheet, unable to locate his hand that should have been there.

His weight shifted as, somewhere, the planets rearranged. And finally I found him. I lay my own left hand—smaller, softer—on his. Not right away, but soon, soon, I realized that he'd already removed his wedding band.

◆◆◆◆

Trinity

Oppie lay awake, lay awake all night he lay awake thinking without a switch to shut him down. What is over the boundary line where space stops, across the edge of time? And who is watching? Emerging on the horizon of his awareness was something splendid, expansive, a lost urge that he couldn't put into words. He had to rein himself in as his thoughts headed towards a place where he didn't want to go. And yet how could he not think about the upcoming field test that for all they knew would end the world? Should he watch it, proud and alone, from on high, the lead soldier, or should he behold the spectacle from a humbly low vantage point, holding hands with his Kitty and bundled up with Peter and baby Tory, perishing as a family man?

As night crept closer to dawn and finally Oppie conceded that he'd never fall asleep, he got out of bed and crawled into the clothes he'd worn the day before. Even the underwear, puddled fabric on the floor. Kitty was a heavy sleeper, conked out on cocktails from last night, so nothing he could do would wake her. As he started down the stairs, a teeny voice asked him, "Daddy, where are you going?" and instead of answering, he said, "Go back to sleep, pal. It's still nighttime."

The purple-dark sky paused before coming aglow with the first light of morning. Oppie could have believed—in that transitional light, on the cusp of a new day, in the luscious hush before the human world awakes—that he and his men had an ally in the old-shouldered mountains as solid as the rock they were made of. He hadn't had the time to decide whether or not he believed in God. It was easy to forget, while peering into the interior of an atom or gaping at the projected effects of the bomb, that they weren't masterminding the universe themselves.

He walked to the Tech Area and on the way encountered not even the sleepiest of souls, not even a cat on the prowl or subatomic scatterings escaped from the lab. But once inside the gate, manned twenty-four hours a day by military guard, a whole city of wakeful humans was busy at work like machine parts in motion together.

"Hey, Boss," he was greeted repeatedly. In return, each time, he stopped to check in on who was doing what, how far along the project had advanced since late night last night when he'd finally gone home, once again, to attempt to sleep.

None of his men was the man he'd arrived as. The skin on their faces sagged but clung, hung on to the

445

bone. Even with a tentative test date already set, and July looming like the end of all time, the scientists were still scrambling to get the design of the bomb right. The gun model had long ago been abandoned in favor of the whopping implosion model. The wives, meanwhile, weren't getting much more or better sleep than their husbands, who were never there, or if there, not there. The grip of silence choked the life out of every marriage, leaving the women gutted and incapable of conversation with each other. When they met in the streets or at the Commissary, their heads wobbled and nodded on spineless necks.

Most of them could still manage to say, "Is my catalogue in?" at the postal pick-up. Too eager to wait for the mail delivery to their doors, they jammed into the small room where the words "Is it...?" flitted around like moths. Lew, the Army employee at work behind the counter, knew what the women needed.

He reached deep into a mail sack and withdrew an 800-pager. Must have weighed nearly two pounds. Betsy got a bite of it in her hand, but then Melody scratched her so Betsy let go, and Melody snatched the catalogue away.

"It's mine!"

"I put my order in three weeks ago!"

"I put mine in four weeks ago!"

No name label could be used as evidence in the dispute. Only the common post office box was printed on the wrapping. The catalogue could have been meant for any of the chorus of claimants reaching out to own it.

In Lew's next handful removed from the mail sack, he noticed an envelope also from Sears and also addressed to no one in particular at P.O. Box 1662, Santa Fe. "Here, Ma'am," he said, offering the envelope to Sally Keene, standing at the outskirts of the fray. She saw that the envelope was from Sears Roebuck though it wasn't one of the coveted catalogues. Despite the number of women crowded nearby, none showed much curiosity about the contents of the letter. So Sally cleared her throat.

"From Sears," she announced, effectively creating an instant audience. She went on to read, "Dear Sir or Madam: We have obliged your many requests for catalogues during recent months, figuring that you lost a copy or two or else were passing them along to your friends. Now, however, the number requested far exceeds what we are willing to supply. Our records indicate that we have sent you 87 copies of our 1945 catalogue. As you can appreciate, wartime shortages make our catalogue more costly than ever to produce; therefore, we will be unable to send you any additional copies this year."

Those evenings the wives spent on their backs, holding their copies of the Sears catalogue above them at arm's length, rolling then to the side and fingering through the pages with sensuous oohs and ahs at the latest styles.

If the nights were long and uneventful outside of

the lab, the days had become hectic. Suddenly the Hill had become a most popular site on the tour circuit of atomic scientists and others with careers related to bomb blasts. The road into town was rutted from traffic, and Dorothy McKibben had booked every room to be had, even asked for favors from her local acquaintances. "Could you put someone up? Just for a couple of days, maybe three," she lied, well aware that the guest would need to be housed until July, when they all just might diminish into cinders.

"What's this for?" the other might ask, and of course Dorothy, sworn to secrecy and having told more untruths than she could ever repent for, had to say, "A visiting cousin." Had all of her prospective hosts compared notes, they would have questioned that she could have had thirty-some cousins, all visiting at the same time.

Dorothy's first call at work this Monday morning concerned that very housing crisis. She had to phone Oppie eight times before she caught him passing through his office, only there to rummage for the last of the cigarettes that he thought he'd seen in a crushed pack in one of his drawers.

"Oppenheimer," he answered.

"Robert, where am I going to put all of these people?"

For one moment he pictured a milling crowd closing in on Dorothy's desk.

"Send 'em on up here," he suggested.

"No, I mean where will all the new arrivals stay?"

"We've got all those shacks out there on-site."

Technically Dorothy knew nothing of the purpose of the project but had long ago surmised what it was. "We're still talking weeks though! They can't live in those shoddy things more than a few days at a time," she said though she hadn't seen them, hadn't been to the site. She hadn't read the Donne verse about a three-personed god or ever experienced maniacal control over matter. Neither had she been flattened like preserved flowers between pages of a Sears catalogue.

"Give me an hour or so." He hung up then fled the phone ring for the rest of the day, confident that Dorothy would solve the housing problem on her own, without him.

He'd seen the buildings himself. Last-minute structures, cruder than the plywood residences on the Hill. The two-hundred-plus miles between Los Alamos and *la Jornada del Muerto* looked to him as the earth might look once blighted by this latest in warfare. So whatever was in fact beyond the window of the vehicle he was riding in, Oppie saw a martian-like terrain repellant to human life, and some central stirring that he'd managed to still would begin to churn.

One day Groves told him, "I'm bringing your brother out here." Frank Oppenheimer had been working at the enrichment plant in Oak Ridge, Tennessee. "He'll be overseeing security at the Trinity site."

Oppie came close to hugging the tight-belted general, who never seemed to lose any weight even during times of extreme stress. Groves would have done just about anything to keep his man safe and happy. He even managed—or Dorothy managed, at his behest—to locate decent quarters for the second Oppenheimers. He turned away during the wordless embrace when the brothers were reunited, allowing them that much privacy.

Of course Frank was driven out to the test site once or twice but otherwise was posted within the wires of the Tech Area. Oppie roamed over to that part of the "T" more often than necessary and tried to see Frank again at night. Being close to his brother reminded him of life beyond work: family, past, the summers in the desert, rides single file along trails through the brush. The softness and earthy colors of nature, not the hard, angular steel of lab tables and cyclotrons.

Like so many of the women at Los Alamos, Frank's wife Jackie had effortlessly earned Kitty's disfavor. So she shuttled back and forth between Los Alamos and Berkeley with their son, one of many unwilling heirs to the work that would culminate on a July day yet to be announced.

The long haul from the Hill to the test site soon became a well-worn path. For security reasons, no one in any of the vehicles was permitted to stop en route, not even to take care of the most basic needs—if a driver, for instance, was surprised by a seizure of stomach cramps, or for water if anyone complained of searing thirst. And on these trucks and other Army vehicles was a constant supply of cables and wires and batteries, as well as staff who were needed to prepare the site, the equipment, the gadget itself.

Bill had told Wanda that he'd be away for four days. She chose to believe that this disappearance was work-related. They had been summoned to the Hill only a month ago and were living in one of the makeshift, second-thought units as crude as shoeboxes and probably no more sturdy.

"What is this place?" she'd asked Bill.

"It's…our new home," he said. He said and she scoffed. No one would want to live far away and in a shoebox without a reason.

"And what exactly was wrong with our last home?" Wanda had come to love the misty blues of Washington State even though she was an East-Coast girl herself. Recollections of the weeping leaves, the teary grass, made her cry like the rain falling from the Washington sky.

No rain would be allowed as zero hour neared. The test couldn't be guaranteed successful with precipitation either in the air or on the ground. Several meteorologists, both on the Hill and outside of New Mexico, were already fine-tuning their forecasts for the upcoming July. And those running the show, breathing down the necks of the weathermen, nudged them on to ever-greater feats. Now it wasn't just accuracy they wanted; they expected these men to actually control the weather: the direction of the breeze, the moisture in the air, the temperature to within a few degrees. No, they didn't come out and say it, but were these not men who'd become accustomed to

451

altering the destinies of small particles, overriding the natural order of existence? So that somewhere along the way they'd forgotten that they were no more than players on the stage.

Still Wanda waited for an answer.

"I can't tell you," Bill didn't say. But she knew he couldn't tell her where or why he was going away for four days. And she was still wondering why they were here, on the Hill, not there, wherever he was going.

Bill was a wiring specialist. Yet he hadn't, Wanda noticed, packed any of his tools. In fact he'd packed quite sparsely, and when she tried to persuade him to bring along his toothbrush he snarled—actually snarled—at her.

What could she reasonably ask for? "Bring me back a hug!" she called out the door.

How she would have loved to discuss this wrinkle in her marriage with other women, other wives, but since coming to Los Alamos, Wanda had noticed that the women seemed lifeless, their eyes defeated. Most all of them carried around a Sears catalogue under one of their arms and murmured through the text as if reading the Bible. Would she, too, become as hollow as they?

Time on the Hill began to crystallize: hard, sharp granules suspended in the thin mountain air. The sense of place became unfocused; the boundaries between here and home, now and then, were suddenly fuzzy and intermittent. And now another dot had been added to the map. Nobody'd been told so, but the wives couldn't otherwise explain their husbands' longer absences from home.

The silence was overwritten with Sears catalogue text. *Too bold? Not this spring! We've softened the bright colors you love... Sleeves, shoulders, strapless. These rugged shoes will be your first choice for treks among the trees.*

Once, while walking in the woods, Dick Glazer had blinked away a cloud of girl and boy scouts foraging in the underbrush for specimens that would earn them each a badge. Was this real? He'd been a scout himself somewhere else long ago and wondered if he might not have wandered mistakenly into his memory.

And the sun-ups, sun-downs, were they real? Those last twelve months, while the scientists had worked to finish the bomb, had been longer than a calendar year. Frequently they'd fallen into crevices and found themselves in unrecorded time. Many of them would swear that in that year they'd become, at their core, old men. Recollections of just the week before were already fraught with nostalgia, and the men felt a sentimental, bittersweet longing to return to the early days in Los Alamos.

But time became swifter, louder as the date of the Trinity test neared. So beyond human experience was the explosion being engineered that no one could foresee with certainty the magnitude of power, of light, of destruction, nor estimate any of these closely enough to be sure what type of measuring devices they'd need. Should they expect a dud sputtering into stillness or a firework display of divine dimensions? Numerous instruments had to be acquired or built to cover all the possibilities.

Up on the Hill, many of the Army men, including the beloved pediatricians, were receiving inoculations before being shipped off to the Pacific. Everywhere there was more war even than there was water to drink or air to breathe. International, concentric circles surrounded the bomb, and at that same center raged a disagreement about whether or not to tell the Russians about the test shot in advance. And if they did. And if they didn't. Setting off a dangerous bomb in the desert was one thing, but provoking a world-wide arms race was quite another. Then there was the question of whether or not to actually unleash the bomb on the enemy. Some among the scientists still wanted it to serve as a threat, no more.

But Oppenheimer, who had once and would later argue the pacifist point of view, had at the crucial moment declared that nothing short of an actual discharge would adequately scare away the Japanese. "They aren't listening, I'm sure of that." He seemed able to see through stone, to see into the future.

"You're flipping on us," Wilson had hissed. Outwardly, Oppie appeared able to withstand his recent unpopularity among the men. But inside his pocket, his fingers worried the old German coin, turned it, turned it.

"This is ugliness, no doubt about it," he said softly, walking away. "But this bomb'll be the last of its kind

454

ever to be exploded." He wasn't eating, sleeping, but always had at least one cigarette going. Smoke issued from his mouth, his nose, his ears. The trademark hat appeared too heavy for his skeletal form.

For months now, the mesa had been wracked by trial explosions in the canyon below, where implosion lenses were being tested. Even at this late date, modifications on the gadget were being made and meanwhile, the base camp was being prepared like the stage set before a theater performance. Groves wondered if there'd ever come a time when all doubts were resolved, all specifications finalized. And why was it taking them so long?

Oppenheimer read the general's mind. "We know so much more," he explained, "than we knew when we started."

Outside the wires of the Tech Area, a small gathering, mostly mothers, surrounded the departing Dr. Barnett, the man who had ushered so many babies into this uncharted world. All of the temps taken, the fevers soothed. "Take care of your children," he said with a shallow smile. Beside him his wife, Shirley, had tensed into taut graciousness and fear.

As more enlistees were shipped off to sea, more men were being moved out to the base camp. In all, seven hundred people were attached to the test-shot operation. Seven hundred bodies sizzled rather than slept at night, chugging gulps of hard water to hydrate themselves, sharing the barracks with scorpions, tarantulas, and the sting of heat.

Twice that summer, practice bombs of conventional explosives were dropped onto the site by B-29s originating from the Alamogordo Air Base. Trinity, alit and mistaken as a target, was spared only by the inaccuracy of the pilots, who struck wide, destroying the carpentry shop and the stables. "Idiots," Groves muttered when he heard, heartened that his own boys hadn't made any such significant mistakes. Almost at once, though, he realized that this was the same Air Force in charge of preparing the pilots who would let his bomb loose on Japan.

No matter, the damaged structures could be rebuilt lickety-split with the same careless craft that had produced most of the homes back on the Hill. New roads were needed between here and there as dust puffed in the tire ruts and stones dinged the undercarriages of the trucks.

Again the Army had created an entire settlement out of desert dust and muscle and the same pride-of-empire that impelled them towards war. Each new arrival would stop and blink at the stark and seemingly uninhabitable base camp, and religious or not, they all hurried to protect themselves with prayers.

Bainbridge had supervised the construction of a hundred-foot tower on which the test bomb would be exploded. They had to get it right this time. This was not an experiment that could be replicated; never could the same exact universe be recreated. The winds would change as would the moods of the spirits. Bainbridge turned away from the tower, surveyed the hot, cranky desert, and when he turned back again, already that world had perished.

Still, with so many uncertainties, Oppenheimer had decided that they should rehearse the test explosion to gauge how far and forceful the radioactive fallout would be. A twenty-foot tall platform, where the explosives would be tested, was soon erected. What would happen when men's righteousness was released into open space? Would any of their equipment be able to measure the momentousness of that historical event?

Spring blossomed at the Trinity site; hundreds of crates of TNT were stacked on the wooden platform of the tower. Dynamite would fill in for the nuclear extravaganza mimicked with just a touch of plutonium added to the mix. The precious element was both difficult to produce and costly. The ten pounds of plutonium stockpiled for the test were worth one million dollars.

By May, Frank was stationed at Trinity, camping out in the extreme heat of that summer. Needing to anticipate both the best and worst outcomes, he charted evacuation routes and arranged for ambulances to be waiting in Albuquerque. The official pessimist, he tried to hide the worst-possible ending from his brother.

Groves observed his head man dwindling. Oppenheimer's weight was way down. His posture was stooped. "Do you want a steak? I can get you steak," Groves offered him in the midst of all kinds of shortages. Thanking the general, Oppenheimer answered that he'd eaten steak just the night before.

"You don't look well," Groves told him.

Again Oppenheimer thanked the general.

What else, what else could Groves do for the frail but sturdy scientist? He had been fussing over Oppie for weeks, worrying about his health, uplifting his morale, wishing him to stay well. Noticing a band of sweat along the sunburned skin below Oppie's eyes and across his nose, the general fought an impulse to take his hankie from his pocket and swab the gaunt face dry.

Instead he asked, "How's the baby?"

"Doing fine. I don't see her much though."

"And—"

"Kitty? Kitty's doing well."

Those blue eyes that had once impressed the general seemed faded or sad. Groves patted his man's back and could feel the rib bones through his shirt. Just that much force unbalanced Oppie and sent him forward one tipsy step.

Groves knew for a fact that the Scientific Director was being recharged with no more than three hours of sleep a night. Though he'd ordered Oppenheimer not to be among those who stayed at the lab all through the night, being at home didn't ensure sleep. It had become harder to keep him away from Ground Zero, to keep the scrawny, star-splittting leader away from the unstable place that just might blow up unpredictably at any time.

Oppie's loneliness was not for women, not even for his wife, nor for the camaraderie of his peers. Now that he was trading in cosmic commodities on such a grand scale, he was, he thought, perhaps lonely for a god to relieve him of such ultimate power. He wouldn't, would never give up, even to the most modest respite. No napping, slacking, steeping in baths. He'd show those Army men, those doubters.

The tick-tick of time measured the gap between now and too late. Oppie passed the pressure on down the line while the world waited in paralysis. The president wants it before Yalta. And it must not rain.

No one was working less than ten- to eighteen-hour days although Hitler had already surrendered. In Europe the war had ended. Boundaries of sovereignty had already been rearranged, and the Russians were likely to begin work on a bomb.

The base camp now was guarded with military police dispatched from the Hill, though the jewel of all weapons had not yet arrived. If Oppie's spindly body was being so ferociously defended, then the bomb must be, too.

I am sorry that we cannot, Oppie wrote in a memo to his men. *We cannot overtly acknowledge your work. There will not…cannot be…*

The babble in the lab became ever more undecipherable even as more of the men were drafted to work at the base camp. Each day, another number of empty lab stools was added to the body count of those reassigned to the Trinity site. Living with them in the barracks were newcomers to the project specializing in measurement or explosives, safety or security.

Could the atmosphere itself be exploded? If so, the universe would then disappear. What do you bet? Will we open our eyes to the sky tomorrow? Some of the scientists had started a betting pool. A buck a bet. How many tons of dynamite would the explosion equal? Such numbers might not exist even in the unused portions of their spacious brains.

Even the usually serious Rabi participated in the pool, putting his money on twenty-thousand tons. "I'm about as sure of this," he began with confidence, "as I am of..." The locked-in air stank of uncertainty.

"I may just shoot myself now," one of the younger graduate students said. Used to anticipating deaths in the thousands, the men hunched over their lab tables weren't fazed by what may have been a suicide threat. And anyway, only one life mattered now. Robert Oppenheimer had become royalty and Groves his protector, hovering, advancing rules pertaining to his prince, existing for one purpose only that had displaced all the intentions and visions of his youth.

* * *

On the evening of July 11, back in Los Alamos, Oppie walked home and then "Goodbye, my Kitty," he said without addressing the possibility that he might never see her again, and yet she inferred the scale of his goodbye. "Here, keep this with you," she said and pressed a four-leafed clover into his palm. "Don't lose it." What more did she mean? "I'll get word to you," he vowed, unless the radioactive message itself reached her first. If he said that she could change the sheets, he told her, she would know that the test had been successful.

The device was ready, the men were ready, the scientists, the technicians, Oppie himself and Groves, Groves was ready, the Army, the president was ready in the Oval Office, and the birds, scattering frantically, were ready, the earth ready to die, the air ready to be tainted, the original sin ready to be topped.

Oppenheimer leaned over the gadget, poised in its place at the top of the tower. If he had turned and squinted, the earthen huts clustered a safe distance from the tower would have looked like a primitive city, the rows of holes in the mountainside at Bandolier.

The rain would rain, then stop, then rain again. By dawn—hopeful, desperate—they scheduled the go-ahead, leaving less than an hour for the big bomb to be armed and for all of the instruments to be gotten ready, for the eyes of the cameras to be cleaned and focused so they could document the revolution that even its creators could, at best, barely imagine.

"How are you doing, Robert?" Bainbridge asked him, not really expecting any answer and certainly not an important one.

But Oppie, wondering himself how he was doing, dove into the deep waters of his being and said, "I'm..." He said, "I'm doing..." He then looked outward at so much desert grandeur about to be destroyed without noticing that Bainbridge had moved on. Everyone was scurrying to his assigned place, to whichever earthen hut would shelter his innocence from the great technological breakthrough, and Oppie was left to stand alone, with only his brother so that they might perish together, together cross the threshold of another life. Seconds had never seemed so long.

Finally the hysteria of billions of atoms inside the huge capsule could not be contained. The spectators who had thought their way to this final outcome could see nothing know nothing else, certainly not any regrets that might occur to them later. Everyone around was warned to lie on his belly, even those wearing suits.

Look away look away! They covered their eyes with their forearms. A noise unlike any before it cracked open the earth.

After the first wave, some sprang to their feet for a better view. A column of dragon's breath ascended, mixing earth with air and fire, and the spent rain, the hesitant rain. And the light, the heat. The explosion thundered hundreds of miles away, ricocheting off the rocks, back and forth, as smoke and cloud roiled the sky. Miles away they could see it. Through slices of filtering glass they'd been sternly instructed to place in front of their eyes. Seven-hundred-some of them inside the huts, watching the world change.

Window panes rattled in their frames and the sky was inflamed with mechanical rage as the cloud of smoke and fire levitated up, up away into space. Was this, then, what prayers looked like? What ambition felt like, a need to be so much more in order finally to become humble?

On a ranch southwest of the Trinity site, cattle-backed burns colored the fur of the herd pure white, and logic failed mightily. Early up, the ranch wife said to her husband, "Look! The sun is rising in the west."

"Whattaya mean?" He'd seen it, too, but wanted her to be the one to say it.

New phenomena of light and color required new words to be created if anyone was ever to speak of that morning when the mountains trembled and the sun seemed to have touched down in the desert. Even a new vocabulary of time was needed to describe the everlasting moment that was over in a fraction of a second. Oppie stood beside Frank. Wondrous and relieved and horrified and disgraced. "It...works," he mumbled, the two words humming around inside his mouth like a fly. Then from the memory-stash of verse surfaced a line that he said aloud, his so-small voice consumed by the predatory rumble that had shaken through all the strata of rock. *I have become death, destroyer of worlds*, and Frank heard the words, not as sounds but as brothers hear brothers even across voiceless separations, and twenty miles away the scientists and technical witnesses were still seeing repetitions of that raging flash of light, an overload of impressions not absorbed by the senses, so even the blind could have perceived that merciless light, the light, the heat. Intense heat could be felt five miles away. And just then the mountains appeared tiny, the desert no more than a quilt-patch of land.

Beautiful beautiful beautiful.

So near a star would have been thought an apparition, but this kindled energy seared through space with tangible speed. The many measuring instruments were suddenly, in unison, animated, busy giving numbers to the lethal atmosphere now tinted purple with the unreal light of a voice soaking through the barrier of matter, though not a voice that any of them could understand except perhaps Oppie, who squinted his eyes and listened past the many languages he'd mastered to a universal undertone, an eerie spiritual beckoning. The genie rose and rose higher, wider, billowing smoke and dirt, a servant become an overlord controlling the next era of the century.

As of now, I am a different person.

In suits, in cowboy boots, in jeans, at desks, in huts, they were all finally freed from the months of imprisonment. They could assume their names again, claim street numbers for themselves.

Would any of them dance again and laugh and drink as they had during the parties at Fuller Lodge when, at that last hour of night, first hour of morning, they could almost hold the whole world in one hand? It was that small, that manageable, that malleable, and we were rulers of that time and place.

Oppie dropped the dull ember of his cigarette. He flexed his fingers and stared incredulously at them, then brought his palms together. (I have blood on my hands.) He wrung his hands as if cleansing them.

"The physicists have known sin," he said, Oppie said, "and this is a knowledge which they cannot lose."

Had he, after all, contributed to the rescue of western civilization? Could he and his scientists have influenced the way war was spoken of, or was their greatest impact that green, glassy residue where the unbearable brightness compressed history into a broken brittle of small, souvenir-sized pieces?

Last call! The final round of drinks had long since been served in the bars and the customers been shooed out into the street. Last call! The spilled beer had been sopped up with mops and with rags. Hurry up, please. It's time. The bartenders want to go home.

Oppie understood then what he hadn't learned from the years of figures on paper and impromptu conferences in the lab. Whether the sheets were changed or not changed. Whether the men watched or looked away. If they'd calculated the rate of expansion correctly seemed irrelevant now, when even death itself was no longer a standard for failure.

And that visionary aim of cooperation among nations, the shared control of nuclear technology was dismissed and ridiculed until some years later, when Oppenheimer was asked by Congress how that ideal might be approached.

"It's too late now," he said. "It should have happened the day after Trinity."

♦♦♦♦

The Day after Trinity

I missed him.

I missed summer, I thought. But then when a sweltering yellow July reminded me how much I disliked heat, I couldn't wait for autumn. My favorite time of year, those aging days, the morose light like a sad song in a minor key. And then finally I understood that I missed Clifford. Though I saw him regularly when he'd pick up the kids or bring them home again, and though I talked with him on the phone several times during the week, I missed his nearness.

But his absences, after all, had been the cause of my dissatisfaction. His investment in our future had excluded present-tense me. To console myself I composed long lists of his faults—how he withdrew in the face of conflict, his ineptitude with tools, his maddening optimism—but then, strangely, I would miss him more. Was it Clifford I missed or the consistent companionship of another adult, the lock of partnership that he and I had experienced during our early days together?

I scrounged for photos of us before we'd married and found only two, both taken by my mother, in which I appeared petulant while Clifford met the camera with an angelic smile. Had I ever been happy? Had I ever stopped guarding myself long enough to let anyone touch me deep inside?

At first Clifford's departure from the apartment felt like the removal of a large, unwanted object—a non-working TV or an oversized armchair. He'd taken with him the alien element in the atmosphere, and I could finally relax beyond the thickly drawn outline of myself. I'd expected to be crushed by the responsibilities of parenting alone but discovered that doing it all without the need to cooperate with anyone else was actually easier.

One day when Sonia and Jasper were napping, the doorbell rang and I charged down the stairs to the door. A uniformed delivery man offered me a package that was meant for one of my downstairs neighbors. I tried to detain him.

"I hear you people have really busy schedules."

"We do," he agreed, already leaving.

"Wait!"

He turned back.

I had nothing, though, to say to him, and so waved him away to resume his route. I was so lonely I wanted to jump out of my skin. Without my son and daughter, their weightless voices and inexact fingers, I might have plunged into deep despair.

My days, segmented by the kids' schedules, lasted into the night. Sonia and Jasper spent only weekends with Clifford, both because of his job and because of the distance between our two homes. He'd rented a place just a three minute-drive from his school, a commute so short that he often biked and sometimes walked there and back, he'd told me.

My family and Alia seemed too far away. The vacant place at the table and beside me in bed taunted me. I wondered if the separation had been too drastic a move. Maybe I'd overreacted to what should have been no more than a fight. Maybe all I'd needed was a week's vacation. And now, "It's all over," I moaned.

"But you aren't divorced, now, are you dear?" Bitty assured me.

Jasper and Sonia were spending that Saturday night with Clifford in his one-bedroom apartment. The crude sleeping setup—sleeping bags on one big mattress on the floor—had earned him the unabashed admiration of his son.

In a flash, my mourning for Clifford could turn into resentment. "Why does he get extra credit for his squalid living conditions?"

"What's that?" Bitty asked me.

"Oh…squalid. Well, it's like…unacceptable. Or worse, substandard and dirty."

To my surprise, when I'd shown up at Bitty's door on "date night," she'd produced half a bottle of a caustic red wine. Who'd drunk the other half-bottle? I wondered. Bitty herself? Edna? A rare visitor? Maybe the son. Apparently the Chianti was Bitty's prescription for healing my misery, or perhaps it just made my complaining more tolerable to her.

Instead of loosening up, after a few sips of wine Bitty revealed a very finicky part of her personality. She wanted me to move the pillow out from behind my back and position it just so against the sofa back. "No, dear, leaning against that brown one. Do you see?" Then she asked for the details of the kids' whereabouts—when they were with whom. And though she didn't take notes, in every other way she acted like a divorce attorney working out the particulars of custody.

"It's good that they're with him, even if they have to sleep right on the floor," she said. "Children need their father." Maybe because I drooped after that last pronouncement, Bitty added, "And you, dear, need a rest now and then."

"Oh, but I miss them." The softness of Sonia's cheek, Jasper's endless questions—every precious trait that had the potential to annoy me.

"Dear, you've got to pray to God to find your way to an answer." She gulped the last inch of wine in her glass all in one swallow. "I can't help but think that your place is with your husband." One of her brows rose to a sharp peak. "I'd be with my own husband still if he hadn't gone and died on me when I was just sixty-four."

The wine accelerated me towards an easy sleep after many nights of insomniac rumination. I would strain to picture my little ones' faces and then to feel Clifford's chapped hand against mine. The idea that he had credited to his coworker—that everyone should be able to have a close relationship with at least one person—was never far from my thoughts. Certainly I couldn't name anyone other than Clifford with whom I'd come anywhere near that worthy goal.

Just as surely as the wine had plunged me into sleep, it caused to me waken in a few hours, feeling mildly nauseous. I burrowed my face into the second pillow on the bed, sniffing for Clifford's scent even though I'd changed the sheets more than once since he'd moved out. Did I long for him or just for a body to fill this vacancy beside me?

I clicked on the lamp on my bedside table and by its diminishing light moved through the hallway and into the kids' room. The sight of their empty beds ravaged me. Disappearance, death, a night away—I couldn't distinguish among these different degrees of loss. My children were gone. I counted them among the many I'd not been able to keep in my life. Family friction, unfinished friendships. Jasper and Sonia were probably delighted with their life with their dad—bouncing on a mattress, eating frosting out of cans—all the pleasures that I, the despotic mother, denied them.

I climbed over the red siderails of Jasper's youth bed and gathered myself into a lump under his covers. Even with my eyes closed, the blocks of color on his sheets penetrated my lids, providing an incongruously bright backdrop to my uneasy dreams that night.

I posted a wall calendar above the desk in the dining room, deciding that I would keep track of the days of my separation. Once I'd survived three months, I'd reward myself somehow—an ice cream sundae or a movie. By then I'd be feeling better, I promised myself at the same time I was skeptical of my own unfounded advice.

The next weekend I offered to bring Jasper and Sonia to Clifford's apartment. So far he'd been doing all the transporting back and forth. I should be sharing the driving with him. And anyway, I wanted a second look at his new home to see just how settled in he was and whether the conditions he was living in resembled a long-term arrangement.

"Why?" he asked disagreeably.

It's only fair, right?"

"Fair? Is any of this fair—to me or to them?"

I ignored the challenge. "Six o'clock, OK? Is it the second turn off of Lawson Lane or the third?"

A pause. "The third."

Clifford's apartment was a replica of the apartment he'd lived in when I met him. He'd claimed only those items of furniture that had previously belonged to him. Not just furniture but the chipped dishware and the wall-hangings and throw blankets that Gail and Dave had picked up during their world travels. The tidiness that I assumed had been trained out of him had recurred here in his own environment, apart from me. His bed was even made, I noticed, the sheets taut and plain white.

Jasper and Sonia spun out into the space of the living room, he more gracefully than she. "Nice, Cliff," I said.

"You've been here before," Clifford reminded me.

"I know."

He didn't perceive this as anything like a social visit, didn't ask if I wanted tea or suggest that I sit down.

"Mama, go home now!" Jasper ordered.

"Go home!" Sonia said after him.

Clifford shrugged. "The people have spoken."

I turned away, mortified.

"Mama, you have to go home so we can be with Daddy!"

Whatever did Jasper find so irresistible about his second home, or was it the opportunity to be motherless that so excited him? Clifford had ended up in the worse of our two apartments even though, by rights, I should have been the one to move out; after all, I'd been the one to upset our lives by insisting that we separate. But we both understood that the kids would do better spending most of their time in the apartment they'd already been living in for a while.

An invasive sadness had found its way into places inside me that should have been unreachable. That weekend while they were with Clifford, I loitered at the grocery store, critiqued each lank string bean before deciding whether to drop it into my bag or reject it. My disembodied self observed a solitary woman roaming through time with no purpose beyond getting to the next minute, and the next.

Maya, whom I'd met during my brief participation in the book group at the library, didn't remember me. I had to prod her with several clues—where I knew her from, what I looked like—before she finally heaved with a groan of recognition.

"Yes, Pauline, I remember you now. Will you be joining our group again?"

Though I'd been overwhelmed by the number of pages that I, as a group member, had been expected to read each week, right now I might do well with the structure of assignments. But I was being detoured. "That's not why I'm calling. We lost touch after I had dinner at your house, and I wanted to see if you might want to get together again."

"You would like to have dinner again at my house?"

"No. No, I'm not inviting myself over. I was thinking we could—"

"Pauline, you are not inviting yourself. I am inviting you."

"You don't have to do that."

"I am leaving in just two days to see my family in India, so I cannot have dinner until maybe three or four weeks. Will you call me then?"

"I will," I said even as I predicted to myself that I would not.

Maybe I should be meeting other men. I thought of

Steve, who'd disappeared from the school with Katie after that first year when I met him. I didn't know any other men in Boston aside from the mail carrier. Now and then I'd sight him and engage him in a conversation so superficial that I couldn't remember it even a minute after it had ended.

What right had I to mourn like a widow over a loss that I'd inflicted on myself? I knew that if Clifford and I were to suddenly get back together, he would be no less distant than he'd been before and I would be no less angry. No, I wasn't ready to persuade him that we should try again. But neither was I ready to let him go. And as far as I knew, Clifford hadn't initiated a divorce or even consulted a lawyer.

The next evening, when Clifford would be bringing Jasper and Sonia back to me, I sat utterly unoccupied on the living room couch and went to the front window each time I heard a car door slam outside. I'd never noticed before the extent of comers and goers on our street. A white car, but not his. A dark-green pickup truck.

And then I heard Jasper's boundless voice in the stairwell. Both his mouth and his sister's glowed with gaudy artificial pink coloring. Instead of running to hug me, Jasper ran into his room and Sonia followed. Clifford, arriving behind them, lingered near the door. He was wearing the outfit he'd always referred to as his work clothes—the jeans spattered with paint, the shirt shredded and gaping with holes. His fine, straight hair was fluttering electrically, uncombed. Obviously he hadn't been concerned with making himself attractive to me.

"Come in. Sit down," I said to him.

We couldn't construct any privacy for ourselves, go into a room and shut the kids out. But I had placed a heap of toys in their bedroom, some resurrected after months of burial, to distract them from our grown-up conversation.

"Why?" Clifford asked suspiciously.

"I want to talk."

He sat, but tentatively, at the edge of the cushion, not committing himself to anything more than a brief exchange.

"I've been thinking about that thing your co-worker said."

I expected that Clifford might ask, "What thing?" but instead he asked, "Which co-worker?"

I couldn't remember the man's name, so I answered the other question. "That thing about being able to get along with one person."

Clifford had to scan his memory for a moment before he said, "Peter." This snippet of wisdom, which had stayed with me and shamed me all these months, must not have had as lasting an impact on Clifford.

"And I've been thinking that maybe, maybe I haven't worked hard enough at it."

Clifford puckered his forehead and leaned towards me. "I've been thinking, too. About what I should have done differently."

And suddenly, as soon as I sensed even the possibility of reconciliation, those old doubts about Clifford began to chatter inside my head. I may even have edged away from him on the couch.

"I'm not sure, though, that I could actually do any of it differently, even if I had the chance," Clifford said.

"What? Why not?" Again I wanted nothing but to have him back.

At the sound of a firm knock on the downstairs door, he stood up and started towards it as if he still lived in the apartment and it was his door being knocked on. But then he stopped himself and allowed me to proceed before him down the stairs.

"Mother wanted me to deliver this to you."

I opened the door partway so Edna could pass me a package wrapped in part of a brown paper bag. She squinted through the screen and spotted Clifford where he stood indecisively halfway down the stairs. "Oh," she said, suggesting to me that Bitty had told her daughter about my marital strife, whether or not Edna was interested in it.

"Edna, I don't think you ever met—" I was about to say "Clifford," but instead I said, "my husband."

"No." Edna gave Clifford a curt nod.

"Thank your mother for me," I told her.

She must have been on her way somewhere because her shiplike car was waiting for her, engine idling, double-parked in front of my building. Clifford returned upstairs ahead of me. "I wouldn't be surprised if she drove that thing down to the waterfront and right into the ocean," Clifford said as he watched her, through the front window, drive away. Then he noticed that the glass he was watching through was cracked.

"How did this happen? It wasn't like this when I left."

I thought of our protracted silences pressing against the glass, seeking escape from the tension. "I don't know. One day it was just…like that."

If this were our own house, I thought, Clifford might attempt to fix the broken window but then botch the repair and break the adjoining panes.

"I'll bet it's an easy fix," he said.

There it was. His ready optimism and my irritation with it. How easily I reverted to my discontent with Clifford even after all this time of missing him so.

"I better go," he said then, as if sensing a shift in my attitude. But instead of heading for the door, he wandered into the hallway. "You changed the sheets," he said, peeking into our bedroom.

"It's been months, Cliffie."

I was beginning to understand what I hadn't learned from the years of living together: that there was something between us, something we shared that was as basic as bread or salt, something beyond the convenience of shared parenting and the efficiency of combined housing costs. I think that Clifford may have understood this all along.

"I'm so sorry about…" A spongy pause absorbed

my tears. I jerked my head up off of his shoulder where he'd gently pressed it to rest. We were standing an inch or so in front of each other, closer than we'd been in months.

"Aren't you going to open it?" he asked me.

I hefted the rectangular package, most likely a book. "I guess so." I removed the wrapping carefully out of respect for Bitty's effort to make the package look like a gift. As I'd predicted, it was a book—a Bible, its leather-look burgundy cover embossed with gold letters. I let the thickness of the pages swish against my thumb.

Sonia tottered into the room and lunged into her father, hugging his leg as if that had been her intended destination. She smiled up at him even as she fought for her balance. Perhaps it was her nature to accept, with grace, all of her limitations. Perhaps she'd inherited her father's unrelenting optimism. Or maybe at just age two she'd developed some courage. Our truths weren't always apparent from the outside. Jasper, the ever enthusiastic and happy boy, was probably troubled about his family's future. And if Clifford sometimes acted unfriendly towards me, if lately he had not always seemed pleased to see me, love, I knew, went much deeper than the gruff crust of his scowling face.

"OK, little girl," he said to Sonia. "Daddy's going home now."

Whether or not we stayed together, I wanted to feel that we'd really tried. For the first time I was beginning to hope that we would, in the end, each find a way back to the other. And if that hope wasn't realized, I'd have to invent a bigger hope. I'd have to hope that even if we didn't stay married, we could continue to care for each other and wish each other well. To hope that love truly was indestructible.

◆◆◆◆

Sources:

American Prometheus The Triumph and Tragedy of J. Robert Oppenheimer, Kai Bird and Martin J. Sherwin

109 East Palace, Jennet Conant

Standing by and Making Do, Jane S. Wilson and Charlotte Serber, editors

The Making of the Atomic Bomb, Richard Rhodes

"Day after Trinity," Jon Else, director

Children of the A-Bomb, Dr. Arata Osada

Hiroshima: Three Witnesses, Richard H. Minear, editor

Laura Mann, midwife

Where the Ground Meets the Sky, Jacqueline Davies

American Academy of Orthopaedic Surgeons, "Your Orthopaedic Connection," http://orthoinfo.aaos.org

Fomite
Burlington, Vermont

Fomite is a literary press whose authors and artists explore the human condition -- political, cultural, personal and historical -- in poetry and prose.

A fomite is a medium capable of transmitting infectious organisms from one individual to another.

Loisaida

by Dan Chodorokoff

Catherine, a young anarchist estranged from her parents and squatting in an abandoned building on New York's Lower East Side is fighting with her boyfriend and conflicted about her work on an underground newspaper. After learning of a developer's plans to demolish a community garden, Catherine builds an alliance with a group of Puerto Rican community activists. Together they confront the confluence of politics, money, and real estate that rule Manhattan. All the while she learns important lessons from her great-grandmother's life in the Yiddish anarchist movement that flourished on the Lower East Side at the turn of the century. In this coming of age story, family saga, and tale of urban politics, Dan Chodorkoff explores the "principle of hope", and examines how memory and imagination inform social change.

ટ**ર** ટ**ર** ટ**ર**

When You Remember Deir Yassin

by R.L Green

When You Remember Deir Yassin is a collection of poems by R. L. Green, an American Jewish writer, on the subject of the occupation and destruction of Palestine. Green comments: "Outspoken Jewish critics of Israeli crimes against humanity have, strangely, been called "anti-Semitic" and as well as the hilariously illogical epithet "self-hating Jews." As a Jewish critic of the Israeli government, I have come to accept it these accusations as a stamp of approval and a badge of honor, signifying my own fealty to a central element of Jewish identity and ethics: one must be a lover of truth and a friend to the oppressed, and stand with the victims of tyranny, not with the tyrants, despite tribal loyalty or self-advancement. These poems were written as expressions of outrage, and of grief, and to encourage my sisters and

Fomite
Burlington, Vermont

brothers of every cultural or national grouping to speak out against injustice, to try to save Palestine, and in so doing, to reclaim for myself my own place as part of the Jewish people."

The poems are offered in the original English with Arabic and Hebrew translations accompanying each poem.

The Co-Conspirator's Tale

by Ron Jacobs

There's a place where love and mistrust are never at peace; where duplicity and deceit are the universal currency. *The Co-Conspirator's Tale* takes place within this nebulous firmament. There are crimes committed by the police in the name of the law. Excess in the name of revolution. The combination leaves death in its wake and the survivors struggling to find justice in a San Francisco Bay Area noir by the author of the underground classic *The Way the Wind Blew:A History of the Weather Underground* and the novel *Short Order Frame Up*.

Kasper Planet: Comix and Tragix

by Peter Schumann

Kasper from Persian **G**hendsh-Bar carrier of **treasures** What treasures Treasures of junk Degrader of the Pre**ciou**sness system Also from India Vidushaka Also medieval subversive thrown out **of** cathedral into marketplace A midget speaking swazzel language which **cops** don't speak

Fomite
Burlington, Vermont

Views Cost Extra

by L.E. Smith

Views that inspire, that calm, or that terrify – all come at some cost to the viewer. In *Views Cost Extra* you will find a New Jersey high school preppy who wants to inhabit the "perfect" cowboy movie, a rural mailman disgusted with the residents of his town who wants to live with the penguins, an ailing screen writer who strikes a deal with Johnny Cash to reverse an old man's failures, an old man who ponders a young man's suicide attempt, a one-armed blind blues singer who wants to reunite with the car that took her arm on the assembly line -- and more. These stories suggest that we must pay something to live even ordinary lives.

The Empty Notebook Interrogates Itself

by Susan Thomas

The Empty Notebook began its life as a very literal metaphor for a few weeks of what the poet thought was writer's block, but was really the struggle of an eccentric persona to take over her working life. It won. And for the next three years everything she wrote came to her in the voice of the Empty Notebook, who, as the notebook began to fill itself, became rather opinionated, changed gender, alternately acted as bully and victim, had many bizarre adventures in exotic locales and developed a somewhat politically-incorrect attitude. It then began to steal the voices and forms of other poets and tried to immortalize itself in various poetry reviews. It is now thrilled to collect itself in one slim volume

Fomite
Burlington, Vermont

My God, What Have We Done?
by Susan Weiss
a world afflicted with war, toxicity, and hunger, does what we do in our private lives really matter? Fifty years after the creation of the atomic bomb at Los Alamos, newlyweds Pauline and Clifford visit that once-secret city on their honeymoon, compelled by Pauline's fascination with Oppenheimer, the soulful scientist. The two stories emerging from this visit reverberate back and forth between the loneliness of a new mother at home in Boston and the isolation of an entire community dedicated to the development of the bomb. While Pauline struggles with unforeseen challenges of family life, Oppenheimer and his crew reckon with forces beyond all imagining.

Finally the years of frantic research on the bomb culminate in a stunning test explosion that echoes a rupture in the couple's marriage. Against the backdrop of a civilization that's out of control, Pauline begins to understand the complex, potentially explosive physics of personal relationships.

At once funny and dead serious, *My God, What Have We Done?* sifts through the ruins left by the bomb in search of a more worthy human achievement.

❧ ❧ ❧

"The activity of art is based on the capacity of people to be infected by the feelings of others." Tolstoy, *What is Art?*

Made in the USA
Charleston, SC
13 September 2011